Praise for
MINDSPEAK/HEARTSPEAK:
A Saga of Quantum Physics, Alternative Universes & Love

In MINDSPEAK/HEARTSPEAK, Nathan drops her protagonist and her readers into a mind-blowing alternate universe on page one—but her strong writing takes us by the hand and leads us along as we not only learn the rules, but closely engage with her heroine, Clarisse. Many surprises follow, but all guided by the sure and clever writing that does the difficult job of making sic-fi/fantasy human and heartfelt.

Gerald DiPego
Author of five novels and many films, including *Phenomenon, The Forgotten, Message in a Bottle, Instinct,* and *Words & Pictures*

Reminiscent of *The Matrix*, Sandy Nathan's action packed thriller keeps the reader captivated from the first page. Clarisse has lost her job because she believes in alternative universes, and then finds herself in a parallel world. Determined to do what it takes to return to her husband and family, Clarisse is committed to survive at any cost. This is Sandy Nathan at her best.

Ayn Cates Sullivan, Ph.D.
Award-winning author of *Legends of the Grail*

A good novel immerses you in the characters' world, whether it is foreign or familiar. Great novels like *MINDSPEAK/HEART-SPEAK* drag you into their world and make the fictional universe palpable. Sandy Nathan grabs readers from page one and pulls them along on a thrilling ride into fantastic realms. With her confident and clear writing, she has created a marvelous combination of science, psychology and espionage.

Kate McGuinness, J.D.
Author of *Terminal Ambition*, A Maggie Mahoney Novel, and the founder of Empowered Women Coaching

Sandy Nathan has the ability to draw her reader right into an alternate reality within the first moments of encountering her prose. Of all her books, *MINDSPEAK/HEARTSPEAK* is the best example, compelling from the get-go. Sandy has the ability to take a normal person like Clarisse, and reveal the "much-larger-than-life" hidden in plain sight that's also there. While exploring unsanctioned, amazing ideas like "alternative realities," Sandy also shows us the pettiness, jealousy and fear of everyday humans like Jack and Ron. Sandy Nathan is a master writer, exploring ideas and universes untouched by other writers. Her skill with plotlines and words is unmatched, all created at a blinding speed. Sandy cannot "not write," something for which I, for one, am most grateful!

Ilene Dillon, M.S.W. "The Emotional Pro"
Host, Full Power Living, author of *The ABCs of Anger*

MINDSPEAK/
HEARTSPEAK

ALSO BY SANDY NATHAN

FICTION
Bloodsong Series:
Numenon: A Tale of Mysticism & Money
(Bloodsong 1)
Mogollon: A Tale of Mysticism & Mayhem
(Bloodsong 2)
Leroy Watches Jr. & the Badass Bull
(A Bloodsong Novella)
In Love by Christmas
(Bloodsong 3)

Earth's End Series:
The Angel & the Brown-Eyed Boy
(Earth's End 1)
Lady Grace & the War for a New World
(Earth's End 2)
The Headman & the Assassin
(Earth's End 3)
The Earth's End Trilogy
(Earth's End 1 to 3 in a single eBook)

NONFICTION & CHILDREN'S LITERATURE
Stepping Off the Edge: A Roadmap for the Soul
Tecolote: The Little Horse That Could

MINDSPEAK/ HEARTSPEAK

A Saga of Quantum Physics,
Alternative Universes & Love

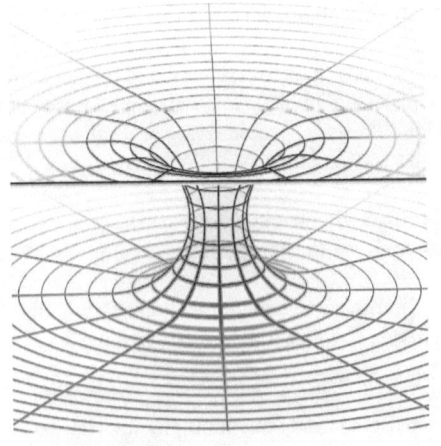

THE BLOODSONG SERIES
SANDY NATHAN

VILASA
PRESS

SANTA YNEZ, CA

Book Cover Design of Print & eBook editions: Yocla Designs, Clarissa Yeo
Interior Design of Book & eBook Editions: Damonza.com

Publisher's Cataloging-in-Publication Data
provided by Five Rainbows Cataloging Services

Names: Nathan, Sandy.
Title: Mindspeak/heartspeak : a saga of quantum physics, alternative realities & love / Sandy Nathan.
Description: Santa Ynez, CA : Vilasa Press, 2016. | Series: Bloodsong series, bk. 4.
Identifiers: LCCN 2016904058 | ISBN 978-1-937927-19-6 (pbk.) | ISBN 978-1-937927-20-2 (ebook)
Subjects: LCSH: Quantum theory—Fiction. | Human-alien encounters—Fiction. | Quests (Expeditions)—Fiction. | Paranormal romance stories. | Suspense fiction. | Science fiction, American. | BISAC: FICTION / Romance / Paranormal / General. | FICTION / Romance / Science Fiction. | FICTION / Science Fiction / Alien Contact. | GSAFD: Love stories. | Epic fiction. | Occult fiction. | Science fiction.
Classification: LCC PS3614.A865 M56 2016 (print) | LCC PS3614.A865 (ebook) | DDC 813/.6—dc23.

To my husband, Barry Nathan,
my best friend and partner for forty-two years.
May we continue to amble down
the trail of life for forty-two more—on our gaited horses.

You can't blame gravity for falling in love.
—Albert Einstein

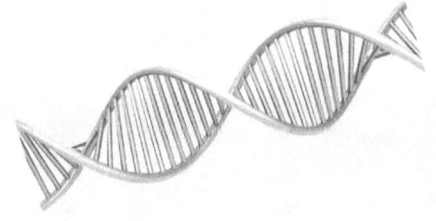

Love is irrelevant. Genetics determine existence.
Your past, future, and entire life is encoded in your DNA.
Pick your ancestors with care.
—Benjamin Hull, MD, PhD

Contents

A NOTE FROM THE AUTHOR

I felt that I should know the place where I stood: a pleasant tree-lined street like those of Palo Alto, CA forty years ago. I'd lived there; I knew the town. This was Palo Alto, and it wasn't. Confused and verging on terror, I ran down streets whose names I'd never heard. The sun shone and birds twittered.

A strange young man approached me. Unkempt, yet still attractive, he looked like he knew some secret I didn't. "What do you want?" he asked.

"I want to go home. I want my husband and family."

"I'll take you."

We wandered along pleasant avenues, the menace growing with every step.

I sat up in bed, choking down panic. And elation. This was a whopper of a nightmare! Most of my books come from dreams. Well, nightmares. Occasionally, they came from out-and-out visions, like the first books of the Bloodsong Series. But this was a prime nightmare. It contained a book—I just had to write it down. I jumped out of bed and began to write. It was two a.m. My husband and I were at our place near Santa Fe, NM.

Has anyone told you that Santa Fe is a Power Spot, a place on the Earth's surface that allows spiritual events and personal breakthroughs to occur? That lets books be born? Have you heard that Santa Fe and the territory around it is a place like the Mogollon Bowl, in the earlier Bloodsong Series books? Well, it is, for those affected by such things.

While my husband slumbered, I spewed words. When I went back to bed, I'd produced the outline of a book. This book. The story morphed as it developed, ending up quite a bit different from what emerged originally. That was the origin of Clarisse and her troubles.

I had the above dream on June 16, 2015. This book will hopefully be released in May 2016, when the story in the text commences. This has been the quickest and easiest literary birth of my twelve books... not that any birth is easy.

If you've come across this novel through reading the previous Bloodsong Series books, you may be scratching your head. The earlier volumes occur in the late 1990s; they're artifacts from recent history, when cell phones resembled bricks and personal computers were primitive and clunky. They feature Native Americans and billionaires, not quantum physics and alternative universes.

You may be wondering where the story you were reading went and what happened to those other characters. I haven't finished telling you that part of the series at all. Don't worry. I do have lots of material to fill in the years from 1997 to 2016. Will Duane and Grandfather and their friends have many adventures. I'm working on writing them now and plan to produce a series of novellas that will take you from the end of *Mogollon: A Tale of Mysticism & Mayhem* to the Meeting's thrilling and terrifying end—and far beyond.

Those will come this year, God willing. But in the meantime, this particular saga demanded that I write it. I hope you'll let me take you forward in time a few years. And, for readers who are new to my work, rest assured that this tale is understandable without having read the previous books.

I feel rather apologetic about making the jump in time, but the explosive way that my work presents itself is undeniable. I can't stop it. For me, writing is like the old academic "publish or perish." Except that it's *me* who publishes or perishes. My soul feels like it will incinerate itself if I don't get my words into print.

MINDSPEAK/HEARTSPEAK is as contemporary as today's lunch. The book starts in late May 2016. Nineteen years have passed since *Mogollon: A Tale of Mysticism & Mayhem,* when the original gang gathered at the

Mogollon Bowl with the great holy man, Grandfather. You may wonder why this book is included in the Bloodsong Series at all; it has new characters and a whole new story. But keep reading, you'll find old friends appearing where you least expect them.

A fun detail in this book: the graphic ornaments at the beginning of the chapters are artists' depictions of Einstein-Rosen Bridges or wormholes, which are tunnels connected to different points of spacetime at each end. They are the theoretical basis of time travel and what Clarisse's work is about.

More tales are coming in the Bloodsong Series, but I believe this one deserves to be told now. Meanwhile, I can think of nothing more rewarding than spinning tales for you!

So, off we go. Let's join Clarisse Hull on the worst day of her life.

Sandy Nathan

SECTION ONE
PALO ALTO, CALIFORNIA

LATE MAY 2016

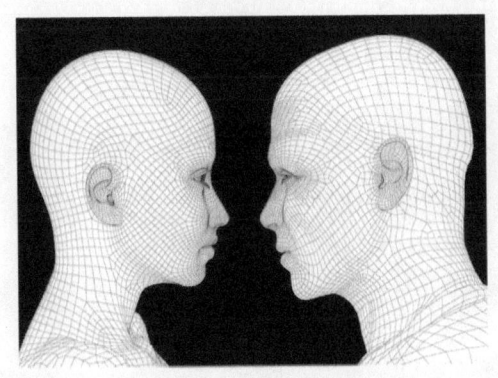

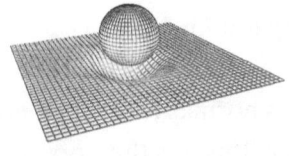

ONE

THE MEETING

CLARISSE STOOD, UNABLE to move, captivated by both the strangeness of the scene and its familiarity. The street looked like the old photos of Palo Alto from her family albums. The houses were small and pushed back from wide streets with generous sidewalks.

She was on a tree-lined thoroughfare. The trees were elms, even though she knew the elms had died off from the blight years ago. Water-guzzling, emerald lawns covered the front yards, nothing like the postage stamp-sized hunks of grass of 2016.

The place was a throwback to Palo Alto of the 1980s or earlier, before the dot.com money hit and new millionaires converted modest neighborhoods into suburban fiefdoms fit for modern royalty. Marring the city's character, as she and so many of her old-timer counterparts thought. Clarisse lived in the most legitimately patrician and authentic Palo Alto neighborhood: Professorville, the enclave of academics and scientists, intellectuals, and whole covens of psychiatrists, all nestled close to the university and downtown. Three generations of Hulls had lived in the ornately elegant Queen Anne Victorian with its deep porches and heavy, gingerbread trim she called home.

What was this street? The sparseness of everything: buildings, trees, traffic. She had to have been standing there for close to a minute, gawking. Nothing moved on the streets. Not a single car had passed; none were in sight. On each block, two or three were parked on the curb, as though placed for effect. She didn't recognize the models; they were like props on some movie set.

No people. Not a single animal. Not a cat or a dog.

The sun blazed and the air sparkled clear and bright. A bird trilled, as if to say everything was normal. More than normal—cheery.

Clarisse wasn't cheery. This was the worst day of her life. She wanted nothing more than to be home with Jack and the boys, in her jeans, sticking her hands in dirt. The vegetable garden had become her refuge this terrible year. She'd met with the committee today. Her fate was sealed.

But she wasn't home. Nowhere near home. The street signs on the corner said "Marble St. and Sawyer Way." She'd lived in Palo Alto all her life and had never heard of these streets. Maybe she was in Midtown, closer to 101 than where she lived and less familiar. Midtown was as close as Palo Alto came to a modest neighborhood.

If she was in Midtown, though, why was she there? How had she gotten there? Poof! Like she'd materialized out of thin air? She'd been walking toward her car after the meeting, and then, here she was. Clarisse was one to think things out before acting. Another person might have bolted, but she needed to consider what was happening.

Where was her car? No sign of it anywhere. She knew why she wore a suit and high heels rather than her usual slacks and blazer. She'd worn ceremonial clothing for the meeting with Dean Dog Turd and his Nazi cohorts. Tears leapt to her eyes at the thought of the dean. The committee had been meeting about her tenure for a year; today's hurdle was to have been the final resolution, the discussion that would give her tenure, or not. And it had been.

What the committee had said was damning enough, but after they'd filed out, the dean kept her for one of his "father confessor" talks. It had turned out to be more of an attack by the "Grand Inquisitor."

"Clarisse, it's not just our questions about the validity of your research. We've gone over these, though I'll summarize them again to make absolutely sure that you comprehend our objections.

"Your theoretical hypothesis posits a universe where every possible outcome plays out at once. What each of us calls reality is a thread of consciousness between alternate worlds. You say that it's possible to discern and follow these threads, allowing individuals or objects to travel in time, backwards and forwards, and to move from one universe to another.

"This is preposterous, Clarisse. It's the stuff of science fiction."

"Or theology. I've had my friends in ..."

"Yes, your friends in the best theological institutes in the country agree with you and have sent their opinions to us. The problem is—you're a physicist. What you suggest is not possible in physics."

"My equations show..."

"Your equations are magnificent. Beautiful mathematics. But there's no connection between your mathematical system and reality *or* your theory. Classical Cartesian fallacy. Because you think alternative universes exist, it does not mean they do. Your math assumes what you seek to prove. You *do* prove it mathematically, based on the false assumption that such alternative worlds exist. It's invalid logic."

"That's not true. In 1927, Werner Heisenberg showed that independent observers are always indivisibly linked with whatever they're trying to observe. My proofs are based on accepted physics almost a hundred years old..."

"You haven't proved anything. Which leaves us dependent upon your experimental results to validate your hypothesis. What results? You've shown us a bunch of images that don't substantiate anything. They could be photos of rippling fountains. Your work is an embarrassment to our profession and the university. Hippies and New Age fanatics may love it, but it's professional suicide. *Your* suicide."

"The experimental results show..."

"That you've been able to create a few undulations of *something* inside a monstrous computer, which unfortunately none of us are able to visit or even see photographs of because it's top secret. What you've done is not enough, Clarisse, to give you tenure."

"That's not true. *No one* has demonstrated what I have." Her face tightened, as did her chest. "Physicists have been talking about alternative universes forever. Back in *1957*, Hugh Everett noted that each time a quantum system is observed, the act of observation might result in different universes being created, one for each possible outcome. That's all I propose.

"What I created in the lab was a wormhole. Every quantum physics comic book talks about wormholes." Her voice rose. The dean nodded and smiled as though humoring a maniac. "Albert Einstein's general theory of relativity establishes forward travel in time unequivocally. It's not a controversial outcome."

"No, Clarisse, it's not controversial. But if a wormhole were to link two times, it could go forward in time only, and the connection would be fleeting and microscopic in size. A person couldn't go through it. It would disappear before any real communication between realities could occur. A wormhole has never been demonstrated in reality. *That's* the physics of it."

"But what if I..." She shut her mouth and clamped it closed, swallowing her words. Top Secret. Top Secret. Top Secret. An alarm flashed in her brain.

"What if you opened one up, kept it open, and went from one world to another? Great job, Clarisse. But you didn't do that." The dean leaned toward her, getting down to the heart of the matter.

"We ruled out tenure this afternoon, but we both know that that isn't what this meeting is about. I'm doing what I must because of what happened this week, and your manner in the classroom.

"I've received numerous complaints from students saying that you terrify them. That you act more like a master sergeant than a professor. This is very serious, Clarisse, and we've talked about it before. But the damning incident calls for swift action. You *struck* a student, Clarisse, and knocked him unconscious."

"I didn't mean to; he came up behind me and grabbed me. I was surprised."

The dean sighed deeply. "He surprised you, so you gave him a concussion."

"I didn't mean to. I just reacted."

"We know something of your background, which is why you're not in jail. Your commanding officer got you off. But you can't remain employed here. The student's parents are filing a lawsuit against you *and* the university. It's all our attorneys can do to keep it from becoming a media circus."

"But I..."

"The other thing is your absences. I know you do government research and that has top priority. You can be called on a moment's notice. That's good for you and our country, but it is not good for your students or this university. We've given you as much leeway as we could, but we can't continue after what happened this week."

"Fuck," she breathed.

"Yes, indeed. Your language is more appropriate to a barracks or gathering of day laborers. We've spoken of *this* before, too. All of these things impair your ability to teach. You are probably the most intellectually gifted member of the faculty. It pains me to inform you that we can no longer use your services. I suggest a research job where you have minimal contact with the public. The committee agrees with me.

"Your termination papers are being drawn. This is termination with cause: your suspicious research techniques and indecipherable results give us grounds to deny tenure, but attacking the student is sufficient cause for dismissal." He looked a bit upbeat as he said, "Unless you care to resign, in which case we can spare everyone a great deal of trouble and embarrassment."

Her jaw tightened. "I'll never resign. You'll have to shoot me to make me quit."

She walked out, rigid.

'Clarisse, you're brilliant, but you'll never amount to anything. You're a disgrace to the Hull name,' her father would have said. *Fuck you very much, Daddy*, she thought. Fortunately, he was dead and would never know. She not only hadn't gotten tenure; she was being fired.

Tears rolled down her cheeks in the safety of the blank, anonymous street. She wiped them with the back of her hand. Clarisse Hull never cried. The dean didn't know what she was really doing in her "government service." He didn't know what she was or what had happened to her, or anything but the glossy spread on her bio. And she couldn't tell him, or anyone else.

She *was* rough on her students, admittedly; they needed it. They were so bright, and so undisciplined. They assumed that life would go on forever with Mommy or Daddy paying the bills and fixing things. That wouldn't happen. She wanted to make them ready.

Now, everything was ruined, but maybe she could fix it. She'd talk to her partner. Maybe they could figure a way out for her. Maybe she could quit, and spend time with the boys and Jack. Grow vegetables. Be a regular person. Not have to work out at the gym in all the time that she wasn't working at something else. Not have to be in super shape just to survive.

Her chest huffed and puffed in dry laughter. No one quit what she did. *Get a hold of yourself, Hull.*

Clarisse rotated her right foot outward slightly, as she did habitually to locate her briefcase. She always set it down there, next to her foot. The damn thing was heavy; she couldn't carry it all the time. Her foot hit nothing. No resistance. Just air. Her eyes shot downward, seeing it wasn't there. She grabbed for the strap of her shoulder bag, always over her left shoulder. Always there, so that she'd held her hand as if gripping the leather. She had no bag. They were both gone!

The absence of her purse and briefcase was more shocking than the nonexistence of her car and finding herself in a foreign neighborhood. Her briefcase held her small laptop, the passwords to her files on the university's mainframes, and memory sticks containing the experiment's initial results—all of them. She had no ID, no card keys, no way of getting into the lab or anywhere on campus. Not to mention keys to her car and her home and her credit cards. She wasn't a person without them.

"Hello! Hello? Is anyone here? Where am I?" she cried. Silence. "Hello? Is anyone home? Help me!" She dashed up a manicured walkway to a small gray house and struck the red door with an iron knocker shaped like a hand. "Hello! Is anyone home?"

The birds were silent a moment, and then continued twittering.

Clarisse scanned the sky. Beautiful, clear blue. Wisps of clouds. Sun leaning toward the west. She lived in the western part of Palo Alto, if one stayed to this side of El Camino. She would follow the sun west. It would take her home to the big, three-story Queen Anne that had housed her professor parents and grandparents, and now her and Jack and the boys. She would go home and it would be unchanged.

Two blocks later, her heel twisted as she half-ran, half-walked to the west, passing streets she'd never heard of and wide, silent boulevards with modest houses. This was a world where people had normal incomes and eighteen-year-old dropouts didn't make eighty million dollars after an IPO.

"Shit!" She'd broken one of her heels. She had jammed her feet into the highest pair she owned to impress the committee with her professionalism. Professionalism was key. She had not fudged the results. She *couldn't* show them all the results she'd gotten, of course; that would be treason. And that kid—he'd stumbled in the computer lab and bumped her hip, grabbing her around the waist to avoid falling. She'd reacted automatically, as she had been trained.

Limping along, carrying her shoes, not worrying that she was shredding the only pair of pantyhose she owned, and possibly the only pair in existence—she had cared about impressing them *that* much—Clarisse wanted to wail.

Why should she be the only one in three generations *not* to get tenure? More than three, her family had been professors and intellectuals before Noah and the *flood*, for Christ's sake. *Jack* had gotten tenure, and his field was squishier than mud. Was she crazy? Sure looked like it now. She wildly searched the antiquated urban landscape. She had to be. Jack had been nudging her to see a psychiatrist, just until her tenure thing was cleared up. She'd been wrangling with the committee for a year, backstage and out of sight, while they tore her professional reputation apart. Half the faculty wouldn't talk to her now, without attending a single meeting and not really knowing what was going on.

"Maybe you can get something that would calm you down a bit and make you feel better?" Jack had smiled so gently, sipping his Merlot.

No. She wouldn't stoop to that. Her father had been a psychiatrist. When she was a kid, he'd stuffed her with pills every time she expressed any feeling at all. But her mother had insisted that she follow her into theoretical physics. Clarisse thanked her stars for that. If she hadn't gone into physics, she would have drowned in her father's psychoactive drugs. She wouldn't be who she was, and she wouldn't have done the experiment that showed her alternative universes existed and that humanity could reach them.

She *had* proof. She just couldn't show it to them because the government owned it, the computer, and her. No one in the university could go near her real experiment. She'd brought in *tons* of funding, too, but they couldn't know about that either. Top Secret meant top secret.

"Damn it!" A crack in the walkway had gouged her toe and almost sent her sprawling. Blood seeped from under the nail. "Damn it!" She stood in the walkway, turning slowly, screaming, "*Where the* fuck *is everyone? What's the matter with this place? How do I get* home?"

When she turned around, he was standing right in front of her. "Shit!" she muttered, jumping back. "Where did you come from? Do you always scare people like that?" Her lips pulled back. She wanted to slug him.

He was thin and vague, like everything in the landscape. His dark, lank hair hung over his forehead, but was short in back. The front separated out in greasy strands. His hands were shoved in his jeans pockets. He wore a navy blue sweater and loafers without socks. He glanced at her with intense dark eyes, not holding her gaze. He could have been any undergraduate, except that she had never seen a person more apologetic. He seemed embarrassed to exist.

"Um… I'm sorry. I've never done this before. They, uh, sent me to take you home." His skin was very fair, almost blue-white, so his brows and lips and the shadow on his jaw stood out. If he hadn't been so cringing and subservient, she would have thought him handsome.

"You're going to take me home?" How? Where? "You know where I live?" He nodded slowly. "Hull House?" Another nod. "All right. Let's go." She pulled herself erect. "Let's go home.

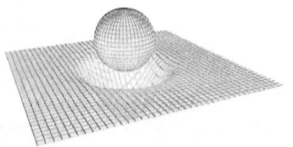

TWO

HOME

THEY WALKED FOR ages, him ranging ahead of her a few steps, looking from side to side as though a doorway might appear between the elms. Or on someone's front lawn. They passed more streets she'd never heard of. Sierra Madre, Jacob's Ladder, Blat. What was that? There was no Blat St. in Palo Alto.

The sun kept moving west, finally nearing the horizon, and she shivered in the evening chill.

"You don't know where you're going, do you?" Only after she stubbed her toe again did Clarisse call a halt. "You've just been leading me around with no idea where you are."

He stopped and ducked his head as though she had struck him. "They said a portal would be nearby. They said I'd see it."

"Who are *they*? Who are *you*?"

"There." His head shot up. "Come with me." He dragged her across the street, not even looking for traffic.

She didn't see anything until she almost hit it. A watery wall, invisible but emanating something. A force field such as her papers postulated might be possible. The evidence she'd found had convinced her and her superiors at the base—but *this* would convince anyone.

"Oh," her voice warbled as he pulled her through the fissure. She turned back. Palo Alto wavered on the other side, dissolving the way the image on the screen of one of her laptops had when she spilled water on it. First, it shattered into chunks of pixels, and then broke into smaller pieces toward the edges, before ending up a dead, gray plain. That's what the street scene behind her did.

Palo Alto, even the fake one, was no more. She and the boy, the *young man*, stood in a huge warehouse. Ceaselessly moving spotlights, like the monsters that swept the skies to announce movies in Hollywood, shone from the ceiling. She blinked, not able to make out anything about where she was.

Instantly, without thought, Clarisse froze, and then relaxed into a fighting stance. Her legs were slightly bent at the knee; her eyes softly focused. Her right hand moved to her weapon. Nothing there. No weapons but herself. Her eyes moved left, where her partner, Ron, should have been. No one—just this scrawny kid. No help at all.

The scene was weird, with the roving lights. Silence. And a strange vibe. Normally, she would have left the room and called for backup. Not possible now.

After a moment, her eyes adjusted and she could see a bit more. The concrete block walls were many stories high, with windows ringing them—two, three, five stories up.

Additional light came into the main hall from the windows marching up the walls. The windows were shaded from the outside; she had no idea what was behind them. She was certain it wasn't the blue sky. Doors dotted some of the upper stories, with metal fire-escape balconies and pull-up ladders.

Why would those on the windows' other side need access to this huge room, that they could create and retract? Who was out there, and what were they doing? What happened in here that they needed to get away from? A sense of danger prickled the hair at the nape of her neck. This building—whatever it was—had much more to it than this vacant space.

Clarisse looked around, jaw loose, eyes scanning. A predator making sure she didn't become prey. The vast hollow cavern was painted white, including the floor. Gray concrete showed through in areas of high use: trails where people walked frequently. Following the gray paths worn on the floor led her eyes to the center of the room. She jerked.

Hundreds of people gathered around tables in the middle of the colossal hall, seemingly frozen as they stared at her and the boy. The flashing lights had hidden them from her. They sat at rows of metal tables fastened to the floor, eating from cafeteria-style trays of food.

They were silent, gawking at her and her companion. When they'd identified them, a cheer went up and their voices rang out. They sounded like young adults, their tones an octave higher than her peers, the faculty.

"Dr. Hull! Dr. Hull! Dr. Hull!" The voices were frenzied, as though she was a celebrity they'd been waiting to meet. An unmistakable violence threaded the syllables with something menacing. "Hull! Hull! Hull!" Shouts filled the air.

"Eli! You did it!" a voice shouted, and was followed by less charitable remarks in a sarcastic tone, "The dufus did the deal." "You're not such a suck after all, Lilypad."

The mass of people stood, leaning toward her.

Clarisse paid no attention to her companion. She moved toward the group automatically, her training taking over. She matched their hostility with her stance. When she got closer, she saw that they *were* young, like her undergraduate students. The supercharged energy she felt when working with Ron came over her.

"Where am I? What is this place? He said he was taking me *home*."

"This is home, ma'am. All the home you'll ever need. I'd like to *welcome* you to your true *home*," drawled one, standing by his tray. He was big, blond, and good-looking. An alpha with a twist of horniness and sadism.

"This isn't my home. I live on Kingsley in Palo Alto. The Hull House. This *isn't* home."

The group froze and their eyes settled on something behind her. She turned as a man's face lit up most of the warehouse's wall. It looked odd, with windows and landings with their metal ladders cutting up his features. The face could have belonged to any senior scientist she'd known. Feral bright eyes, close-trimmed beard, and mustache, a bald head and the air of someone who would do and had done *anything* to get where he was.

"Welcome, Dr. Hull. Greeting such an august intellect is a pleasure.

What you call home is no longer safe for you. You are safe here, and will be able to continue your research in peace, with all the resources you need at your command. *We* understand your theories and the validity of your experimentation. But we can get into that tomorrow when you start work."

"What do you mean, 'start work'? I never said I'd work for you. Who are you? Why have you brought me here?" The words shot out of her mouth. She stood, clenched hands at her sides.

"Oh, my!" A dry chuckle came from the face on the wall, his lips pursed and his brows raised in surprise. "You are as feisty as reputed. Well, you will work for us, if you want to see ..." Another wall in the big room lit up. Jack and the boys were in the kitchen, talking. Her fifteen-year-old son, Ricky, was at the breakfast bar while thirteen-year-old Jimmy snagged a piece of pizza. Her husband, Jack, stood, his piece of pizza dripping cheese. He was speaking. The boys in the clothes they'd worn to school that morning. They looked concerned. There was no sound.

"What are you doing? Threatening me? Saying I'll never get back to them?"

"Oh, I didn't say that, Dr. Hull. But... how *will* you get back? Without us? Perhaps you should cooperate."

"Cooperate with what? What do you want me to do? Why am I here?"

"You're here because we want you here. That's enough reason. As a corollary, though, you should know that the merit of your research has been noted. You show the greatest promise of any theoretician we've investigated. You should be able to attain our goals."

"What are your goals? What do you want?"

"You have to ask? With your background?" He laughed heartily at that, then cut the mirth and said seriously. "Let's get to practical matters.

"Elias has been trained for you. He is assigned to you and will fulfill your personal needs. I know this has been an unsettling day. Elias will show you to your room and bring you supper. Tomorrow, you may begin work."

The face disappeared, leaving the window-pocked wall.

"Who was that?" She turned to the crowd, incredulous.

"It's Him. *They've* been waiting for you," Elias whispered, studying the floor before his toes.

"Who's *him*? Who are *they*?" she barked.

"Questions, questions, Dr. H," the blond surfer broke in with his broad smirk. He looked her up and down. "They should have given you to me. I'd answer your questions *and* take care of your *needs*." The kid leered at her, his intentions clear. He was a predator.

Clarisse knew she had one second to achieve dominance or she'd be his bitch as long as she was there. She walked up toward him quickly. He grinned and reached for her with his right hand aimed directly at her breast.

She grabbed his middle finger and wrenched it back, pressure centered on the middle knuckle. His eyes widened and he shrieked. She kept up the pressure until he dropped to his knees. "This is a very simple hold," she said quietly. "I can control your pain easily, like this." A tweak, and he dropped his head toward the floor, whimpering.

"Please. Don't hurt me. I didn't mean…"

"Oh, you *meant* it. You should have done your homework, lover boy." She jammed the joint harder. He howled.

"Don't break it, please." Sobbing, begging.

One last tweak, eliciting a final yelp from her adversary, and she let go abruptly, stepping back. He flopped on the floor, gasping. The group jumped away from her.

"My name is Dr. Clarisse Hull. You will address me as Dr. Hull. You will *never* say anything to me like this idiot did. None of you will come within six feet of me without my permission. Do you understand?" She bellowed at the group. "Get up, you sniveling fool." She would have kicked him, but her bare foot wouldn't do much damage.

"You ought to do more thorough research on people you bring to this place." She'd addressed the bunch of them, suddenly sure that there had been more like her. This scene had been played out many times, but with a different outcome than now. The mob's hostile elation when she'd first entered was very different from the guarded deference their faces and bodies expressed now.

Other people—faculty members, scientists, and researchers—had been brought here. The others had not fared well in their initial meetings with this gang. But why had they been brought here?

"I have a reputation of being hard on my students. I do not tolerate insubordination or rudeness. If you cross me, I will go after you, no holds barred."

Clarisse spun toward the mousy boy who'd accompanied her. "You and I are going to have a long talk. Take me to my room and get me something to eat. And some Scotch."

His face kept working, but he seemed unable to move.

"What's the matter with you? The big face on the wall said you were supposed to get me what I need."

The warehouse's long sidewall was dotted with institutional double doors leading to wide corridors. They looked like the metal-clad versions in hospitals—big and impregnable. Each set had large numbers in an elegant font painted above it. Elias, what the apparition on the wall had called her companion, led her to corridor one.

"Headin' up the *corridor*, Lily? You gonna score tonight?" she heard from the group. It wasn't the blond boy's voice. Her display of an elementary interrogation technique hadn't quelled the insurrection. She should have gone after the speaker, but she didn't have it in her. The enormity of the day hit her.

She'd been denied tenure and fired—all but the paperwork and formal announcement were complete. Her research was deemed fraudulent. She'd been transported to a computer-generated facsimile of her hometown. Picked up by a—what was Elias? A robot? A mentally disabled person? A fucking asshole?

And she'd lost it with a perfect stranger, setting up a contentious relationship in a place she hadn't been for ten minutes. Her husband and boys were on the other side of a great divide that she could only grasp through mathematics. How could she get home to them? Were they okay?

Jesus Christ. She was fucked.

She and Elias moved down the corridor in silence. Long and all white, the walls were apparently some kind of plastic. Doors like those in hotels dotted each side. The image of the man's face appeared again on the blank wall opposite room 132. "Dr. Hull, this is your quarters. We trust it will be satisfactory. If you need anything, inform Elias. Welcome to our community."

The disturbing visage faded and Elias fumbled with a card key.

"Give me that." She swiped it and opened the door.

Her room was surprisingly large—a roomy studio apartment rather than a dorm cube. Its cement block walls and concrete floor were painted the obligatory white. Everything else in the apartment was also white. It gave the place a bleached, weird look. A huge bed, large enough for an orgy, was shoved against the rear wall. Doors leading to what she assumed were a closet and bath pierced the left wall. A sitting area with a sofa and chairs and a dining table with four chairs filled the middle. A kitchen too small to cook much of anything filled the far corner. Everything she needed to live indefinitely was here.

She gasped and ran to the bed. Her briefcase and purse lay on it. "Oh, thank God." She opened the case. The printouts and memory sticks were there, as well as her small laptop. She clutched the computer to her chest. Tears came. She didn't stop them.

She made the decision then, or rather, she *was* the decision. It came from her depths, inalienable, unalterable, and immutable. She would do *anything* necessary to escape this hideous place. Steal, lie, and kill. Destroy anything in her path. She would escape and find her way back to Jack and the boys no matter what she had to do.

At this point, she wasn't able to consider niceties. Will I betray my country? Will I betray myself? Will I let my body be used, or use it to attain my goal? How far will I really go?

Tears covered all of that. Clarisse was alone.

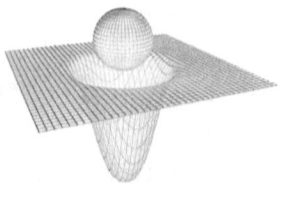

THREE

LILYPAD

"DR. HULL, I'VE got dinner." Elias' voice came through a speaker on the wall. "I can't open the door."

She let him in. He carried a heavily laden tray. The dinner plates had plastic domes over them.

"They saved this for us. I'll get there earlier tomorrow and get more." He put the tray on the table and laid out two plates and silverware, arranging the settings so precisely that her grandmother would have approved.

He was eating with her? Well, he'd missed dinner with the others. Why not this once? She would question him and send him on his way.

"Where's the Scotch? I need that more than this shit." He'd brought her a smallish portion of what looked like packaged mac and cheese, and a wilted salad of iceberg lettuce, plus a glass of green Kool-Aid.

Flinching as though her words were blows, Elias kept his eyes on his own plate. "We don't have Scotch."

"How about a bottle of wine? You could score me one of those, couldn't you?" Fury arose in her again. She felt like pummeling him.

"We don't have alcoholic beverages." Eyes down, speaking in a monotone. "They have found that the guests do better without them."

"*They*—the big guy on the wall." A nod. "The guests. So there *are* more than me?" Another nod. "How many more?"

He looked like he'd choke on his tongue. He was scared to death, and she was scaring him more. He sat, hunched over, not touching his meal of orange plastic goo. She'd never seen anyone so cowed.

Yes, I have. In the camps, she thought. *Did they know about her past? What she'd really been doing the last twenty years when everyone thought her sequestered in her lab?*

Clarisse's eyes narrowed. She got up silently and picked up her laptop from the bed. She powered it up, searching for internet access. Could she call Jack? Ron? No access at all. She turned it off anyway, something telling her that whoever ran this place was an expert at snooping. She stood next to him as he sat stooped and staring. She set the laptop on the table and wrote:

Is this room bugged? He nodded.

Visual or aural? Or both? He pointed to aural.

Do you know where the bug is? He shook his head.

How loudly can we speak without being heard?

"Like this," a barely audible whisper.

Where am I?

He typed back: *Home.*

NO! Where is this place?

He flashed a glance at her and typed again. *Where your research said.*

An alternate universe? A nod.

"*What the fuck!? I was* right!" she exclaimed. If the dean and committee could see her *now.*

He typed, *We do not swear.*

"I FUCKING DO! I fucking swear whenever I fucking feel like it," she shouted, her temper seeking release after the events of the day.

He flinched again. She would have continued grilling him, but his stomach growled.

She looked at him, finally seeing him. He wasn't slight; he was emaciated.

"Let's eat." She pointed at his plate. His portion was smaller than hers. He waited until she'd taken a bite, then politely speared a bit of macaroni and carefully put it in his mouth.

She smiled. *My Grandma would love your table manners,* she

thought. Thinking about her grandmother reminded her of Hull House and the other people who weren't there. *Jack. Ricky. Jimmy.* Her husband and boys. Where were *they?* How could she get back to them?

She kept eating… the shit looked *better* than it tasted. The boy continued to eat methodically, as though every bite was measured and his plate could be taken away at any moment.

She stabbed a soggy hunk of lettuce. "How do you get iceberg lettuce to taste *worse* than it already does? This is crap." A swig of Kool-Aid. She forced herself to swallow it.

"Now I know what they mean by 'Don't drink the Kool-Aid.' This stuff will kill you! This meal has a negative nutritional quotient." She shoved her dinner to Elias. And shouted into the middle of the room.

"If you want me to work for you, you'd better feed me right. And him. I don't want to look at a scarecrow. For breakfast, I want two, no— *three*, eggs scrambled light. Extra thick bacon. And two English muffins with butter and jam. And good coffee. That's for each of us.

"None of this, 'they ran out' shit. You want me; you feed me. And you pay me, too."

"Eat," she whispered, pushing her plate to him. "Eat it all, and stop monkeying around."

He ate. He *was* starved. He was so hungry that even the terror engendered by her shouted breakfast order couldn't stop him from consuming every scrap of the slop in front of him. He belched softly, then blinked, eyes popping. Did *anything* not scare this kid?

"Better?" She regarded him, noticing more. The bluish cast to his face. Natural, maybe, from lack of sunlight. Or something else? His sweater was too small; his wrist protruded from it. A blue stain ringed his arm just above the carpal bone. A bruise from a restraint.

They'd beaten the crap out of him. She couldn't take anymore. "Elias, I've got to get some sleep. Why don't you go to your dorm and I'll see you tomorrow?"

That produced the big freak-out of the day. He almost stopped breathing, but reached for her computer.

I am trained to take care of your needs. They created me for you. Do you want me to make you feel better?

What? she mouthed, then typed. *What do you mean by that? Fuck me?*

His bluish skin turned violet as he blushed. *If you wish.*

I DON'T WISH. I'M MARRIED. I DO NOT CHEAT ON MY HUS-BAND AND HE DOESN'T CHEAT ON ME. GET OUT OF HERE. She typed it, but her message shouted just the same.

Elias stood trembling, the whipped dog to the nth degree. He took a step toward the door, cast a beseeching look at her, and then typed some more.

I'm sorry to have displeased you. I beg you to let me stay here. I won't touch you. You won't know I'm here. I will stay in the closet. Please let me stay.

Cogs turned in her mind. The scene out in the hall. Blondie, the handsome thug, bullying him. His bruised wrist.

Will they get you if you aren't with me?

Yes. If I leave here, I will not have done what I have been trained to do. I will be a failure.

What will they do?

She erased that immediately upon writing it. She knew what they'd do. Nice alternative universe she'd come to. But Clarisse needed to get a better look at him to tell how bad it was.

"Okay. Show me around our apartment."

The two doors were exactly what she'd thought. One opened to a large, walk-in closet. Women's clothes hung on one side. A few men's outfits, jeans, shirts, and a sport coat, sparsely populated the other.

"You can sleep in here on the sofa cushions," she whispered in his ear, noticing something else about him when she got close.

They went into the bathroom. All white, very functional and modern, like a three-star motel.

"Good. I'm going to take a shower. And so are you when I'm done. You stink."

He backed away, shaking his head.

"Oh, yeah, buddy. You're here for my needs and I need to have you smell better. Take a shower and wash your hair. Put on this bathrobe when you're clean," two terry-cloth robes hung on the back of the door, "then come out. I want to look at you."

"You don't have to show me anything you don't want to," she whispered. Then, louder, "Turn your back and let the top of the robe fall down so I can see you." The robe exposed a study of his bone structure; every bone in his back showed. Vertebrae, ribs, shoulder blades. And the bruises. Blue-black new ones, yellow-green older ones. Made by a length of hose, most likely.

She estimated two severe beatings, several weeks apart, one recent, plus starvation... for how long? A long time. The definition of the bones wouldn't have been so severe if he'd undergone a brief, intense deprivation of food and water. She yanked the robe down so she could see his buttocks.

Lashes from a... she didn't know what. Nothing like wire, or anything that would cut the skin. A riding crop? So many things could do that. New and older wounds.

"Pull your robe up." She stood back from him, her whisper barely audible. "Anything worse than that in front?" He tried to double-up. "Nope. Face the music, Eli. Turn around." Those were probably electrical burns on his chest. She pulled the robe shut. Deep bruises from metal cuffs on his wrists and ankles. She'd seen his wrists when he ate, but the ankles. The extent of it...

She couldn't look at anymore. Keeping her voice and demeanor neutral, she began a very quiet interrogation.

"Who did this to you?" He looked at the floor. "*Tell me.* How do you expect me to help you?"

"They did."

"The people in the hall?" A nod. "Why?" He blushed again.

"They wanted to kill me."

"That's obvious. Why?"

He couldn't meet her eyes, looking away while his body jumped like a hooked fish on a pier. Clarisse tried another track. "Those windows in the big room with the fire escapes on them. Why are they there? Do people need to escape?"

Another nod. "Yes. Sometimes." Silence.

"Come on, Elias, help me out."

"During the games, they put the ladders down. If the prizes are good enough, they can climb up. They never are."

"The prizes...?

"People like you... and sometimes us. Please..." He panted and looked like he might faint.

"Okay. One more question—why did they try to kill you?"

"For you. They wanted me to die for you..."

"That doesn't make any sense at all..." Clary shut up in the nick of time. His eyelids fluttered. She caught him as his eyes rolled back. Trauma, she thought. Clarisse was the world's greatest expert on trauma. That was enough. She'd find out the rest later. She dragged him a couple of steps and laid him on the bed. He seemed out cold, but she couldn't stop thinking.

Why beat the crap out of her personal servant? They'd *created* him just for her? They had to know all about her background.

When she got it a second later, she fought the urge to fold up like him. But she didn't.

"Okay, Eli, off to bed." He stirred and looked around. She pointed at the sofa and lifted a cushion, jerking her head toward the closet door. They made up a bed for him on the floor.

"See you in the morning," she whispered. "I'll try to debug this place then."

The bed loomed. What was Jack doing now? And the boys? Had they called the police yet? The cops wouldn't take a missing person's report for twenty-four hours, would they? She only knew about things like that from TV. In the years she and Jack had been together, she had been away from her family a fair amount of time. She left to work or go to conferences to present papers; her absences were always planned. She never departed without giving them itineraries and letting them know when she'd be back. Or saying goodbye. She never just disappeared. They'd realize she was late. Then missing. They'd start looking for her. They'd find her car.

But they wouldn't find her, because her research was correct. Parallel universes *did* exist and she was stuck in the mother of all of them. *Oh, God.*

Pulling the covers and sheets back, Clarisse carefully inspected the bed before getting in. Her heart pounded. It did every time she was away from her own bed. She had a phobia, picked up in a hotel in New York City. She'd gotten in late from a night presentation. When she'd thrown back the covers to get into bed, it had been swarming with black insects. She didn't just change rooms; she demanded the Presidential Suite and pitched a fit they'd never forget.

Clarisse was more afraid of bedbugs than almost anything. She'd rather face a beating like that boy had had than get into a bed full of bugs that would creep out to suck her blood while she was unconscious.

Sleeping alone was also a problem. Jack was so big and comforting. With him next to her, Clarisse felt like nothing could hurt her. The world was a safe place and all was good. She'd developed rituals to compensate. She curled up on her left side and grabbed the corner of her pillow with her left hand. She could sleep alone if she held the pillow corner in her left hand and her right thumb and forefinger rubbed the spread.

Why had they beaten Elias? To show her what they'd do to her if she didn't cooperate. Clarisse worked the coverlet frantically. She couldn't see it coming, couldn't stop it.

Everything erupted within her, 3-D and real. The sights and smells, the physical impact. Explosions shaking the earth. The stench of blood and entrails. Dust tossed up from hell. Wind pounding everything, inescapably. Clarisse was twenty-two years old and it was the year 2000. She was in Iran, doing covert work for Uncle Sam—looking for evidence of weapons of mass destruction.

She was reliving what happened for the millionth time. She couldn't tell a flashback from reality and they never stopped coming—her two truths.

The blast tossed her as if she was nothing, the way it did the bricks and walls and buildings of the village. She flew, and then everything was black.

Clarisse came out of it in a hut of pocked mud bricks. The roof and top portion of the walls were blown off. She couldn't move, discovering quickly that her arms were tied behind her. They'd put her where she could see the middle of the dirt floor. The assailants didn't bother to cover their faces.

They had a man tied to a chair. He slumped to the side, his face a swollen, blackened, bloody mass. Every part of him was a bloody mess. She wouldn't have recognized him except for his slim build and the shape of his head. His dark hair fell to the side. It was *Alex*. His hair was matted with blood. They had *Alex*.

One of them shouted at her in Farsi. Stuff was all around: a car battery and jumper cables. The tire iron. Pliers. A fire and red-hot tongs. They used them on him, slapping her and grabbing her head to make her watch. Laughing and chattering, pointing their guns. AK-47s, pistols.

She recoiled with each of his screams. Making noise hurt; taking a breath seared her ribs. The explosion must have broken her ribs. She didn't care about her pain; she kept shouting, "Don't hurt him! I'll tell you what you want. Leave him alone."

They took her into another mud-walled room and she gave them everything she knew. "Don't hurt him anymore."

When she had nothing more to spill, the leader said in British-accented English, "Do you want to see your friend again? We spared him for you." They dragged her into the room where Alex was.

"See? He is alive." He swung the tire iron once, striking Alex across the middle of his face. "Now he is dead."

She heard the sound of breaking bones—the fine bones of his lovely face. Blood spurting silently. Uproarious laughter. Her sobs. They made those ululating sounds of joy.

They kept her in the room with his body while they checked out what she had said. All of it was wrong. Her trainers had said she was unbreakable, but the government had given her bad intel anyway. They must have known no one is unbreakable—so what they gave her was incorrect and couldn't hurt them.

She'd never been beaten before. Strange, how sounds carried through the pain and how blows were distinct, no matter how many of them there were. They kicked out her teeth. They did worse than that. When she came to, she was kneeling in the dirt with a bag over her head. She fell forward again, unconscious.

"We got you, Lieutenant. You're going home." Blue eyes greeted her when he pulled the sack off her head. He was a big man in camo-cloth, just like her. She looked around, befuddled. A ring of dead insurgents all shot to hell circled her. One of them had a machete.

A second more and they would have beheaded her.

"Oh, my God," Clarisse gasped. These people knew about her. They'd beat *him* if she didn't produce for them. Clarisse ran for the bathroom and leaned over the toilet. A few orange blobs floated in it when she flushed.

They knew what had happened. Did they know she had carried Alex's child? That he was her older son, Ricky, back in Palo Alto? Did they know the rest? That her younger boy, Jimmy, wasn't Jack's either? Did they know everything that had happened before she met Jack?

She clawed her way back to the bed, frantically feeling the pillowcase with her left hand, the bedspread with her right.

Everything melded into one scene: the flashback from Iran, being where she was. The committee meeting and the dean that morning, losing tenure, her reputation, and her job. Thought crazy for trying to prove that the universe was only one among an infinite number, linked by threads. Crazy?! She was *right!*

She was right, but the alternate world she had found was hell. She'd been hijacked to her past. A beautiful young man—Elias was beautiful, she could see that now that he was clean and his hair was washed—had been starved and beaten to prepare him to *serve her needs?* No. It was so *she'd* do what they wanted. They'd beat *him* to death if she didn't follow orders.

Sobs came out of nowhere. Clarisse called for her husband. "Jack. Jack. Help me. Please help me." The room was bugged, but she couldn't hold anything back. They wanted her to work for them and thought they had to do *that* to Elias to get her to do it… She held a pillow to her face, biting it, trying to get control.

"Shh, Dr. Hull. I'm here." He'd slipped into bed so silently, she hadn't known he was there. "I'll help you."

"No!"

"I won't do anything you don't want. I can help you. I'm trained." His hands touched her shoulders and they relaxed. Her ribs convulsed and more sobs came. "Shh. You're all right. I'm here."

He stroked her head and the back of her neck. Relaxed her shoulders. The tears and shaking dissolved into him. She slept.

When Clarisse awakened, they lay together, bodies cupped. He was still asleep. She carefully disengaged and looked at him. He was beautiful. Clear, pale skin, long black eyelashes against his cheeks. Lovely bones. The sweetest expression. No fear now.

He left her breathless, captivated. Within a minute of his touching her the night before, Clarisse had known that they would be lovers.

And that she would lose everything she had.

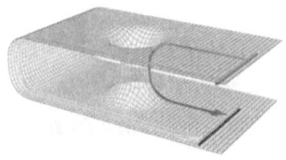

FOUR

JACK

JACK ABERCROMBIE WISHED that his father-in-law had slid into his grave with his mouth shut. But Benjamin Zachary Hull, MD, PhD never held his peace about anything. On the night he'd died, he'd told Jack the truth, heedless of what it did to his son-in-law.

As a result, Jack paced in front of the big bay window of the magnificent Queen Anne Victorian with its onion-shaped dome, widow's walk, and commodious porches. He walked around the historical monument where he lived with his wife and two children, more upset than he had ever been. He peeked out of the curtains in the front parlor and scanned the street for the fiftieth time. His mouth was dry and his stomach churned. Those pains in his heart were beginning. He hoped that he didn't end up in the hospital, the way he had when Clarisse's father died.

Where was she? It was ten at night. Where would she have gone? She hadn't called him, which was weird in itself, but he knew about the disastrous results of her committee meeting and what had happened subsequently. She'd been fired because she'd decked that kid. The whole campus knew. Concerned friends had been calling all afternoon and into the night. The sympathetic callers were faculty; they understood. Maybe they'd wanted to do the same thing to a few students. Their well-wishers knew everything, except where his wife was.

Clarisse would have to leave Palo Alto. Finding another academic job would be hard anywhere, given the reason for her firing. There were always think tanks and research institutes, though. And the research she did for the military, whatever it was. She could just move into that full time.

If she'd falsified her data or experimental results, her career would be ruined, even in a think tank where she'd spend her life in a cubicle, but that couldn't be the case. Jack was sure whatever she did was correct, but physicists spoke a different language than him. They were all "dark matter" and "black holes" and expanding universes. A problem with her results was possible, but he knew she'd never fake them. He knew her *that* well, at least.

Of course, she'd be upset. He'd expected she'd go to the gym at her karate studio and work out the equivalent of a marathon. That was the first place he called, looking for her. The staff hadn't seen her. He asked for her teacher, the *sensei,* but he was still at his "day job" at Moffett Field. Her karate class didn't meet that night, anyway.

As time went by, he became more desperate, and called her sensei on his cell phone. Jack and the boys called her karate teacher Obi-Wan-Kenobi. All of them felt one down in the face of her devotion to the man. She respected the eighth-level black belt more than she had her father.

Obi-Wan said, "I haven't heard from her. Have you tried her teaching assistants? Maybe she'd go out with them and…"

Get drunk. A logical move for anyone. Likely to have very bad consequences for Clarisse.

Should he call the cops? No. Not yet.

This was so unnecessary. He had had news that would fix everything. All of their lives: his, hers, and the boys'. A magic cure had materialized that very afternoon. He had been so excited, waiting for her to get home so he could tell her. It made what happened with the committee pale to insignificance. She could have a new career, a new professional life. None of what had happened in California would matter.

Jack stalked around the room, then into the kitchen where the remains of the pizza he'd ordered for them sat in its box. He tore off a section and ate it, standing up.

Jimmy came in from the library—known as the TV room in other households. They did have a TV in there, but it was only used for programs on PBS.

"When is Mom coming home, Dad?" The thirteen-year-old looked as worried as Jack felt. But he had been too young to know what had happened, hadn't he? Ricky, his fifteen-year-old brother, might remember. No... Ricky had been a toddler, and Jimmy not even a baby that other time. They wouldn't be able to recall their mother's previous disappearance.

"I don't know where she is, Jimmy. But I'm sure she'll be back soon."

"Ricky and I don't think so, Dad. She's never late and she always tells us way ahead if she has to leave to work. Ricky's searching the net upstairs. For signs."

"Signs. What signs?"

"I don't know, Dad. Anything. If there's anything, he'll find it."

That was true. Ricky was a tech genius. Colleges were already making him scholarship offers.

"Why don't you go up and help him, Jimmy? Give you something to do. I'll make some calls."

"He's on his third iteration of..." some tech mumbo-jumbo came out of his son's mouth. Jack didn't understand Clarisse's boys, either. "I knew it wouldn't work, but he wanted to try it anyway." He looked up, eyelids fluttering a little. "Good. He got it. That was the algorithm I told him to use." The boy left. Jack watched him go. He was the picture of his mother: slim, dark-haired, and beautifully formed. Driven, just like his brother. With the same oddities as their mother.

Ricky and Jimmy could have been full brothers, rather than half. They were equally gifted. Jack found them a bit spooky in how well they got along. So close, so connected, almost as if they read each other's thoughts. Like Jimmy had just done with that algorithm. And the way they could communicate with their mother even when she wasn't there. Very strange. They joked about it, calling it *mindspeak*.

But he had no time to worry about the boys. Now it was Clarisse's turn for being the focus of his undivided anxiety.

Jack poured himself a finger of Scotch and pondered. Clarisse had never disappeared like this on him. Which was not to say that she wasn't capable of it, given what her father had told him.

He was thrown back into the dreadful night when Ben had died and told Jack the truth, dumping the family secret and curse on him.

He could have lived with Clarisse's explanations and been fine. She *had* told him the truth before that, sort of. But she hadn't told him all of it, and not the part that really mattered.

He'd once exclaimed that she had the most beautiful teeth he had ever seen. She said they were implants. She'd had an accident and lost all of them.

Clarisse didn't tell him that the "accident" had happened when she was on a covert op for the U.S. government in Iran, sniffing out possible weapons of mass destruction. Nor did she tell him that she'd been the only survivor.

Someone had *kicked out* his wife's teeth. Who? Agents of the Iranian government? Terrorists wanting nuclear materials for their own bomb? Or had her team been trapped between Iraqi and Iranian forces? They'd been having a vicious civil war at the time.

Her father had said the feds refused to tell him who it was.

"They beat her so badly it's a wonder she lived. It's a wonder Ricky survived. She was four months pregnant with him. They tortured Ricky's father to death in front of her. His name was Alex Caldwell. Clarisse told me he was 'the love of her life.'"

Why had Ben told him that? All of it, but especially about "the love of her life"? Clarisse was the love of *his* life, his goddess and obsession. He knew she had never loved him the same way, but why did her father have to tell him about that other man?

"I'm telling you this because I'm dying. Since her mother died, I'm the only one who knows her real story.

"When I've been on the job, she's done well. When I've let go of her... Well, the escapade in Iran was just part of it. You should know the rest."

And Ben let him know the rest. Jack sat next to the old man's death-bed, barely able to breathe, mouth hanging open, hands clutching the chair arms. His head moved from side to side. *No. Don't tell me any more.* His father-in-law kept talking.

"Clarisse always was willful, but she went over the line after she got her bachelor's degree. The girl was brilliant; top honors with a double major in pre-med and physics. She could have gone to graduate school anywhere."

Jack had seen smiles like Ben's before. His father wore that grin when one of his horses won a championship.

"I wanted her to go into medicine, like me. We quarreled. She joined the military because they promised to make her a physicist. She didn't have to run off. I would have backed down if I knew what she'd do."

The old man had rocked back suddenly, hacking and gagging, eventually spitting bloody phlegm into a container that Jack barely got in place in time. Ben Hull was fading along with the evening. Fading with Jack's spirits. And everything he believed about his beautiful wife.

"She ran off to spite me and ended up in Iran."

As though remembering an important fact, Ben threw in, "The Caldwell boy was brilliant, by the way. Math and physics, like Clarisse. The military said they saw no limit as to what he could have achieved with them, had he lived. Shows in his son. Ricky's IQ is beyond even his mother's. Genetics. That's what life's about." Another attack of coughing.

"I want you to know about her so you can take care of her, Jack. They're putting me on morphine tonight. Talking to you is the last thing I have to do before they take my mind away. When that's gone, my life is over. You're just what she needs, Jack! Stable. Authentic. Honest. I'm so glad she found you. You can continue my role."

He was a babysitter and stooge. What about Jack's work? His writing and teaching? He'd been nominated for the Pulitzer. Didn't the old man know that?

The crack between him and Clarisse materialized next to Ben's deathbed.

"Thank you, Jack. You've given me peace of mind."

A nurse came in and put a morphine drip into the IV port in the back of Ben's hand.

His father-in-law said nothing more to anyone. Ben Hull, MD, PhD, managed to inject himself with a lethal dose during the night. How was never determined.

Jack ended up in the hospital the next day. His heart hurt as if it was cracking open. He'd fallen to the floor and the ambulance had hauled him off.

His hospital visit leaked over the campus, increasing his social and intellectual capital. He cared so much about his esteemed father-in-law that he'd been hospitalized with anguish.

Jack had grieved, but not for Ben—for the beautiful woman he thought he'd married. He'd lost her when Ben relieved himself of the truth, and *all* the truth. And now he'd really lost her. He hadn't done the thankless job Ben had left for him; he hadn't kept her safe. Her disappearance was his fault.

The government had transported Clarisse back from Iran and put her in one of their hospitals. Ben had her moved to Stanford. He'd pulled strings and gotten her a medical discharge from whatever clandestine branch of the armed forces had ensnared her.

Frantic and having flashbacks almost daily, Clarisse delivered baby Ricky three months after getting home. She moved into the family mansion with the baby, and she went wild.

Clarisse was an alcoholic. Jack knew that. She'd told him about it. He knew she went to a therapist because of it, and she went to AA meetings, sometimes several times a week. Clarisse didn't drink. He curtailed his drinking when he was home to make it easier on her.

Her hard drinking had started when she grieved for the man Jack would never meet and couldn't match.

"But, she found a cure somehow. Stopped drinking, pulled herself together." The old man nodded wisely at Jack, imparting a secret. "She was very wild in those days, Jack. Running around with *men*." Jack gaped. He hadn't known about that. "But Clarisse got into the doctoral program in physics. No help from her mother, either." Her father continued; he was not going to let Jack out of hearing a single sordid fact.

Speaking of his deceased wife, the condescending old goat had smiled broadly. Clarisse's mother had been even more prominent than her dying husband. A Nobel prize-winning physicist. Jack had never seen Ben in the light he revealed that night. The intellectual snobbery and pretension. The conviction that smart people were superior to everyone, and he was superior to all of them.

"Everything was fine until Clarisse went to a ten-day conference in New York City. A physics conference, but there was lots of drinking and late parties.

"She disappeared from one. People told me she had been flirting with any number of men, and was very drunk. They saw her get into a car with four. She was so inebriated she could barely walk. It was *not* an abduction."

He shook his head. "We had no word of her for almost ten days. Eleanor and I were beside ourselves. Thank God, we were there to care for little Ricky. She abandoned him without a thought."

"What happened?" The woman Jack had married was a responsible physicist, a professor at one of the world's best institutions, not a drunken slut.

"They found her in a little town in Wyoming, incoherent and high on something. LSD, maybe. She had nothing. No purse, money, identification, credit cards. She was also pregnant." Jack gasped. "With Jimmy. She refused an abortion."

Jack groaned and put his face in his hands.

"It's not all that bad, Jack," the old man consoled him. "The four men she left with were all top physicists. They went to Clarisse's hotel room. The police gathered DNA samples and identified the men. I had Jimmy tested when he was born." He beamed as widely as a dying man could. "Jimmy's father is a professor at a major East Coast university. Wants nothing to do with Jimmy or that night. Signed off custody. So, our girl pulled off another good one."

Jack's mouth opened and he shook his head. "What?"

"I don't mean to sound callous, Jack, but that happened years ago. She's been a model of propriety since."

"Wait a minute. How did she get to Wyoming? Who took her things? That *had* to be an abduction."

"I have no idea who else was involved or if it was voluntary on her part. The authorities couldn't find anything and she didn't know. Whatever they gave her produced amnesia."

Ben seemed less disturbed by Clarisse's abduction than thrilled that she'd produced a brilliant baby from the incident. Jack had seen that elation dozens of times in his cattle and horse-producing father. A champion offspring was worth whatever it took to create it.

"We brought her home. She pulled herself together with the new baby. She became the woman you met and married. Finished her PhD. Worked her way to associate professor. Started showing her true colors—until she got into this alternate universe crap. That's for hippies and New Age idiots.

"That's why I'm telling you this, Jack. If her pet, and very shaky, research fails, she could do it all again. Promise me you'll take care of her..." the fading man beseeched, a wreck with rheumy old eyes, shaky hands, and a cancer-ridden body.

"Sure, Ben. I'll do whatever you ask."

"Get her to give up that alternate universe nonsense. It's her pathology speaking."

Here he was. Four years after Ben had died, in the middle of the disaster he'd expected since that night. He'd promised to make her forget about alternative universes; they were her delusion. A fantasy. He'd tried to talk to her about it, but didn't understand her mathematics-laced explanations of why the area was so important. He didn't understand the passion she felt for the subject. He didn't understand *her*, and he didn't like her very much ever since his father had told him the truth.

Jack wiped his eyes. She wasn't interested in him. Her projects and nameless missions were more important to her than their marriage. Those and her goddamned karate studio—and teacher.

He'd lain in bed alone on so many nights, aching for her, wanting and needing her. And she was not there.

Yet, everything changed when she *was* there. Clarisse was so breathtakingly present, so focused and attentive, no other woman could compete. In minutes, she made up for every slight with a smile and a kiss. With all of herself. The gift of her love.

He'd never forget her, but Alex Caldwell had been the love of her life. To Clarisse, he was a faithful babysitter. Fortunately, Jack had fallen in love with her boys. That filled some of the emptiness in his heart. When they'd started calling him "Dad" and "Daddy," Jack had thought he'd melt. He made sure they had what they needed—loving, most of all.

In his books, Jack wrote about complicated feelings and relationships with astonishing ease. He could write about such tangles because he lived in one. He also knew that no easy out existed; he couldn't walk away. His father-in-law's revelations about Clarisse had driven a spike into the heart of their marriage. Ricky and Jimmy were part of what held them together, but not all. Despite his pain and disappointment, Jack still loved his wife madly. She took his breath with her beauty and brains. Just seeing her made him want to tear off her clothes. More than that, she was Clarisse Hull, of the famous Hulls. Jack wanted world-class success as much as the next man. With Clarisse as his wife, tenure at a major university, and a couple of important book awards, he'd hit the bigtime. The Oklahoma rancher's son had made it to the top. She was a trophy, and he intended to keep her, aching heart and all.

The phone rang and he answered, "Yes, this is Dr. Abercrombie. No, I haven't seen my wife… I was about to call the police."

When Jack hung up, he held onto the wall for a few seconds. The campus police had found Clarisse's car sitting in the parking lot where she'd left it that morning. No sign of a break-in. No sign of her.

It was all his fault. If he'd made her happier, loved her more, and done what her father had said, this wouldn't have happened.

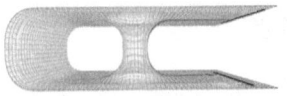

FIVE

Dr. Hull

WHEN ELIAS STIRRED in the bed, Clarisse was standing on a chair and waving a wand-like instrument along the wall where it met the ceiling. The bug was very clever, built into the room's construction. She wouldn't be able to remove it, but she could disable it.

Her laptop was already booted up. What she needed to do was create a surge that would blow out their system, and the eardrums of anyone listening. Which she could do with a little programming. Her fingers flew on the keyboard.

Elias shoved himself into a sitting position in the bed, eyes bulging. She put her finger to her mouth, shushing him, and hit enter. She laughed aloud; her instrument's controls shot off the chart, and then the panel showed that the wall had stopped broadcasting.

"Ultra-sonic," she said to Elias. "We can't hear it, but I'm sure they did. We'll have about fifteen minutes before they reboot. Tell me about this place so we have a chance in hell of getting out of it. Where are we?"

"Home."

"Oh, come on. This isn't your home. You weren't born here. Where do you come from?"

"I don't know."

"Come on. We're wasting time. *Were you born here?*"

He shuddered with terror.

"Come on, Elias; we need to work together if we're going to escape. How did you get here?"

He jolted at that. "I don't know where I came from or how I got here."

"How did the others get here?"

"They were here."

"All of them, no new arrivals since you've been here?"

"All the ones younger than me are newer. If someone goes up a corridor and doesn't come back, new ones appear, like you did."

"Out of nowhere?" He nodded. "So the number is always the same." Another nod. *Suggests a finite number of people can be supported by this world,* she thought. *How many?* "Where do the new people come from?"

He shook his head. "I don't know. No one can remember. Just me. I can remember a little."

"What do you remember about your life before?"

He shook his head. "I remember some things. A red door. A thing like a hand on it."

She'd knocked at a door like that when she'd been lost the day before. "A gray house, small, with a red door and black knocker, like a hand."

He nodded. "I see it in dreams sometimes."

Palo Alto, sometime between 1970 and 1980. Where in Palo Alto? she thought.

"Is that how you found me yesterday? On that street?"

"Yes. I went to the house."

"How did you get there?"

"I thought about it."

"You thought about it and you were there?"

"Yes."

"Can everyone do that, come and go when they want by thinking about it?"

"No. No one can do it, except me, yesterday. I couldn't do it before that. Once people are here, no one leaves, unless they..."

"Die."

He nodded. "People go up the corridors if they get married, but I think they die."

"Why?"

"Because they never come back. This place—there's nothing but what you see. I've looked through the windows in the doors to the corridors. There's nothing but white."

"No back alleys or escape routes? Nothing outside the windows up above?"

"No. I don't think there's anything, even air, if they don't put it there for some reason."

"That face on the wall. Is he all we see of the aliens? A human face that we can relate to?" He nodded.

Great. How the fuck could *she* get back?

"Do you remember anything else about the place you went yesterday?"

His face was so beautiful, aching planes and huge, clear eyes. "When I was sleeping last night, I remembered someone lived in the house. I felt her." His eyes misted.

"Your mother?"

He nodded. "I think so. I think they took me from there and put me here."

"How old were you?"

"Ten." The answer came with no hesitation.

"You remembered?"

"Yes, because you're here. I remember more with you here." He gazed at her, worship in his eyes.

"Me? Well, that's me, Super Clarisse. Let's see what else you can remember. How old are you now?"

He shook his head. "I don't know for sure. There's no time here. You wake up, there's the day, then the night. Sometimes, you can see rain and clouds through the windows on the top. And you can see the stars. I don't know if they're real, or they put them there. I calculated the years when they taught me about the stars just before you came. I think I'm twenty-two."

"You've been here twelve years. In that big room?"

"Yes. There's no other place, except the corridors. We only get to leave when our person comes."

"Your person."

"Yes, the person you were created for." He couldn't hold her gaze, looking away.

"Me. I'm your person."

"Yes."

"What does that mean?"

"I was made for you. I match you. I will help you do your work. They taught me. I know what you know."

"You got a PhD in physics in this hole and can replicate my work?" Pissed her off, this shillyshallying. Also, the effrontery.

"I know what you know." He directed his speech at the floor.

"They have classes out there?"

"No. They put what you know in me."

"Oh, shit. Listen, Elias, the power's going to be off a lot at this rate. You have to tell me more, faster. How did they do that?"

"How did they bring *you* here?"

That rocked her back. "I don't know. I'll have to do more work to figure it out. Fuck. Well, my research was right, anyway."

The ominous, academic face appeared on one wall of her room. "Dr...."

She pointed the wand attached to her computer at it, and the image broke up the same way her view of Palo Alto had the day before. "You're not allowed in here, in any way. Butt out."

"Dr. Hull, we will take stern measures if you do not comply." The voice entered the room from no apparent place.

"You mean you'll beat the crap out of me if I don't do what you want?"

She could feel a hint of mirth in his tone. "Oh, no, Dr. Hull; you know what we'll do."

"Beat the crap out of Elias. No, you won't. I won't let you."

"How will you be able to stop us, my good doctor?"

"I'm not 'your good' anything. I'll stop you by killing him first. I can kill him before you can get the door open. You should know that. And I can kill myself just as fast.

"El and I are going to eat breakfast. Someone's outside with it now, right?" She could feel him back off, wondering how she knew that. He didn't know *all* of her talents. Those were the stuff of legend, and the Hull genius. "I thought so. We're going to eat breakfast, and then El is going to show me to whatever laboratory you've cobbled together for me.

"I'll see if I can do what you want with it."

"How do you know what we want?"

"Any moron could figure out what you want. You kidnapped me and are holding me captive to do what you can't—create larger and more stable portals to my world so your people, or whatever you are, can get through and take over. And so you can go back and forth at will. You may have a variation on the scenario, but that's the general plan, yes?"

A laugh rippled through the air. The voice didn't speak again.

"Dr. Hull, I have your breakfast," a chirpy teenaged girl's voice said from the intercom to the hallway. "I can't open the door."

The girl was blond, doe-eyed, and the female equivalent of the surfer-boy whose finger Clarisse had bent back. She entered the room with a laden tray, and looked around surreptitiously with a smirk on her face. Her eyes lingered on the bed, then flashed to Elias with a knowing smile.

"We didn't fuck last night," Clarisse barked. "And we *won't,* so tell your friends to quit keeping score. Put that down and get out... Wait!"

Clarisse went to the table and took plastic covers off the dishes. Exactly what she had ordered. She sipped the coffee. "Fine. We'll have the same tomorrow. We'll eat lunch in the lab. I'll have a salad. What do you want, El?"

Elias looked like he might faint.

"He's a little shy. He'll have a double cheeseburger and double fries. And milk. Whole for him, nonfat for me. We want lamb chops and sweet potato fries for dinner, with ice cream. Double ice cream. We'll eat here. Got it?"

The girl flapped her jaw like Elias.

"One other thing. If you or anyone else in that zoo you live in lays a hand on him," a wave at Elias, "I will kill them. Understand that? I will kill whoever it is. You, or your pretty boyfriend or anyone. And don't think you can gang up on me. You can't. By the end of the day, I will have trained Elias so that we are an unbeatable team.

"Go back to waiting for your prince to come."

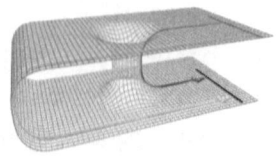

SIX

CURIOUSER
AND CURIOUSER

THE BLACK CAR first appeared less than twenty-four hours after Clarisse disappeared. The boys said it cruised the house a couple of times that afternoon. They weren't home most afternoons, but they happened to be that one. Having their mom disappear had knocked their cockiness down a notch.

A black car pulled up in front of the house and two men came to the door.

Jack had just come back from the police station, where he'd filled out more forms. They were doing all the usual police things, but had no clue as to his wife's whereabouts.

He poured himself a Scotch just before the doorbell rang. He looked through one of the glass panels next to the front door and ditched the Scotch in the kitchen. They looked like FBI. In every movie he'd seen about the FBI, the agents looked like that. Two of them, a team, wearing black suits with white shirts. Short hair, super clean-cut and straight looking. He was terrified.

They showed their identification. FBI, as he had thought. They came in. One pulled a sheath of papers out of his briefcase. It was an extremely inclusive search warrant. As Jack sputtered, a crew emerged from a large van covered with the logos of a window-cleaning establishment.

"Where is Dr. Hull's office?" one asked.

Jack pointed.

"And your bedroom is…"

"It's upstairs. What are you doing? You can't…"

"We can, Dr. Abercrombie," said the FBI man. "Read the warrants. We are impounding all of Dr. Hull's belongings."

"Why?"

"We are not at liberty to say. This is a national security matter."

They began trooping through the house, taking Clarisse's computers and everything in her office, including a framed picture of him with the boys.

"Why do you need that? Stop this! All of it. I want my attorney."

"Call whoever you want, Dr. Abercrombie. We'll wait." The asshole had a *smirk* on his face, as though he knew what was going to happen. Jack called his attorney.

"Todd, I need your help right now. I've got some men here who say they're FBI. They're taking Clarisse's things."

"Let me talk to them."

He handed the receiver to the sneering goon. He could hear Todd's voice rising and falling. The FBI guy's amused expression never changed as he responded to the attorney.

"I've got the warrant. You're welcome to examine it."

Todd was there in less than fifteen minutes, in a jacket and tie. One thing about living in Professorville—all the professionals in town were minutes away. Plus, Clarisse's disappearance was notorious by this time; anyone would have put on a coat and tie to get in on the drama. Todd read the warrant. Pages and pages of it. When he hit the end, he looked up and said, "It's legal, Jack. They have the right to do this."

"I don't understand. Clarisse wasn't involved in anything touching national security. She was interested in alternative universes. She might as well have been studying faeries and magic wands. Nothing of what she did was even the slightest bit a national security matter. You can't…" Jack turned to the FBI man, who had pulled out a recorder.

"Would you repeat what you just said, Dr....?"

"That's it," his attorney snapped. "My client has nothing to say. Do what's permitted by the warrant." He took Jack into the kitchen, where the boys sat staring out into the entrance hall over the latest pizza he'd ordered.

"Jack, do you know anything about what she was involved in? Her real research?"

"No. She was writing science fiction with equations... Hey, stop that," he ran into the entrance hall, where a couple of gorillas walked toward the front door, bearing the wooden rod from their closet. All of Clarisse's clothes hung on it.

"What are you doing? How could her *jeans* be involved in *anything*? Stop it."

Another guy followed with a big box of her shoes.

"What are you doing? You can't take those!"

His attorney put his hand on Jack's arm. "They can, Jack."

The next day, he went to Todd's office. It was a nice place, a Victorian on Cowper.

"What's going on?" he asked, only slightly less shell-shocked than the night before.

"From what I've been able to find, Clarisse isn't in trouble, but her research was top, top secret. The feds don't know where she is. The government fears that terrorists may have kidnapped her to make her divulge what she knows. It's bad, Jack."

"She didn't do anything wrong?" He was stunned. He'd never imagined that terrorists would kidnap her.

"She has a military background. Were you aware of that?"

"Yes, her father told me. That was years ago."

"Perhaps. Maybe not. She did her research at Moffett Field, didn't she?"

"Yes. She had government grants. They had cheap space and lots of free personnel. I never could figure out why they wanted her there."

The attorney frowned. "Jack, it might be a good time to take a sabbatical. You wanted to go to Greece, didn't you? Why don't you take the boys and have a year's holiday?"

Jack went home, flabbergasted. He'd always assumed Clarisse's research was nonsense. Some people didn't; she was quite the media figure. Whenever she spoke, the venue had to hire extra security. She had groupies and fan sites on the net.

Clarisse had been arguing with her tenure committee for a year, pointing out that if *they* didn't think what she was doing was legitimate, a lot of people *did*, and were making her life miserable, so it had to have some validity. The committee wasn't receptive to her arguments. Whatever originated outside of their hallowed circles was nonsense.

"That's pop-sci foolishness, Clarisse," she'd told him the dean said. "People get worked up over what happens on social media. Facebook and Twitter. Even I've read of people receiving death threats because of innocent tweets. That doesn't mean we grant them tenure. Hire security people and give us some real research to examine."

Clarisse had responded to part of the dean's advice. The family's computers and phones were protected by firewalls the boys had set up. A secretary went through her emails. Some were from fans idolizing her. Clarisse got a lot of hate mail, too. She'd been stalked online and once had talked of hiring someone celebrities used in Hollywood to keep the nuts away to protect her.

Why hadn't he taken it seriously? Because of Ben. Her father had disparaged her work and treated it like a joke. Eventually, he had, too. Jack hadn't felt that way in the beginning; he'd been starry-eyed over Clarisse's talk of quantum physics and wormholes. All that jargon, and the way some of the students worshiped her. He'd been one of her groupies.

Years of living in Hull House with her famous parents and their disdain for their daughter had gotten to him. The process was insidious, and fueled with late-night brandies with Ben and Eleanor's clever but snide jabs at their daughter. He lived in a poisonous cloud, and it tainted him.

Why did Ben and Eleanor hate their daughter so? Jack hadn't seen it before Clarisse disappeared, but now the hatred screamed like a siren. They were a cold family prizing intellect above all else. He'd never seen her parents make a physical display of affection to anyone, public or private. Why didn't Clarisse walk out? She must have felt the poison. He'd almost gotten her to leave when they'd discovered that Ben had been experimenting on the boys. Jack had been furious enough to pack up, but she wouldn't go. Clarisse had raged, *and* stayed.

She was tied to her parents and the house with golden chains. What was the keystone that kept the toxic game going? Why did his in-laws want to destroy the public's opinion of Clarisse? And *his* of her? Why was that piece so important?

The part of Jack that had written those insightful books came forth. He knew all about complicated entanglements. Dark motivations. Lies that became truth. Ben and Eleanor were covering something up, something involving them and not their daughter. She had to be the unstable maniac for them to play loving, concerned parents coddling an explosive, if brilliant, liability. They were hiding something, but what?

The FBI had a very different reaction to the public response to Clarisse's work than the elder Hulls.' They took it very, very, seriously and started calling him or coming over every day as they went through her computer or the stuff in her closet. The agents presented him with printed-out reams of the most vicious, violent emails directed at his wife.

"Did you know about this, Dr. Abercrombie? Do you know who these people are? Look at their screen names. Many of them make repeated threats," one of the black-suited wonders said. They were almost ludicrously serious, but when he read what maniacs threatened her with, the joking was knocked out of him. This *was* serious.

Every alarm went off in his brain. Why had he accepted Ben's description of Clarisse's earlier disappearance? A drunken, drug-induced orgy that she had initiated? Part of him had railed against his father-in-law's innuendo when he'd heard it. But he hadn't verbalized his feelings. The Clarisse he knew was a dedicated scientist; he should have fought her father's words tooth and nail. God, he'd been such a wimp. Maybe she'd been abducted then, too. Maybe her departure from the hotel with the four men had been a kidnapping.

Which was why he decided to find out what his wife really *was* doing. The FBI had her computers and working materials, but he remembered that most of her papers had been published in physics journals. He looked them up online... And couldn't read a one. He hadn't known that math had that many symbols, or what they meant. He could barely read the synopses and responses from colleagues. The readers' responses printed in the journals broke down like the emails: some were wildly positive and others as charged with hate as the worst online stalker's venom. The physicists just couched their anger in jargon and more of those unintelligible symbols.

Jack knew all about academic journals and those who lived in them. Some intellectuals lived their lives by waging footnote wars in professional periodicals. They wrote hateful responses to articles they disagreed with. The article's author often responded. The responses were included in reprints, so that the footnotes ended up being longer than the articles they elaborated upon. Usually, the comments and responses were so obtuse that only a few could understand what the combatants were saying, but their rancor stank. At least in his field, they spoke English.

Clarisse hadn't written any popular material, but he remembered that she had spoken at TED, this being short for 'Technology, Entertainment, Design,' a group of conferences held by some non-profit foundation. "Ideas Worth Spreading" was its slogan. The concept behind the meetings was to bring together leading minds and provide a sort of university in a day, or a couple of days, so leaders of business, science, and the arts could stay abreast of current developments in a very short period.

Jack hadn't gone, for reasons that had seemed valid at the time. He felt that TED was fundamentally flawed—the product of Silicon Valley prodigies who had made too much money without developing the maturity of true leaders. TED was the fruit of egomaniacs who thought that an afternoon of lectures could teach and illuminate better than the intellectual community could with its thousands of years of experience.

Also, they charged a bloody fortune and wouldn't comp him a seat, even with Clarisse speaking.

He and his father-in-law had felt exactly the same. They sat in the library one night, cigars and brandy in hand, and vented their feelings. The longer they ranted, the more absurd Clarisse's invitation seemed.

Ben was adamant that no one in the family go. "Pop culture, that's all it is! Hubris! Folly!"

Now that Clarisse had disappeared, Jack couldn't figure out why he hadn't attended. How many men's wives were invited to speak at such a thing? Darker motivations arose as he sat with his devastation. He was jealous of his wife. He'd never been invited to speak where people would pay thousands to hear his thoughts. He didn't even have a fan group or Facebook page. Not a single stalker.

So Jack didn't go when Clarisse gave her talk, nor did he watch the DVD of Clarisse's speech, nor did he look it up online.

The FBI had taken the DVD, so he looked TED up online. The speakers included everyone from Bill Clinton to Bill Gates, and onto a raft of Nobel Prize-winners. Important and substantial people. Why hadn't he taken it seriously? He found the video of her talk.

Clarisse looked stunning on the screen. She wore a plain black dress that couldn't hide her trim figure. She was outlined clearly against a gray curtain background. Even in such somber surroundings, she was gorgeous. His heart grabbed when he saw her. Every negative thought he'd had vanished before her loveliness.

"Clarisse, what am I going to do without you?"

When he saw how compelling and vibrant she was on the screen, what her father had said seemed preposterous. Had the old man ever *seen* his daughter? Tears ran down Jack's cheeks as he listened to Clarisse's clear, intelligent, thoughtful voice. He could have howled; the pain of her absence was unbearable.

"We say that alternative universes don't exist. We have enough trouble dealing with *this* one. Explaining it. Measuring it. Controlling it. We think that the possibility of alternative universes, existing in the same time and place as ours, is fodder for science fiction.

"What if they aren't, though? Who hasn't awakened from a dream that seemed as real as the world we're in? Who hasn't driven into an unfamiliar neighborhood and known exactly where he was? Who hasn't been cruising along and all of a sudden been totally lost, as though in a new place? Sensations of déjà vu—I've been here before—are common. Yet we discount them.

"I've had these experiences, perhaps more than most…"

Perhaps because you got your head bashed in, were in a coma, and could have died, Jack thought.

"… and I thought… What if it's real? What if as many worlds as we can conceive stack upon themselves in a time/space reality that is beyond what current physics can conceive? It's an impossible question." She laughed merrily. "Well, if you know my family, that's exactly the kind of problem we look for. I talked to my dad about it, and my mom, and they encouraged me to pursue the concept."

Jack paused the video. They'd encouraged her? He'd never heard Eleanor Hull say anything encouraging to anyone about anything. Ben had never said a positive word about Clarisse's work in the years Jack had known him. He'd openly mocked it on his deathbed and told Jack to make her stop.

Why? Did they know something? A chill ran over him. What if the elder Hulls had been using him for more than a babysitter?

Jesus, he'd start believing in conspiracy theories next.

He turned on the DVD again, fuzzing out. He fast-forwarded through pieces of it. Equations flashed on a screen behind her. He couldn't understand them and was too rattled to comprehend her explanations. The crowd must have understood, though, as they started jumping up and down and screaming, applauding like maniacs.

"I have shown that alternative universes are mathematically possible," Clarisse smiled at the audience. "Now all I have to do is prove that they exist physically and that we can go to them." She held up her hands, quieting the crowd.

"There's something to be aware of, though. You know the old sci-fi nostrum, 'We come bearing gifts'? If we access other worlds, they may not bear gifts. They may not want us, with our troubled planet. Or, they may want our planet, but not us. They may not be friends on a similar journey. They may open their arms and greet us, or they may *not.*

"We don't know what's out there, or in there, in our minds and souls. Caution is advised before we sign up for a recreational journey.

"Dante Alighieri may have said it best in *The Divine Comedy*:

'*Relinqvīte omnem spem, vōs qvī intrātis.*' Abandon hope, all ye who enter here.

"The universe isn't necessarily friendly, nor is it safe. This isn't a New Age 'ain't it wonderful' dream that I'm courting. It's a level of reality no one knows."

The applause was tentative and first, and then a groundswell.

Jack shut off the machine. *Lord have mercy, what was Clarisse involved with?*

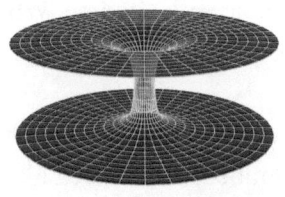

SEVEN

OBI-WAN-KENOBI

T HE NEXT DAY, Jack got a sitter from the agency they used to watch the boys. He had to find out something and it could take a while.

He took Alma St. to Shoreline Boulevard, and then surface roads toward Moffett Field. The Bayshore Freeway would be a nightmare at rush hour, but it generally was.

Also, Jack didn't want to see any trace of the "Googleplex," Google's spectacular *global* headquarters to the east of the freeway. *Global.* He couldn't stand the hubris and inflation that *was* Silicon Valley. He turned east on Moffett Boulevard, driving toward the NASA Ames Research Center. Moffett Field was operated by NASA now, not the Navy.

Why did the word NASA jump out at him today? Space research. Then the sign for Carnegie Mellon University, Silicon Valley. A high-level tech university. Why hadn't he thought it strange that a karate teacher should have his studio so close to a federal airfield surrounded by major scientific institutions?

Obi-Wan-Kenobi also had a name: Ron Weistheimer. His studio was a warehouse bordering Moffett Field, as close as they'd allow. Clarisse had liked it there because her lab was in the military complex. She could karate her brains out and then go back to work.

Jack scowled. He was going to find out about *everything* tonight. He wished he was big and tough and could beat the shit out of Ron. He was sure Ron had something to do with Clarisse's disappearance. Worse, he'd suspected Ron of having an affair with her from the minute he'd met him. He was doing *something* with Clarisse. When he saw them together at Ron's karate tournaments, they had an easy comradery he'd seen only between lovers.

Ron Weistheimer revolted Jack; he was everything the professor hated. Tall, muscular, and long-limbed, Ron moved like a superhero, taking over every space he occupied. He seemed invincible and all-knowing, a military man without conscience, but with tremendous and canny, applied intelligence. Not a shred of fat existed on his frame. His laser intensity made him resemble a vicious bird of prey, except when he was with Clarisse. When he'd seen Ron with Clarisse at the interminable karate tournaments, he smiled. That turned him into a nightmarish jack-o-lantern.

Ron's face was all that made him bearable to Jack—he was supremely ugly. Jack couldn't imagine how many times a nose would have to be broken to look like his, or why Ron didn't get it fixed. The outside edges of his ears were thickened and lumpy, resembling cauliflower. His knuckles were scarred and smashed, the joints of his hands enlarged almost past bending. Jack didn't want to think about how he'd gotten into this state or what the rest of his body looked like. Still, the imperfections made Ron seem vulnerable, and possibly human.

Jack parked in the empty lot in front of the studio and steeled himself for their meeting. He'd arranged to meet Ron after work when the place was closed. It was a big, blocky building, a two-story tilt-up constructed of slabs of concrete poured on the ground and then tilted into place. That was the predominant architectural style of Silicon Valley. He'd been there for Obi-Wan's karate tournaments and exhibitions. Clarisse was always the star, though the boys were getting good.

He walked into a tall cube of a room, straight from the street. The dojo. It was big. Had to be expensive as hell to rent. There was no second story; it was all open space. The walls were padded with black, cloth-covered stuff, up to way over his head. Could anyone throw an opponent that high? He wanted to chuckle, as he always did when he was here. Clarisse took Ron so seriously; you would have thought he was her father-confessor. Now Jack's breath caught. What had this ape done with Clarisse?

"Come on back, Jack," Ron's absurdly assured, masculine voice called through a speaker. "Straight through the dojo to the back."

Jack did as directed. At the rear of the big open space—where they pummeled and kicked each other—was a corridor. On one side was a weight room, something you'd expect to have seen Arnold Schwarzenegger running in the 1970s. On the hallway's other side were locker rooms. Straight back was Ron's office. He'd never seen it; Jack had never ventured past the dojo during the karate competitions he'd attended as a parental duty.

The back wall was painted burgundy. A big photo of an Asian guy sitting cross-legged with his eyes closed was centered in the wall with an altar under it. Jack assumed he was the master of their school. Candles and stuff were arrayed on the altar. The rest of the walls were black. Ron had a rosewood desk and cabinets set up on the left. He sat in an ultra-modern leather chair on the right. It was a grouping, like an upscale living room. All of it was expensive, and much more so than he'd expect a guy running a karate studio to be able to afford.

"Take off your shoes," Ron said. "Take a chair. You want some Scotch? Pour yourself some if you do." He waved at a table with a bunch of crystal decanters and heavy glasses. "Bring the bottle over here. We're going to need it."

Jack stared at Ron, reassured by his ugliness. Even more reassured when he took a close look at him and realized that the guy was probably more upset than he was.

"It's been days. I thought you'd be here sooner. I'm fucking out of my gourd. How are you?" Ron's voice rasped.

Jack doubled the amount of Scotch in his glass and picked up the decanter. "You don't know where she is?"

"Do I look like I know where she is?" Ron's ruddy skin was gray-tinged. Bags pouched under his eyes. "I've barely slept since she disappeared. No one knows where she is. No one on the fucking planet."

Jack sat down, clutching the decanter and his glass. He took a swig and then launched. "I thought she ran off with you. I thought you were having an affair."

Ron let out a donkey bray, almost spraying his Scotch over the coffee table. "That's the stupidest thing I've ever heard. Do you know how much I envy you? I'd give anything to have Clarisse love me like she does you. You don't have any idea how much she cares, do you?"

Jack blinked. "No." He wanted to say more, but his thoughts wouldn't coalesce into words. *You're sleeping with my wife... You've kidnapped her... You're holding her somewhere... Give her back to me...* The thoughts didn't make any sense, but they were as powerful as the grief and loss that claimed him. This man had had something to do with...

"I've been so jealous of you. She comes home to you every night. She's in your bed; she loves you. Jesus Christ! What did you do to get so lucky?" Ron barked words that expressed what was going on inside *him*. He glared at Jack, his blue eyes magnetic.

He hadn't considered himself lucky since Ben had broken the charm.

"You've got the most beautiful, brainy, talented woman in the world loving you like you were the second Jesus, and you don't get what you've got. Clarisse would *never* cheat on you, and certainly not with me."

Jack sat and stared. "What?"

"You heard me. You probably thought we were banging our brains out whenever she was gone." He tilted his ugly head, lips parting in his cracked version of a smile.

"You stinking..." Jack was on his feet, stumbling across the Persian rug between their seats. Ron didn't bother standing, just waving his hand in response. Jack plopped back in his seat.

"We weren't, so kill that thought. You can hate me all you want, but it's time to take off the gloves and tell each other the truth. Do you know where she is?"

"No. I told you I didn't."

"No idea where she'd go if she wanted to run away and hide? If she was being pursued?"

"No. Why should she be pursued?" He thought of all the crazies writing those terrible emails. "Her research."

"Her research, yes."

"Do you work with her on that?"

"I can't tell you, Jack. We're in top secret-land."

"You work on the base."

"There and other places."

"But it's all top secret. You can't tell me."

"That's right, buddy. Even now, I can't tell you anything you don't already know." He rolled his eyes around the room significantly.

"Are we being recorded?" Jack looked around, wild-eyed.

"Let me say only: don't fart. They've probably got a smell-meter hooked up."

"We're being recorded. You're interrogating me..."

"No. I am *not* doing that, nor will I allow anyone to do that on my watch."

"Oh, shit." Clarisse was involved in something serious. But he'd known that, hadn't he? "What can you tell me?"

"I can tell you that I've loved your wife since I took that bag off of her head in Iran."

"*You* did that? You were *there*?"

"I can tell you about her being in Iran because your father-in-law already told you. I can't tell you any more."

"But you're in the service." What branch? Moffett Field had originally been a Navy base, but the base had been closed as a military facility since the late '90s. Or had it? Nothing about Ron bore any insignia of rank or corps, but he was as military as any general decked out with stars. "Clarisse was in the service, a long time ago. In Iran."

Jack parroted what his father-in-law had told him. He glanced at Ron, who sat perfectly still, a knowing look on his face. Something about his posture said something. Jack jerked, getting his message almost by thought waves.

"She's *still* in the military? How? She never said a thing about it. I know she did experiments on the base, went to meetings, and spoke at conferences a lot, but that was about physics. Wasn't it?"

Ron painfully folded his fingers and polished the nails against his shirt. "Can't talk about it, Jack. Some things never end. Some never happened." He looked at Jack with astonishingly blue eyes, his only attractive feature. "I'm here to find out what you know and facilitate getting her back. Did she have any friends that she might have gone to?"

"Friends? What friends? When did she have time? When she wasn't working, she was asleep, or with you." Jack's eyes narrowed. Clarisse and Ron had done something together. "You worked with her, didn't you? Away from the base."

"Can't say, Jack. There's secret, and then top secret. Then, so secret not even our president knows. They call it covert ops." Every inch of Ron's body spoke, and Jack was receiving. He worked with Clarisse on military things. She wasn't gone as much as she was because of her laboratory; she'd been doing something with Ron. She was still in the service. Covert ops.

"She was your partner. Like on TV cop shows. You did missions or something together."

"Top secret. No can tell."

"Tell me, for fuck's sake! She's my wife."

"Yeah, she's your wife. You lucky SOB. I'm just a grunt for Uncle Sam. You got the real prize."

"I don't understand. Why did she want *me*? I'm not a commando. I'm not a karate... *person*. I'm not *you*."

"Of course you're not me! She knows me. Knows what runs me. It runs her. She loves you, man, because you're the only frigging *normal* person in her world.

"She is my partner. That's as much as I can say. We gotta move through this faster. No one knows where she is. Nobody above me, or below me. No one in our world or anywhere on the planet. I've checked. She's up shit's creek, wherever she is. I hope she's as unbreakable as they say, because she's got a ton of classified information in that pretty skull.

"You need to get into the real world, Jack. The assholes at the university didn't believe in what Clarisse was doing. Shows how stupid they are. On my side, *squadrons* of people like me, and *our* scientists, and guys above me up to the top levels of government, take her word as gospel. We've known the implications of her experiments for years, and we've been preparing for the inevitable breakthrough. We *never* expected a warm and cozy visit from outer space, and neither did she.

"The folks here who run her lab and take care of her experiments while she's with me or home being 'mom' have discovered you're in danger. Or rather, the boys are in danger. Someone has found a way to pierce reality from the other direction. Exactly what she said was possible has happened. They've snatched her up. She'll fight until they turn her into cat chow, and she won't give anything up.

"But if they can do what they did in the way that they did it, they aren't friendlies. Don't expect ransom notes, Jack. Don't expect her to come back, either, unless she can find a way. If she can, she will, but I don't know if she can. Remember that she loves you and the boys more than anything on Earth."

Jack couldn't assimilate what Ron was saying. He'd come here thinking that Clarisse had run off with her karate teacher, or he'd kidnapped her. Or something. He was so fucking confused he didn't know what he thought. What he'd found was much worse than any imagining.

"She's my boss," Ron volunteered.

That was too much. Jack felt dizzy.

Ron grabbed Jack's glass as it fell. "Put your head between your knees. Get your head down. I've got a lot more to tell you."

Gasping, Jack struggled to sit up. Ron held his head down. "Get some oxygen to your brain. You're going to need it."

When they started talking again, Ron sat closer, forearms on his knees, talking more seriously than anyone Jack had ever heard.

"They want her DNA, Jack. First, they did what her research said could be done—created a hole in reality. They did that by putting superior resources into the investigation. The government's been feeding her crumbs. She needed some big bucks. She does have a computer here, a mother that you would not believe, but not enough money to staff it. So they're taking it down soon, in a couple of months. That's *not* top secret.

"Whoever got her did what she said was possible, and they tracked her as the theory's originator—and discovered the Hull genius. Her parents, grandparents, how far back? All geniuses. Ricky and Jimmy's fathers— geniuses. With psychic powers—you know that as well as I do. Mindspeak. You've heard them talk about it."

"I don't…" Jack sputtered.

"They'll come for the boys. You're safe because, well, you don't have that multigenerational Hull over-the-top intelligence *or* 'mindspeak.' But the boys do."

Jack sat there, blinking and opening and closing his mouth. Ron filled his glass, almost to the brim. "Drink. There's more. Dr. Óskar Erland, Jimmy's dad, has disappeared."

"How did you know he was Jimmy's dad?"

"Same way you did. Ben Hull told me."

"Clarisse's *father*?"

"Yeah, the old shit was proud that his grandson had been sired by a Nobel laureate. Sort of a family tradition."

"He *told* you?"

"Ben shot off his mouth wherever he thought he could impress someone. I was on duty when he broke the news to some generals."

A yelp of anguish escaped Jack. Ben had been around generals? Why would a psychiatrist and biogenetic researcher be around generals? What did Ben have to do with the armed forces?

"Yeah, the old man was a certified MD, PhD piece of shit. Erland disappeared the same way Clarisse did—no trace. They're *collecting*, Jack.

"Here's the deal: the boys have to be put in protective custody. They can't be anywhere *anyone* knows where they are. Now. You have to move out of that house, now. You've got the feds on your ass, you've got us on your ass, and the energy readings around your house—using Clarisse's own meters—are getting wonky. They're going to come for the boys soon.

"You are going to call up Oxford University and take that job they offered you."

"How did you know about that?" Jack spilled Scotch on his slacks. "No one knew about that. I was going to tell Clarisse when she got home. She didn't have to get tenure."

"But she didn't come home. You have to tell Oxford yes or no soon, don't you?"

"Yes, but how did you find out?"

"Welcome to our world, Professor Abercrombie. No secrets. Nothing is hidden. We know everything. *And* we don't exist. Everyone in the intelligence community knows that the University of Oxford made you an offer of a professorship, or whatever they call it in England.

"You're going to take it and move, tonight. Your belongings are being packed. The boys can't go to England with you; it's too exposed. They'd be taken."

"What do you mean? They have to go with me. They're my sons. They've lost their mother and now me? No. Absolutely not."

"I'm sorry, Jack. That's how it has to be. We know you worked hard to get that offer from Oxford. And so does the entire clandestine world. You have to go there and show up. The boys need to be far removed from the world and protected."

"Why?"

"Because whoever got Clarisse wants them, I told you that. And you being out in the open at Oxford is as important to the overall intelligence scheme as the boys being hidden. If Clarisse escapes, she needs a safe harbor that she can find, someone she really trusts. You're it. She'll come to you in England and we'll protect her. And you. You're a top-level security property now.

"You need to say goodbye to the boys. They're in the dojo now, waiting to say goodbye. You have ten minutes before your plane leaves."

"What? What are you saying? You haven't told me... why. Anything. I can watch out for the boys. You can't take them."

"Oh, yes, we can. Do you know who their babysitter is?"

"A graduate student. I got him from a service Clarisse and I use."

"Have you used him before?"

"No, our regular guy is in finals. They sent me someone new. They're vetted and safe..."

"No, they're not. You left Jimmy and Ricky with an operative for the Russian government. He's suspected of offing a few of his subjects."

"No!" Jack jumped up again. Ron pulled him down.

"They're safe. We picked them up, and the 'babysitter.' The heat is on, Jack. You can't *possibly* deal with this. You're out of your league."

"I let a Russian spy..."

"And assassin..."

"Watch the boys?" Jack sputtered.

"Yeah. Go say goodbye to Ricky and Jimmy, Jack. You'll see them again when it's safe."

"When?"

"Maybe never, Jack. The world may never be safe again."

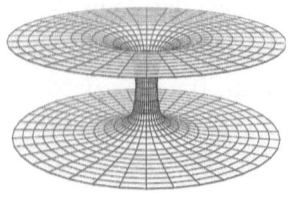

EIGHT

THE LAB

"OKAY, WE'RE OFF." Clarisse tweaked her instrument to knock out *their* bugs. She and El had finished a huge breakfast, most of which she'd passed to him. "We'll go to the lab now. Act stupid, like you know *nothing*. I may be mean to you and say nasty things. It's for effect—please don't think I mean what I'm saying. I have to convince them I'm the baddest motherfucker they've ever seen and that they can't push me around." Elias looked mystified, so she went on.

"Why do you think I'm here? So you can 'take care of' me? No. They grabbed me because they know about my project. Anyone who could make a fake Palo Alto, send you to it, find me, and then bring us back here—to this obviously phony Earth—can find out about my research. I make holes in what people call reality; that's what I've done in the lab. They want that. They also probably know about what I do with Ron. Black ops. I don't think that kid was all jacked up last night because they expected Cinderella.

"Why would an alien intelligence grab someone like me? To make holes in existence big enough for them to go through and grab my world. Pretty logical, huh? I think so, and so does the team I've been working with at the base for the last *six* years. That's what we prepared for." She trembled slightly in rage, or eagerness. Clarisse didn't know, beyond that she felt the same way when she and Ron were on a mission.

"They want me to open bigger holes, and then go through them and lead the charge to victory with the thugs they've assembled. I need to convince them that I can do that, but that I'm so tough, they can't *make* me do anything. That's how I'll stay alive, and so will you."

"How do you know that?"

She chuckled. "Anyone with half a brain could figure it out. Now we have to give them what they want, without giving it to them, and stay alive."

A knock at the door. She opened it and *that* face appeared on the wall opposite. "I trust your repast was satisfactory, Dr. Hull?"

"Better than dinner, which was hog swill. We need to talk about nutrition. You have a whole crowd of young people out there. I'm amazed they don't all have rickets from the crap you feed them."

"We feed them well."

"No, you don't. You feed them shit, and not enough of that, so they have to fight for food or they look like that drowned rat. He must be on the bottom of the totem pole." She'd indicated Elias.

"You don't know the first thing about feeding humans. We need fresh fruits and vegetables. High quality protein. If you're shanghaiing all these *people,* why don't you beam up some topsoil and vegetables? And a cow and some chickens. *I'll* make you a garden worth having— and enough protein so that people can thrive. I'm an expert gardener."

She turned to Elias. "Don't let blow-hard scare you." He was frozen, staring at the face on the wall. "Look, don't be afraid to talk back to a bully. It's all they understand. Come on."

They left their room, walking along the bright, all-white hallway away from the main warehouse. Panels in the ceiling provided light. Clarisse didn't know what the walls were made of. Maybe plastic. The floor was concrete, like the big depository where they'd entered. Except that here, the walls, ceiling, floor, and everything looked brand new. No marks, no mars, no sign of having existed before this moment appeared on any surface.

"Wait a minute," Clarisse stopped. The face on the wall accompanied them, slipping along the slick surface of the hallway effortlessly. "This corridor looks like it just materialized out of the 'white plastic' factory. You're making this place as you go, to suit your needs."

The haughty face stopped, regarding her with surprise. "You are observant, Dr. Hull."

"Never forget it." She squared her shoulders. "We walked into a barracks last night. Obviously, your people had been living there quite a while. They're your army." The eyebrows on the face rose a bit. "Don't be coy. Why else would that hostile gang be in that hall *but* to overpower something? You brought me here to make bigger holes into my reality and then lead them through to take over."

"I'm surprised that you could discern our mission so easily." The face's eyebrows rose and an amused smile appeared on his lips. "I'm sorry we're so transparent."

"This is one of those '*Duh?*' situations. Why else would you bring me here? I think you're powerless to do anything but light up walls. Isn't that right, Elias?" She turned to the young man. His face went dead white and he stifled a gasp. She was jacked up in commando mode and let his reaction slip.

"You expect me to train the undisciplined, ignorant gangsters you've allowed to run rampant out there into a force capable of attaining a military objective. Am I right, Dad?"

The scientist's face jerked, eyes twinkling and the corners of his mouth turning up.

"I'll take that as a yes. You made a few mistakes. You assembled a bunch of people, but they're not capable of attaining your goals."

"Why not? They're strong and healthy."

She scoffed. "If Blondie and his friends somehow make it into my world, the only thing they will do is get shot by the cops. If your troops get lucky and raise some dust, they'll call out the National Guard, and *they'll* really off them. You need physical and mental training for your army to be anything more than *useless*. And you need weaponry, and knowledge of how to use it. I can provide that. For a price. I don't come cheap."

"You'll help us?" An expectant buzzard's face lit up the wall.

"We'll see. Show me what you've got. Where's the computer? I can't do *anything* without the computer. It's what makes the holes and keeps them open. Me without the computer gets you zilch."

The corridor dead-ended into a shiny, white wall. The projected face turned left and moved down another hallway. At the end were double doors, sealed by airlocks. She pushed through the seal and entered a small cubicle with Elias. Inside, the face filled one wall. It looked like a very large space was beyond it. A large, never-before-entered space that had just materialized.

"This is the computer?" The doors looked like those leading to her own computer. Elias started to walk through. "No, El, wait. They have to decontaminate us. You haven't been here before?" The face looked on from the wall. Clarisse realized that her impression was right—*no one* in this world had been in there before.

A whoosh surrounded them, then a mist of something, and then another whoosh. Clarisse took a suit from a cabinet that opened on the side of the chamber. "Suit up, and we can enter the computer."

She put her suit over her slacks and shirt. "Go on, El. It's painless." When she had on a sterile suit, with her shoes covered and an elastic-edged cap covering her hair, she turned to him. "Aren't you a sight?"

He was obviously embarrassed and confused, but had followed her lead.

"It's not designer, but it's the best we can do. We have to be allergen, dust, and germ-free to enter." She turned to the face on the wall. "How many of these suits did you bring? Everyone entering needs a new one each time. You can't wash these." The face on the wall pulled away, brows rising. He was surprised he'd overlooked something. "Yeah, well, every-one can make a mistake. Put 'clean suits' on the shopping list.

"Okay, El, let's hit it." She opened the rear doors and walked into a refrigerator. It was thirty degrees inside, at best. She faced a huge machine.

The computer was a giant cube nestled into a space built to fit its bulk. She craned her neck to see the top. The thing was almost two hun-dred feet high, and as wide and deep. Apparently identical to hers. Gave her chills every time she saw it. The middle of the massive machine had been bored out so that a cylinder fifty feet wide pierced it front to back.

LED light tubes followed the edges of the circular cuts. The computer's workings were exposed in the empty tube. Layers of metal with bright electrical impulses running through them were stacked two hundred feet high, with the cutout drum running down the middle.

The whole thing rippled with electrical energy and light. It thrilled her. Elias stood, not needing to act to look stupid. His mouth hung open and his eyes blinked about every three seconds.

"Well, looks like you got it all." Clarisse remarked to the face as she walked up to the cube. "I hope you did a 'copy and replace.' They'll definitely notice that it's missing at Moffett." She entered a small glass enclosure on the side of the cube closest to her. She inspected a wall of dials and knobs, nodding. Bending down, she ran her fingers along a metal door and, pushing the corner, popped it open. She adjusted something, then closed the cabinet door and left the control booth, surveying the machine carefully before backing off to look at the whole thing.

Similar control modules existed on each corner, with others every hundred feet around the perimeter: three on each side, including corners. Metal scaffolding wrapped around the machine to reach the higher levels; similar controls existed on the scaffolding. Three vertical levels allowed every section of the computer to be maintained and controlled separately. Each control module was surrounded by a clear glass booth.

"Well, you got it all, and it runs. There's only one problem." She stood opposite the wall where *his* face shone in obvious delight at their prodigious accomplishment.

"What is that, Dr. Hull?" He raised his brows as though it was impossible that he might have missed something. His expression reminded her of the one she'd seen on her father's face all her life.

"I can't run it by myself. Even if I trained my friend here," a nod to Elias, "I couldn't do it. I should have one technician on each of those modules around the clock. Nine control stations on each level, times three levels. Twenty-seven techs at a time. The computer needs round-the-clock monitoring to keep it going. Humans need to sleep and rest. I'll need three shifts, or 81 people, absolute minimum, to run the computer. And extras for illness or if people don't work out. Plus more analysts for the data. And some scientists of my caliber to troubleshoot and bounce ideas around.

"I need a *trained* crew."

He was silent, and then said, "Can you train the people in the warehouse?"

"Your *army*? They're supposed to be your army *and* your computer operators? That's a big job. Fortunately, I am one of the few who can do it, but it will take time. Elias told me you've given him the equivalent of a PhD in physics. If you have, I'll find out soon. He'll be the person I debrief. The others don't need as much education, but they do need technical acumen and theory, plus computer skills."

"We can do that, Dr. Hull. I gather you want to select your own crew?"

"Absolutely."

"Do it now. I will educate them to your specifications and you can begin training them immediately."

Elias squeaked and jumped in front of her, shaking his head. "It's how...," he held out his hands, exposing his bruised wrists.

"You did *that* to him to put my PhD into him? You stinking bastard. I'm done. I won't work with you at all."

She stormed back into the decontamination chamber, shedding her "clean coat" as she went. Elias followed closely behind her.

"I won't work with monsters like you. If you think I'll allow..."

"Dr. Hull," the dry voice intoned.

"What?" She turned.

Elias was lying on his back, clutching his throat as though he was being strangled. He *was* being strangled; the creature on the wall was killing him without laying a hand on him.

Clarisse jumped, spun Elias over onto his stomach, and jammed the knuckles of her index fingers into the point where his skull met his backbone. Elias instantly went limp.

"Have you heard of a 'kill spot'?" The face on the wall backed away, eyes wide, mouth open. "He'll be dead in one second if I push harder. If you're stupid enough to think I won't kill him..." She gazed murderously at the face.

A shudder went through Elias' body and it relaxed profoundly. He was unconscious. "Oh, you believed me and let go. Smart call.

"He's *mine*. No one kills him but me."

She turned El over. He gasped and retched.

"Come on, Elias; dying isn't that bad." To the face on the wall, "If you pull any strong-arm stuff, I will kill him *and* myself. *And*—I'll take as much of this place with me as I can. You don't know what I can do."

She pulled Elias to his feet and slapped him hard on both cheeks. "Come back. We have lots to do." He pulled himself erect, staggering. She pulled him along. The face on the wall lagged behind them, bewildered. She turned around. The face had the slack jaw and flat cheeks of true befuddlement. Elias continued to gag as they moved toward their room.

"I like Pops as a name for you," Clarisse remarked cheerily. "You remind me of my dad. Of course, I'd never have called *him* Pops. He had no sense of humor." They'd reached corridor one.

"What we're going to do next is go back into the schoolyard and pick us some soldiers. Say, one hundred and forty of them, to allow for breakage. El, you're going to get me the good ones. None of that shit that I had to tame the first night. Smart ones who understand they have to follow orders.

"But first, El and I are having lunch."

Clarisse pulled out her device and zapped the surveillance system the minute they got into their room. Her hands shook. "I'm sorry, El. I have to show him I'm tough and willing to kill. That I'm not afraid of him." She plopped down at the table, unable to stand up. Her bravado had disappeared.

El sat next to her, looking wasted. "You should be afraid of him, Dr. Hull. He can hurt you very badly. Please, don't talk to him the way you do."

"It's all I know, El. Guts, balls, straight ahead. The best defense is a good offense. Shit, the best defense *and* offense is a good offense. That's how I live."

El sat, biting his lips, looking more terrified than ever. "He can hurt you, and you can't stop him. Please, don't make him angry."

That stopped the conversation cold.

"Can we get out of here, El? Have you tried?" she asked a minute or two later. They sat at the table, lunches laid out in front of them. She stared at him, trying to extract everything he knew with her eyes.

"No one has escaped. I'm the only one who's gone out, but I could only go to find you and come back. There was no other place to go."

"How about through the windows in the main room? Climb up the ladders on the fire escapes and get out. Has anyone tried that?"

He shook his head sadly. "No. No one gets out that way. During the games, they let the ladders down. The prizes run, jump, and try to get up. Sometimes they do, but they put them back down so they get caught. No one gets away."

"The games? Prizes?"

"Yes. It's when they punish bad people. People who failed—they didn't accomplish their tasks."

"You said that's what they would call you if I didn't let you stay last night."

"Yes, I would be a failure and would become a prize."

"What's that?"

"It's someone we are allowed to hunt. They put them in the center of the room. Everyone gathers around. They ring a bell, and the prizes run. We always catch the prize. They put the ladders down so that the prizes can jump for them and try to get away. It makes the game more fun."

"Fun?"

He nodded solemnly.

"Have you been in the game?"

"Everyone has. You have to, or you become a prize."

"Who are the prizes? Why...?"

"The prizes are everyone who fails, and the scientists who fail. If they don't do what they're supposed to do when they come here, they become prizes."

"Scientists."

"Yes. Like you, but their experiments didn't work. Some of them became prizes."

Clarisse slumped. "What happens to the prizes?"

Elias looked down. "I've never caught one. I only get what they give me."

"What do they do to them, Elias!" She grabbed his forearms over the table.

"Eat them." The words were barely audible.

"Oh, no."

"There's no meat. I'm sorry. I would never hurt you. Please."

She ran to the door and grabbed the handle. Locked. Clarisse wanted to scream. She was locked in hell and shared her bed with a cannibal. How could she get out? Her body quaked. She had to get herself under control. They had to think she was invulnerable.

The toughest woman in the world couldn't be a prize. Could she? She'd better show the aliens right now.

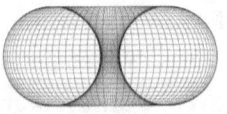

NINE

JACK

THE BOYS WERE in the dojo, dressed in those tight jeans kids liked and their sloppy plaid flannel shirts. He had ten minutes to say goodbye. They were their cool teenage selves at first.

"Hey, Dad." Ricky said, jerking his head back and standing with his arms crossed.

"Hey, Dad." Jimmy also said, copying his older brother, but failing to achieve his studied nonchalance. They stayed at arm's length for a moment, faces working with feeling.

Jimmy cracked first. He ran to Jack, speaking as though he was telling him what he didn't know. "They took Mom, Dad. Bad guys have her. She can't get free. Ron doesn't know where she is, Dad. What are we going to do?"

And Jimmy was in his arms, his tears staining Jack's shirt and tweed coat with its suede elbows. He'd dressed like a damned professor to confront the man he'd thought was his wife's lover! As though that would impress Ron. But his son was in his arms...

"Sweetie, we'll figure it out. There's got to be a way to find her. Ron and his people will find her. Don't cry, son." Jimmy cried anyway, which was exactly what he needed to do.

"They say they're taking us away, so we'll be safe. But we want to be with you. *You're* where we're safe." Jimmy clawed at Jack, wild-eyed. "We can't lose Mom *and* you, too. Oh, Dad. Don't go."

"They say that it's me putting you in danger. That whoever took Mom will watch me, because they know she'll come home to me."

"They'll come for *all* of us. We're a family. They can't take *you*."

"I'm going to England, guys. Not so far away. It's a civilized country. I'll be teaching at Oxford, what I always wanted to do. It's my dream. I was going to tell you all about my new job the night Mom disappeared." Jack heard his voice rumble in his chest. He wanted to roll into a ball like a baby and cry. "It *will* be a dream come true. They'll get Mom back, and you can join me. We'll live in England and be happy."

Ricky's eyes narrowed. "That's cool, Dad. But they're going to leave you in the open so Mom can find you? Who's going to keep *you* safe?" When Ricky cracked, it was with anger. "They're using you as bait."

"Ricky, they'll keep me safe. It's okay, honey. Don't worry." Jack opened his arms and the fifteen-year-old yanked himself farther away.

"They *won't* keep you safe. Look what they did with Mom. They can't keep shit safe!" Ricky's tears were tinged with fire.

"They'll find Mom. They have all the might of the United States government behind them. All sorts of scientists and specialists. We'll get back together. They'll keep you safe—Ron is pledged to that. You'll be with him. I'll be in Oxford, which is a stodgy old town. I'll be teaching and writing, as boring and safe as you can get.

"We'll be back together soon. Maybe we'll spend Christmas at Papa Jack's ranch in Montana, or he'll come to England to be with us. Jolly Olde England! All of us together! Papa Jack, too. Would you like that?"

A burst of joy passed over their faces at the mention of their grandfather. The boys loved Jack's tall, rugged father. Their blood grandfather, Grandpa Hull, had called forth none of the love they felt for their step-grandfather. Papa Jack had two ranches, one in Oklahoma where he did his cattle and horse breeding business. And the real ranch in Montana, his "hunting ranch." It was just like the old West, complete with cowhands and adventures. That was where their family had their best times.

"But *Mom*. How can she be with us in *Jolly Olde England*? Or in Montana? She's not free, and they don't know how to get her free."

When Ricky finally let go, he cracked harder than Jimmy. His sobs broke Jack's heart.

Jack tried to calm him. "Ron says she has all sorts of special training. If anyone can get free, it's Mom.

"But, Dad, what if they *hurt* her? What if they *torture* her? She got tortured once, before I was born. Did you know that?" Jack nodded.

"What if they *torture* her? *They can't torture Mom!*"

Ricky screamed more than cried when he let his feelings out, but he ended up in the same place his younger brother had—Jack's arms.

"Look. We're going to have to be brave until they find her," he said. "We'll be fine. We'll move to England and be a family again. We are a family now. Ron says your mother can do things we can't believe in both martial arts and in computers. If she can get free, she will.

"Don't worry, boys. It will be fine. I love you."

It ended with tears and hugs, ten minutes after it started. Ron hustled him away and some person materialized from nowhere to stay with the boys. They went to him smiling; they must have known him from karate.

Ron hustled him out of a hidden door in a corner of his office, down a long flight of stairs and through a gray concrete passageway, at least ten feet wide and just as high. It had steel doors at the ends and at every hundred feet along its length. More locked doors opened along the tunnel, going somewhere, feeding a maze of underground passages. Jack had had no idea such a world existed under the apparently placid surface of the base. After a seemingly endless run, the tunnel ended at an elevator that took them to the surface.

They were in one of the three enormous hangars that dominated the landscape when you passed Moffett Field on the Bayshore Freeway. Moffett had been a naval air station, but it had been demilitarized back in the 90s. A while ago, 2014, Jack thought, Google had leased most of the biggest hangar to house its planes. They weren't in the Google airport; the hangar they were in had no resemblance to a civilian installation.

Jack had thought the other buildings were pretty much deserted and that military activity had ceased. That was untrue; the place bustled. A bunch of big planes dotted the hangar he was in. They got into a gray one; Jack couldn't think well enough to notice much more about it.

Ron hustled him into a seat, saying words that Jack could barely decipher. "This is all going to hit you in a while and you're going to need help. We'll give it to you; make sure you take it. Don't try to play the Lone Ranger.

"The boys will be with me. I don't know where we're going, but I'll lay down my life for them. Know that."

Jack's ribs and chest began a disconcerting filling and emptying, a bellows movement that he couldn't control. Tears leapt in his eyes.

"Go ahead, buddy. Cry. This one's worth it. I don't have much time, but I'll be your contact. News will come through me, no one else. If someone says they're calling with a message from me, don't believe them. Report it. I'm your contact, period. You're one of us now.

"If I can get a secure enough connection, I'll make sure you see the boys or at least talk to them as much as possible. We've got you a safe house in Oxford, near where you'll be teaching. It's swept for bugs, and we'll keep it swept, and guarded 24/7. And *you* will be guarded.

"I'm sorry we got to know each other better in these circumstances, but it is what it is."

"How can she… cope? What if they torture her? What do they want?"

Ron made a tsk noise and pulled away with the faintest glimmer of… what? Superiority? 'I know her better than you?'

"You don't know your wife, Jack. I told you in my office that she's got skills you don't know about. She's so tough, nails are afraid of her. Clarisse knows how to take care of herself, way better than you. And she loves *you*, you and the boys. She'll come back to you, if she can."

He patted Jack's forearm, a gesture meant to reassure him, Jack supposed. "When you get a chance, watch the TV show *24*. Clarisse is Jack Bauer on meth."

Ron backed away unceremoniously and left the plane. Jack's brain barely worked, but he had so many more questions. What kind of plane was this? It was a military plane, but what branch? It was just a gray plane. The section where he sat hardly had any windows. He had seen some numbers painted on its exterior, but nothing inside or out that indicated whether it was Air Force or Navy, or even a "Secret Force That's So Undercover that No One Knows It Exists."

After Ron left and the plane took off, he sat staring. Thoughts formed slowly, like smoke-rings blown through congealing concrete.

Faces, names. Clarisse. Ben. Eleanor. The lies he'd been told by all of them. He'd thought he was a family member, but his wife had a secret life as a commando, or something. Ben had hung out with generals. Why? What business did a psychiatrist and geneticist have with high-level military officers? What about Eleanor? Was she a secret agent, too? She had government contracts. The three of them seemed to have kept him around as a prop to indicate their normality, but he'd never been in the game. Or the family.

And Clarisse. She was gone. A captive. *Oh, God. Ricky. Jimmy. Oh, God.* They were his family. His ribs did that galloping, gasping thing again. Now he couldn't move. Couldn't speak. His heart hurt like it was rupturing and his ribs jumped around, moving out of his control.

Jack sat stiffly, clutching his briefcase to his chest with both hands. He stared straight ahead, across the open space. After a while, he looked around and found that it helped to examine his surroundings. He had never seen an airplane configured like this one: rows of seats in back where he was, and then a large area with nothing in it. The empty area had what looked like cargo doors on each side.

A wall, such as would separate the pilot from the travelers on a regular jet, ended the passenger area, if that's where he was. *This* wall cordoned off a third of the plane. *Something like a super first-class,* he would have thought, had his mind been able to form words instead of impressions. But Jack wasn't able to think.

If his brain had worked better, he might have postulated that they used the wide doors on each side of the empty area for parachute jumping. Except they were about thirty thousand feet above the Atlantic Ocean. That was far too high for a jump. Even with his intellect disabled, though, Jack knew he was on a military plane. They'd left from Moffett Field.

A few hours before, his life had exploded in ruins.

Now he couldn't move. The pain in his heart ratcheted up so that he couldn't make a sound. His hand went to his chest. His ribs kept jerking in and out, beyond his control

He slumped to his side. The briefcase clattered to the floor.

A sharp and painful smell like a punch to his nostrils assaulted him. His head jerked back, eyes watering. A woman stood over him, holding a cracked ampule.

"Dr. Abercrombie. Can you hear me?" She peered at him. Her face seemed too round, her eyes too intense and dark. More of that powerful, painful smell and the world jelled again, sort of. The woman wore a white lab coat with 'Rachelle Schwartz, MD' embroidered on it. She was a doctor.

"You fainted. You've been through a great deal. We're going to do a work-up on you. You may be in shock." She wrapped a cloth around his arm and took his blood pressure.

"Yes. You're lucky you were here," another said. Several other lab-coated people appeared from the front of the plane and began doing things to him. Taking blood.

Jack found himself leaning back in his chair with his shirt unbuttoned, pants unzipped and pulled open, and sticky tags attached to leads and a beeping machine. They were doing an electrocardiogram.

"Your heart rhythm is a bit off. Stress, but maybe more. The length between the…" Something. More words. He had no idea, "is too long. This can lead to possibly fatal cardiac arrhythmias.

"Does anyone else in your family have heart problems?"

"Uh. No. … Yes." He shook his head. "What am I thinking? My dad. He had a heart attack a few years ago. He takes medication."

"I bet he's got what you have," the doctor nodded knowingly. "It's hereditary and can be a killer, untreated."

Jack gasped.

"Don't worry. We've got you. We'll get you stable and keep you there. You need to lose this," she indicated his belly, "if you want to live. And you do. You have a great need to stay alive and healthy. Your family depends upon you, now more than ever."

His ribs began doing that out-of-control pumping thing. He bent over, gasping, feeling his tears on his hands. "I just… I mean…"

"You mean that you're in shock and grieving. We will take care of you and put you on our diet and health regime when we reach England. However, we're going to make a quick stop in a minute and we need to move you to the front cabin."

They landed. The side doors of the plane opened. Wide stairs were deployed and heat blasted in like a firestorm. He could hear people outside, and sharp voices, mostly men. Urgency cut through the words.

"Okay. We're moving you forward," said the doctor. Two big guys, far bigger than he would have expected male nurses to be, emerged from the compartment. They propped him up and guided him to the doorway splitting the berth, bringing the monitor attached to his chest with them.

He turned his head to the door to the outside as the first stretcher was hauled in. An IV bag hung from a stand. The person on the gurney was covered with sheets, but blood seeped through the bandages on his head. Jack couldn't see a head or face—just bloodstained white gauze.

A bunch of men and women in desert camouflage uniforms jumped through the two side doors. They dropped legs from the stretcher and attached them to moorings in the plane's floor. Others poured through the doors with more wounded people. Only a few seemed able to moan or make any noise. Their carriers were affixed to the floor as the first stretcher had been and the soldiers hustled around, putting up IVs and fastening machines to their patients. Still more stretchers with people covered in white sheets poured in. Their stillness and stained bandages were more horrifying than seeing actual wounds might have been.

The orderlies propelled Jack through the door to the front cabin and shut it behind him.

This was a hospital ship. They had just picked up a load of terribly injured people who had been on an ultra-clandestine mission that had blown up, literally. *Jesus Christ.*

He thought about how long they'd been flying. They'd made one stop somewhere to refuel. He thought Florida, maybe. He couldn't see much through the tiny windows. It was green out there, and flat.

Then they'd flown across the Atlantic. They were going to England;

the Atlantic had to have been the broad body of water beneath them. Where had they landed to pick up the injured? On a flat, dry desert with searing heat.

That could be almost anywhere around the Mediterranean. Where was there so much turmoil that the U.S. might send in a secret force?

Everywhere… It was 2016. Syria. Iran. Yemen. Sudan. Lebanon. Libya. Afghanistan, Iraq, Pakistan. The whole Middle East. Parts of Russia. China. That didn't go near the whole New World and its drug-dominated cultures of violence.

This had to be a Mediterranean-based operation, though, and the people in the back were the losers in whatever had happened.

Had Clarisse done things like this? Had she been wounded? No. She would have come home with major damage. He remembered her returning from karate tournaments with nasty bruises. He'd tried to keep her from going to them, but she wouldn't hear of it.

All that time, she'd been on covert ops, not competing for trophies. Another lie.

He grabbed his heart. The orderly jumped to the monitor, then inserted a syringe into an IV port in his hand.

"You'll relax now. We can't let your blood pressure get any higher. Would you like to watch TV or something?"

"On my computer?" he said, eyelids drooping.

"No, the big screen." He indicated a screen covering most of the wall that led to the cockpit.

"Uh. Yeah."

"What would you like to watch?"

"Is there a program called *24*?"

"You bet there is. The most badass program ever made. The number one favorite of the U.S. military everywhere. And cops. All the good guys like it."

"I'd like to see it."

"Good choice. Which year?"

"Start from the beginning."

The final landing was at a military base in the British countryside, *not* Heathrow. By that time, he'd watched four episodes of *24*.

In those hours, Jack had vicariously participated in more death and destruction than he'd seen since birth, including all the shots of maiming and disaster shown in the major magazines and every news show he'd viewed. He thought *24* was a hideously perfect example of popular culture gone wrong.

It thrilled him. He was a writer. He'd won several prestigious writing awards and had been short-listed for the Pulitzer. Jack's books were elegant, meticulously plotted and beautifully written sagas of personal development. He was interested in issues of social class, and how it impacted and crippled human beings. His writing was his political statement: compassionate, kind, and steely in its clarity of vision. He wrote literary fiction—fiction for grown-ups. He'd read somewhere that only three thousand true readers still existed, people who would understand subtle nuances and work their way through difficult text. Maybe that was so.

His last book, *Realms of Magic,* had sold twenty-five hundred copies before it was announced as a contender for the Pulitzer. After that, it had sold another thirty-two thousand. Given the time involved, he would have made more working by the hour at any fast food joint than he had on *Realms.*

Jack depended on the largesse of the Hull family for the major part of his living. The university was one of the highest paying in the world, but it couldn't match Palo Alto housing prices. The university provided subsidized housing for professors. Profs in the scientific and tech fields didn't need it as much. They were paid more than his compatriots in the humanities. They could also find lucrative consulting jobs outside the University's halls. Literature professors like him were near the bottom of the heap—they had no market value in a nonacademic setting. What he made would have been great back in Oklahoma, but it was barely enough to live on in Silicon Valley. By himself, Jack couldn't have bought any sort of house in Palo Alto. He would never have lived in the magnificent Hull House, attended the opera, and eaten at the fine restaurants he and Clary frequented.

Feelings boiled inside him, emerging with an intensity he hadn't known he felt. Except for Clarisse's penchant for opera and upscale dining, the Hulls' generosity wouldn't keep a Chihuahua in chops. They were all cheapskates. They gave him socks for Christmas. Of course, they didn't believe in God, so the holiday was wasted on them.

When the medical staff had gotten the patients stabilized, some of them came into the compartment where Jack had been watching Jack Bauer take apart and then fix the universe. When they saw he had *24* playing, they sat down with avid interest. As time passed, they clapped and commented on every "good scene."

"I've watched this whole series four times, and I can't get over this part, where Jack Bauer..."

The star mesmerized them. Jack had never heard of him. Kiefer Sutherland. What a terrible name for a boy child. That was a yogurt-based drink, wasn't it? Sutherland had a misaligned, long face. He was skinny. A hero of this sort of thing should be bulkier, he thought, more like a body builder or athlete.

Jack pulled out his computer and did a search. He was Donald Sutherland's son. Donald had been a bit of a pacifist earlier in his life, Jack read. His son played a mass murderer who was exonerated because he served the United States and the forces of good. He could take any level of torture and dish it out just as well. People loved him; the faces of the medical staff and the few bandaged-up soldiers there showed something close to devotion. The man was a hero.

Jack did another search on his computer. Some internet page about celebrity wealth said Kiefer Sutherland was worth sixty-five million. The monitor attached to his chest beeped and an orderly came over and checked it.

"*24* too much for you, sir?"

"Yes, it is." Sixty-five million. Dr. Jack Abercrombie had about fifty thousand in the bank—the fruit of a lifetime's labor. He had a PhD and had held some jobs that were prestigious to a bunch of over-brained farts. He had written five elegant, superbly composed novels that had earned nothing. He also owned his car outright.

Jack had no equity in Hull House. No share in the Hull fortune, which was only an alleged fortune to him. He never saw any bank statements and never would, either. The prenuptial agreement he'd signed precluded that.

The credits to an episode rolled by. Jack wondered how much the screenwriters made. He went back to his computer. A final search revealed that, while screenwriters were among the lower-paid denizens of Hollywood, they out-earned all but the most popular fiction writers.

The writers of *24* made whatever they did with two lines of dialogue: "There's no time" and "Trust me." The series consisted of those words repeated again and again, plus scenes of people dashing through high-tech-looking places or warehouses that blew up. The professor in him was outraged and stunned.

The sound of a detonation from the screen caused him to look up and see the skinny actor wreaking mayhem on some hapless city. Ron had said that Clarisse was "Jack Bauer on meth," but this was all trickery and special effects.

Clarisse was nonviolent, despite her karate habit. She took spiders out of the house and put them in the garden that filled most of the mansion's back acre. His wife gave the garden's produce to homeless shelters. Clarisse was a grower and cultivator—a kind, loving person.

Explosions burst from the screen. Sound effects deafened him. Jack Bauer leapt out of the chaos, carrying a small child. The gang in the compartment cheered.

Clarisse *couldn't* do that. She was a tiny little woman. She didn't have special effects, stunt doubles, and phony guns.

She had the real thing.

Oh, God. This can't be happening.

TEN

RICKY & JIMMY'S NEW HOME

RON TOOK RICKY and Jimmy to their new quarters at the base. The boys were practically dizzy by the time they got there, going through a secret door in Ron's offices, down an elevator, through a maze of corridors, and up again into one of the huge hangars. They didn't see any airplanes in this place, though it was obviously made for aviation. Part of the huge space was partitioned off, going all the way to the roof of the gigantic building. A enormous cube over two hundred feet high and just as deep and wide enclosed something. The walls were solid—no windows allowed them to see what was inside, but a bunch of doors ringed the lower level. Many people must go in and out, all the way around.

"That's your mom's computer," Ron said, hustling them along. "Top secret, even for you. Let's go."

The boys ogled the structure before Ron hustled them into another elevator. This was as close to their mom's brainchild as they had come. She couldn't show it to them—even on her computer.

The new elevator dumped them into another concrete corridor, a new part of a secret maze. They navigated the labyrinth, Ricky and Jimmy pulling closer together as they traveled. It was creepy. They walked down a dismal, gray corridor. *All* concrete—walls, ceiling, and floor.

"Is this place earthquake proof?" Ricky asked. He had been born almost on the San Andreas Fault and had felt earthquakes all his life. No earthquake-savvy person would live in a building made of materials that would crush him if the ground rattled and rolled. Which it would.

"Oh, yeah. It's to code all the way. You're so far down, nothing but an atomic bomb could reach you. That was the idea behind these quarters, and nothing else."

Right, thought Ricky to Jimmy.

Yeah. Bring on the torture chamber, Jimmy thought back.

Steel doors marched down the corridor, identical pairs on each side like a high security prison. Steel-framed entries with complicated key-pads marched along by each door. This was a jail.

"Uh, doesn't seem to be much natural light down here," Ricky said. "My mom is big on natural light."

"And I don't think we're gonna get much exercise, either. I don't see a gym."

"This isn't a jail, boys. You'll eat with me or whoever's on duty. You've got laundry service and a housekeeper. You can work out in the gym after hours, when I'm with you. You'll have school delivered to your lap-tops." Ron glanced at the dolly they dragged. It carried as much as they'd been able to grab from their rooms in five minutes. They'd brought their computers and tech stuff. Not many clothes.

"I'll get you new skivvies and all." Ron stopped at a steel door and apologized before admitting them to their new quarters. "I'm sorry, guys; this is the best we could do for right now. It is *very* secure."

Ron opened the door to their rooms. Two of them, next to each other with a connecting door, like adjoining rooms in a motel. Single beds with gray woolen blankets. Pegs for hanging their stuff. Tables set up as computer stations. Some chairs. Fluorescent lights.

"Not fancy, but okay." Ron waved a hand, ensuring that they saw the whole miserable scene.

The boys stood, stunned. They had lived in the magnificent Hull House all their lives. High ceilings, ornate moldings, pillars, mullioned windows, bay windows... wall-to-wall windows. Persian carpets and antique furniture. Gorgeous, old-growth trees outside. More than an acre of their mother's veggie garden in back and plantings all around, bursting with color and life. Not to mention the fabulous neighborhood surrounding their house.

"You expect us to live here?"

"Yeah. I expect you to live here and recognize that Uncle Sam is spending a shitload of money to put you up here and keep you from being *really* kidnapped by assholes who would consider this a palace." Ron glared at them, changing from lovable Uncle Ron to someone else. "Your mom's a warrior, boys. She and I trained you to be warriors. So suck it up and learn to *love concrete!*"

He left. They heard the keypad working from the outside. They were locked in.

This is bad, Jimmy, Ricky thought to his brother. They used silent speech, mindspeak, whenever they didn't want to be heard.

I've never seen Ron like that.

No. He's probably like that more than the nice guy we know.

What are we going to do?

Get out of here as fast as we can. Is it bugged?

I'll find out. Jimmy booted up his computer and pulled out a couple of devices from one of his cases. He set them up. *Okay, talk, Ricky.*

"Oo-oh, say can you see through the dawn's early light..." Ricky had a very nice tenor voice and he knew the entire national anthem, which he sang.

Jimmy's screen showed wavy lines spiking up and down.

If this place was any more bugged, we'd be begging for Raid.

Fuck, as Mom would say.

Double fuck. But let's not swear. It reminds me of her too much.

They sat around, dejected.

What are we going to do? Jimmy thought.

Hang out, watch for openings, and when one comes, escape. We should both remember real hard how Ron changed when we said we didn't like these cells.

Yeah. He's a cop...

Worse than that, Jimmy.

Do you think Mom was like that when she was working with him?

Yep. I have a feeling we don't know a lot about Mom. We may be in for some surprises. But Jimmy, we've got each other. He reached out and grabbed his brother's hands. *We gotta hang tight.* Tears formed in Ricky's eyes, blurring his vision. Fortunately, they were also in Jimmy's eyes, so he didn't see his big brother as being a wimp.

This is going to be worse than the other time, when they experimented on us, isn't it? Jimmy communicated soundlessly.

I think so. This time, we won't have Mom or Dad to stop it.

We'll have to stop it.

Best way to do that is not let it get started.

Ricky, it was so... awful. Jimmy reached out for his brother and they hugged awkwardly. *The metal band they put around our heads, and the electricity.*

Grandpa Hull telling us we had to do it for posterity. We had a gift. We owed it to the universe.

But what they did hurt.

And Mom came in like Superwoman when she found out.

Dad yelled at Grandpa Hull. I've never heard him do that, ever.

Oh, God, Jimmy, what are we going to do? What if they decide to experiment on us and no one helps us?

They held each other and cried, shoulders shaking, weeping becoming sobbing as they lost control. The day finally overwhelmed them.

"Boys, are you all right?" A woman's deep voice came through the intercom. "I'm coming in."

Someone in a black uniform entered. She was big, like she worked out all the time, but also big like... one of Papa Jack's prize heifers. "That's prime beef on the hoof, boys," he'd say about them.

The lady was. She had enormous bazoomies and big hips jutting out. Her face, though... was a kind face.

"You poor boys. You've gone through so much. I'm going to be watching out for you." They were sitting on the itchy gray blanket on one of the beds. She walked over. "May I sit with you?"

"Uh. Sure."

She handed out Kleenex from a stash in her pocket. "I do know how you feel. I lost both my parents in a terrorist attack. In Paris, of all places. I know what you're going through, sort of. My version. I'll help you as much as I can.

"I'm with the FBI. I get people settled into the witness protection program. Hopefully, I'll be doing that with your family. I'm not your mom or dad, but I'll be here for you."

That made them cry more. Ricky pulled himself out of it and sat stiffly, hands in fists, breath coming in and out of his clenched teeth.

"You're not going to experiment on us again, are you?" he asked.

"What?!" Her eyes bulged and she sat up. "Who experimented on you?"

"Our Grandpa Hull and a bunch of scientists. He said that we owed it to the world and the generations. They needed to know just how smart we were and if we were psychic…" Ricky pulled himself up hard. He was talking about it too much.

"They put wires on us and a thing around our heads and put electricity through it." Jimmy couldn't stop himself. "To see something… but we never found out what."

"Why would anyone do that? No! That will *not* happen to you here. We're keeping you safe here. If you need anything, ask for Annie. I'm on duty, well, feels like all the time. I'm here for you, boys. I'm not your mom, but… I'll try. Would you like some ice cream?"

They nodded enthusiastically.

Okay. That's our first break. Ricky thought, then licked his ice cream dish.

Yeah. We can con her. Seems a shame.

We'll be nice when we do it. Hey, bro. That smile you gave her was supreme. The "I'm the cutest kid in the world smile."

Jimmy shrugged. *What can I say? It's a gift.*

We should go to bed.

Yeah. I don't want to sleep in the other room, though.

The beds are bolted to the floor, but we can undo them tomorrow.

Can I sleep with you? Jimmy asked. Ricky nodded.

Two big boys settling into a narrow bunk was hard. All that was coursing through their minds made sleep impossible, almost.

What are you remembering? Jimmy thought.

Grandpa Hull's face when he put the electrodes on my head. He didn't care about hurting me; he cared about how the reports came out.

I remember Mom, too. She ran into the lab, tore the wires off us, and screamed at the techs.

I love her. And I miss her.

I miss Dad, too. He was majorly pissed at Grandpa Hull.

Mom and Dad really worked together then.

Yeah. But they don't go together very well, do they?

No. But I love them.

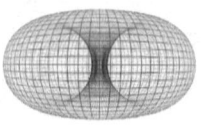

ELEVEN

THE TEAM

"E L, TAKE EXACTLY three bites of your burger. Chew it carefully. You need protein and water going into battle. Too much food will make you sick."

After the happy news about the games and cannibalization that Elias had shared, Clarisse turned to what would happen after lunch. What she was about to do should convince her hosts that she would be a most unpalatable prize.

How about Elias? Could he help her? He had to have been abused for years. Could she turn him into an asset? Right now? Could he become a warrior and help her? She'd gotten local people to fight back on several missions. Had she ever transformed *anyone* so fast?

Dark faces with shining white teeth came to her. Tall, elegant tribal women in Somalia, captured to be sold as slaves. They'd been broken when she and Ron had gotten to the slavers' encampment, but they understood what to do fast when the two of them overwhelmed the guards. Clarisse had skewered one of their captors. She went crazy, gutting him like she had wanted to do to her attackers back in Iran. When fighting, she was always back in Iran. She showed the captive women how to use sticks and stones to kill. How to work together and not cower in fright when attacked. To know that death was nothing to be feared.

When the raiding party came back, the slavers got a big surprise. The women were soldiers, not victims. The good guys won that battle. She hoped they had made it home to their families.

But she had had time to work with those women. Days had passed while the hunting party was out capturing another batch. She had no time with Elias. Would he see that he could fight back?

Their lunches were on trays in their room. Clarisse lifted the cover, and nodded. "Good, that little tart can take orders. Give me half of your burger." She consumed three bites of the meat substitute only, and then put it back on the tray. "Drink one of those water bottles. A small one. Then put this stuff in the refrigerator."

She went into the closet and came out wearing a long-sleeved black shirt and pants. "Do you have anything darker?" He nodded. "Put it on."

"I want you to point out to me anyone with the self-control and intelligence to work for me. That's on the computer and personally. The good guys.

"But first, we'll need to clean house. Have you ever killed anyone, El?"

He jerked back, shaking his head.

"We're going to kill people today. It's not what I want, but it's what's going to happen. I want you to do whatever you must to show me the bad guys, even if they're pretty little girls. Pull them out. Make them reveal themselves.

"And if they don't show themselves, you tell me who they are. Anyone that needs to go, goes now." She attached pouches and sheaths to her belt, handy technological devices she kept in her briefcase and carried everywhere. She pulled out a rod that just fit into the case and twisted it open. It proved to be a formidable-looking club, which she stuck in a holster at her waist. "I wish I had a helmet, but this will have to do." Clarisse pulled on a black Kevlar mask that had been folded in her briefcase. His eyes went wide. "Sort of like Darth Vader, isn't it?

"Put this on, too." She gave him a Kevlar vest. "Wish I had two, but you can only fit so many emergency supplies in a briefcase.

"This is for you." She handed him a tool that fit neatly into his palm. "Hold it so they can't see it. I'll show you what it does." Clarisse took the device and pushed a button. A two-sided blade about five inches long snapped out. It had deeply serrated edges.

"You can cut a guy's head off with this. I have. But look at this," she retracted the blade and pushed another button, and a flat, sharp rod about two inches wide leapt out. "This is so great. You can kill someone, just pushing the button. Hold it against his neck and push the release. Best is in front, here," she indicated on her own neck. "You get the wind-pipe *and* the jugular and carotid. That's your instant death option.

"Use that first. Do *not* get inside anyone's reach. The ones I saw had no technique, but lots of strength. If one grabs you, you could get in trouble. Or, if they get you, gut them with that first blade. I can show you a lot more, and I will, but we don't have time now. Ready?"

"Oh! What do *they* have in the way of weapons?"

"Sharpened spoons and silverware. And big serving spoons. They gang up so you can't fight them."

"I should be able to handle spoons. Anything else? Do they give them special weapons?"

He shook his head. "They don't interfere with anything. But the 'bad guys' never lose. Maybe they help them, some way I can't see."

"Sounds like gang heaven."

They walked to the door to corridor one that led to the big ware-house where she and Elias had entered initially.

They slipped into the hall silently, hugging the wall. The face on the wall spoke when they entered.

"Dr. Hull is going to select some of you to work with her on our proj-ect. She'll handpick the best of you, so present her your finest attributes." The now-familiar old scientist's face filled the huge sidewall, interrupted by fire escapes and windows, plus doorways to somewhere. His smile radiated malevolent joy.

Clarisse glanced up. "Motherfucker," she spat. "Okay, El. Go smoke 'em out." She held back, hoping the roving spotlights and her dark cos-tume would keep her hidden.

Elias walked out slowly, head down, eyelids blinking like he was try-ing to use them as wings and take off. If he could have retracted into himself, his posture indicated he would have. Clarisse stayed way back, waiting until the last minute.

"Aw, Lilypad; glad to have you back." The blond surfer practically slurped his words. He stuck his tongue out and waggled it from side to side.

"Did Dr. Hull kick you out?" A burly, dark-haired young man.

"Couldn't you fill her *needs*?" Blondie's girlfriend, Barbie. Nasty bitch.

"We'll take you back, Lilypad. You fill *our* needs." Surfer boy again. This caused uproarious laughter from a disconcertingly large number of people. Clarisse estimated that up to fifty laughed—as many young men as women. Had they all used him?

"Yeah," a thin blond kid came out of the pack, sadism written all over him. He was wiry and athletic-looking. "Would you like a welcome back party? How about now?" He walked toward Elias with a proprietary attitude. "You're mine, aren't you, Lilypad? All white and soft. And you sing so pretty." He squealed like someone in pain. "Like a baby."

Smiles and giggles moved around the room. "A party! A Lilypad party!"

She pulled back and to the side, drawing one of her weapons and calibrating it. She could take out the entire group. Elias continued to shuffle toward the assembly, head down. Trembling. It pissed her off, but she didn't want to move too soon.

"I'm so glad you're back, Lily. I got blue balls waiting for you." The skinny, sadistic kid was fast, streaking toward El. The others, twenty hard-core killers, followed in a bunch. Some wavered just behind those, laughing. The majority pulled away, watching as though mesmerized.

The whipcord thin blond kid was close to El, making kissing noises. "Come on, baby. It's been *soooo* long." Laughter surrounded them.

"El, if you want him, take him," she said just loudly enough for Elias to hear.

The boy jumped toward El, grabbing the back of his neck and pulling his head down toward his crotch. She thought that Elias had caved in, but the wiry guy stood up abruptly, grabbing his neck. The handle of El's knife protruded from his throat. Blood spurted. Elias stepped back and his opponent fell.

"Stop where you are!" She stepped out fully. "On the floor with your hands behind your heads! Get down, all of you, and no one will get hurt."

Blondie and his girlfriend looked around, identifying Clarisse as she came out of the shadows. "Oh, it's Dr. Hull! Wanna get *Hulled, Clarisse*?" The boy swept his arm. "Come on, she can't get all of us!" They ran toward her.

She detonated her weapon. The front batch dropped where they were. A few latecomers staggered and then fell to their knees before flopping on their sides. They kicked a while and then were still. "The rest of you, on your knees, hands behind your heads. If you run, I'll kill you." They did as she said, moaning. "Shut the fuck up. Do you think I care how you feel? You people don't deserve shit."

She reached El. "You okay? Good. Excellent work. We'll debrief later. You want to take some souvenirs? Looks like you two have a history. Cut off one of his ears. Or both. If you smoked, I'd say cut off his balls and use the sack for tobacco. But you don't smoke."

El looked at her, bug-eyed.

"This is your last chance, kiddo. All he did to you, you should cut out his guts.

"Not your style? It is mine." Clarisse pulled a six-inch Bowie knife from her belt and eviscerated Elias' persecutor. "Amazing how guts stink, isn't it? Sure you don't want that pouch?" El shook his head violently.

"Okay, Elias, my man. Let's do job interviews. Anyone who ever fucked you when you didn't want it, point them out. Don't bother if they're dead."

He pointed out fourteen; she shot them with the electronic device as he went through the crowd. "Better living electronically, I always say. You can get through airports, whatever, with this, no problem. But as you can see, it's deadly." El pointed out a few more and Clarisse kept shooting.

"No, El. You wanted it," a simpering redhead said.

"Did you?" she asked. He shook his head. Flash. "All gone."

"See, you can think of me as the wrath of God. Also justice. I am both. You do bad, you hurt my friends, you die. I don't take prisoners.

"I've been doing this for a long time, I'm good at it. I like it. Now, how do I separate the good ones from the rest of you douche bags? El, point out the good ones."

When Elias moved toward them, the people who had taunted him or hadn't helped him cried out, "El, we didn't mean to. It was all in fun. Please, El... We're sorry..."

"I didn't do anything, El. I never..."

He had the stones to do it. El kicked them off his legs as they grabbed him and told her whom to shoot. "This one, these two. That one. Those..."

"No, El, I didn't mean to..." Some of them pleaded and cried.

"Good job, El." He earned his chops that day. When they saw that he couldn't be dissuaded, they sobbed and tried to get away. Elias kept pointing, unmoved by blood or screams. She kept shooting.

They ended up with just over a hundred who Elias thought would work out. An equal-sized bunch he had doubts about, but they hadn't harmed him personally. They hadn't helped him either. None of them had.

"I need a hundred and forty of you to staff my project. You'll end up trained technicians with abilities you can't imagine. If you betray me, or Elias, I will kill you. And not quickly like this bunch.

"I'm going to go through the maybes and see if I can sniff out a few of you worth saving." She walked through the cringing crowd and pulled out fifty. "You're the second string. You get trained if I think you won't destroy my work.

"The rest of you are junk.

"Hey, Pops! What shall I do with the junk? They're not worth feeding."

The scientist's appalled face appeared on the wall. "Dr. Hull! What have you done?"

"I've done you a favor. You should have done it ages ago and restored order to this hellhole. You knew what I was doing; you were watching.

"Now, Pops, where's the garbage can? Shall I torch the duds that are still standing here, or wait until they grow up like Blondie and his friends?"

His eyes widened, and blinked and blinked and blinked. The mouth opened and closed.

"Decisiveness is a soldier's best weapon. Commit, Pops."

The face disappeared.

"I take that as a 'go ahead and off them.'" She pulled the weapon she'd killed Blondie and the thugs with. "Oh, one thing, before I clean up—and this applies to all of you. I understand that some of you—the *deceased* portion of your group—had some fun at Elias' expense. Not one of you helped him, you cowardly bastards.

"Apologize to him. Now! All at once, and individually."

Elias' head moved from side to side and he frantically mouthed, "No."

"Okay, El. Got it. Getting raped is an embarrassing experience for a man. It's not much for a woman, either. So say a nice, 'We're sorry that we were rat-fink cowards and didn't help you, Elias' and I'll call it a day. Be sincere."

"We're sorry, Elias."

"We should have helped you."

"We were scared."

"Okay. Good job, guys." And then she torched those who hadn't been chosen to work on her computer.

"Clean up! We need clean up! Thorough cleansing! Get all this junk out of here."

The face appeared on the wall. A shudder ran through the warehouse. The bodies and all the gore was gone.

"Wow, El. Why do these people need me? They do it all with mirrors."

El shook so badly he could barely stand. "They like hurting..." he whispered. She heard him, but had no time to question him about it.

"Okay, people. Listen up. Work starts tomorrow. I'm going to get you in shape mentally and physically to run this world. You work for *me*. *No interference.* We're going to get you in shape to do a job, which will include growing decent food to eat.

"Tomorrow, 8 a.m. Here, in the warehouse. You, El, and me.

"Hey, Pops, I want oatmeal and whole milk for them for breakfast, and fresh fruit. Some kind of protein. Hardboiled eggs, cheese. You should have some slack in your food budget now and be able to supply all of them.

"That's it. Welcome to my team!"

TWELVE

CLARY AND EL

C LARISSE STARTED TO jog the minute she banged through the doors to corridor one. The back of her hand went to her mouth and she panted explosively. By the time she got halfway to their room, she was at a full run. She swiped the lock and dashed inside, not bothering to wait for Elias or for the door to close.

"Oh, God." She threw herself on her knees and clutched the rim of the toilet, ribs pumping, gasping, and retching. All she'd eaten was three bites of burger. What came out of her wasn't much, but she couldn't stop gagging. Couldn't stop... but finally did when something else became more important.

She tore her clothes off, stowing her weapons belt carefully. She set it down where it couldn't get wet, but left the rest of her grisly garments where they fell.

The water tingled as it came from the showerhead, wet, but not soothing or cleansing. She washed herself frantically, shampooed her hair again and again. Hands shaking, body shaking, trembling with the horror of what she had done. Clarisse grabbed one of the robes on the back of the door and threw it on, and then dashed for the bed.

She burrowed under the covers on her hands and knees and rolled into a ball. A pillow filled her mouth and absorbed her sobs. She didn't know how long she cried or where El was. Didn't know until she couldn't hold the screams back. Screams erupted, seemingly having been hiding under the sobs.

"Oh, oh, oh, God! Help me! Oh, God! Help me! Jack! Where are you? Help." The pillow couldn't muffle anything. Her captors could hear her. She had to shut up, but she couldn't. She couldn't find her magic wand to knock out their systems. All she could do was scream.

"Clary, it's me." El got into bed behind her, as he'd done before. "I used your device to jam their bugs. They didn't hear you." He had a terry robe on and his hair was wet.

"Oh, El. Hold me. Oh, what I did. I can't believe it, El. I killed all those people. No due process, no trials, nothing. I just murdered them. I sounded like I didn't care, but I *do,* El. Oh, God. I've never done anything like that. Oh God. What am I going to do? I don't know what to do. I don't know how to get out of here."

"Go ahead and cry, Clary. I'm here. I'll hold you."

She did, for a long time, not registering that he'd called her 'Clary' or that his hands exuded that soft balm. It came out of all of him.

"Thank you, El." She didn't know how much later it was when she raised a tear-tracked face, and spoke with swollen lips. "I bet they wouldn't believe that I'm a softie. I don't even kill bugs at home. I thought I'd do *anything* to escape here—lie or *anything.* But I don't think I can. Oh, God. I *killed* all those people."

"I'm glad you killed them." His mouth compressed and his jaw hardened. "I didn't like seeing it, but I'm glad you did it. They were bad, Clary."

That caught her attention. *No one* called her Clary, or any nicknames. She didn't permit it. He looked at her with soft, intelligent eyes.

"Can I call you that?"

She paused. "Yeah. I guess." Then everything that had happened and that she had learned about his life fell in on her again. She reached toward him. "El, what they did to *you.* Oh, that was so awful. Did that really happen?"

He pulled back and turned his face from her. She could feel the tremor running through him. He would have run, but she grabbed his arm.

"For years, huh?" she asked. He trembled harder. "El, it's not okay. I'll never say it was okay, but you can get over it. Sort of." She held him next to her in the bed, hanging onto him so he didn't flee. Every muscle in his thin body tensed to run.

"I'm going to tell you something that only a few people know. Only my parents, a bunch of doctors, and Ron Weistheimer, my partner in the military, knew what really happened to me." She forced herself to speak. "I was on a covert op years ago, when I was twenty-two. My first. It went bad and we fell into hostile hands. They tortured my partner to death." She stopped, breathing hard and long. Wiping her eyes, she continued.

"His name was Alex. He was my first love, the love of my life, and my son Ricky's father. I thought I could save him by telling them everything I knew. I did tell them, too, but it turned out I'd been given bad intel, so that I couldn't damage the group if I broke. When they found out what I said was garbage, they beat me. First, the entire village, I don't know how many men, maybe ten or fifteen, raped me. They spent a long time doing it. I was pregnant with Ricky. I thank God that they didn't kill him. They almost killed me.

"Ron saved me. He saved me and loved me through it—not as my lover, but as a person who could make a woman almost raped to death want to live. My father suppressed that information. I think that having a daughter who'd been gang raped was too much for his lordship. Hulls don't get fucked over; they figure a way out. I couldn't and I didn't.

"My husband thinks I'm an alcoholic; I go to a therapist and meetings every week. I told him that's what I was doing. I'm not an alcoholic, though I understand the appeal. I go to a sexual violence survivors' group and trauma counseling. That's almost sixteen years post-rape. I'm a lot better, except for when something gets triggered."

She softened her grip on his arm, laying a hand gently on the sleeve of his robe. "I understand, El. I know what it's like to be treated like less than garbage. To be used by people who know what they're doing to you and love it."

El stiffened and looked at her. Dark eyes, damp hair falling over his forehead. Beautiful bones. His eyes were closed, squeezed tight. Drops formed and trickled down his cheeks. He fell forward without warning, clutching at her. "Oh." That's all he said. The rest were silent wails. So restrained, so deeply repressed. Finally, he choked out a few words, "I couldn't... stop them." A moan.

She pulled him close and ran her hand down the back of his head. "Go ahead and cry, El. You deserve to."

After a long while, he was limp, lying next to her. "I'm sorry."

"Why are you sorry?"

"I'm sorry to bother you."

"You're not bothering me. I would have killed them if I'd been there, El. I want you to know that."

He nodded. "I wish you had. I wish I could kill them. Would you teach me how to kill? I don't want that to happen again, to anyone."

"Definitely. I think that's one reason I'm here, in the grand scheme of things. To turn you into the most badass killer this world has ever seen. Maybe *all* the worlds.

"But that's the only fucking reason I can figure for me being here."

They were drifting toward sleep when she heard his voice.

"Clary, I love you."

"I know you do, El. Just remember that I'm married and faithful to my husband."

"I know that. I love you for that."

"I think I love you, too, El. Just for yourself."

"When you leave here, take me with you."

"If I leave here, I won't leave without you. And I want to take all the humans with me."

She fell asleep with him in her arms. The softness of him, his soothing sweetness, infused her soul. He was so like... Alex. She'd been in heaven when he held her. The way she was now.

El didn't feel like an abused kid as she held him. He felt like the man he *could* be. The only time she'd felt so happy had been with Alex.

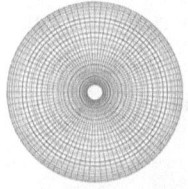

THIRTEEN

JACK HITS OXFORD

BEFORE LANDING, JACK did a bit more surfing the web, trying to figure out where they were going. He found that the United States had six bases, or "sites" as the military preferred to call them, in Great Britain, all operating under the rubric of the Royal Air Force. The largest had about *sixteen thousand* employees. Why did the U.S. need six bases in a friendly country, one of their closest allies? How could they need tens of thousands of employees there?

Jack was a researcher; he couldn't stop digging once he'd started a project. The U.S. was reputed to have more than *one thousand bases* around the globe. The figure was nebulous. Might have been a few hundred more. That didn't include bases of fewer than ten acres or valued at less than ten million dollars. The thousand-plus number excluded more than four hundred bases in Afghanistan and another four hundred in Iraq. But those weren't substantiated anywhere. They even had a name for it. Baseworld blackout described sites that existed, but weren't tallied.

The articles he'd read were from 2011. How many existed today, now that the wars were sort of over and troops were on the way home? Jack was a liberal who'd somehow managed to find and hold onto his principles despite his ultraconservative upbringing. He saw no need for the military. In his opinion, all the wars and "police actions" since WWII had been a colossal waste of human lives and money.

Jack staggered off the plane, somewhere. He'd given up trying to figure out at which base they'd landed. The medical crew unloaded the injured soldiers first. As they disembarked, the soldiers in the front section nodded to him gravely, treating him as a colleague. Somehow, his presence on the plane and the monitor on his chest had made him one of them. A wounded soldier.

That was the fucking truth.

They put him in a car right outside the plane's ramp and someone drove him into the night. Someone had packed a few suitcases for him back in Palo Alto, but he didn't have to go through Customs. He turned his head and watched some buildings and a control tower disappear behind a high fence.

"Where are we going?" he asked the driver. They were in a plain black car. It was a new Ford, but Jack didn't know the model. Biggish. The windows were darkened, but not black. Jack had anticipated being hauled around in a blacked-out, bulletproof SUV that could out-perform the vehicles he'd seen in Jack Bauer's terrifying programs. This one seemed stodgy. The driver's voice made him jump when he started talking.

"We're on our way to your manse in Oxford, Dr. Abercrombie. I am Albert Jordan, your staff liaison. I will connect you to the base and to operations. I'll make sure your household functions smoothly. And I'll drive for you." Both hands were firmly on the wheel. "Can't shake hands just yet." He smiled. Albert had an accent, but Jack didn't think it was English. Australian?

"I'm going to explain where we're going and what's going to happen. As well as why. The world—my world, the covert world—has known of your wife's work for years. She's one of us, and she's published widely, though only what she was allowed to reveal. We figured that eventually she'd poke through into another reality, or they'd use her findings to poke into ours. Looks like that's what happened."

"You knew for years?" Jack swallowed hard.

"Yes. You've been protected while in your Palo Alto residence. We knew about the offer from Oxford long before they made it. The international team was activated to guard you here. They're waiting for us."

"Why? I thought Clarisse and the boys were the targets."

"They are. The boys are hidden so deep no one can get to them. We could hide you the same way, except for one thing..." He glanced over at Jack.

"What?"

"Clarisse. If Clarisse gets loose, she'll stay underground. She won't trust any of her contacts, figuring they leaked something that let the bad guys get her. Which is true. Someone turned over something about her computer that told them how valuable it was, where it was, and where she was. They couldn't grab her unless someone told them her schedule. We don't know who did it, but we'll find out.

"If she escapes, she'll head for the one person she knows would never betray her. You. We need you where she can find you, out in the open."

"Christ. I was a patsy for the Hulls, and now I'm bait." Jack shook his head. "I won't do it. You want to catch Clarisse and lock her up... or something. I won't be any part of that."

"More like, we want to give her a medal. We don't want to *catch* Clarisse, Jack; we want to save her." Jack harrumphed. "If she escapes, who do you think will be right behind her?"

Jack's jaw loosened as he got it. "Whoever captured her?"

"Yes, either international terrorists—the easy option—or extraterrestrial marauders who want our planet. We think it will be the latter. The bad guys she wrote about for so long are real, and they snatched her up.

"You're *her* only chance at freedom. When we've got her, and have whoever leaked her research, we can protect her, and you."

"What will you do?"

"We'll relocate your family and give you identities no one can break, and guard you for the rest of your lives."

"You'll lock us up."

"You were locked up the moment Clarisse disappeared. The question is do you want to be sequestered, or dead? They *will* kill you."

"How do you know that? How do you know any of this?"

Night had fallen almost imperceptibly as they drove. Darkness surrounded the car. They were on a narrow city street surrounded by stone buildings two or three stories high. He saw the name "Cowley Road" on a street sign when they turned onto a smaller street. No curb existed; no one could stop for more than an instant. This lane had much less traffic than Cowley Road, which was all that allowed them to stop at all.

"We'll go over that later. Dr. Abercrombie, this is your residence. I'll hand you over to your staff and park the car. Parking's a problem here, eh? The guys who built medieval towns didn't plan for modern transportation. Mr. Paige will take you in."

Jack stumbled out of the car. A tall, stiff-looking Brit in a black suit and tie greeted him.

"How do you do, Dr. Abercrombie? Fulton Paige, here. I'll be looking after you during your stay with us. Please come with me into the residence." He spoke with the authority of a member of the House of Lords.

Jack had a vague sense of having walked into a downscale episode of *Downton Abbey*. The house wasn't grand and luxurious, like the famous Abbey or the spectacular Hull House. But it still had something. It was an old row house, packed into an ancient, busy municipality. The houses on the street were jammed shoulder to shoulder.

His house was fronted with stone like all the others; a few steps led to a paneled doorway with a tiny overhang that might have provided some shelter from rain. The canopy was held up by a couple of meager columns. The front windows indicated three stories. His wasn't a big house, but nice enough. Some residences on the street, like the places on each side of his, were ludicrous in their narrowness.

Paige led him to the front door, opened it, and stood aside for him to enter. Jack did. He felt like someone should lift him and carry him over the threshold. Or he should have been able to pick up Clarisse and walk into their new life together. Tears sprang to his eyes.

He was at Oxford! Jack was sure this house was much nicer than he could afford by himself. But he was here. He was going to be teaching in this ancient, prestigious place. He, Jack Abercrombie Jr., son of Jack Abercrombie Sr., the owner and breeder of Abercrombie's Blue Tomorrow III, the bull that had swept the competitions over all of his long life, would teach at Oxford. The Oklahoma cattle rancher's boy who no one had expected much from because he was too chubby and bookish had hit it big.

All that was missing was his beautiful wife and boys.

The small crowd in the entry hall kept him from dissolving into mawkish joy/sadness/regret/grief.

"This is…" Fulton Paige introduced him to his household staff. He had a bunch of commandos posing as chief housekeeper, maid, cook, and kitchen maid. Paige was his butler.

Midway through the introductions, Albert Jordan walked in, having stashed the car somewhere. Jordan immediately took over. "I'm your chauffeur. You'll find you need me here, to find a place to stow the car, if nothing else." He smiled.

Jordan addressed the group. "Dr. Abercrombie's safety is our business. Dr.…"

"Please, call me Jack."

"Dr. Abercrombie," Jordan ignored him, "you need to know that everyone here is a specially trained commando able to operate the defense systems of the home and protect you from any conceivable threat. We have top-secret security clearances and represent the intelligence agencies of several nations. We have leased the homes on each side of this one to provide for your greater security. They are also being guarded."

Jack gaped. "Why? How did you do all this so fast?"

Jordan snorted. "Fast? Our project has been ongoing for years, Doctor. What happened to your wife merely caused us to actualize our plans."

"Do you think I'm in that much danger?"

"Yes. That's why we're here. And we have to intercept your wife, if she escapes. Let me show you around."

Jack walked through the house: entrance hall with a narrow but still lavish stairway going up, living room on one side, dining room behind it, and kitchen behind that. A wood-paneled library. A paneled door tucked into one corner turned out to be a soundproofed entrance guarding a cavern-like space with computer monitors ringing it. A bunch of other bleeping machines was stacked around. A tech nodded when they entered, and then stood and bowed curtly to Albert Jordan and then Jack.

"This is the control center for the house. Monitors will be watching the screens around the clock, searching for unauthorized frequencies and disruption. This building is reinforced; the windows and walls are bulletproofed. It's engineered to survive a direct hit by a missile."

Jack wanted to guffaw; this was so unnecessary.

"Jack, I think I'll start calling you that rather than Dr. Abercrombie. We need to remove all barriers between us. I am your new right arm. What we're doing is very necessary. Ron Weistheimer will be calling you on the phone in your room in a few minutes. All the phones are secure and checked for bugs hourly, by the way. There's been a development in your wife's case."

Jack's heart grabbed again. He clutched his chest involuntarily.

His new chauffeur/handler nodded as though he'd been briefed on everything that had happened to Jack since Clarisse had disappeared, maybe before that. "You experienced chest pains on the flight over. Our cardiologist is here to examine you. Dr. Indra will check you now. Then you can talk to Ron and get some sleep. Your orientation at Oxford is tomorrow, if you are up to it. Just a minute or two with the warden of your college—you chaps call the warden the dean in America. Or the president of the college, perhaps. But you only need to go if you're up to it."

Jack walked up the stairs. In all the TV series, fancy English houses had ancestor portraits on the staircase walls. His own humble ancestors didn't warrant them, but he giggled as he thought for a moment that he should ask his dad to send poster-sized photos of his prize bulls, Abercrombie's Blue Tomorrow I through III. Maybe some of the best cows. The creatures who'd put him where he was—his true forbearers.

He approached his bedroom. It was obviously the one with the tidy, brown-skinned woman with glasses and a lab coat standing in the doorway. She took his vital signs, attached another heart monitor to his chest, and did an EKG.

"We'll monitor you until the morning. Just to be careful. I have instructed the cook on your dietary needs. We'll begin your diet and exercise regimen tomorrow."

"I don't want to lose weight. I've always been fat."

"Yes, and you have always been alive. Soon, you will be fat and dead.

Trust me." Her head waggled from side to side, as was the custom in India. "Continuing as you are is not an option. You will die."

"But you're not my doctor."

"Oh, yes, I am. Several governments are funding you, this house, and everything in it. You are no longer in charge of your life. As my patient, you will do what I say." Her tiny brown face was surprisingly commanding as she scowled a few inches in front of his nose.

"You may take your call from that phone. Push the panic button if you need me." The doctor indicated a bulky, wired-in phone on a small table next to a large wing-backed chair and left the room.

He sat in the chair and the phone rang. The clarity of sound and the thick cord attached to the wall told him that it was as soundproof and secure as the rest of the house.

"Jack, how are you?" Ron's voice, sounding strained, greeted him.

"Been better. I've just been told that if I don't lose weight and get in shape, I'll die. That's if the bad guys don't get me." Ron didn't laugh at his joke.

"House okay?"

"Amazing."

"Good. Go slow and settle in tight. There's some news on Clarisse's disappearance."

"Tell me!"

"A homeless man who hung out in the woods near the physics building came forth early on and said he'd seen Clarisse disappear into thin air on the way to the parking lot. You know about those woods?"

"Yes." The campus had stands of oaks throughout. Not too many homeless people lived in them, but they liked to gather and lie in their shade on hot afternoons. Clarisse brought them bags of the vegetables she grew.

"The police discounted his story as a hallucination and didn't tell me about him. The guy has a few arrests for loitering and public drunkenness. Plus a few drug busts; pot, mostly. They thought he was drunk and seeing things.

"I asked them for *everything, especially* what they thought was irrelevant. First thing up was the homeless guy's report. I didn't discount it at all. I spent the afternoon with him, and we went to the spot with some of Clarisse's team from the base."

"What happened?" Jack's heart pounded. He looked for a bell to call the doctor, but—later. He had to hear what had happened.

"He said that he's seen 'the force field' across the path before. It looks like the air is a sheet of shimmering water. He's seen it four times, and crept up to look at it. It didn't disappear. He put his hand through it, and nothing happened.

"It was across the path that Clarisse normally took to get to her car. He's seen *her* often. She's a big favorite among the homeless crowd. The tomatoes. Plus, she's nice to them.

"Clarisse walked out of the building, down the path. The shimmering, invisible wall was there. He said you don't notice it unless you know what you're looking for. She walked into it and disappeared. No grab, no bad guys, just poof!"

"Oh, my God." The monitor attached to his chest started beeping wildly. He looked around frantically and unplugged it. He had to hear this.

"Yeah. It's our worst nightmare. Her research must have alerted some other entity from another world. They snatched her, and obviously just her, because they could have taken the homeless guy and didn't.

"What will they do with her?"

"I expect they'll force her to bring them here. They're hostiles, Jack. Just what Clarisse said in her TED talk. They're not from a warm, fuzzy world. The homeless guy hadn't seen the force field since, and he's been watching that walkway and everything around it. They got what they wanted and split."

A noise came out of Jack.

"Don't freak out. I've got the boys; they're safe and guarded. We're working as hard as possible to get her computer functioning the way she could and bust some holes in reality to find her. If it's possible to get her back, we will."

"What if you can't?"

"She's toast, and maybe our planet is, too. But let's not go there. We've got a cover story for you. People are going to ask where Clarisse and the boys are. Your friends know that she didn't get tenure and was very upset—we asked them. They volunteered that the tenure committee had been indiscreet about leaking what went on in that meeting. Half the campus knew what happened. So we talked to the committee and dean, too. We did *not* tell anyone not to talk about happened—just not to put it online. Which assured that it would happen. Now, everyone knows that her research was being questioned along with her professional reputation and that she got fired.

"Your cover is built on that. Clarisse was so upset that she took the boys and split. She's gone on an impromptu vacation. They're making an itinerary and setting up a paper trail of tickets and receipts for her. I'll get it to you. She's in Thailand, unless they come up with somewhere better. She's on the beach, licking her wounds. She knows all about your new position at Oxford and is delighted for you. Just needs a little alone time with her kids before moving to England with you. She's going to join you in a few weeks. That's what you tell anyone who asks. Everything's fine. You're fine. Clarisse and the boys are fine. If anyone asks if you've talked to them, say yes. 'Bad cell reception, but I heard from her the other day.' Like that.

"I'll be in touch when I've got more."

FOURTEEN

THE GARDEN OF EDEN

"WOW, POPS! YOU got it right!" Clarisse looked at the leafy plot, astonished. "Those pasty-faced excuses for human beings in the hall will brighten up when they get the nutrition in these veggies. And you brought over my entire garden."

He'd gotten *all* of it, the acre-plus of her organic growing field. This was the real thing, not a facsimile. Clarisse stood in the middle of a brilliantly lit plain of white, plastic-like stuff. Her vegetable patch from Hull House sat in the middle, rows of fruit trees marching across the rear of the raised beds. Good old dirt filled in between the planters.

The vault of the sky was vast white space. ""I hope you got the light spectrum right, or all this stuff is going to die. You'll need to simulate day and night, and seasons."

"Oh, rest assured, Dr. Hull; the spectrum is consistent with that of your home. We have arranged a match to your latitude and longitude on Earth. The light will dim and rise as though powered by your sun and the rotation of your planet." Pops smiled benevolently from the glare above her.

"That's a relief. Did you feed the cat while you were at the house?"

"I was not aware that you had a cat, Dr. Hull." Pops' brow furrowed in dismay. She'd caught him. She didn't have a cat, though an assortment of alley cats greeted her every time she entered the backyard.

"Well, someone will feed him. Now, what's all this? You delivered imperfection?"

She examined a damaged area on one of the raised beds. In her one experiment with mechanized agriculture, she had bought a small tractor which she'd promptly run into the side of one of the raised beds. A couple of planks had splintered.

One of her interns had replaced them, demonstrating that a skilled graduate student in physics was not necessarily a good carpenter. The replacement boards were set crooked, and sported enough battering from his hammer to qualify for Family Services aid. She'd left the mess there because the student had been so pleased with his handiwork. And now it was here, wherever that was. This *was* her garden.

She walked around, noticing one imperfect detail after another. Did her real fruit and vegetable patch still exist? Or had they taken its vitality along with its topsoil?

"Really nice, Pops. I should be able to transform those weak-ass ninnies into something approaching soldiers with these veggies. And low fat, high quality protein. Plus six months of hard training. What about a gym? I need one of those, too. Use Ron's as a model."

El stood by, staring at the greenery as though he'd never seen leaves before. She realized that he hadn't, except during his excursion to pick her up. She'd seen no greenery in the white world. He followed her around, gaping, while Pops gloated from the sky, or whatever it was.

"The gym should be in place later today," he exulted. "I'm glad you found our little effort satisfactory, Dr. Hull. We're working on cattle and chickens. When would you like to introduce your troops to the computer?"

Clarisse expected him to start drooling, the jackass was so eager.

"I wouldn't let those bozos near an electric toothbrush, much less my computer. They don't know topsoil from dog shit." She turned to El. "Check your shoes, kiddo." He looked at the bottom of his shoe and wrinkled his nose.

"What is it?" Brown mush protruded from the grooves in his tennies.

"Dog shit. Someone left the gate open again. They come in looking for squirrels." To Pops, she said, "See what I mean? That's dog shit on his shoe. He doesn't know what it is." The look on Pops' face said he didn't either. "You want to trust a multi-billion dollar installation to someone who doesn't know what dog shit is?"

The expression on Pops' face said he didn't.

"We need a little remedial education, but El and I will check the computer later today. Right now, we'll bring in a few of the kids and learn about weeding and snails. If you've got uncooked oatmeal—and I hope you do, because the breakfast menu is the same tomorrow—we'll make escargot. Put the snails in oatmeal for few days; they'll eat it and clean out their digestive systems. Bingo! You've got high quality, high-class protein. Especially when sautéed with my giant garlic, which is right here."

She stopped at some luxuriant stalks. The tops were tied in preparation for harvest. "I developed this variety myself—Hull King Giant Garlic. I possess a wealth of agricultural knowledge." She smiled. "I was forced to diversify from physics and academia or go crazy. I chose topsoil and tomatoes as therapy. Humans need to exercise more than their brains or they go nuts."

Clarisse continued to walk between the raised beds. She'd folded over the stalks of the garlic the day before they'd kidnapped her. This was her garden, leaf for leaf.

Which provided additional substantiation of what she'd surmised earlier. They could take people and things from her world very effectively. She'd seen no evidence that they could go from this world into hers except for when they'd sent El for her. But they'd sent him to some made-up world, not directly to her world. They'd sent her there, too. She didn't know how. But that's what they wanted her for—to make her computer capable of opening larger portals between their worlds. Then to train an army and take them to Earth.

Clarisse looked up. The sky was a dome, or an infinite space. Clear white light bathed the garden. No sun shone up there. The only natural things were the plants, soil, and her and El.

"El, go pick the five people in the hall you think are best—smartest, most reliable and trustworthy—and bring them here."

"Okay, gang," she said after El introduced his choices. "The chard should be about the same size as what you buy at the grocery store... which you don't know, never having been to grocery stores... About this long," she indicated about one foot with her hands. "Or a little more. Start picking the leaves at the bottom of the plant. Bend the leaf outward until you hear a cracking noise, then twist it fast, like this, and pull it off." She gave a demo.

"We'll only take what we need for today. Leave the top of the plant alone. The upper leaves will continue to grow and be available for the future."

"El, you demonstrate." His eyes bulged as though she'd asked him to sprout wings. "Don't be afraid of vegetables." She laughed. "Do what I did."

The five students, plus El, harvested a large heap of leaves.

"Okay, Pops. There's the green vegetable for dinner. Troops! Did you gather the snails, as I told you? Don't give me those looks. Wait until you see the caterpillars that live on tomatoes. Snails are cute! Put the snails in the tray of oatmeal. We'll have us some escargot in a couple of days.

"Now, tomatoes." She led them to another raised bed. Luxuriant, fuzzy-leafed tomato plants overflowed messy rows in a green tangle. Wooden sticks supported the stalks and twine, and wire mesh helped support the heavily laden limbs. "I've never worried about *pretty* in my garden. I use twine or whatever I've got to hold them up.

"Okay. Pick only the orange to red tomatoes. Let the greener ones ripen, which hopefully they will in this fake sun." She let them work until they'd picked a substantial and colorful heap of vegetables. "That's it. We've harvested enough for today. You may go back to the hall. We'll start working out whenever the gym..."

"Dr. Hull," Pops beamed from the white expanse above them, "the gym is complete. You may use it now."

"I need to do an inspection. I also need to eat lunch. But, thank you. Troopers, back to the pit. I'll be inspecting your quarters right after I look at the gym. I want everything clean, neat, and stowed. If the gym passes muster, we'll start working out tomorrow. That is, after *you* pass my muster and do your first drill. You'll be on your way to being effective soldiers in *my* army. You are dismissed."

"El," Clarisse said, but then abruptly stopped speaking. They were in their room eating lunch. "Oh, shit." She got up to get her device and zap the bug so they could talk.

"It's all right, Clary. I reprogrammed it."

"*You* reprogrammed it?"

"Yes. They changed their algorithm, using a slightly different frequency. I wanted to catch it before..."

"*You* reprogrammed it? I didn't give you permission to do that or touch my equipment." Anger flared inside her.

"Clar... you were making sounds at night. I didn't want them to hear you."

"*Sounds?*"

"You were crying for Jack and your children. I didn't want them to hear."

Her eyes widened. "In my sleep?" He nodded. "Oh, no." She bit her lip. "I used to have flashbacks... about..." She couldn't say Alex's name.

"Is it all right if I fix things like that, if I have to?"

"Yes. Don't let them hear me crying. They have to think I'm Superwoman. But how did you do it? I've never instructed you on my equipment."

He shrugged. "I just know how. I told you what they did."

"They put everything I know in you?"

"About physics, not about gardening or anything else."

"Okay. We'll have to discuss this, but later. I need to make a trip to the computer and make sure it's working right. And I need to do something else." She rolled her eyes at the ceiling, raising her brows.

"They can't hear us."

"Good. I need to recharge my weapon. I can do that with the main computer, but I need a distraction so they don't notice what I'm doing."

"Where do you recharge it?"

"There's a port on each of the monitor stations, down near the floor. I can plug the big gun in there, and then recharge the others from it. It will take about three minutes, once it's in the socket. Can you think of anything you could do that would keep them from wondering what I'm up to? Short of starting a fire?"

El's brow furrowed. "Yes. I know something that would work. Do you have to do anything while it recharges?"

"No, just plug it in and wait. While we're waiting, maybe I'll be able to figure out a way to use the computer to go home, with you and whoever else won't destroy the planet." Clary bit her lips. She wanted to go home as much as she wanted to breathe.

The computer was as splendid as ever, seen through the windows of the changing room. Lights streamed along the edges of the layers, pulsing throughout the cutout cylinder and down the middle. Colossal and impressive. And surrounded by freezing air.

Clarisse moved to the paneled compartment where the clean suits were kept.

An unctuous voice broke the silence. Pops spoke from the wall. "Oh, no need for that, Dr. Hull. We've adjusted conditions in the computer's environs so that clean suits are unnecessary. They were such a bother."

"You've made the computer able to cleanse itself of contaminants so people can enter without protection? That's impossible."

"Not so, my dear doctor. We can do many things. Though, we were unable to adjust the temperature all the way up to what you will find comfortable. It's fifty degrees."

"You didn't ask me before doing this? You could have destroyed the computer!" Wild-eyed, she was ready to fight.

"No, we would not harm it. We were sure of that. And, if our filtering operation had harmed the computer, we could simply have imported another copy from Moffett Field. The way we did this one."

His gloating face was almost more than she could take. But she had a fail-safe; if the computer was ruined somehow, she could get another. She could get home.

"Well, if you can always get another... Let's go, El. Maintenance time." She hoped her voice didn't quake the way her heart was.

Clarisse and El entered the clear glass monitor stations, one by one. Pops floated on a wall outside, observing their activities with great interest. Clarisse checked all the monitors, on all the floors.

"They're working perfectly. One more and we're done," she said, beckoning El to enter the final enclosure with her. She gazed at him searchingly and nodded. *Do it now.*

El lunged at her, grasping her around the upper body and pinning her arms to her sides. His lips smashed into her face. "What are you...?"

He was *kissing* her, which became obvious fast. Kissing her passionately, while feeling her back and hips. He was way more skilled than she'd thought he'd be, and stronger.

"What the fuck are you doing?" She twisted away and stood facing him. "What do you think..."

He lunged again, succeeding in maneuvering her back to the side of the machine that contained the port she'd told him about. She struggled, but when she got what he was up to, she allowed him to pull her to the floor. He kept kissing and groping, putting on a show that anyone would believe. She put one on, too, once she got her gun moored in its receptacle.

"Stop it! El!" She pulled away, turning from side to side on the floor. He kept her down, maneuvering himself between her legs.

"No! You *can't* do that!" He grabbed her hands and pressed the lower part of his body into her, moving in an unmistakable rhythm. "STOP IT!"

He kissed her, pinning her face and mouth with his. She fought for a moment and then felt his hand along her side, rubbing her breast. He stroked her slowly, once, twice, hands moving across her chest. He reached her nipple.

Like a spark, the whole thing changed. She began kissing him back. "El," she breathed, and his hand kept moving. "El..." His lips were soft. She couldn't stop.

When they finally broke off, he whispered, "Don't forget the..." He moved his head toward the port containing her weapon and shoved her in that direction with his thighs and torso.

She collected the gun, stowed it quickly, and rose. When she was steady on her feet, she turned to him, blazing.

"You stinking son of a bitch." The sound of her palm slapping his face

ricocheted around the cubicle. "You *asshole*! *Never* do that again!" Following him, she pointed toward the door to the computer. "Get out of here." Then she carefully secured the door to the cubicle—as upset as she was, she'd never neglect her machine.

"Never touch me! Get out of my sight. I never want to see you again." She stormed from the computer facility, furious. El slunk behind.

Pops' face glowed with absolute delight.

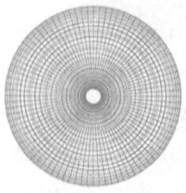

FIFTEEN

DR. ÓSKAR ERLAND

J ACK EXAMINED HIS magnificent room. Dark wood paneling, a canopied bed with tapestry hangings, a crackling fireplace, and big wingback chairs. All his life, his soul had cried for this classy, romantic place.

He couldn't sleep and he couldn't stand sitting here alone. His bags had been delivered, along with his laptop. Jack couldn't be idle while Clarisse was potentially being tortured. He had to do something to help find her. He was a superb researcher. How about doing a little background checking? Maybe he could unearth something the pros had missed.

Booting up his PC, Jack looked around. He was in jail, yes, but he was also the bait in an international manhunt—or womanhunt. That was so weird. Who would want an oversized, middle-aged wordsmith? A boring wordsmith. Even his brilliant red hair was dulling; gray streaked it.

His screensaver lit up and filled the laptop's screen. Clarisse and the boys grinned at him from their backyard. They held one of those enormous tomato-eating caterpillars like it was a hunting trophy. He blinked back tears and pulled up a search engine as fast as he could.

What stuck out in his mind on this day of shattering revelations? Ron had said something about Ben Hull and Eleanor, his ice queen wife, and where they fit into this mystery, but not much. More shockingly, Dr. Óskar Erland had disappeared. Ron had announced the fact, and never gone back to it. Jack never read the popular press, but Erland's disappearance would have been headline news. A vanishing Nobel Prize winner who'd "cracked DNA," leading to huge changes in the prosecution of criminals, settling paternity, and resolving fertility issues, was big news.

He'd heard Erland speak, years before. He'd been ancient then, and sounded like a Nazi, saying genes determined *everything*. He'd stopped just short of, "You ought to eliminate everyone but the very brightest people."

Erland and Ben Hull had been great buddies, both sporting 'MD, PhD' after their names and sharing a fervent belief in the power of genetics.

Jack searched "Óskar Erland" and was flooded with information. The man had died two years earlier. That *had* been headline news—in 2014.

What? Jack thought, *how could he disappear "just like Clarisse," when he's been dead for years?*

All the crazy whack-a-doodle shit he'd heard all day flooded him. Ron had said, "I'll be in touch when I've got more."

Fuck that. Jack couldn't wait. How could he reach that lying thug? The wired-to-death phone they'd spoken on probably had more listeners than the Oklahoma party lines his dad talked about. Jack felt for his cell phone in his pocket.

"Weistheimer, what are you up to?" he shouted when Ron answered right away.

"Do you know what time it is here?"

"I don't care, ol' buddy *Ron*," he gave it his best Oklahoma drawl. "Tell me how Óskar Erland could disappear just like Clarisse? *He died two years ago!*"

"Oh. You found out."

"Of course, I found out. I'm not stupid. How much of what you told me today was bullshit?"

Ron sighed long and hard over Jack's cell phone. "I haven't told you everything, but what I did tell you was accurate."

"Tell me what you didn't say, starting with Erland. *How* can a corpse disappear?"

"Just like that. It was as though he was still alive. His experiments were still going on. But things were tampered with, changed. All of his projects had national security aspects. We thought he might have staged his own death, so he could operate freely, without surveillance.

"Jack, are you there?"

"I'm listening." Jack was so angry he could barely think. His jaws clenched. More bullshit.

"We exhumed his body. It wasn't there."

"That's impossible. An embalmed body is not going anywhere. It can't be resuscitated. Nothing, including black magic, can bring back a corpse soaked in formaldehyde."

"That's true. Erland wasn't embalmed. His burial instructions were very specific. He was not embalmed. His body was rigged with devices to keep fluids moving. He had life support systems we've never seen in that casket. That's how we know his disappearance was recent; our forensics people tested the fluids. They indicated living biological material had been there, and it ceased to be 'fresh' when Clarisse disappeared. Which is when Erland must have really died, or been resuscitated, and disappeared."

"This is great, Ron. Now you're telling me that Óskar Erland rose from the dead, escaped from his coffin and grave... was he in a crypt or the ground?"

"Crypt, but not inside. The cemetery featured an area with wings of crypts stacked in rows, outside. The burial instructions specified that, and a million other things. Bottom line being, if he got out somehow, he could walk away."

"So he did. Or maybe he beamed up." Rage flashed through Jack. He hated Ron Weistheimer; he'd always hated him. Their little bonding session that afternoon had softened him a bit, but this...

He burst out, "Thanks for telling me, Ron. My wife has been kidnapped by aliens who are capable of raising the dead. You bastard! Why are you telling me this shit? Next, you'll be telling me that my in-laws are secret agents. Eleanor really made atomic bombs and Ben was an expert on torture."

"They were, Jack. That's the part I didn't tell you."

"FUCK YOU, RON. If you think I'm going to believe a single fucking thing you ever say to me again, you're out of your..."

The pain was so bad he thought he'd die. Jack grabbed his chest and fumbled at the nightstand until he hit the panic button. "Help me..." he managed to say before falling to the floor.

SIXTEEN

WORKING OUT

E LIAS RAN AFTER Clary, who headed back to their room as fast as she could fly. He had to stop her, he had to tell her he hadn't meant it, that it was just that he'd known it would work… But she *was* as mad as she'd seemed after he kissed her. Would she ever forgive him?

"Dr. Hull, the gymnasium is ready," Pops announced from the wall as Clarisse rocketed out of the computer room. A grin decorated his face; Elias had never seen him so happy. He'd thought that El would do his real job soon.

Hearing Pops, Clarisse stopped her headlong flight. "Where is the gym?"

"Right here," Pops chortled. The doors appeared on the wall.

Clarisse spun left and banged through the newly existent entryway. She examined the space, head moving up and down and turning in a circle to scrutinize the entire room. When she finished her survey, she whistled.

"Well, Pops, you've got copy-and-paste down great. I hope Ron has something left."

"Don't worry, Dr. Hull; your friend will never notice we've been there."

Elias cringed at Pops' certainty. He was dangerous when he was so pleased with himself.

"Oh, *Ron* will notice; don't *you* worry." She stalked around the very large, square room with black, padded walls twice the height of a human being. Above the padding was white space, seeming to extend forever.

Elias cowered in the doorway. He'd never seen a place like this. Clarisse obviously had. She continued across the big room and into the corridor on the other side. He tiptoed behind her. The room on their left had clear windows allowing him to look in. Different sizes of round metal wheels on long poles were placed on racks around the room. A big bag, the size of a person, hung on chains in one corner. Near it was a much smaller bag suspended from a metal arm extending out above his head.

Elias tried to disappear while Clary did a lightning-fast survey of the room through the window. "You've brought the weight room over." She spun and opened the doors across the hallway behind her. "Locker room and showers." She turned to her left. The hall ended. "You left out Ron's office. I need an office to keep records on the soldiers."

"We thought the workout facilities sufficient."

"They're not. I want Ron's office by tomorrow."

"Very good, Dr...."

She was already in the room with all the big metal wheels on rods, opening a tall cabinet. She pulled out a white roll and wrapped tape around her knuckles.

Elias crept up. "I'm sorry, Dr. Hull," he knew better than to call her Clary in her current state. "I thought what I did was a good idea."

"It was a great idea. But I don't want to see you again. Move out of our room."

"But I..." He couldn't move out. If he moved back into the hall, even the sanitized people there would kill him. He would be the prize of prizes. If she kicked him out, he'd have failed. Failure wasn't permitted.

"I don't care where you go or what you do. Just so it's not with me." She jerked her head toward the wall where Pops had been. "Ask him for a room. He seemed to love what you did. Now, leave me alone."

She started jumping rope, slowly at first and then quickly, and then so fast that he couldn't follow her feet. The rope made a rat-at-tat, rat-at-tat noise, never missing a beat. She was doing little dance steps and movements as she jumped. Not out of any happiness. Clary was enraged. He hadn't seen her this way, even when she'd killed all the people. Then she'd been deadly and directed, and now she was so angry he couldn't talk to her. Why?

"I didn't know I'd like it, Clary," he wanted to say. "It was just for show."

But it was more than that. He'd wanted to kiss her since they'd showed him images of her and announced she was his person. He hadn't been able to stop thinking about her. They took him to a white room and covered the walls with pictures of Clary, still and moving. Pictures of her going through her day. Of her and her children, in her garden, with her husband. Even he charmed Elias. A family. More of her. Teaching physics in a lab. They kept him there for ages, whispering stories about her and her life. Showing her with her parents.

He wanted her to smile at him the way she did at Jack. He wanted her eyes to light up the way they did with the boys. He wanted to go to the beach with her. He wanted to go to the beach, period. He could remember very little besides the big white room.

El wanted *everything*—a house, children. A wife. *Clary* for his wife. Happiness. Freedom. A way out. He'd do anything to get out of this place, even what they wanted. *Especially* that.

He'd wanted to kiss her since the confused day when they'd sent him to Earth and he'd seen her on the street. He'd never felt what he felt for her. Perhaps it was love. He thought it was love. Everything she said or did toward him struck him, magnified. A cross word would have him close to tears. Approval made his heart thump and seem to jump in his chest. He'd thought he was doing well, making her happy.

But he had wrecked it all.

Clary was sweating hard when she stopped jumping and put padded gloves on her hands. She moved to a small brown bag hanging from a stand. Punching it tentatively at first, she established a rhythm the way she had with the rope. The small brown sack rocked with each punch, sometimes hitting the brace above it and then swinging back to her glove.

Rat-ta-ty, ra-ta-ty, ra-ta-ty, faster and faster until he *couldn't* see the bag. He watched her. Her face said she was killing whomever that bag represented, killing them again and again. The speed of her, and the ferocity. She wasn't the Clary he'd slept with and loved; she was someone else.

A fierce cry burst from her lips. She gave the bag one more punch— Wham! It hit the metal arm that held it. She spun, racing across the room to the much larger bag, the size of a person from below the knee to head-height.

It was anchored above and below by chains. She launched at it, hitting it not with her hands, but leaping into the air and striking it with both feet.

Wham! She rebounded and attacked the bag with hands, feet, and knees. She punched it with her head, all so fast he couldn't track her movements. He was surprised the bag didn't burst as she assaulted it. She was screaming, making guttural noises that didn't mean anything, except that she wanted to kill.

As abruptly as she'd done everything since he'd kissed her, she turned and ran toward the padded wall of the big room they'd entered at the beginning. She ran, legs pumping up and down, covering ground. He'd never seen anyone run this fast, or like this. Like she was running toward something. Death, perhaps. Or life. He thought she'd run into the wall. She didn't.

In one expertly timed leap, Clarisse jumped, hitting the wall with her feet above where her head would have been. Screaming, she ran up the wall a few more steps, flipped in the air, kicking behind her—left foot, right foot, left foot—before landing. The kicks would have hit an opponent in the head, chest, and belly. She could have killed him.

Shrieking, she did the run and flip five times on different spots along the wall.

"I'm done." She turned and banged through the gym doors, heading back to their room. Her room.

He slunk behind her. She had shown him how ferocious she was. How she could kill him. But he didn't know why she hated him so much. He'd kissed her, and touched her. But she knew he loved her. His idea was good. He knew *they* would love it. They would think he was getting on with his job. They didn't notice her recharging her gun at all.

He got into their room just because the door hadn't shut all the way when he arrived. She was in the shower. He looked around helplessly and made the bed. He was dusting when dinner came. He took the trays and arranged the food on the table.

"I'm sorry, Dr. Hull," he said when she emerged from the bathroom. She had on jeans and a shirt.

"I'm glad, Elias. Get out. Take your dinner and get out."

"But…"

"Get out."

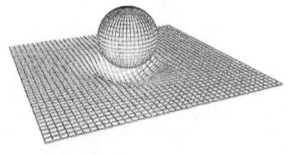

SEVENTEEN

JACK VS. OXFORD, ROUND ONE

JACK DID NOT do his introductory round at the university the next day, as planned. Nor did he breach the hallowed halls the day after that, or even the next week. He hadn't had a heart attack—merely an "episode." One of the stress-related attacks he'd had earlier in his life, but on a grander scale.

Dr. Indra and her beeping machine friends kept him down and starving, but full of fluids. His recovery was not pretty, but it was effective.

"You've lost eight pounds, Dr. Abercrombie. Only forty-five more to go." Dr. Indra said, her face tight. She was not much fun. Neither was he.

"I don't have to do what you say. I'm a private citizen."

"Ah, Mr. Private Citizen, do you know that the entire team—your staff at this house, and those guarding you outside this building, others you'll never see, and your health staff, primarily *me* at the moment, were assembled to keep you safe? Do you know that our various governments pay us handsomely? Those governments will be very unhappy if you are in anything but first-rate health. You are a key element of a multinational military operation. We need you alive until your wife surfaces and comes to you.

"You will do what I say until that happens, because you're going to die if you don't. I do not allow my patients to die, and especially not those who are required to attain military objectives. The rest of the team is similarly committed to keeping you from killing yourself, however you may try."

"So I can die after Clarisse comes back?"

"Yes. You will be a real private citizen again, free to live in ways that will kill you."

He couldn't get the dour Dr. Indra to smile over anything. And so the days passed; she had Jack chugging water, walking on a treadmill, eating grass clippings, and peeing up a storm.

He discovered a humorous streak in himself, though, having his father send the files for the portraits of Abercrombie's Blue Tomorrow I, II, and III, as well as his top five cows. "You can send them by email, Dad. Remember, I showed you how to do attachments. Send as big as you've got. I want to show some of these British lords what a real bull looks like."

"Oh, son. Do you think they'll appreciate them?" His dad's voice quivered.

"Dad, somewhere around here, there's a Lord Hereford," he pronounced the word the way the English would, Hair-ah-ford. "His people invented the Húr-ferd breed," Jack said, pronouncing it the way any good American cattleman would. "He must know what a great bull looks like."

"Oh, son, having that lord see my bull—*our* bull, he belongs to all of us—would mean so much to me."

"If I can do it, Dad, I will." Jack hung up, mystified. His desire to spoof the Brits had led to one of the closest moments he could remember with his father.

The images of the cattle, blown up and framed in fancy frames like ancestor portraits, were hung along the stairway as he prepared for his meeting with the warden of his college— which, true, was one of Oxford's smaller and more obscure colleges, but it offered the D.Phil. (doctoral degree) and had all its bona fides. He wished that Oxford had invited him into one of the larger, more prestigious colleges, such as Wadham. Maybe if he'd had better book sales… Jack smiled at his joke. Nothing could bring him down.

One of the reasons he felt so good was that his caretakers had sent over a little something to ease his pain.

Dr. Alma Bertrand-Elverton was a true MD. That was rare in Britain, most of them being MBChBs or MBBSs, abbreviations for Bachelor of Medicine or Bachelor of Surgery. In the labyrinth of British education, a medical doctor had to obtain one of the lesser degrees, termed a bachelor's degree, which was equivalent to medical school in the United States. If they were talented and worked many more years, they became MDs.

Alma was a psychiatrist, sent by whoever was taking such good care of him, to alleviate his stress. She did. Jack felt much better after expressing his terror, fear, loss, and the scathing anger that was beginning to rise within him over his wife's deceit. And her parents' total denigration of his worth. And being cut out of all the family wealth by that prenuptial agreement Clarisse had popped on him. He could make his own way, but what would happen when the shadow military stopped supporting him? They would, he knew. Would he end up in some tiny flat, making his own toast?

"My father loved his bull more than me, Alma. That was hard to stomach. But Ben and Eleanor loved *everything* more than me. That makes me want to puke."

Jack was angry, and he hadn't realized it.

"So you gained weight and had heart 'episodes.'" The wise Alma could say things like this without sounding condescending. "How does that make you feel?"

Angry. Jack realized he was moving into his *angry* period. His fury was underlain by guilt because he was pissed off at his abducted wife, who was potentially being tortured at that moment.

"Jack," she said, and he was glad that they were 'Jack and Alma' instead of some formal British nonsense, "you're going to feel angry and you're going to feel guilty. Survivor's guilt, it's called. They took her and not you."

"They didn't *want* me. I have nothing to offer them. That's why I'm running around loose. I'm nothing."

"Even not being abducted fuels your sense of worthlessness." She was right.

He could barely breathe when he mouthed the words, "What will I do if she doesn't come back? What if they kill her?"

"You'll go on, Jack, and live. You've done all this to get here; don't lose it now. You have so much to give the world, and Oxford. I've read your most recent book, *Realms of Magic*. It's excellent. You could be a psychiatrist, you understand people so well. Maybe it's time for you to understand Jack Abercrombie." She smiled at him, that very intelligent face with its piercing, all-knowing eyes seeming to inhale his state of being.

An idea for a new book arose then; the heroine would be like her. Brilliant, insightful, utterly honest. And not an exercise freak or operative for anything but her own psychiatric practice.

Alma Bertrand-Elverton was not as beautiful as Clarisse. She was older than his wife, more his own age. Mid-to-late forties. It felt good to see some gray hair in her flyaway mocha-colored bun. Nor did she have a super-athlete's perfect body, which also made him feel less inadequate, given his rotund state.

She had more. She showed up every day at the appointed time and listened to him, making astute comments that indicated she knew what he was going through more than he did. She was there for him the first time he broke down, and he knew she would be there every time it happened.

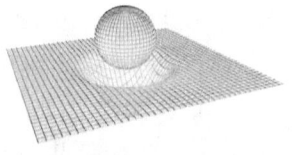

EIGHTEEN

GETTING REAL

S ITTING ON THE floor in the hall, Elias nibbled a little, too upset to eat. They had been friends. He should have told her what he was going to do, but he'd wanted her reaction to be unrehearsed. It was; she'd kissed him back. That had been real.

Just as real as the fact that she hated him now. It was Jack. She was married and wanted to be faithful. He had tempted her.

He knew a great deal about people and relationships, all learned in the jungle of the big hall. He'd survived there from the time he'd been stolen until now—twelve years. He knew of the intricacies of bonds between people. He knew everything there was to know about sex. He'd never had girlfriend, though; they didn't allow it. Nor had they allowed the boys who wanted him to stake anything but a transitory claim. They'd allowed others to pair up, but not him.

He wished he could have had someone of his own, and some role other than what he had. Elias knew that some couples had been faithful in the big room. Which made it sadder when they brought their special people up from Earth and tore the lovers apart. But everyone knew that, eventually, they would bring their people to them and they would go live up a corridor. Once they entered a corridor, no one ever came back. He was the first to reemerge.

He knew about couples coming untwined on their own, too, and cases where one person loved the other more than he or she was loved back. Someone new could lure them away.

And there were people who didn't love anyone, and just loved fucking whoever they could. The people who'd used him loved him like that, as though he was a special toy. They'd said they loved him, and sometimes he'd said it back. But it wasn't true.

He knew he didn't love Clary like that. It was more.

When he heard someone coming to collect the dinner trays, he left his outside the door and hid, farther up the corridor.

He was exhausted and wanted to sleep, but knew Clary wouldn't let him in. Elias curled up with his back to their door. If they discovered him in the night, they'd kill him. If he went back into the hall, they'd kill him. What difference did it make?

"El, would you come in?" He had to have been sleeping when he heard her voice from a speaker. When he stood up, the door was unlocked.

The lights were dim and the bed was a mess. Clary sat cross-legged in the middle of it, head hung forward, hands limp in front of her. She had on baggy sweats. She didn't acknowledge him for several long moments.

"I'm a terrible mother." She spoke to the sheets in front of her. He would not have recognized her voice. Timid. Broken. Clary was broken. "I'm a worse wife. I was never home. Work was more important to me than the boys. Nannies raised them. And my parents. All they did was reinforce the idea that work was more important than them and that what I was doing was right. I practically ignored Jack."

As he moved closer, he could see her tear-stained face, swollen and blotchy. She looked up.

"I don't love Jack. I never loved him." She shrugged. "My marriage is the biggest lie of my life. I married him because he loved me so much. He is a good man, stable and kind. What I needed—a normal person. Jack is big, cuddly, and sweet. The boys needed a father.

"I never loved him." She paused, her face screwed up in anguish. Her breath came in pants as she labored to express herself, hands clawing at the bedspread. "But, no. That's not true. I came to love him—I do love him. It's so complicated. I *do* love Jack, but not like I loved... I loved *Alex*. I *can't* love anyone else..."

She didn't cry hard, the way she had before. She just folded over and got smaller. He could watch her disappear. "Everything about my life is a lie. I'm in love with someone who's dead. It was my fault." She struck the bed in front of her with a fist, a weak blow, as though the Clary of that afternoon had perished.

"I let him die. Alex, the man I really loved, is dead because of me.

"I made myself into this *thing*," she tossed her head in the direction of the gym and indicated her rock-hard body with her hands, "because I thought, if I was tough enough, I could have saved him. I could roll back the clock and save him.

"*Isn't that funny?*" She sounded a little hysterical. He didn't reply. "God, I wish I had something to drink. I said I wasn't an alcoholic, but maybe I am a little bit." She laughed, breathless and broken. "That's like being a little bit pregnant." Another bitter laugh. "They want you to make me pregnant, don't they?"

He nodded.

"I knew that from the start, the way I know everything." She raised her head a bit and sniffed. "There's lots about me you don't know. We've kept the boys apart from other kids as much as possible. Part of it is their intelligence; other kids don't interest them much. But part of it is them. They know things that people haven't said, and they feel things that haven't happened, but do. They're always right.

"They get that from me. I get it from my mother and grandmother. The Hull genius is more than genius. It's fucking freaky psychic shit. We call it 'mindspeak.' At home, I can hear their thoughts whenever I want to—or when they let me. They're getting cagey about it. And I know what others want without being told. I knew from the start what they wanted with you and me. They want me to lead an army and take over the world, but you and I are in their breeding program. They want you to make me pregnant. All the humans are here for that. All that business about going up corridors and not coming back. Those were couples who failed to produce babies that *they* could get into, babies who could read minds like you and I."

Elias stared at her. "How did you know?"

She laughed. "El. I'm a *genius*. I just told you that. That's what geniuses do. Figure things out that regular people can't. I made that computer. I figured out the basic outlines of this place in an instant. It's called an intuitive flash. That's where I live. If I didn't tell you about it, so what? It's obvious. What the fuck do aliens do in every sci-fi movie made? They breed with humans. I knew everything the minute I got the scene here. Going up corridors when you get married?

"What a pack of bullshit. They were breeding people, but none of them had the horsepower Pops and his friends wanted. Don't deny it, El. I can read your mind sometimes. *We've* got what they want. And I knew they'd somehow get into our baby and have a super-charged addition to their army. That's what they wanted with all the scientists they've chosen and the people out there. We're breeding stock, making hybrids of humans and them.

"Well, my friend Elias, that will never happen. I'm sterile. After I had Jimmy, I had my tubes tied. No one can use me for breeding."

El didn't know a great deal about female anatomy or fertility, other than what he'd found out in the hall. None of the women "had their tubes tied." If they got pregnant, when it showed, they disappeared up a corridor and were never seen again. New women appeared in the hall and things went on as usual.

"When I was in the hospital after having Jimmy, I had the doctor fuse my fallopian tubes. They do it with an electrical charge that seals the tubes. Fertilized eggs can't get into my womb and grow. That's it. I wouldn't have an abortion, even after what happened, but I wouldn't let it happen again."

"You can't have babies."

"Not after what happened—or '*what Clarisse did*.'" His face scrunched, trying to understand. "Oh, you don't know my horrible secret, do you? I'm the whore of Babylon."

"I don't know who that is…" His eyes narrowed, as though that could make him understand.

"She was a prostitute. She had sex with all sorts of men for money. That's what my dad made me out to be. Because of what happened."

"You had sex with men for money?"

"No! When Ricky was two, I disappeared. I showed up ten days later in some town in Wyoming, out of my mind on drugs. My father told Jack all about it—I know because we haven't been the same since. My dad wrecked the pretense that was my marriage.

"But El, I didn't run off with a bunch of men and come back pregnant like my dad told Jack. I was rufied." He didn't know what that was. "Rohypnol is a sedative known as the 'date rape drug.' A guy wants a woman but doesn't have what it takes to get her in bed on his own. So he gives her Rohypnol and takes it from there."

"I don't understand."

"Not a lot of rufie out in the hall, I bet. I went to a physics conference. I drank one cocktail—one—and passed out. That was the last I remembered until I woke up in Wyoming. Someone put Rohypnol in my drink. They kept me drugged up until they were done with me.

"Jimmy's father is Óskar Erland, an expert in biogenetics. My father found that out from DNA tests. I was impregnated to produce the next generation of genius Hulls. I think my father had something to do with my 'escapade.' I just wish he'd had the balls to say, 'I want to breed you to Óskar. You two are a great cross. We'll use AI.'"

El's head moved from side to side, trying to keep from understanding what she was saying.

"Artificial insemination. They do it with animals." She shrank more. "I married Jack because I felt safe with him. But I never loved him. He deserves someone who really loves him." Her jaws clattered and she shivered, head to foot.

"Clary, let me hold you. I can make you feel better."

"I don't deserve to feel better. I'm shit. My life is shit. I'm no good."

Eventually, she let him hold her. "Hold me, El. Nothing else."

"I know."

They drifted for a while. She reached up and ran her fingers through his hair, then dropped her hand to his lips. He kissed the back of her fingers.

"I liked you kissing me, El."

"I know," his whisper came, barely audible. "It wasn't your fault that you couldn't save Alex, Clary."

She froze, as though not registering what he'd said. Her nostrils widened and deflated as she breathed in and out, faster and more frantically. "Ohhh," a sound came from her, not a sound a person should make. Anguish.

"He died." She said that a dozen times, clutching his chest, sobbing hard at first and then unable to make much noise, until, "He died right in front of me. I couldn't..."

"It wasn't your fault."

Clary didn't break; she shattered. But he was ready and held her, whispering and stroking her hair. And in his mind's eye, Elias could see Alex in that hut, ruined and bleeding. He could see him and feel the crowbar across the middle of his face.

She didn't know everything about *him*, either. He also knew things ahead of time. He knew people's secrets without being told. That's why he'd survived in the hall. That's why they'd found her for him. They matched.

Everything was a setup in the white world.

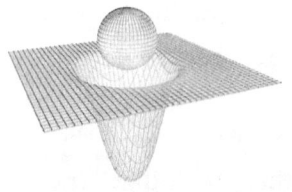

NINETEEN

OXFORD FOR REAL

T HE DAY THAT Alma and Dr. Indra finally deemed Jack well enough to go to work dawned. He headed toward the college in anticipation, but with a big dollop of fear. The town thrilled him. Rather than being a complex of buildings on a big campus, the way American universities were, Oxford was a group of thirty-eight colleges dotted around a medieval city that was also inhabited by a hundred thousand or so very lively people.

Every journey into the city filled him with awe. The ancient buildings with their spires. The history that had transpired in the place practically oozed from the stone facades. Art and literature had been born here, along with every type of intellectual activity. The bustling modern-day streets with their mix of antique buildings and contemporary mass transit thrilled him. Very lively pubs and museums dotted the avenues. *People* lived in this historic place. It was a wonderland for the Oklahoma rancher's son.

He hadn't seen much of the town—just what was visible from the car on a few exploratory ventures from his house. Alma, who was a stern taskmaster, wanted him to do some trial runs to manage his anxiety when he actually showed up for his job. She'd ordered Albert Jordan, his chauffer and primary babysitter, to drive him around Oxford and his college to prepare.

When the day came, Albert Jordan pulled into a narrow drive on one side of a U-shaped group of buildings. Paved walkways rimmed and crossed the space between them. Bright green lawn filled in between the paths, and austere plantings backed up to structures. The college consisted of three-storied structures with steep-pitched roofs dotted with chimneys. A tower with spires graced the long building at the back, which connected the other two wings. The buildings were weathered, buff-colored stone with small-paned windows stacked in rows. Historic and Oxford to the nth degree. This was his college. No sign announced its identity.

"Go in that door. A sign inside will say the building is closed. That's for the public. Turn left and keep going. The warden's office is on the second floor, butting up against the spire. You can see it there," Albert pointed. "You should know, Jack, that operatives are following you. You won't be able to see them, I hope, because the bad guys won't either if they're hidden."

"Do we really need...?"

"Yes, we do. Starting now." He nodded to a normally scruffy looking student who stood outside his door. Albert unlocked it. "He'll get you to the warden's in one piece."

"How do you do, Jack?" The warden came out from behind her desk and extended her hand. Her office was large, paneled in ancient oak, and lined with books, seeming somber with the cloud-dampened light coming in the leaded windows. Most of the time he'd been in England, rain had pelted down, or been about to.

"I'm very well, Jeanette." Again, no Dr. to Dr. bullshit. They knew each other. He'd met Jeanette several times when he'd been interviewing for the job.

He never had had to tell Clarisse where he was going when he'd interviewed. She wasn't home. Off doing something. Research, she'd said. Maybe she'd really been napalming villages or rescuing trapped spies. He'd told the boys he was going to conferences. They never questioned him. The invisible man. He coughed to cover his feelings. He had so many, these days.

He'd met the warden, Jeanette Thorthope-Glennes, D.Phil. on his first interviewing voyage. She didn't look even vaguely the way he had expected. She was a she, not a he, first off. She had hair, not a shiny bald skull. She didn't wear glasses and wasn't fat. Jeanette was a very pleasant woman of about fifty, and yes, she was a little dowdy. Fashion was not her strong point; she looked as though the last time she'd thought about clothes had been shortly after her birth. Today, she was frumpier than ever.

"Please, be seated." She ushered him to a wingback leather chair by a fireplace and sat opposite him. "Well, Jack, I'm glad to see that you've been given a clean bill of health after your episode," Jeanette said. "Rather an alarming start."

"Yes, it was."

She was curious as hell as to what had happened to their new American Fellow, but wouldn't ask.

"Little rocky around the ol' homestead," he quipped, using his Oklahoma accent, which he had relegated to the bottom recesses of the verbal portion of his cerebral cortex.

She lit up, hearing his enunciation. "Oh, I see. Fine now, yes?"

"Yes, ma'am, jus' fine." More Oklahoma drawl and Southern(ish, Oklahoma not being strictly a Southern state) manners.

The warden lit up more. Jack realized something. He was looking for a way to be a success in this ancient British institution. How could an American with his background do it? Answer: Be an American Fellow from an Oklahoma cattle ranch. *Be himself.* The revelation dawned like Clarisse's smile—a brilliant stroke.

"Well, you begin next week. I'll refresh you on how our teaching process works here at Oxford, Jack."

He was glad of that. She'd explained it before, but so much had happened to him, outside and in, since he'd interviewed, he was fuzzier than his old wool sweater.

"Oxford works much differently than American colleges. You won't be teaching classes of groups of students. You'll be tutoring students in the college on a one-on-one basis. You'll be called a 'tutor' here in the college. You'll give your students assignments and meet with them every week to terrorize them." He jerked, relaxing as he saw her smile. "British humor, Jack. Talk to the other tutors about how hard to push them. You'll also be giving university-wide lectures, which are open to all of the colleges and students. There, you'll be referred to as 'professor.'"

Jack's eyes might have bulged a bit.

"I know, it is quite different, but I'm sure you'll adapt. You'll be teaching a roughly equivalent load to what you had in California, Jack. Your university-wide lectures on modern American literature are scheduled. And," she sighed, "there's been a development. Our American studies program has requested you to lecture on the United States as you see it. Its literature, of course, but also the country as you see it in relationship to the world."

"I can't do that. That's for a poly-sci prof, ma'am."

"No, it's for the author of *Realms of Magic*. The Pulitzer Prize people may have missed what they had, but I assure you, Jack, we at Oxford have not." She nodded sagely. "We have high hopes for y'all." The frumpy woman winked at him.

The meeting gave Jack a reason to live. He was appreciated. He might have a life of his own one day, one where he wasn't a decoy to pull in Clarisse. The possibility gave him a moment's respite from thinking about her. His every breath, every thought, revolved around her, otherwise.

Jack lived in horror of what might be happening to his wife, alternating terror with anger at her and her family's lies and deceit. Sadness and loneliness laced the whole mess. He missed her bright smile during the day and her soft warmth at night. He missed her intelligence. Her toughness wasn't all of her; she also had softness and kindness that took his breath, and heart. Thinking of their nights made him dissolve.

As long as he thought about how much he missed Clarisse, the loss of the boys didn't threaten to drive him insane.

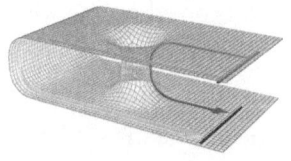

TWENTY

PULLING THE PLUG

"YOU'RE SURE IT will work?" Ron Weistheimer asked Ricky. Ron, Jimmy, and Ricky stood in his office at the rear of the dojo, behind his desk. The seismic registers had told Ron that *something* had happened to the dojo, weight room, and lockers, but he didn't know what. His office was untouched—he felt sure that whatever held Clarisse captive had caused the disturbance and that it would come back for the office. She knew what it contained and she'd want it.

"No, I'm *not* certain that what we made will work," Ricky said, with that too serious, not-yet-a-man-but-not-a-boy-either voice. He hit a key on his laptop. A tiny *zap* let them know that something had happened. "We can talk now. I just cut the bugs."

"My office isn't bugged," Ron exclaimed.

"If the bugs were any bigger, they'd be running around like cockroaches. Don't be so sure your clearance really clears you, Ron."

Hearing Clarisse's boy admonish him was weird, but not too weird. Ron knew the Hull boys very well.

Ricky continued, "You have Mom's computer here at the base for me to work from, and I have her secret protocols on my laptop. The FBI didn't take *that*. They didn't think a kid could do what I can."

"*We* can," Jimmy said. The boys smiled. "The feds can't outguess a whole family of Hulls. Mom had her work backed up everywhere. Even in our *toaster*."

The three of them chuckled. "She used to lecture us on what she was doing at the breakfast table. From the time we were little kids."

"Do you know what your mom's big computer is, basically?" Ron asked. He was way over his head with the Hulls. "What does it do? I'm not clear about that. No one is. She insisted on doing things alone."

The boys looked at him, brows knit, and heads cocked a bit. "Do you know anything about quantum physics, Ron?" Ricky asked.

"Or post-Einsteinian physics?"

Ron shook his head, looking mystified.

"Do you know anything about the theoretical basis of wormholes?"

"Worm holes? In the ground?" Ron shook his head. "No. I don't know anything about any of that."

"That's why Mom didn't talk about what her computer did much. It's hard for people to understand. And what she was doing with the theory is *top secret*." Ricky rubbed his mouth with his hand, his forehead furrowing in concentration as he decided whether to enlighten Ron.

"Just Google it, Ron. They've got tons of videos and articles about wormholes. Cartoons, even, that everyone can understand," Jimmy explained patiently.

"Can't you explain it? I don't even get cartoons about this stuff."

"Well, we'll try. This is old theory. Back in 1935, Einstein and Rosen used the theory of general relativity to posit paths through the fabric of space-time. Einstein-Rosen bridges, or wormholes, join two points in space and time.

"Theoretically, the fabric of existence can fold back upon itself. Wormholes bridge sections of time and space. Wormholes look like tornadoes dropping from a plain and joining with another tornado coming from the opposite direction. The tube in the middle is the wormhole.

"Traveling through one could reduce the time needed to travel between distant places. Like, you could travel between planets almost instantly."

"They could also allow for *time travel*, Ron," Jimmy said excitedly. "They're cool."

"Google it, Ron," Ricky added, studying Ron's bewildered expression.

"The theory can explain a lot. Travel at the speed of light. Time travel—time is different on one side of the wormhole from the other. Elapsed time of ten minutes here might be ten years on the other side."

"So, wherever Mom is, time may be passing slower than here."

"Or faster. We don't know. She may think she's been gone for years."

"There's more. The mouths of the wormholes could be *black holes,* like from collapsing dying stars." Jimmy's eyes glowed.

"But wormholes don't have to be black holes. And they're theoretical only. If they even exist, *the* biggest problem with wormholes according to all the physicists is their size. They're tiny, sub molecular. A person couldn't fit into one. And they collapse, so if someone *did* fit into one, it could disappear, and so would they."

"Also, you can't go back in time with a wormhole; it's just a shortcut forward." Jimmy spoke excitedly, enthralled.

"Most scientists think travel between times and alternate universes is impossible. That's why what Mom did is so important. Her computer recognizes the unstable and submicroscopic nature of wormholes. She went far beyond the theoretical frontier. She not only found wormholes, she made them large and stable and created a way to transport things through them. That's what her computer does."

"She didn't tell us any of this, Ron. It's classified, and she never broke that. But Jimmy and I have been studying her briefs since we've been here. Mom's computer tears objects placed in its central core into sub-atomic fragments and sends them through a big wormhole that's induced through electromagnetic forces that it generates."

"It's an atom smasher," Jimmy said.

"That's basically it," Ricky added. "Putting Mom's theory in words, the universe is like a bunch of stacked blankets, threads arranged in layers, all intertwined. Each layer is a reality, an alternate universe." He held out his hands, fingers at ninety-degree angles, to indicate the warp and woof of the threads. "But they're not flat layers, and the *matter,* really anti-matter, of each reality can bleed into the next layer.

"So you have an infinitely large stack of threads and blankets all existing in their own separate worlds, but matter is also able to slip from reality to reality, from blanket to blanket. That's what Mom says the universe is. It's wormholes, whether in consciousness or the physical world, that let you travel."

Ron looked punchy.

"It doesn't matter that you don't understand it; Jimmy and I do."

"She always made sure that we knew what she was doing, wherever she was," Jimmy added. "To go from one reality to another, sometimes you don't need anything. Sometimes people just slip onto another 'blanket' for a while, or a long while. Mom thought time travel and travelers were common, and natural."

"For some people."

"Yes, not everyone."

"But if you can't do it by yourself, or you want to take a lot of people along, you need enough energy to *break through* the layers of the blankets. For that, you need *lots* of energy." Ricky said.

"The kind atom smashers make. Mom's computer isn't just a computer—it's based on the old Cyclotron in Berkeley, but it doesn't need radioactive materials. It's a gun that swirls atoms and parts of atoms around so fast that they become capable of breaking the bounds of time and space."

"They create portals, where anything can travel between worlds at will."

"Like whatever it was that snatched Mom."

"Yeah. And she *has* created stable, long-lasting portals in her experiments." The boys scowled, working hard to explain their mother's achievement. "She *has* sent things through them, but she's never been able to retrieve anything. It's what she was trying to do when they grabbed her. We keep hoping we'll find something on her computer or somewhere that will explain how to get things back."

Ron stared at them. "I've worked with Clarisse for years, and she never explained it that clearly."

"She didn't *want* you to understand. You'd take it to the generals, and what happened wouldn't be what she wanted," Ricky said grimly.

Ron had to acknowledge that that was true. Their superiors would manipulate Clarisse's work to serve defense. He and Clarisse didn't have compatible goals all the time. "The computer is an atom smasher?"

"But not a radioactive one. It needs to be as big as it is to contain all the energy needed to pulverize matter into subatomic parts," Ricky explained. "It works. The biggest problem with it is where do you go when you go through a portal and how do you get back? That's what's kept her from experimenting more. Besides getting funding to keep the computer open. It needs a big staff. They're always threatening to shut her down."

"She has sent things through the portal—messages, and her papers. Magazines. Nothing alive; she didn't want to kill anything. Whatever it was she sent disappeared, but never came back. She didn't know where it went."

"We think the bad guys who grabbed her picked up what she sent and were able to trace her through it." Jimmy scowled.

"I've never heard of this. Where did she send this stuff from?"

"The middle of the big cylinder in the computer. The open space is the center of the energy vortex. That's where she took the photos of things disappearing that she couldn't show anyone. That's why she lost tenure. *She should* have been hailed as the greatest physicist ever. Greater than Einstein or *anyone*. Mom did what no one has been able to do." A thundercloud boomed from Jimmy's face.

"That's true, Jimmy. She's never gotten credit for how great she is, but we need to tell Ron the rest so he can help us get her back." Ricky looked at Ron, wild-eyed. "You could stuff the hole with people…"

"In theory," Jimmy added.

"Yes, in theory… and take the whole bunch of them somewhere. But no one's ever tried it."

Ron thought. "It's big enough to hold a *lot* of people."

"Yes, hundreds, maybe a thousand," Ricky nodded.

"But that isn't our problem now," Jimmy brought them back to task sharply. "That isn't why we're here. We're trying to plant something in the dojo office that Mom can use to contact us. So let's do it." Jimmy looked around angrily.

Ron jerked. He'd never felt any aggression from the boys before, but Jimmy's glance was like a laser. They would be formidable enemies. "Hey, guys. I'm on your side. I want your mom back safe and sound... Now, what about this invention that you want to plant here in my office?"

"We created this..." Ricky held out something that looked like a latest generation electronic game player. "We'll hide it here in your office, and when the aliens come back and copy the office, the module will go to the alternate universe with everything else.

"That's what they were doing with the dojo and gym and stuff. Copying them and taking them to where they are, we'd bet anything." The boys nodded in unison.

"You're sure?"

"Of course. If they'd *taken* the dojo, it wouldn't be there. But it is. Therefore, if they did anything—and they did, the seismic data shows it—they copied it. And they'll copy this, too." He held up the game console. "There will be one here, and one there, wherever that is. Just like the computer and the rest of the gym." He looked at Ron as though he was a dope.

Ron was dumbfounded by what they said, and by their presence. The way they sat, the position of their heads, the way they moved; they seemed almost like carbon copies of the same person, moving in unison. The boys worked together, like a tag-team. The Hull boys exuded *an aura* of knowledge of stuff he didn't and couldn't know.

Worse, the way they responded sometimes was eerie; he had the feeling they could read each other's minds. Along with their mother's. Clarisse sometimes seemed otherworldly, too. The three of them were spooky when you saw them working together.

He didn't have any kids, so Ricky and Jimmy were Ron's surrogate children. Given a choice, he'd rather have regular kids who played baseball instead of hacking top-secret computers and sending psychic messages.

"If we used Mom's work correctly, the game should play here, on our console, in our world. It should work there, too."

Ricky carefully placed the game in the top right drawer of Ron's desk. "This is the first place she'll look when the office gets there. But we won't know if it got there and can broadcast back until she plays the game and our end registers what she does.

"The game uses stuff only she'll know about; the bad guys won't understand it, but she will. And we can both use the screens to write messages. In code, of course."

"Great job, boys. Okay, guys, let's call it a night."

Ron took them back to their bunker bedroom at the base and tucked them in. They were hidden in the perfect place—under everyone's nose in the headquarters at Moffett. Ron kept close to them during the day. Although apparently and publicly closed as a military base, Moffett Field wasn't, quite.

Ricky and Jimmy were allowed limited access to their mother's computer, but only at night and when the regular employees were gone. Weird as it seemed, they'd never seen it before. The powers that be had kept them away while their mother was around. Now, the kids acted as though they'd been raised with it.

The general staff kept them fed, did their wash, and cleaned their rooms. True, their rooms were underground cells and Ricky and Jimmy were locked in at night, but they were safe from bad guys. And the boys were kept under surveillance 24/7. No telling what *they* might do.

This night, Ron locked their door from the outside panel and went off to complete the one remaining task of his day.

"I think it's almost time to pull the plug," Ron spoke into a receiver from his own underground bunker. The room was darkened; white noise filled the air, despite the ultra-secure line he was using. He wore big, padded headphones; the voice on the other end was not audible in the room. Ron looked like he was talking to himself, except that his statements had pauses between them, indicating he was conversing.

He had to report to his superior officer, but he restricted what he conveyed. Ron didn't feel competent to explain what the boys had said Clarisse's computer was. He could barely explain what he'd done with them that afternoon, and he sure as hell didn't want to open up the can of worms of illuminating Clarisse's masterpiece to his boss.

"Sir, the seismic equipment showed something happening to Clarisse's computer a while back, as I briefed you. We were *not* able to ascertain what happened, but we put the boys on it. Yes, Clarisse's boys, Ricky and Jimmy. They know almost as much as she does. They've come up with the theory that whatever or whoever has their mother has somehow copied the computer and set up an alias somewhere, wherever they are. Not an empty alias; an identical, physical copy. Last night, the seismic meters noted activity in the dojo and gym, but not my office. I knew Clarisse would want my office and send her captors back to get it. We needed to create a way of passing messages between her and us."

He chuckled, listening to the muffled voice on the other end of the line. "No, sir, not a string with two tin cans, but the 2016 version of that. It had to be powerful enough to pierce alternate realities. And it had to look like something I might have as a matter of course. Yes, sir, the boys created a video game based on their dreams. They both dream of a red door in a little gray house, but the door opens into nothingness. The boys designed a game based on their dreams and what they've done that only the family knows about. She'll be able to send us coded messages, if it works.

"They got it stashed in my desk just in time. The seismic data indicate that they did come for my office, minutes ago. So they've got the game. That's why I called you. We need to see if she responds and anything shows up on our side. If she tells us they're hostile and heading for us, the country needs to go on red alert. And we need to find that house with the red door. It's the key. Ricky and Jimmy say it's in Palo Alto. We need to find it. If Clarisse can't contain them, we don't want a force of alien hostiles showing up somewhere in town."

"It's worse than that, sir. The intelligence world knows something's happening here. We've got electronic snoops—Chinese, Russian. Middle Eastern. Mercenaries. Even our friends are trying to figure out what we're doing. Everyone knows it has something to do with Clarisse Hull. It may be time for Clarisse and the boys to die."

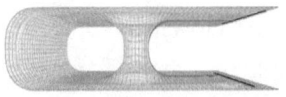

TWENTY-ONE

BASIC TRAINING

"YOU NEED TO be ready to effectuate our plans in six weeks." Pops' face filled the sidewall of the main warehouse. His raised brows and little smile gave him a jaunty look that was out of keeping with their grim topic.

"I *can't* turn them into an effective military force in six weeks." Clary barked at the wall. Her troops were arrayed in rows, all of them standing at attention with their hands behind their backs, their faces emotionless.

"Basic training in your military is six weeks," Pops said, maintaining his smile and perky air. "I've given you everything you asked for. They should be ready in six weeks." He was taunting her.

"*Our* military starts with people who are healthy. These were malnourished, lacking in any discipline, and illiterate. Basic training is *basic*: to make ordinary foot soldiers that can mop floors and shoot a gun. You do have guns, don't you? Ordnance? Because if we're going to storm Earth, they *will* fight back."

"You'll have everything you need when the time comes, Dr. Hull. You'll have the 'big picture.' That is the human way of putting it, isn't it? I'll fill you in with all the details you don't have now." His smile was blindingly sanguine. "Don't worry."

"*The details I don't have now.* How about *all* of them? We're going to 'beam down' to Earth, assuming I can pull that off, and take over.

From where? That fake Palo Alto you sent El to? This whole thing is so bogus..."

Clary exploded. Everything that had been clamoring inside her burst out, all the whispered worries hiding in the synapses of her brain leaping forth. "What about *supplies?* How will we feed...? Do you have any idea how you'll transport people on Earth? You can't even breathe there."

"Don't worry, my dear," Pops giggled at her eruption. "My goodness, I've never seen you so distressed. All the mysteries will come clear..."

"How about you tell me these mysteries now? How can they learn to shoot without guns?"

Pops sighed mightily. "Oh, Dr. Hull. You are so old-fashioned. Even I know that your military doesn't depend upon 'boots on the ground.' You'll program your lovely computer to take care of all opposition. You can do it! *Try.*"

"*No one* can make soldiers out of this bunch in six weeks, much less teach half of them enough to maintain the computer while the rest go through alternative realities. Or use it for a weapon. It's not made for that. And most of them can't *read!*" Clarisse was furious. "*You* created the mess here. If you'd done some basic research on what humans need to thrive, they'd all have been fed properly, deloused and wormed, and know how to read! For God's sakes, couldn't you just Google 'humans as pets' or something?"

Pops frowned. "We have an expert on humans."

"Who? Dr. Mengele?"

"I am not familiar with that doctor. We have had Dr. Óskar Erland advising us. He is a Nobel Prize winner. You have heard of him?"

Clary went white, stepping back.

"Of course, you have heard of him. You are here because he knows you so well. He said you were the most intelligent woman on Earth. The only one who could make our project succeed. Dr. Erland created the human side of our program and guided us."

"You should fire him. He doesn't know shit about anything but lab rats. *Sick* lab rats, like him." Clary felt her pulse racing. Óskar Erland. Jimmy's dad. The man who'd rufied her and done God knew what else.

Rage burst inside her, masking the terror Óskar's name engendered. Her fight instinct swamped her urge to flee.

"We have no intention of firing him. He is resting from his journey from your world and will soon join you to complete the mission."

"What?! I won't work with him!"

"He will be your co-commander in our effort. I recognize that sharing the spotlight may be difficult for one used to being pampered as you have been, but share it you will. Dr. Erland says it will take six weeks. That's what you've got."

He smiled happily, as cheerful as she'd seen him, laughing at her. The menacing face faded slowly, but he added something before disappearing. "As a favor to you, I'll make them literate. What grade level would you like?"

"Master's in physics or higher."

Clarisse had her soldiers make five laps around the warehouse, this followed by a drill including push-ups, abdominal crunches, and leg raises.

"That's it for tonight. Sleep well, boys and girls; you're going to wake up little physicists." She yelled the last part at the wall, exuding sarcasm. "Oh, I need some techs, too, Pops! And computer jocks!"

She barely made it to their room before doubling over in terror. El was right behind her.

He spoke softly. "Clary, I'm here. I won't let him hurt you."

She looked at her young mascot. How could he protect her?

He'd changed; it was true. El had said that figuring out how much time had passed was hard in the warehouse. The time and date displays of the computer and all electronic devices were blank. Days and nights slipped into each other. Seasons could have passed.

El's body provided the most obvious indication of how long she'd been here. He had put on significant weight and muscle. Gaining that kind of muscle mass would take months. Had she been here that long? She need only look at her young partner's arms and torso.

His voice still sounded like a traumatized teenager.

"I need to think, El. Can you take a powder for a while?" she asked. His brows knit, not understanding. "Give me a moment alone?"

"I can go to the computer lab. They wouldn't mind me going there if I look like I'm working. Are you okay?"

"Yeah. I need to think." As scared as she was, something wasn't right. *Lots* weren't right.

Why was Pops so cheery? They were talking about a military invasion of an unknown planet in six weeks. They needed to discuss ordnance. Transport. Battle plans. Objectives. Where they were going, for certain. Yet, he gloated, as if he knew something she didn't. She'd missed something *huge*.

Óskar Erland was here. *That* was huge. Would that make Pops so happy? Apparently, but why? Since Erland had abducted her years before, Clary had made sure she knew where that asshole was at all times. He had died two years ago. The day he'd died was every holiday that existed rolled together for Clary.

Óskar was here? Resting from his journey. Why did he need to rest after coming here? She hadn't.

Shit. They'd brought him back from the dead. That was beyond any technology she'd heard of. *They* brought people back from the dead and went back in time to get them. They popped realities like some popped drugs... *Oh, no.* She rolled into a ball on the bed, hiding her head in her arms.

"Clary, it's El. Let me in."

She hit a switch and the door opened.

El sat next to her on the bed, putting an arm around her. "I'll help you."

How could he help her? He wasn't healed from what had happened to him. The size of the trauma moving inside *her* would stop a freight train. He had to be fighting an eruption like Mt. Vesuvius.

"El, I know you want to help me, but you can't. I've been in therapy for seventeen years and I still get flashbacks. I don't even know what happened, just that it scared me so badly. Let's go to bed."

They'd slept together after her earlier meltdown, but it had been as brother and sister. She knew El wanted more, but she couldn't give it. She wouldn't betray Jack. She loved El more than anyone but Alex, but she'd be faithful to Jack no matter what. She wasn't a slut. Nothing Óskar Erland and his friends could do could make her one.

"Clary, Clary! Wake up!" El shook her. "You were screaming. What's the matter?"

She awakened, covered with sweat, heart pounding and lurching in her chest. She threw the covers off. "Oh, God, El. They're everywhere. They're crawling on me. They're biting me!" Clary struck at her legs, trying to dislodge the bedbugs.

They were firmly attached everywhere: calves, thighs, and feet. They covered her abdomen, sucking her blood. She couldn't get them to let go. Clary tore at her body. Hundreds more massed in the bed, waiting to drain her dry.

El grabbed her shoulders. "Clary, there's nothing there. It's *them*. Dr. Erland has told them what you're afraid of. They're trying to break you."

She could hear him, but the racing heart didn't go away, nor the specter of bedbugs surrounding her, waiting for her to go to sleep so they could destroy her. "El! El! Help me..." She grabbed at him. This time she didn't object to his touch.

He ran his hands down her legs, swept an arm over the bed, and then covered her eyes. "See, Clary. They're gone. They were never there. You're safe. I'll keep you safe."

"Oh, my God, El. I've never been so afraid."

He pulled her down, head on his shoulder, and stroked her. "I'll keep you safe, Clary. Do you remember anything else? Where you were? What happened?"

"Just the bedbugs. They were all over." She paused. "I was in a log cabin. The bed sagged like the middle might sit on the floor. It had a cowboy headboard and wood paneled walls. The bugs hid in the cracks." Sitting up, she said, "El. It was where I was when they found me. When I disappeared and got pregnant with Jimmy. I couldn't remember a thing about it before. They're opening up all those memories, El. Oh, no..."

"Go to sleep, Clary. I'll guard you."

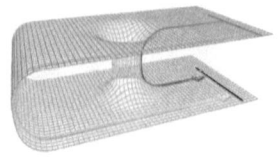

TWENTY-TWO

INVENTION IS A MOTHER

"WHERE DID YOU get it?" Jimmy held up what bore every stamp of being their mother's latest, secret invention. Neither boy had seen it before. The rectangular object was about the size of a cigar box, covered with complicated, soldered patterns of wires. It had a number of ports for power and communicating with other electronic devices, as well as colored glass inlays like jewels.

They couldn't see any way of opening the thing; it was welded shut. Neither of them had the faintest idea of what it did, but it was pretty and looked very sturdy, like you could play a major league football game with it and not damage a thing.

"It was in a cardboard box labelled 'crafts projects' that the FBI took out of our house. They cleared it yesterday. Ron brought it here so we could have it. 'Memories of home to make us feel better.'" The boys laughed. Their mother *never* did crafts, but she did build things and hide them in improbable places. "There's the carton it came in." Ricky indicated a big cardboard box that was jammed with crumpled papers.

The boys dove into it. Scraps of newsprint covered with their mother's mathematical symbols were wadded into the box with other smaller objects, similar to the larger decorated rectangle. All were covered with fine wire fused together in ornamental patterns. Glass insets. No visible way to open them or use them for anything esisted. They looked like decorative trinkets a hobbyist might make, as the FBI had concluded.

Jimmy powered up his laptop. The objects glittered to life, flashing light from the glass portals indicating electrical movement inside the boxes. "They're connected to a computer."

"What do they do?"

"Beats me." Jimmy typed a bit on his laptop; the "craft projects" did one thing—glittered faster.

"They're controlled by something else. Let's look at Mom's notes." They plowed through the messy box, assured that it was their mother's latest output. That's how she worked. Total mess to a super-neat final product. Among the crumpled newspapers packing the box were wadded up sheets of butcher paper covered with their mother's writing.

"Okay. Now we're getting somewhere." The FBI agents who had cleared the box and its contents were not as familiar with the Greek alphabet and notes written in it, or symbols of higher mathematics and physics, as were Ricky and Jimmy. "See, here's the order she tossed them in." The page number was written in Greek numerals at the lower left of each page, in mirror image. They arranged the pages, flattening them out.

"Geez. Do you see what she's doing?" Jimmy asked.

"Yep. It's the theoretical schemata to interface with and control the big computer. And notes for writing code to make it do what she wants."

"She's written instructions for it to find and retrieve the stuff she sent out. That little jewel box is the key to retrieving things from other universes."

"God, she's smart."

"Yep.

"Was she able to actually do it?"

"Dunno." He found a memory stick stuck in a container for chewing gum. "Ahah! The Rosetta Stone." Ricky plugged the stick into the port on his laptop. He scanned the contents, then downloaded them into a secret partition on his hard drive. The boys sat in front of the black screen, looking at lines of white programming code interrupted with colored lines indicating commands.

"This code controls a small computer, hidden in here," Ricky patted the largest decorative box. "I bet this tiny box controls the big computer in Moffett. This is her latest work. She hid it under everyone's noses."

"And these hook the bigger pieces," Jimmy held up several USB cords with male and female connectors on each end. These were wrapped with wads of fuzzy pipe cleaners in a plastic box of craft glue, sequins, and other junk. In the same box, a bunch of fancy hairclips flashed. They bore the coiled wire exterior and the glittering glass of the boxes.

Ricky studied the objects. "Okay, Mom, what are you trying to tell us? What does all this do?"

They found it on the last crumpled page in the box, written in their mother's compact handwriting. "She did it! She figured out how to get things back from alternate universes."

"Yeah, she did it. The code on my computer is inside that fancy box. It gives the big computer directions to find these little things." Rickey held up a hairclip. "If she puts one of these things on something she sends into an alternate universe, the computer can track it."

"But not retrieve it. These drawings," Jimmy leafed through the crumpled papers on the floor, "show these things were drawn early on. She must have designed the other pieces in the box later."

They got down on their hands and knees and looked at the drawings.

"The other boxes are retrievers, Jimmy! She can put the little clips on things and send them out and track them, but the three bigger boxes can call them back."

"How?" Back onto their hands and knees...

"Those three pieces plug into the main computer, in the hollow central core."

"That's a problem."

"Yeah. Have you ever seen the computer?"

"Just when you did, when they brought us here. They won't let us anywhere near it, and neither would Mom. She said the inside is dangerous if the computer's operating."

"Which it always is."

"Ricky, do Mom's equations indicate how big an object she can bring back?"

"No. She must have just sent out little stuff, though."

"Shit."

The boys sat by the laptop, going over the lines of code their mother had written to program the box-like device. Code that was presumably nestled in its pretty and impregnable depths, waiting for activation by installation in the main computer. They pored over the sheets of paper, growing quieter as the idea grew within them.

Finally, dead silence.

"Ricky, if they had one of these set up on the machine the aliens copied, maybe we could use this," Jimmy said, holding up the decorative box, "to bring the whole computer back here."

"If it could move that much."

"What if *their computer* was powered up, and trying to come back to us?"

The big computer was a metal and glass cube, two-hundred feet on each edge. Monstrous.

"It's impossible. That little box couldn't move anything that big."

"Atom bombs are pretty small these days, but look what they can do. And that little box controls Mom's *computer,* which is huge. *It* could be programed to retrieve, too."

"We'll think about it, but first we have to put all this stuff away where no one, including Ron, can find it."

"Do we tell him about it?"

"If it's the only way."

"It's so impossible, Jimmy. We have to make one just like this when we can barely read the code that made it, don't know what's in it, or where to get the stuff to make another one. Then we have to get it to Mom in an alternate universe."

"Bleak."

"At best."

"Let's get to work."

"Mom developed a couple of things at home, Ron," Jimmy said softly. He'd carefully debugged their room for the meeting. Turned out, they needed Ron's help, and were reluctantly asking for it. "She developed a module that will allow her to communicate from her computer here, in this reality, to stuff she sent out to another reality, wherever that might be. It's hardware... well, here it is—" Jimmy held up something that looked like a little girl's hair clip. "It's a tracking device. Ricky, write something on your computer."

The little bauble blinked and shimmered.

"It's wireless. She doesn't usually do wireless, because of security, but she had to for this. She made a few of them, all similar. But this is her masterpiece."

Jimmy held out the wire-covered, jeweled cigar box. They had it hooked up with the other boxes. All of them flashed in rhythm.

"This will give whatever's got one of her trackers on it instructions to come back home. Do you understand what this means?"

Ron didn't.

"If they have one of these things on the other computer," Jimmy held up the jeweled carton, "we can activate this one, and make the whole computer come back. Whoever could fit in the center hole would come, too."

"How could that little box do that?" Ron didn't hide his skepticism.

"Bombs smaller than this could blow up one of the hangars. If we could program the computer on the other side to work in unison, that would probably double the amount of power," Ricky added.

"And we could tell Mom and anyone else over there to get in the middle of the machine."

"We can save her, Ron! We can save anyone over there! We really can!" Ricky's boyishness showed with his enthusiasm.

"We've already done more on the code. We just have to get inside Mom's computer and install this in the empty core." He held up the jeweled box and its attachments. "She left instructions for how to do it."

"She was so close, Ron! She almost got results that no other scientist could come near. Mom wrote–writes—brilliant code. We'll show you. I think we could use this to get her back. If we've got this in the computer here."

"And she can get another one on the other side installed in the other computer..."

"Maybe we could move things between them. People and anything else."

"What do you think?" The boys looked at him like almost twin owls.

"It's impossible. Those little hair bow things have never been used to track *anything*. You don't know if that jewelry box does anything. They won't let you near the computer, much less to install anything in it.

"They don't have the stuff to make those on the other end. And even if you made one of those things—which I don't think you can—how are you going to get it to them? I don't have another office Clarisse will want to beam over. It's crazy and impossible."

Ricky gave Ron a hard look. "You won't help us?"

"I didn't say that. I said it was crazy. Now hide all that shit and don't let anyone find it."

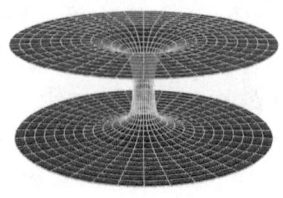

TWENTY-THREE

THE TRUTH
ABOUT SCHOLARS

C LARISSE WAS SHOT from guns and ready to go the next day. She marched into the warehouse and to her assembled troops at eight a.m.

"Form ranks!" They lined up pretty well, considering most seemed terminally hungover. "So, are you scientists now? Everyone ready to rock 'n' roll with physics? Let's have a quiz. Pops!" The face appeared. "I need a surface to write on and something to write with." A podium with markers appeared next to the rear wall.

"I'll start with you, El. In differential equations, what's lambda?" She wrote a character on the shiny, white wall with a red marker. "Starting with, did I write upper or lower case?"

"Lambda is the eleventh letter in the Greek alphabet. The letter you wrote is lower case. It means a lot of things, depending on what field you use it in. In physics, electronic engineering, or mathematics, it indicates the wavelength of any wave. It can be the density of occurrences in any time distribution, or..."

"I asked for what it means in differential equations."

"In mathematical optimization, it represents the Lagrangian multiplier."

"There you go! Explain what that is and write the equations showing how it's used." Clary held out the marker.

El took it and spoke slowly, as though verbalizing information presented to him internally for the first time. "If you want to maximize or minimize a function subject to constraints, the form is:

"maximize $f(x, y)$

"subject to $g(x, y) = 0$."

He gathered steam, explaining the method of Lagrange multipliers in optimization and writing equations on the wall. His eyes sparkled as he wrote. He was realizing the implications of what he was putting on the wall as the symbols emerged.

"...To incorporate these conditions into one equation, we introduce an auxiliary function

$\mathcal{L}(x, y, \lambda) = f(x, y) + \lambda \cdot g(x, y)$, and solve:

$\nabla_{x, y, \lambda} \mathcal{L}(x, y, \lambda) = 0$.

"This is the method of Lagrange multipliers.

"Note that $\lambda \mathcal{L}(x, y, \lambda) = 0$ implies $g(x, y) = 0$."

El stopped, looking at the equations he'd written with amazement.

"Excellent, El. Pops wasn't bullshitting me about what you know. Next! El, give her the marker." Clary went down the line.

"What's your name?"

"Rachel, Dr. Hull."

"Great. Rachel, explain the difference between quantum mechanics and Newtonian physics, and when you would use each. Tell me how lambda figures into that determination."

And Rachel did.

"We gotta go faster. First row, grab markers and totally differentiate this equation..." She moved to one end of the wall and started throwing symbols on the wall. "Let's go! We haven't got all day." Clary laughed. She loved teaching. "Actually, we do have all day, but let's move it."

Eventually, all one hundred and forty of them lined up at the wall in groups and answered questions Clary posed. They covered the wall with their answers. The rainbow of colored markers and Greek letters and mathematical symbols created a spectacularly brilliant graphic display.

"Goddam! Look at that wall! That is beautiful! *That's* what turns me on!" Clary paced up and down. The colored markings made a composition in contemporary art.

"Okay. Let's write some code!" Clary grinned as she studied the wall. It presented evidence of differential equations well learned by well over a hundred minds. "Here's a section of code controlling that computer. There's something wrong with it. Tell me what?" And they did.

"How many of you know computers? I asked for a few techs..." Turned out, they all wrote code. "I'm going to download this..." She had a handheld computer clipped to her belt, a mini. Clary pointed it at the adjoining wall and code appeared on it. "I've been working on this. It's an address book app that maps locations anywhere. But it's bogged down here." She pointed to the writing on the wall.

"Anybody who can solve this can make ten million bucks in Silicon Valley right now. The location doesn't even have to be on Earth. It's the app of the decade." They went at it, and solved it.

"Wow! Pops, you delivered!" she shouted into the air. Each one was as competent as Elias. All closed their eyes and turned away from the wall when they were done, indicating splitting headaches.

The gang was one hundred percent educated: a pack of physicists, computer scientists, and technicians. They seemed shocked that they knew what they did, even with their hangovers.

"You guys, you gotta be proud of yourselves! What you just did is amazing! *I'm* proud of you. You make my university students look like slugs."

Clary noticed something. They looked down when she walked by, deferential, but brightened at her praise. Smiles appeared. She liked seeing them like this.

Her night of terror with the imagined bedbugs had changed her. Maybe it was knowing that the years-dead Óskar Erland was alive and on the premises somewhere. She saw the truth. Her people exhibited a little pride at their intellectual achievement, but mostly, all she could see in her troop's eyes was fear. They were as petrified of *her* as she was of the illusory bugs. This wasn't right.

Something had changed inside Clary. She could see that these were *people*—human beings.

When she'd killed however many hundred it had been earlier, she'd done it in a jacked-up combat rage. No remorse for that, until later. Now, the evil she'd done seemed to have fully penetrated her mind and soul. These were *people,* just like her and El. And they were terrified of her.

I'm not listening to myself, she thought. *I'm only listening to my fear.*

Their fear came in like the foghorns of the San Francisco Bay, booming through her bones. She'd been roaring around like an avenging spirit, training them for something even she didn't understand. They didn't know what they were supposed to do in six weeks. To them, she was a crazy murderer, flogging them to purposeless feats. She'd been blind.

She wanted to save herself and El. Why not the rest of them, too? The good ones. Not all of them were good-hearted and trustworthy—she could feel that.

Pops was up to something. What did he have planned? Sure as hell, they wouldn't be properly equipped for the attack. He had some kind of double-cross in mind.

Maybe she and El could organize the others and give Pops a surprise he'd never forget. Clary beckoned to El and whispered in his ear. "Let them know that I want to save them. I'm acting mean because of Pops. I'm working on a way out of here; that's what the attack will be. Make sure the others know about this—the ones you can trust, only."

After her inspection, she drilled them out on the warehouse floor, simple routines as fit their exhaustion. As she did, El moved among them, whispering to a few as though giving instructions in the exercises. They each looked startled in turn when he walked away.

Clarisse took them to a simulated computer lab she'd convinced Pops to set up. "You don't want beginners to fuck up the computer, do you?"

Setting them to easy tasks, such as booting up the machine with its complicated protocols, Clary managed to use up a day. One less day of the six-week allotment, but one more day of time wasted before they destroyed Earth—if that was what this was really about.

Having educated recruits made things worse. Clarisse couldn't stall because of inadequate personnel, and a subtle undercurrent of nods and hand movements said the bad apples were planning something. Insurrection, most likely.

She was planning something, too. Saving some of them. The ones El had talked to looked at her with gratitude, but they were only a quarter of the total.

Swell. She had educated troops, most of whom wanted to kill her. Very shortly, they'd be able to run the computer without her. Óskar Erland, who wasn't a physicist or computer expert, could even run the lab if he had physicists and staff to back him up. And they'd all figure this out very soon.

If she didn't head it off, another bloodbath was brewing. What could she do to stop it? Put another impossible to break password on the computer? Install a sensor that would respond only to her? When would she set this up? In her spare time?

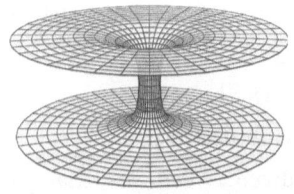

TWENTY-FOUR

A TALK WITH DAD

"DAAD?" RICKY'S VOICE shook. Jack could feel the effort it was taking him to keep it from shaking more.

"Hi, guy. You guys okay?" Jack's voice croaked. He sat in his study in Oxford with a set of special headphones. A thick cord led from the phone to the wall. The cord was thick as an umbilicus. A lifeline? Yeah. The only thing holding him to the life he'd known.

"We're fine. Oh, Daddy, we miss you." Jimmy jumped in. "They aren't doing anything to find Mom and they won't let us help. They keep us locked up..."

"Shut up, Jimmy. If you say that, they won't let us talk to Dad anymore!" Ricky whispered viciously. "We're safe, Dad. And we're fine."

"We found something that might help Mom, and they won't let us near her computer." Jimmy's voice rose with urgency.

"Either Jimmy or I could install it in a minute, Dad. It's something she made that we found. She solved the problem of getting things back from other universes," Ricky added.

"But they treat us like kids."

"Shut up, Jimmy. Ron's coming back. He'll hear us."

"Oh, come on, Ricky. So many people are listening in on this phone. It's like Mom's roses, crawling with little green things." He raised his voice. "All of you snooping, we have something that Mom made that might be able to get her back."

"Jimmy, Ricky, is Ron there?" Jack croaked into the phone.

"I just walked in, Jack."

"What is this about? The boys have something that could save Clarisse, but you people won't let them use it?"

Ron hemmed and hawed. "Well, yes, that's true. There's a protocol..."

"For Christ's sake, Ron. Those assholes could be torturing my wife right now and you're twiddling your thumbs." Jack's breathing became labored.

"Oh, Dad! Don't have a heart attack!"

"All they have to do is shut off part of the computer for a couple of minutes and I'll install it," Ricky said.

"We have our own technicians," Ron sputtered.

"You have the world's greatest experts on my wife's work sitting with you, and you're diddling about staff? God in heaven. Let the boys do what they need to do!" Jack shouted into the receiver.

"Y'all listenin' t' this?" He switched to his best Oklahoma drawl, addressing the silent listeners to their conversation. He'd learned at Oxford that displaying his roots had a greater effect than trying to be the blue blood he wasn't. "Get off your butts and git my wife back. Uncle Sam is paying you plenty for your brains. Use 'em, don't sit on 'em!

"Now, I want to talk to my boys. Do they feed you well? You have clothes and everything you need?"

"Yeah, but we could use more computer time and some hardware..."

"We write our own software, but we could use some..." Ricky rattled off some obscure pieces of hardware.

Totally rattled, Jack erupted. "But you're okay? You're safe?" This talk had not reassured him at all.

"We couldn't get any safer if we were in jail."

"I'll talk to Ron when we're done."

"*Dad! Are* you *okay? Are* you *happy?*" Jimmy burst out.

"Oh, sweetheart. I won't be happy until Mom's back and we're all together. But I'm okay. I've got a nice house. More servants than you can imagine—a butler, even."

"A butler? Like on *Masterpiece?*"

"Just like that."

"How's England, Dad? Do you like it?"

"I love it, guys. I think we could be happy here when we get Mom back. I love England, and the people. And I really love Oxford. My books are even selling!"

"Wow, Dad! Way to go!"

"If they'd *let* us install Mom's hardware, maybe we could get her *back…*"

Something in Jack's line began beeping.

"Jack, that's as much time as we've got. Any longer can be tracked," Ron cut in.

"Ron, let the boys do whatever they need to do to rescue my wife."

"We'll discuss it, Jack…"

"You'll do much more than that." Jack's voice was hard. During the conversation, Jack had realized that he could do something to determine his family's fate. He'd realized he had power. "You know, Ron, I've been feeling chatty lately. *The UK Guardian* and half a dozen newspapers want to do interviews with me. Do you think they'd be interested in knowing what really happened to Clarisse? Huh?"

"Jack…" Ron's sputtered, "I've got to get off…"

"Do *get off*, Ron. Get off your fat ass and save my wife." Anger vibrated through Jack's being.

"Do you think the UK papers would want to know about the boys' discovery and what y'all *aren't* doing with it? I bet papers all over the world would jump on that. I've been asked to be on TV, too. I bet I could fill up a whole hour on how your protocols leave an innocent woman at risk, while lyin' about her t' everybody."

"This isn't the time, Jack."

"*Fucking A,* it's the time, Ron. The *only* time. I can call *The Guardian* right now."

Jimmy almost shrieked. "Dad! Are you safe? You're out in the open. Are they guarding *you*?"

"Jimmy, honey, they've got undercover operatives outside my office, on the paths. I'm okay, boys. All I need is for us to get back together."

"Okay, Dad." Both said, "I love you," at once. "We'll never forget you, no matter what happens."

Jack could almost hear their tears falling. That's when he knew he'd never see his boys again. "I know, guys. You're the best boys on the planet. I love you with all my heart. Stay safe. I'll always love you, too."

Sitting at a table in a concrete block room with Jimmy and Ricky and a fancy phone, Ron's chest was rigid. He coughed into his hand, choked up. "I'm going to work on getting people to look at your mom's invention. I don't think they realize how important it is."

The boys nodded, looking at him with those sharp, dark eyes, seeing his lack of certainty. "Ron, is Dad really safe?"

"Kids, the only people in the world safer than your dad are you two. He's protected by the best we've got. And you've got all this," Ron indicated the bunker around them. "And me. I've got your back. I'd give up my life for you. I won't let anything happen to you."

They listened, unblinking.

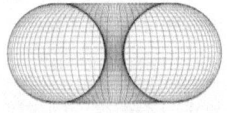

TWENTY-FIVE

WHERE DID ALL THE SCIENTISTS GO?

WHEN THEY GOT back to their room, she cornered El. "How did they make them all scientists? They couldn't read yesterday."

He shook his head. "I don't know, Clary. I don't know how I knew what I did, or how all those equations came to me."

"Did they put that in you last night?"

"No, when they told me you were coming."

"Why did they wait to do up this batch?"

"I don't know, Clary. Maybe because they didn't think you would need them so trained. Or just because you wanted them to be scientists. Pops seems to do what you want."

"He didn't do that for the other scientists that were here?" She had to get to the bottom of this.

"No. They were afraid and they couldn't do what Pops thought they could do. They didn't last long."

"Did the other scientists end up *prizes*?"

El averted his head, but he didn't balk. "Some were, if they caused trouble or their experiments failed. The others, they tried to change."

"What does that mean? What did they do to them?"

"They tried to beat the human out of them. But it killed them."

"What does *that* mean?"

He hesitated, his head moving from side to side involuntarily. *Don't ask me about this.*

"What is *'beating the human out of them'*?"

He glanced at her, eyes pleading. *Don't make me talk about this.*

"I have to know, El. Óskar Erland is here. They're going to bring us together soon. I don't know why he's here or what they intend. What did they do to the others?"

El spoke, averting his eyes. "They brought scientists here who supposedly knew what you do. But they didn't. Pops was very angry, but they decided to use them anyway. They killed them, trying to get inside of them."

"Get inside of them?"

"Yes. They tried to use their bodies."

"*What?*"

"Clary, *they're* nothing. Just energy and power. They don't have bodies. That's why they need you, and me and all the others in the warehouse. They need us for bodies so they can do things on Earth."

"They don't have bodies? There's not a whole bunch of *them* sitting around somewhere?" He shook his head. "They did all this with 'no hands'?" A nod at their room. "All of this, the whole place? If they can make this, why don't they just go to Earth themselves and do whatever they want?"

"I don't know, Clary. How could I know why they do what they do? I just know what I see. I know they are very powerful, but they don't have bodies so they can't manipulate objects; control computers and cars and things. You can see it—they had the people in the hall beat me and kill the prizes. They could send me to Earth—or somewhere—and back, but they don't go themselves. I think the atmosphere on Earth is too thick—they'll drown. Or maybe it's poisonous to them. So they don't just go down by themselves.

"There's no air here, Clary. You know that, don't you? Just what they put here, where we're living and in the warehouse. They haven't been able to go to Earth. But they can see it... and they *want* it."

"How do *you* know all this?" The fact that he had pieced such a story together was almost as incredible as the story itself.

"I watch and listen. Sometimes I can hear them *talking*, Clary, like I can hear your thoughts."

She startled. "What!?"

"I've always been able to read your thoughts, the way you told me that you and Jimmy and Ricky can. I can't read your thoughts all the time, but I can when you need me."

He *was* there every time she needed him. Had she told him about Jimmy, Ricky, and her? Clarisse didn't remember. "How do you know..."

He cut her off, holding his head. "You ask me all these questions. *I don't know that what I said about them is true, Clary.* I've been by myself, since I was a little kid, trying to make sense of what they do. Trying to find a way to stay alive. I'm telling you what I *think*.

"I think they like to hurt people. This is a game to them, all of it. Bringing people and scientists here, trying to get them to break into Earth. Killing them. Having *games*. It's all *fun* for them. It gives them something to do. I don't think they really want the Earth; they want the *game*. If they got a way to get to Earth, I think they'd kill all the humans here, or see that we died trying to take over."

"This is great," Clary said. "I was hijacked into a spiritual world, except that the spirit is evil and sadistic and delights in destruction. Is that it?"

"I don't know what sadistic means."

"It means feeling pleasure at the pain of other people or animals."

"Yes, they are sadistic."

"I knew there was a no reason to believe in God. This takes the cake."

"Clary, I think they'll kill us in the end. That's what they do. Kill and destroy. If they got to Earth, that's what they'd do to it. Make it like here. Hurt everyone. Kill everyone. Take what's there and wreck everything beautiful. And then move on to the next planet.

"But they can't go to Earth and live without bodies. *Don't ask me why. I don't know*." He turned away from her, shaken and upset. "My head hurts. This hurts me." His hands went to his temples. She could see them trembling.

"I'm sorry. I'm trying to understand, too. They want us to function for them on Earth. And they want me to get them there?"

"Yes."

"How do you know all this?"

His eyes blazed. "I told you, I *don't* know for sure. It's what I think. I'm like *you*, Clary, and Ricky and Jimmy. I know things that are floating…" He grabbed in front of him, as though grabbing at an invisible thread.

"When they've mined me of everything I know, they'll kill me," Clary whispered.

"Not you. They'll try to put part of themselves into you and everyone they want to go to Earth—and it's *one*, Clary—there is only one of them. They're *a* spirit. What they want to put in isn't a part; it's *all* of them in a tiny package. There's just one of them."

"So Pops goes back to his hangout and hangs out with himself."

"Not himself or herself. Just *self*. He knows everything."

"He doesn't know how to get onto Earth. Or how to work machines or manage people or get into human bodies. All his experiments have failed. And you never said what 'beating the human out' meant."

El had such sad eyes. He looked down, long eyelashes almost sweeping his cheekbones. "A part of him or them somehow goes into a person. Then they beat the human so its spirit leaves the body. That part of them takes the body."

"Spirit leaves? You mean the person dies? Beaten to death? By whom? How do they beat someone to death if they don't have bodies?"

"The people that you killed beat the scientists until their spirits left."

"They did this to *all* the scientists? How many?"

"Seven… that I know about. The people that beat the scientists *liked* killing them. They bragged about it when they got back to the hall. That's how I know what they did. I wasn't one of the ones who did it; I didn't see. But they talked about it when they got back to the hall.

"Pops took them to a special place to 'change' the scientists. They call it 'changing' or 'beating out the human.'"

She grimaced in disbelief and revulsion. "*Beating out the human.* Did anyone 'change'?"

"No one came back but me. They took me. Before you came, they showed me pictures of you, and videos. They said you were my wife and you would be coming. I was very excited. Getting married is what everyone lives for. We get to leave the hall and get more food."

He smiled at her, glancing up from under his brows. Scared and shy. And in love with her.

Oh, El, she thought. *Don't fall in love with me, El.* But he already had.

"There are many places here," he continued. "They appear when they need them." She nodded, having seen doors open in walls and whole wings of the white world materialize.

"They took me to a big room and tried to put part of them in me. They looked like a cloudy sky. That's what I thought of when I saw it. Clouds against brightness, with the clouds spinning in a circle."

"Like a tornado, or hurricane?"

"I guess. The circle of clouds was very large, and went round and round above me. A finger came out and touched my chest. That's all I remember." He held his hands out, palms up. "It didn't hurt, but I don't remember anymore.

"Then people from the hall came in and tried to beat me, the human, out. They sang when they hit me, 'Beat him! Kill him! Beat the human dead!'

"I didn't die. They tried again later, and I still didn't die. I remember how much it hurt and how sick I was afterward." He shrugged, as though recounting a ritualized murder attempt was an everyday occurrence. "They finally put me in the hall so everyone could try to kill me. They did that before you came."

"*That's* what happened to you before I got here? You looked like you were ninety percent dead. That was why? To make you part alien for *me*?" He nodded. "But you didn't die? Are you an alien? Do you have an extraterrestrial inside?"

He shook his head. "I don't think so. I don't feel any different. I don't hear any other voices or feel like someone else wants me to do anything I don't want to. Their experiment doesn't work. All it does is kill people. And then you saved me. *That's* why I didn't die."

Clary took a huge breath. "Well, I guess I did save you. I'm sorry, El, that you've had such a rotten life. But Jesus Christ! They killed all those people trying to get bodies?"

"Yes, but it didn't work, even with me."

"But they keep trying." He nodded, and Clary went on. "When I enable the computer to transport everyone in the hall, they'll 'beat the human out of us,' fill in the empty space with themselves, and attack Earth. Pretty much what I thought, but worse." She thought for a moment. "You said they'd do that to you and all the rest, but not me. What would they do to me?"

"I think they'll give you to Dr. Erland. You were supposed to be my wife, but I think they'll give you to him."

"Oh, El, no. Oh, God." She collapsed. "Oh, no." Nothing was left of Clary but terror.

He jumped forward and held her. She clung to him.

"Hold me, Clary. I'll take care of you."

She began to relax, falling into him. That sweet essence came from him. When she was breathing normally, he let go and moved away from her.

"Clary, will you marry me?"

"What?"

"I love you. No one will ever love you more than I do. We're going to die. I want to marry you before we do. That's the only thing I want."

"Oh, El, you're so sweet." She stroked his cheek. "I'm still married to Jack. I love you, you know I do, but I haven't given up on going home."

"Would you marry me if you had?"

"You're twenty-two. I'm thirty-eight. That's sixteen years older. When you're fifty, I'll be sixty-six. An old lady. You're closer to my son's ages than mine. Let's not talk about this, okay? We have enough on our plates."

"Dr. Hull," Pops' enthusiastic voice burst into their private moment. "I'm glad to announce that we have successfully completed installation of Ron Weistheimer's office behind the gymnasium. You may inspect it if you wish."

"Holy smokin' hot dogs," Clary said, standing behind Ron's desk in the newly materialized office, complete with burgundy and black walls, the portrait of the Asian master, and all the leather furniture. "You got the whole thing, Pops! If you'd brought Ron and a squadron, we could have a party!"

Clarisse moved around the office with its attractive rosewood furniture and leather seating groupings. She stopped behind Ron's big desk and opened the drawers, noting something Ron would never have had. "Yep, you even got his game console. Ron's a gamer, a little known secret."

"A gamer, Dr. Hull?" Pop's face showed up against a paneled wall holding an entertainment center.

"Yep. Total videogame addict." She sat down at the desk. "I'd better get to work." She opened Ron's laptop and set up a link to the main computer. "I'm going to download a few records from the big computer to this laptop, and make notes on our students' progress. Okay with you?"

Pops smiled. "Certainly. We have another surprise for you when you're done."

Clarisse knew exactly what that was—Óskar Erland, MD, PhD.

"Sure, Pops. Give me a minute." She extracted the videogame from Ron's desk with a wide smile. "Ron's got a new version of *Red Dragon* loaded. Look at this, El. You ever played this?" She nudged him to get his attention, a tad harder than needed, alerting him to be cautious.

El studied the miniature screen. A realistic rendering of the house with the red door covered it. He stiffened, but didn't show his surprise.

"You ever played this game, El? You've never played *any* game, have you? Well, we'll have to play one before walking the plank."

She tapped the door and it opened, revealing floating clouds with text on them.

One flashed, "MAYDAY. MAYDAY. MAYDAY." It asked if she was in desperate peril. Her finger hit the button.

Reeling after hearing that they would most likely be beaten to death for their bodies, and certain that if they got to Earth alive it would be as bloodthirsty aliens, Clary hit the screen again. Or she would be married off to Óskar Erland. She hit the control again, and again.

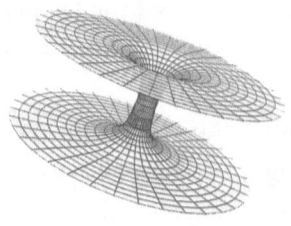

TWENTY-SIX

THE WHOLE TRUTH

"WE'RE HERE TO discuss the data from the videogame we sent to the other world," Ricky said. He and Jimmy sat in their bunker room with Ron, who looked dazed. "My mom found the game and played it. The thing we put in the desk in your office, remember?" Ricky spoke slowly, studying Ron. He didn't look too hot.

"When I opened the drawer, the game was turned backward in the drawer; she did that so we'd know she'd played it. It worked—our console recorded all her answers. I've downloaded the results onto my laptop. You were there. That's what we're going to look at now. Got it?"

Ricky spoke slowly and deliberately, aware that older people didn't relate to his world. Also, most of them lost it by the time they got to be Ron's age.

Ron had been losing it all week. His superiors had not liked the boys' dad threatening to blow their cover to the media. They'd gotten permission to install their mom's sparkling thingy very fast, but Ron had been worked over badly in the process. His superiors didn't take well to coercion.

Ricky wondered if there would be any blowback—his new word, meaning repercussions—on Dad.

"You just installed that glittery box thing in the main computer a few minutes ago." Ron really was confused. "What was *that*? How does it relate to the game box in the drawer?"

"That was *another thing*, Ron; we just installed something my mom made before they grabbed her. The bunch of jewel boxes joined together. She had it at our house. The FBI cleared it. Your superiors cleared it. We talked about it with Dad. Remember?"

Ron could barely muster a nod. The uproar was over that. Everyone on the base seemed ready to explode.

Ricky smiled. His dad's threat to talk to the newspapers had worked. The installation had been a piece of cake. They'd shut the monstrous machine down so he could put the thingy inside the cylindrical tunnel at the computer's core. Jimmy had assisted him with code transmitted from his laptop. The techs had started up the mainframe again; all was well. They had finished minutes before their meeting with Ron.

Whatever their mom's newly installed device did, it was doing it. Its interior lights happily flashed and danced. Like the rest of the computer. It was amazing to see, with ropes and patterns of light moving and glittering. His *mom* had built that!

"When do we get the results from what you just put in?" Ron swallowed hard, slipping a finger between his neck and his collar. He was *sweating*!

"There are *two* devices, Ron. The one in the videogame. And the one I just installed in the computer. We don't have any results from the one I just installed—it *just* went in."

"We don't know what it does, anyway," Jimmy added, unhelpfully. Ron's eyes bulged.

"But why...?"

"We think the thing we just installed can call its mate home from the other world. But we're still working on it. It's a prototype—it's got some glitches. May need a booster, some new code."

"But we'll get it going! Don't worry," Jimmy's voice squeaked.

"I sure as hell hope you do, because the next barbecue you smell around here will be my cojones. Do you know what they..."

"I've got a pretty good idea, Ron. But let's look at what we've got. Maybe it will make it all worthwhile. The other thing is doable, we just have to make a copy of what I installed and get it to Mom. And make what we've got work.

"Let's look at what we got off the videogame."

They clustered around his laptop.

Ron drummed his fingers on the desk, barely able to sit still. He let out an explosive breath and said, "I'll have a proper briefing with my boss later, but, Jesus, I can't stand twiddling my thumbs. If we wait for them to analyze the data and formulate an official response, I'll die. Let's look at it and not act on the intelligence."

"Great idea, Ron. We'll just take a peek and do nothing." Jimmy smiled beatifically.

The game screens decoded themselves as questions on Ricky's laptop, moving from the first response in the game to the last. The first question was most obvious. 'Are you in extreme danger—is this mayday?'

MAYDAY? Affirmative. She'd hit that box four times.

Are you in danger? Affirmative. Critical.

Can you get free? Negative. Trying to set up computer to escape, but aliens will come with.

Do aliens pose threat to USA? Affirmative. Repeated four times.

Can we help you? Negative. Secure Earth.

Earth? Ron thought. *The whole planet?*

Estimated attack date and time: Six weeks less two days.

What can we do? Find house with red door and establish safe zone. Neutralize anyone coming from it on attack date, including me. All are hostiles and aliens, including me.

Do you have a game plan? Neutralize hostiles and secure human population.

What should we do? Fortify and guard my computer. Save yourselves.

Then the context skipped. Another player signed on, someone named Elias, and wrote a few words on separate pages:

1538. Clara. Sterling Gardens. 1956. Jessellyn. Roses.

That was the end of the message.

"It's really bad," said Jimmy.

"Yeah. About as bad as it can be," Ron agreed.

"We need to find that house with the red door," Ricky said, jumping up. "Come on, Ron. I know where it is. It's still daylight. We have lots of time."

"Where is it?" Ron asked.

"Clara Drive is in Midtown. One of my friends lives there. I bet 1538 is the address. We know what the house looks like; it's the cover of the game, from our dreams. We can find it. Let's go."

Ron was out in the parking lot before he questioned what he was doing. He should call his superiors. This required analysis. Back-up. Using his brain.

He followed the two teenagers, his concern for their mother clouding his judgment.

He'd loved Clarisse Hull all of his adult life. Yeah, she was the most badass woman he'd ever met, but one had to spend time with her and watch her soften to know who she really was. One had to see her smile as she talked about the boys and about Jack. Ron could tell they didn't have a marriage made in heaven, but it was a hell of a lot better than anything he'd managed. When she backed him up on a job, no one was more trustworthy. He even got the idea that she cared about him from the soft smile she gave him occasionally.

He drove down the surface streets to Palo Alto, as everyone did at that hour. US 101 was hell. So were the surface streets.

They arrived at 1538 Clara Dr. as the sun was going down. A supermodern, two-story, totally pimped-out house, painted taupe with a shiny black door, occupied the small city lot. A Tesla was parked in the driveway with a Land Rover closer to the garage, which was set in the back of the lot like in old-fashioned houses. The dwelling covered most of the parcel of land, with a thin strip of water-saving shrubbery around the edge.

A huge sycamore sat in the parking strip, tilting up the sidewalk. Ron held up the drawing of the house with the red door. The fork of the tree's lower branches matched the one in their picture, but it was ten times the size. That fork was the only thing that matched their image.

Jimmy jumped out of the car the minute it slowed down and ran to the front door. He rang the bell.

"Stop, Jimmy; you're not supposed to…" Ron was right behind him, but not fast enough. Ricky elbowed in front of him. Ron stood, stupidly, unable to will himself to stop what was happening, but close enough to see and hear it all go down.

A cultured, accented woman's voice answered through an intercom, "Yes?"

"My mom is inside. Let me in."

"No one is here, young man. Who are you?"

"It's my mom! She's in there! You've got her."

Ricky caught up with him and said, "Jimmy, it's not right. This isn't the house. Look at the picture. It's wrong."

Jimmy shrieked. "*It is right.* That's the number Elias said. It's here. They've disguised it. *She's here.*"

"She's not here. It's the *wrong* place." Ricky shouted into the speaker by the front door. "So sorry, ma'am. We're trying to find my mom. My brother's got the wrong address."

"But I don't. Can't you feel it? This is the place."

"No, it's not. This isn't small. There aren't roses."

Jimmy looked around. "*There.* That's it, across the street. It looks just like it."

He pointed to a much smaller, obviously original tract house with a large front yard. But it was not shaped like the drawing, nor did it have the red door or the tree. The front yard looked like a weed-growing experiment. Broken blinds filled the windows.

Jimmy ran toward it. "It's the one. See, it just needs paint. It's the one."

"It's not. It's not the same shape. There's no tree." Ricky grabbed his younger brother and tried to haul him back to the car. Jimmy pulled away and fought as hard as he could. Ricky escalated his use of force.

Ron shook himself into action. This was very bad. He shouldn't have brought them. They were supposed to be in Thailand with their mother. No one could see them here. He should have told his command where he was going. He pulled out his cell and barked into it. Jimmy started swinging at Ricky.

"You always stop me. Don't you want Mom back? We have to find her. *They'll kill her.*"

People were looking out of the windows, and a few ventured out to their driveways.

"Boys, what's going on here?" a bald man said. "Do you need help? Is your mother in trouble?"

"Let go of me!" Jimmy pulled away and swung at Ricky, hitting him in the nose. Blood spurted, coming out of Ricky's nose and mouth. "Oh! I'm sorry!"

"You're not sorry, you stinking creep. You always do that."

"No, it was an accident."

Ricky jumped at his brother, murder on his face. Jimmy took off running, straight for 1538 Clara. Ricky was right behind him, swinging his fists at his brother's back, trying to hit him.

"If I get my hands on you…" Blood poured down Ricky's face.

"Oh, please, lady. Please, let me in! My brother is going to kill me!"

Surprisingly, the door opened. A tall, perfectly groomed Asian woman stood in the opening. "Go away, hoodlum boys. You not from this neighborhood. Go."

Ricky rammed into Jimmy, who fell into the house, knocking the woman aside. Jimmy got up and ran into the interior.

Ron sprinted to the house and burst into the door, picking up the Asian lady and heading into the house. "I'm sorry, ma'am; they're upset." He charged into the living room after the boys. They'd stopped fighting and were doing a superfast and efficient search.

"Jimmy! Ricky! What are you up to? Whatever it is, stop it. We have to get back. This is not safe." Ron grabbed their upper arms and pulled them out of the house, toward the car.

"I call police, you bad, dirty boys. You are robbers!" She had a cell in her hand and a nasty smirk on her face. "We see who is upset." She began cursing them in Cantonese, or Mandarin, or something.

In the middle of the walkway, Jimmy jerked away from Ron and screamed at him. "Let go of me! You can't tell me what to do! You're *not* my *dad!*"

Ron grabbed him again, this time putting Jimmy in a football hold under his arm. A crowd had gathered on the curb.

"Jimmy, shut up," Ricky whispered. "People are staring." And getting out their cell phones and videoing what was going on.

"You're *not* my dad! You can't make me do anything. Let go of me! I want to find my *mom*! I know she's here. They're going to kill her! We have to save her! *You are not my* dad! *You don't have any right to touch me!*"

Ron watched in horror as Jimmy blew up.

"You have to get in the car, now! This is not good." Ron glanced around. He saw three people filming them on their phones. Another one had an honest-to-God video camera set up on a tripod. "Jimmy, get a hold of yourself." He shook the boy.

"DON'T TOUCH ME!" Jimmy whirled and attacked Ron. "*You* can't touch me. I want my *mom*!" He burst into tears.

"Jimmy, I know…"

"You *don't* know anything. She's not *your* mom! She's not *your* wife! You're not in *our* family." He wailed, tears falling everywhere.

Someone approached, a big guy in sweats. A weight lifter. "What are you doing? Are you trying to abduct these boys? They don't want to go with you, buddy, so piss off." He stood, fists on his hips, glaring at Ron. "Did you hit that kid?" Speaking of Ricky, of the spouting nose.

Oh, fuck, Ron thought as black and white City of Palo Alto Police patrol cars flashing every light any law enforcement vehicle could possibly have approached from both directions.

"See, Jimmy!" Ricky hissed. "I told you you'd pull a screamer one day and get us in trouble. Now they'll put Ron in jail and us in juvie. Then we *really* won't be able to find Mom."

Jimmy screamed. "No!" He whirled at the assembled neighbors, most of whom were pointing their cell phones at them. "It's okay. I mean… my mom… Oh, Ron, what do we do now?"

"Step away from the juvenile," the first cop drew out his pistol and approached Ron. "Put your hands above your head. Step away from the boy." To Jimmy, "Are you okay, son? Did he hurt you?"

"No." Tiny little voice, like Ron had just beaten the crap out of him.

"I'm sorry, officer." Ricky stepped in. "My brother gets upset some-times. When he forgets his meds. He's a little nervous. My mom plays bridge around here, but we didn't have the address right. Jimmy had a fit because of it."

"Who is this man, son?" The officer paid no attention to Ricky, focusing on Ron.

Ron waved his hands, trying to figure out how to pull his badge without being shot. Or say anything without revealing who he was and for whom he worked.

"He's our Uncle Ron. He's babysitting for us until Mom gets back."

"From playing *bridge*?" The officer drew closer, still aiming his weapon at Ron. "Step away from the perp, boys. *Alleged perp*. We have reports of physical violence involving minors and an attempted kidnap-ping. As well as home intrusion and attempted burglary."

"The violence is right. Look what my brother did to me," Ricky was as quick a liar as he was anything else. He had a scraped elbow and blood all over his face. A good shiner blossomed under his left eye. "He's my little brother, but he's the mean one. He used to chase me around the house, biting me when we were little. Uncle Ron was trying to break it up."

The officer turned to the crowd. "Is that what you people saw?"

By this time, four patrolmen were closing in on Ron, weapons drawn. Cop cars filled Clara Dr. Shouts from old forty-year-old yup-pies and real old ladies and twenty-year-olds who'd just bought their first house in cash from their IPO earnings contradicted each other.

"That boy break into my house. He say I am holding mother hos-tage," said the stylish woman from 1538 Clara Dr. "I never hold anyone hostage. They do this to get in my house. Are robbers."

"No, the guy grabbed the kids and tried to get them in his car. He's a pervert." From a bald guy with an iPad. "I've got it right here."

"This is obvious gang activity," said a super-slim dude in Day-Glo spandex who was perched on a high-tech bike. "They're coming in from..."

That's when the black car arrived. It was unmarked, had totally blacked-out windows, and a license plate, which identified it as..., nothing anyone had seen before, except the cops. They backed away, lowering their weapons and bowing slightly.

Another totally black car arrived.

A voice came from the first black car. "Ladies and gentlemen, this is a matter of national security. Please hand your recording devices and phones to the officers, who will collect them."

The doors to the second car opened and black-clad cat burglars with ski masks swarmed out, relieving the residents of their cellphones and anything that could record anything. Other black-clad people, this time in suits and ties, and bearing clipboards, followed and approached every person in the crowd. The voice in the first black car said something in police jargon, and all the officers kept the neighbors from leaving. "Until they sign the release."

"Your devices will be returned to the Palo Alto Police Department when they have been examined. In the interest of national security, this incident did not happen. You will not mention it. You will forget it. Our attorneys are circulating, explaining your legal rights. They are simple. You have none."

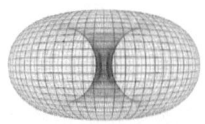

TWENTY-SEVEN

NOTHING BUT THE TRUTH

R ON'S CHEEKS FLAMED when he got back to his subter-
ranean office and called in his report. He held his big headphones away from his ears so he could withstand the voice
screaming at him from the other side as he received a dressing down
such as he'd never had before.

"No, sir. Yes, sir. I am an idiot, sir."

"Weistheimer, as of this moment, you will do only what you are
assigned to by your superiors. That's me. Consider yourself disciplined
and get back to work."

Ron breathed for the first time since taking the call. He hadn't been
removed from the case, but he had been demoted to the sub-janitorial
level. The voice dropped an octave.

"But Ron, think with your head, not your dick from now on."

Ron gasped. "Yes, sir."

"Son, I know how it is. I've been in love with Clarisse Hull most of
my life, like you and every other man in the service. Beautiful, deadly.
Brilliant. And a muff too tough. No one could get through to her. Perfect combination to drive men crazy. Now, use your brain, and get her
back. Decode whatever that game's message said. Get her back, and then
kill her."

Later that morning, Ron, the boys, and a few research operatives met in a war room deep in the base. Their analysis centered on the portion of the transmission from Elias.

"Who's that?"

"A friendly."

"Maybe. But he wrote: *1538. Clara. Sterling Gardens. 1956. Jessellyn. Roses.* What does that mean?"

Ricky took the lead. "I still think the '1538 Clara' was the address of the house. Those houses are old. Maybe it's from when it was built."

"Yeah. 1956." Jimmy had behaved nicely since his breakdown, Ron thought.

"We need to research that area," Ron spoke slowly as he considered the issues involved. "When was that house built? Who built it? Who was Jessellyn and what did roses have to do with it? There weren't any at the house yesterday."

Clarisse's giant computer purred consolingly from the other side of a glass wall. Ron and the others could hear it from their meeting room. Ron didn't know what it was doing, but it did it all the time. Searching for holes in reality, he guessed. Maybe for a way back for its creator.

He didn't know which was worse. Clarisse held by hostiles or what he'd been ordered to do. He would never kill Clarisse Hull. Ron made his voice strong as he directed the meeting, all the while thinking, *I'll go so dark no one can find me. I'll never hurt her.*

"Okay. We need information on the house at 1538 Clara Drive. Where do we look?"

"The Palo Alto Building Department for permits."

"The County Assessor's Department."

"The County Recorder's Office for change in ownership."

"The Coroner's Office for deaths."

"No, Social Security keeps those records."

"Newspapers? Do any go back that far?"

"The Palo Alto Garden Club? Or the Rose Society?"

"How about asking Elias?" Ricky was ever the direct one.

"Let's do them all," Ron said. "Ricky and Jimmy, you get to work on the next go-round for the game you made. It has to be so obscure that *no one* but Clarisse will get what it really is."

"We've already done that. Only Hulls can get it."

"Great. Do that." Ron felt uneasy. The boys were so smart that they'd think up something that the most experienced computer jock could never figure out. They were out of his control.

He'd been around them for years, teaching them karate and letting them use his office to hang out. But he didn't know them. The two were a closed set; their secrets stayed between them. He tried to deflect the talk. Lots of it cropped up around the base, and *anywhere* they were for any length of time. 'They were psychic and had supernatural powers.' 'They were more than geniuses; they were from outer space.' Crap like that followed them.

Sometimes it seemed real to Ron. Like now. Jimmy had run back to that house as though he knew no woman could resist a beautiful, bloody boy being chased by a larger boy, apparently in fear of his life. Ron shook his head. They had gamed him, as well as her.

"The original house was built in 1951," one of the operatives reported. "It was part of a development called Sterling Gardens. That's documented by the assessor's office, Palo Alto Planning, and the County Recorder."

He put a scan of a yellowed newspaper ad up on the screen. "Historical Society had this. Someone's grandma kept it." They gasped. The screen showed a simple, black and white drawing of the house with the red door. "Top of the line for 1951: three bedrooms, one bath. Six thousand square-foot lot. The full price was $9,250. $1,175 down and $58.78 a month."

The three of them leaned toward the big screen and gaped. "That's *all*?"

"Man, it would be more than two million now," Ron commented, shaking his head.

After commenting on the amazing inflation of Palo Alto housing prices, they focused on the screen.

"The house in that picture is the one in our dreams," Ricky said.

"Yeah, exactly," Jimmy echoed.

"But what does it mean? How did Elias know about it?"

"Who's Elias?"

"That's the nine-billion-dollar question."

"It's the portal, just like we made it in our game," Ricky said. "I don't know how we dreamt about it, but that's the place they will come and go through."

"In 1956? We better hope not," Ron said. "We're in 2016, sixty years later. We can't defend an invasion in 1956. We can't even tell them to defend themselves. We're totally fucked if that's the entry point."

"Maybe it means something else. Who bought the house originally? What happened to them? What about the roses and Jessellyn?"

They went back to work.

"Okay. The first buyers were Bryan Jackson Dalton and his wife Jessellyn Bell Bertram Dalton," an operative reported. "We know that because the builder interviewed them and there was an article in the paper about it. The Daltons won a prize for being the first to buy in the subdivision—a house full of furniture. The developer was known for giving prizes that people would want and the media would notice. Bryan Dalton was killed just two years later in 1953, in Korea."

Everyone groaned.

"Yeah. Sad," the operative went on. "Jessellyn stayed in the house after her husband's death. This was where the newspaper archives came in handy. The big crime of the year in 1956 was Jessellyn's son, Robert Quinn Dalton, disappearing from their yard. No trace, no clues, and no ransom note. The case was never closed formally. He was ten at the time."

"Did he get snatched up by the bad guys? Maybe they were testing the portal?" Ricky asked.

"Maybe. It's consistent with what happened to Clarisse. Boom! Gone. No trace."

"What was the boy's name again?"

"Robert. Bobby Dalton."

"Anything about roses or Jessellyn?" Ron asked.

"Yeah," said another agent. "Social Security shows her death in 1960, four years after her son disappeared. She was thirty-five years old." Everyone in the group took a deep breath. "Yeah. She was so young."

"The Rose Society filled in the rest. Jessellyn loved roses. She was the president of the society when Bobby was snatched. It's still very active in Palo Alto. Their secretary had copies of the old newsletters. They had an article about Jessellyn after she died.

"Jessellyn's death was a suicide, though it's not stated. A friend wrote a letter defending her, which was printed in a later newsletter. She wrote, 'Anyone would do what Jessellyn did. First, she lost her husband, then her son was kidnapped, and then her parents were killed driving out from Georgia to be with her. She had no one. Who could stand that?'"

Ron could feel a pall over the room. The bad guys had killed Jessellyn when they'd abducted her son.

"Why would they snatch Bobby?" Ron reflected a moment. "Why would anyone but a perv snatch him? School records, anyone? For a ten-year-old?"

A little later, they knew. Bobby had been screened as having a genius-level IQ. Even back then, Palo Alto Unified had identified the smart ones.

Clarisse was a genius, and so was everyone in her family, including the two boys sitting near him. Ron thought some more. Had they snatched Bobby as a mate for Clarisse? He'd be seventy now. Not much good for breeding baby geniuses. What else could it be? Was Bobby going to create some masterpiece they'd want that Clarisse could take over?

"Somebody get me that list of missing scientists." There had to be some pattern. Ron would find it or die. "The meeting's adjourned until we have more data."

Ron left, bothered by everything. He'd been ordered to *kill* Clarisse. He wouldn't do it, ever. He'd walk away from his life's career and keep her safe. And the boys. The way the boys had acted bothered him, too. Yes, they were upset about their mom. Yes, this was the first concrete evidence they'd gotten that she still existed. Yes, Elias had given that address, if it was an address. Could have been his girlfriend's birthdate, though, or anything.

Why had they taken off like that on Clara Dr., together? Why had Ricky hit Jimmy? The blow had been designed to create a lot of blood flow but not much damage. And the boys never fought, despite what Ricky had said. That had been a staged maneuver. They'd acted as though they had a plan to get into that house. They'd looked around plenty in the moments they were inside. When they got back, they were happy. They'd found out something. They hadn't told him anything, and they wouldn't.

He'd had the same spooky feeling about the Hull boys before, almost as if they knew what the other was thinking. The way they moved in the dojo showed they could anticipate each other's' actions in a way *no one* could.

Something about them. And the rumors. But those were just rumors. But how did they have an image of a house in their dreams that it had taken the team hours to unearth? And the image was correct.

He'd get to the bottom of it. But first, he had to call Jack. It was time.

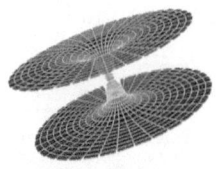

TWENTY-EIGHT

OFFING CLARISSE

J ACK KNEW SOMETHING was up when Albert Jordan drove him
to the RAF base where he had landed when arriving in Britain. He'd
been teaching for over a term, and he'd never been taken anywhere,
other than tourist sites. Plus, Albert lacked his normal jovial demeanor.
Jack expected he'd be taken to task about threatening whoever his guard-
ians were, regarding talking to the media about Clarisse.

"What's all this, Albert? Why couldn't I take the call at home?"

"Top secret, mate. That's all I was told." Clamped lips. Jack knew that
Albert had been told a hell of a lot more than that.

Jack sat in a grey-walled concrete room like a cell. An interrogation room,
he'd bet. He wore big headphones and had a tiny mic near his lips, both
plugged into the wall via cords. Nothing wireless in the setup. This was as
secure as it got.

When Ron's voice came in, it sounded like he was in the chair next
to him.

"Jack, we've had some developments. It's time to fake Clarisse's death,
and that of the boys."

"Why?!"

"The heat's on and it's getting too close." Jack could feel Ron sweating
on the other end. "I screwed up. We got some intelligence about Clarisse.

Instead of waiting for it to be processed and handled through channels, I jumped in the car with the boys to check it out. Total disaster. We were found out, but more than that, we found out how hot the search for Clarisse is."

"What did you find out?"

"All I can tell you, even with this setup—" Ron was obviously on a contraption like Jack's, "—is that we've found a way to communicate with Clarisse. She's in deep doo-doo. That's all I can say, Jack."

"We already knew that."

"Yeah, but now we know how deep and what color. It's bad.

"There was another problem. The intel referred to a local address. Like an asshole, I took the boys there. They jumped out of the car and tried to find their mom. They got in a tussle. I tried to break it up and get them into the car, but it looked like an attempted abduction. Neighbors called the cops. Big problem.

"Half the world videos everything that happens to them now. *All* the people there videoed what happened."

"They took pictures of Jimmy and Ricky! Are they in danger?"

"Yeah. But they have been all along. My people confiscated all the recording devices with the intention of wiping off any footage of the boys and returning the devices. Except... we got more than we bargained for. We have the legal authority to examine records on those devices.

"The team did that, and got their eyebrows scorched."

"What do you mean?"

"It's Silicon Valley, Jack. What do we do best?"

"I don't know; I was a professor. We don't count as true residents."

"Steal, copy, and sell the results. It's the land of espionage. We found out many interested parties were searching for Clarisse and the boys. In the few minutes the boys were out on the street, the industrial spies had already sent photos of Ricky and Jimmy to their bosses. The damage was done *before* we grabbed the cellphones."

"Their bosses? Who?" Jack felt panic rising in his chest. His heart throbbed.

"The usual suspects. The Chinese. Russians. Middle East. 'Other Asian.' Everyone wants Clarisse, and the boys. We set up tight alibis for them, but in our world, no one believes anything. Hostiles are checking out the stand-ins we planted in Thailand, but they're also watching us. What we got off the phones and tablets and every other thing was communication between people *in that neighborhood,* a normal middle-class neighborhood, for Silicon Valley, and hostiles."

"Silicon Valley has spies for hostile governments?"

"Most of them are industrial spies looking for a little competitive advantage. We make money here in the Valley, Jack. It attracts flies. The industrial spies feed into their governments. They're interested in more than just money. They're interested in Clarisse."

"Why is her disappearance such a big deal? I've never understood that. She was an assistant professor denied tenure and *fired.* Plus, she was being sued by the parents of that student she decked. Why should anyone want her that badly?"

Ron chuckled. "You didn't know your wife, Jack. She was a hell of a lot more than a failed academic. Someone leaked a copy of Clarisse's experiment and preliminary plans for her computer. Her department and peers at the university thought it was bogus—because they didn't know *all* the results she got from alternate realities. Governments, including ours, accept her research outcomes as absolutely real and valid. And they think she can do it again, for them."

"But she was kidnapped by some *force.*"

"Yes. The rumor mill has it a bit different. Hostiles think she knows how to go into alternate realities. And now, maybe the future. They think she went on her own, pissed over the tenure thing. And there's all the rest. The nut cases that wrote the death threats, the New Age faerie queens who think she's a saint. Look at Twitter and Facebook. She's got fan sites. They're boiling."

"Why would a government care so much about this, Ron? Say there *are* alternative universes and Clarisse is in one. Why is that a matter of state importance? Why should governments fight over it?"

Ron sighed. "Jack, you're the writer. Use your imagination. What if a hostile force existed in some other dimension and planned to use Clarisse to get them back over here to take over the world? That *is* what Clarisse's intel indicated was happening, between you and me."

"But, Ron…"

"Listen to me. Did you know that a typhoon of unprecedented strength is heading across the Indian Ocean toward Thailand and approximately three thousand miles of coastline in Southeast Asia? It's fueled by an underwater earthquake and expected to hit land in about five hours."

"What? That just happened a couple of years ago."

"Nope, longer than that. It was in 2004. A quarter of a million people died. The waves caused by that earthquake hit the shores with the equivalent of twenty-three thousand Hiroshima-type bombs. This one is bigger."

"How is that possible?"

"It's easy, Jack. There's a fault under the ocean. It ruptured and shook again. They do that. It's climate change, buddy. Droughts in California, flooding the whole Midwest. Snowstorms from hell. New York City underwater. And we haven't had 'the Big One' here on the West Coast yet.

"People with a political agenda deny climate change, but no one with a brain can ignore the evidence. The planet is practically exploding. And you know that our military and 'protective forces' are not going to bury their heads and let it happen. On the one hand, Clarisse's bad guys could come here and take over. That's the obvious fear. But what if the opposite happened? What if it got so bad that *we* had to split the planet for somewhere better?"

"Leave the planet through Clarisse's portals to escape climate change? That's crazy."

"Not so crazy, Jack, but that's the peaceful interpretation. What if world leaders knew that none of the peace initiatives in process now would work? What if we ended up in full-scale war?"

"Nuclear war?"

"Sure. Nine countries are known to have nuclear weapons; a handful more claim to have them. Who knows how many bozos can press a button and blow us up? Nuclear war is very possible. With today's political climate, where 'back down and look like a pussy' is the prevailing mindset, it's more likely now than ever. Being able to use the hole Clarisse went through if we needed to bail is strategic knowledge. Priceless.

"I don't have the answers, Jack. I know the amount of heat on my end says our politicians may think we're heading for something truly devastating. Maybe our leaders are scrambling to get prepared. Otherwise known as 'save their asses.' Clarisse is priceless now. The whole dark world wants her. And they want the boys. Do you know how fast rumors spread, fueled by the internet?"

"I've seen a few things about tweets turning into disasters for people," Jack replied.

"They can do more than that. They can destroy lives—and create legends. Ricky and Jimmy are believed to be boy geniuses who know as much as their mother. That's not from speculation—that's from what we took off all the cell phones and crap we confiscated.

"The texts and emails on those devices show that the boys have achieved legendary status. These bozos are saying that they worked alongside their mother, developing her computer and doing her research. They say she trained them to take her place. The Hulls have so much money no one can count it. They're warlords who plan on taking over the world. It's the *gamer* mentality, Jack."

"Gamer?"

"People who play video games all the time start to think reality is like that. Warlords, super powers, magic. Kill or be killed. Wham! Shoot 'em!

"That's what's happened. In the popular mind, Ricky and Jimmy have become like superheroes from those damn videogames. This complicates things enormously.

"You've seen them communicate without speaking, or move things or do stuff that can't be done? I know you have. *I* have." Ron barked out the words. "Today, in Palo Alto, I saw them pull off an entire play without a word between them."

Jack didn't respond, finally saying softly, "They're very smart, quiet boys. They were always home, with their sitters, or with you in the dojo. Clarisse didn't train the boys to do anything; they barely saw her. They saw more of you, in the dojo."

"Except they didn't, Jack. I was gone a lot with Clarisse, working. They were in the dojo, yes, but what were they doing? They were in my office after karate class or working out. My students checked on them once in a while. They said they were 'doing homework.' Every time."

"Yes, they're good students."

"Jack, they could knock off their homework in fifteen minutes. My people spot-checked them. They *were* doing homework for hours every day, though; it was out on my desk or their computers."

"So?"

"You don't know about my office. And I'm not going to tell you about it. Point being, the boys could have been doing *anything* in the virtual world, including what's said about them."

"They could have been in on the creation of that computer?"

"They could have been, but I don't think they were. But what I think doesn't matter. It's 'gone viral' as they say. If Clarisse were to come back now, maniacs would grab her, lock her up somewhere, and force her to duplicate her computer. Or grab the boys and force them to do it."

Jack reeled.

"And Jack, if she busts into this world with a band of hostiles, *we* will kill her and whoever she brings with her. In the new intel, she said that she'd be one of them if she came back."

Jack couldn't open his mouth to object.

"We have to make the world think they're dead. If they really believe that, 'interested parties' will go away. If Clarisse ever manages to get back from wherever she is and we can ascertain that she isn't an alien, she might be able to carry on a life, with a new identity. Or something."

"That doesn't make any sense. If she's a cult figure, her death will make her *more* of a legend. There'll be sightings everywhere, like Elvis. And the speculation as to how her death occurred *will* last forever. Like what happened with JFK. And what about the boys? Do you plan on having them disappear, too?"

"The boys will be safer if they're thought dead. We'll move them somewhere where no one can find them. We'll go on with our investigation and try to recover Clarisse, but it will be carried out in secret."

"That's completely insane! What possible good could come from taking them underground?"

"Don't think we're abandoning our search—*our* government wants her for all the reasons I outlined. Climate change. Nuclear war. A way for the top guns to escape if the planet is destroyed."

Jack couldn't speak. Or think. Or...

"This is such bullshit!" Words burst from him. "Our congressmen and the president are looking for a rabbit hole to duck out through after they've destroyed our world with a secret atomic war? And *Clarisse* is at the center of it? You guys are ready to shoot her if she somehow manages to escape? *What the fuck?"* Jack had never used the phrase before, but he meant it now.

"That's the truth. And it *is* the truth, Jack."

"What?"

"What you said. I can't say anymore."

The president of the United States planned to skip the planet after he and the other world leaders blew it up? They needed Clarisse to show them the way? So they had to pretend to kill her and the boys to keep foreign spies from getting her first? That's what Ron had said. Jack stared straight ahead.

Ron continued, "Their deaths are going to have to be real in every way that anyone could see or find out about.

"Clarisse and the boys are going to die in the tsunami that is about to hit the resort where they're staying. We are going to plant, and have been planting, videos, photos, tickets—a paper trail—showing they're there. We have look-alike operatives doing tourist stuff very visibly. We can show the world that they're in Thailand and have been there since Clarisse disappeared.

"You *will* have to identify bodies. We'll send you images that look very similar to your family—just say, 'Yes, it's them,' and sign an affidavit. We'll do them up with DNA and the right blood types. The images you see will *not* be your family, Jack, but they will look like them."

"Can I see the boys again?"

"Not in the flesh, Jack, until this is cleared up."

"That is not acceptable. They're my kids."

"You'd rather have them alive than dead, wouldn't you?"

"Yes, but..."

"Hostiles will watch for evidence of you contacting them, or trying to. They'll be watching *you*, even with our security. This has to be real. They are *dead*. You can't contact them."

"Why? I'm talking to you and it's safe. Why can't I talk to them the way I am with you now?"

"It has to *be* real, Jack. You have to look like you've lost your family. You have to be grief-stricken. You can't do that if you're chatting with the boys on the phone every week. It has to look and feel and *be* real to anyone who's watching. And they are watching, Jack. Maybe someday you can talk to the kids again…"

"What? I can't…"

"Clarisse will be officially dead. Her living trust will be read and her assets will be distributed as it stipulates. We'll have our attorney bring it to you; you don't have to come back here."

"But… But… But…"

"Legally, you will be a single man. The safest thing for Clarisse and the boys is that you consider yourself single and act like it. I suggest you process your grief and get on with your life."

"I'm not single. I'm married to Clarisse. Ricky and Jimmy are my sons."

Ron was silent for a long moment. "Jack, we don't know each other well. I wish we did so I could do this better. Clarisse isn't coming back. The intel we've got indicates that if she does, she'll be one of them. And we'll kill her."

"She'd never change sides! She's the most true-blue woman in the world! She would never betray her country!"

"She may not have any choice, Jack. They may overpower her."

"She'd kill herself…"

"Yeah, the woman we know would. But Jack, this is bigger than anyone knows."

Something inside of Jack grew ill. He realized who and what he was dealing with. Ron and whoever was behind him were not friends. "Don't shoot her, Ron, if she gets back. She'd never…"

"Jack. This wasn't my decision. There's nothing you or I can do about it. I have to hang up. Consider yourself a single man."

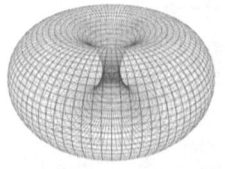

TWENTY-NINE

SUPERHEROES

"OH, MA'AM. THAT'S so nice of you." Jimmy's eyes filled. The tears bridged his lower lids and spilled down his face. "I didn't have any pictures of my mom. Or anything."

"You're such good boys. The FBI cleared your mother's computer. I'm afraid you'll find everything gone, except for family pictures and some poetry your mother wrote. It's beautiful. I couldn't stand it if you two boys were deprived of it." Annie, the lumpy FBI operative, had returned, bearing gifts.

"I'm happy I was able to help. The FBI is behind you boys. It may not feel like it here," she swept her hand to indicate the concrete walls of their room, and what had seemed like miles of matching corridors beyond. They were several stories beneath the surface of the old Navy base's asphalt landing fields.

"But this is safest for you at the moment." She handed over a backpack stuffed with something rectangular. He unearthed a huge laptop, probably the mother of all portable computers. And an electronic tablet, also bigger than standard. "But now, you'll have your family photos and vacation videos. I know you boys have lost so much…"

Jimmy's shoulders shook. "Oh, ma'am." She opened her arms, and he ran to her and hugged her. Then he pulled away, embarrassed. "I'm sorry. I didn't mean…"

"Sweetheart, you deserve a hug." And she gave him one again. "I meant what I said. Don't believe anything you hear about them experimenting on you. I won't allow it."

The boy grabbed Annie. "Please, don't let them. They hurt us."

Later that evening, Ricky and Jimmy sat in their bunker. It was a dead concrete cave whose steel door was locked from the outside. It was a jail, but everyone made such a big deal about how it was for their safety. If it was for their safety, why couldn't they get out if they needed to?

Ricky took a wand-like device, the same as his mother had held in her briefcase, and swept the room. They set up white noise—a band called Turtle Suck playing at full volume into the bug. The base had installed a more sophisticated bug that morning, after they'd discovered the boys had dismantled the old one and stuck it to the wall with chewing gum.

Ricky and Jimmy put on big headphones and sat over their laptops, apparently doing homework. Though they were locked up, their keepers were going through the motions of normality. They had school online and got to get out of their room to work out at the dojo or go to appointments.

The log outside the door said that someone came here while I was at the dentist. Ricky asked his brother in mindspeak. Jimmy practically vibrated with excitement; he had a story to tell.

We hit the jackpot, Ricky. That nice FBI lady did us a favor. When they were hauling us away, I looked at her like this. Jimmy's face took on the most pathetic expression. Tears formed again, and ran down his cheeks. He'd perfected the crying-on-cue skill years before, watching old videos of Lee Strasberg teaching Method Acting.

I told her, 'I just want to see my mom. I don't have any pictures of her. They took them all. I'll never see her again…' And I boo-hooed. Jimmy reveled in his ability to move people. *I told her all the family pictures were on mom's big computer, and her tablet. The feds took them. 'I'll never get them back…' It was classic. I also meant it.*

That's what Grandpa Hull said was the best way to lie, Ricky silently responded to his brother. *Whatever you say should be the truth and you should mean it. Just don't say all of it or why.*

Yep. Grandpa was right about a lot of things. Thing is, I didn't like playing Annie like that. I like her. And she brought us a care package from Mom. Jimmy hauled out the gigantic PC and equally oversized tablet. He opened the laptop and booted it up.

Holy shit! It's Mom's big laptop. You have the controls to the big computer in the hangar.

Yeah. The lady said they scrubbed them, but... The boys burst into laughter. No one could scrub their mom's computer but her. *We got all her code, and the family pictures. I couldn't look at them by myself. But if you're here, I'd like to see her again.*

They opened the computer to their family photos. They paraded by on a carousel. Their mom and dad together, dancing at Grandma and Grandpa Hull's club in San Francisco. The family at the beach on a rare day off. A video of their mom taking them to their only horseback riding lesson. She looked petrified. Mom doing one of her amazing kicks in Ron's dojo. The three of them in karate togs.

Both were sobbing when Ron walked in. "Hey, guys, what's happening?"

"The FBI lady gave us our family albums back, Ron," Jimmy made his voice shake. "I want my *mom...*" He started to get up to get a hug from his sensei, but pulled himself back on his bed, holding his hands in tight fists.

"Oh, man. I know that hurts. I'll see that no one takes that laptop from you, no matter what."

"Or the tablet," Ricky flicked the screen and a smiling portrait of Clarisse blasted across it. She was so beautiful and vibrantly alive that Ron jerked backward.

"Oh, my God." He raised his hand as if to protect himself. "The tablet and laptop are yours, wherever you end up."

"We're moving? We wanted to stay with you."

"Well, that little trip to Clara Dr. stirred up a hornet's nest. They have to find somewhere safer for you."

"What could be safer than this, Ron?" Ricky indicated the concrete dugout around them.

"I don't know, Ricky. I don't think anyone else does, either. They're working on it. It will be a few days."

"Will you come with us?"

"If I can. They're pretty mad at me right now."

"Ron, did you know that, years ago, our Grandpa Hull let scientists experiment on us? They put electrodes on us and things around our heads."

"And put electric current through them. It *really* hurt."

"Don't let them do that to us, please. Kill us before you let them do that."

"Boys! I will *never* let anyone do that to you," Ron exclaimed.

"But you knew about it." The speed with which he'd responded and his lack of emotional reaction told them he knew *all* about it.

"Be safe. They're watching you, and listening," Ron lowered his voice to barely audible. "Act like normal kids. Don't be silent for long periods like you're talking without using words. Talk aloud. Ask if you can play basketball or something regular kids would do. Don't try talking to your mom… the way you do, with your minds. They have recordings of her brainwaves. Your grandpa did a little 'measurement' on her, too. Talk to…" Ron stopped.

To Elias. They don't have readings on him, Jimmy thought to his brother. *And don't try to use mindspeak to Mom. They'll know.*

"Use that game, but don't use it with her…"

"I thought you said you'd keep us safe," said Ricky.

"I will. I'll try my damnedest. But after Clara Drive…"

"They're going to kill Mom, you know that?" Ricky said when Ron left. He didn't bother to cloak their communication at all. What was the use? "They'll be all nicey-nicey, but if she shows up, they'll kill her and everyone with her."

"Yeah. She said she'd be an alien if she comes back."

"But what if she isn't an alien? What if she escapes? She's smarter than anyone."

"They'll kill her anyway. They may kill us, too, Jimmy. Their 'safe' place may be *dead*."

"Yeah. Let's save her and get out of here."

"The only thing that's going to help is to make a copy of that thing of Mom's that I installed in the main computer. No one's said much about it, because it doesn't seem to do anything but flash, but if there was another one on the other side…"

"We could get Mom back." They sat quietly. "There's just one problem—we don't know what was in that device or how to make another one, much less how to get it to her world."

Ricky typed a while, shadowed by Jimmy on the iPad.

"Let's bust this thing open, Jimbo. I'm going to contact Elias."

"I think he's Bobby Dalton, snatched up in 1956."

"It's time, isn't it, little brother?"

"Yep. Grandpa said a day would come for the Hull brothers to show the world what they are."

"It's now."

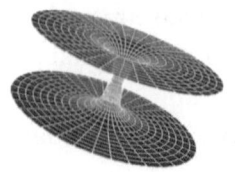

THIRTY

MAYDAY

CLARISSE AND ELIAS sat at Ron's desk in the facsimile office. She made busy-work notes on the files for her troops, covering for El. He was the real reason they were in the office. He played the videogame like crazy.

"See, modern technology has corrupted you already. You're becoming a gamer and you've only held a console once before."

"It's fun. It's faster this time. It's about roses. I didn't know I knew anything about roses."

Clarisse waved her "jammer rod" around the room and asked, "El, where did you get all those things you typed into the game the last time?"

"I don't know. The words just came to me. I didn't think about them."

"Do you know what they meant?"

"No. I just typed them out without thinking. Like this. These are all roses, the game is to match the roses and write the name of the variety. I know them."

"Huh. We'll have to go over what you said on the game. You may remember more. And how you know so much about roses."

El's face went white. He bent over and grabbed his head in his hands. "Oh. It hurts."

"What?"

"My head. It hurts. And my eyes. Everything's so bright." He lurched forward. She barely got the wastebasket under his mouth before he vomited. "My stomach…"

"That sounds like a migraine, El. Alex used to get them. Do you?"

"I've never had one. Oh, I'm so sick." He doubled over in the desk chair, trying to cover his eyes and ears. "The light is so bright. Everything's so loud."

"We'd better get you to bed. Do you have a doctor here?"

"*No* doctor. Pops is the doctor."

She got him up and helped him walk to their room.

"Dr. Hull," Pops' face with its unctuous, manipulative expression showed up on the wall. "Elias is ill? That's unusual. Our humans usually are perfectly healthy. Maybe he knows he's not doing his job and feels guilty."

"He's got a migraine, probably from the stress of being spied on all the time. What do you want?"

"We have a new member of our community. I'd like to introduce him to you. But I don't really need to, do I? You know him. Put Elias to bed and meet me here in the office. I'll be here with Dr. Erland."

"Do you have medication for migraines? El's got one. They can last for days."

"Sorry. I don't know anything about human care. I'll expect you in your office within fifteen minutes." He smiled malevolently and his face disappeared.

"El, this is the best I can do." She had him tucked into bed with a wet rag on his forehead. "I put some ice cubes in the rag. If you lower the temperature of your head relative to your body, it may help. Here's the wastebasket if you feel sick. I wouldn't leave you, but I don't want him alone in that office, with everything that's in there and the game."

"Okay, Pops. Let's say 'hi' to Dr. Óskar Erland." Clarisse swung into the office, horrified to see a man in his forties behind the desk, holding the video game. He stood with his legs braced, strong and robust. Athletic.

"*Óskar?*" She hunched without thinking. "*You're* Óskar Erland?"

The stranger laughed. She knew that dry laugh and the spite behind it. "Ah, yes, it's the distinguished Dr. Hull. I am Óskar Erland."

"But you were..."

"I was seventy-four when I saw you last, and ailing. I should have been eighty-eight at this meeting, if I were not in my grave. But our friends can be very accommodating if you're nice to them. You should try it. They can do much more than shuffle things from one reality to another."

Clarisse stood stiffly.

"They can take people from one time to another, and move them from death to life with no loss of cognitive ability *or* temporal knowledge. I remember *everything* from my past, and yours, too. Our lives overlapped for a while, didn't they?" He chuckled and tossed the game back in its drawer.

"You were twenty-four back then, the loveliest woman I'd ever seen. Except for now. Most women lose their beauty as they age. You have not. You're radiant."

"Shut up, you perverted asshole."

"Oh, you're remembering a bit of our time together. You should start remembering more. Our friends, or Pops, as you call their representative, have started to remove the memory blocks from your mind. I understand you've been troubled with nightmares." He chuckled. "Bedbugs! Who would have thought an Amazon like you could be terrified of bugs! Your next days and weeks should become very lively."

Clarisse stood without moving, fighting the urge to put her hands over her ears. El had told her that her memories were Pops and Erland working to destroy her. She knew it was true, but didn't want to admit it.

"You'll come to want me, Clarisse. I don't want all of you, just a little bit. A few hours, and then you'll belong to our hosts. A few hours that you'll never forget. Which is how it was meant to be."

"Get out! Get out of my office! Never come back!"

"But we're going to be working together, my dear, working on the *real* reason that we're here. The *real* experiment. You've been mistaken as to their purpose."

"I will *never* work with you. Never in your life. Not if the sun falls out of the sky. Not if the devil walks the Earth..."

"That may happen, my dear. You don't know all that's planned. You don't have 'the big picture.'"

"Get out! Don't come near me!" She ran toward him, ready to strike.

"All right! I know what a formidable adversary you are. But you won't be for long, Clarisse. They will destroy you. And our bond will be complete and permanent, as it should have been long ago. And then you'll be nothing."

"GET OUT! GET THE FUCK OUT OF HERE OR I'LL CUT OFF YOUR HEAD." A knife appeared in her hand; she had no idea from where, but she was never unarmed.

"All right. No need to let that famous temper flare..." As she watched, Erland faltered, leaning toward the desk and bracing himself. He paled.

"Well, I see that I am no match for your hostility yet. I will be at the height of my powers soon; we'll meet then. And out meeting will have a different outcome." He left the room, staggering slightly, but still a man in his forties with a formidable physique. He wasn't fully adjusted to being alive. What would she do when he was?

"Oh, El. I don't know what to do. Oh, my God." Clarisse charged into their room and flipped the deadbolt before looking for him. He was on the bed, the rag on his head, just his chin and mouth showing. He was so still that she forgot Óskar Erland and ran to him.

"El, are you okay? Oh, El, what did they do to you? Baby, are you okay?"

His skin was pasty and damp. El was completely unconscious.

"Oh, baby, I never should have left." She fished his hand from under the covers and squeezed it, taking the wet rag and wiping his face.

"What did they do to you, El? El, don't leave me. I'm scared. I can't handle this." She climbed into bed next to him, pushing herself into his side. He was warm, at least, and breathing. "El, this is awful. I can't..." She clung to him, shaking, until sleep overcame her.

"CLARY! CLARY! WAKE up. It's okay." El shook her shoulder.

She realized she was screaming. "The bugs, El. They're all over me.

Help me." She tried to get them off, clawing at her legs, shoving them away from her on the bed.

"Clary, they're not real. It's something *they're* doing. They're trying to break you." He spoke slowly, as though not all there.

She grabbed El. "They *are* breaking me. Óskar Erland is here. He's not much older than I am. He wants me. Oh, God, El! What am I going to do? He said I'd start to remember what happened when he kidnapped me.

"I *can* remember, already. Men, lots of them. And him. They're like shadows, but I can see them. And he said they were going to take my power away. Oh, El. What am I going to do?"

El responded slowly. When he did, he was dreamy and removed, talking as though drugged. She wanted to shake him, but remembered that Alex had been this way when he'd had migraines. He hadn't had them often, but she'd never forget what he went through with them.

"Clary, someone is trying to help us," El whispered as though he was looking into an unseen space inside. "I saw him. When I had the head-ache, I went somewhere. There was lots of light. So much it made me sick. Someone was there. He said he was sorry for the headache; he'd never done what he was doing before. He'd calibrate better the next time.

"He asked me what I knew about this place. It was very fast, like thinking, but faster. He said they were going to help us.

"He told me things. My mother's name was Gerrilyn. She liked roses. He said you couldn't go back the way we came. In the message you left in the first game, you said you would be an alien. They believe that and will kill you if they find you."

"I thought I would be turned into one of them. That's why I said that."

"We can't go back to Palo Alto. But Clary, there's something else."

"What?"

"It was Jimmy who was talking. He said he and Ricky are going to help us."

"My Jimmy contacted you in a migraine?"

"He said he didn't mean to make me have a migraine. It wouldn't hurt next time. But yes, it was Jimmy."

"Holy God in heaven! The boys are going to help us?"

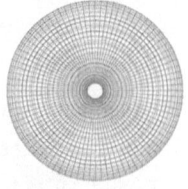

THIRTY-ONE

CLARISSE'S LAST WILL AND TESTAMENT

T HE TYPHOON CAME and did its horrific damage, leaving behind glassy clear water in the lagoons and destruction like the wreckage of unwelcome relatives on land. Jack expected to be notified of his family's faked demise within hours of the news of the disaster. He wasn't.

He went to meet with his students as scheduled—woodenly, he thought. The students didn't seem to mind, or notice. He taught like a department store mannequin for a few days, afraid to breathe.

"You're so British, Dr. Abercrombie," one said. "All stiff upper lip."

"Tha's me. A Brit, through and through," he said in his Oklahoma drawl.

They laughed. The British kids seemed to love that part of him. He loved them. His charges were from all over the world, and different economic strata. He'd thought he'd be teaching the sons and daughters of the aristocracy and nobility, but Oxford wasn't like that anymore. These students were a cross-section of British youngsters and international students.

The building where he worked had also surprised him. The ancient edifice wasn't gloomy, even with its small windows and the ever-present threat of rain dimming the sun. Lights hung from the high ceiling with tulip-shaped glass shades directing the light down. His office was an intimately scaled, well-lighted place for learning, and the students had taken to him instantly.

Jack could have kissed the young woman he was tutoring when she held out a copy of an old hardback and asked him to autograph it. *A Faraway Ruse* was his first book. *Ruse* had sold fewer than eight thousand copies. It had won the Lancaster Award, the Bingham Prize, and been shortlisted for the Booker, but after a round of stellar testimonials and reviews, it had disappeared from existence. Only to reappear in this girl's hands, years later.

"Dr. Abercrombie, I don't know how you could write this. The language. The feelings. They're so simple, but they ring so true. I love the part where the boy realizes that his mother is going to die." She opened the book and read the passage to him.

"'It was real. David had heard them say words about how serious it was; he'd heard the diagnosis. The nurse moved in and his mother had the IV attached to her arm. But all the time, it wasn't real. He was part of a play they were putting on, a family play. Everything would be fine. When he saw the blood trickle from her nose, unnoticed, like part of the play, he realized it was real. His mother was dying. It would be soon.'"

Jack's eyes filled—no stopping his feelings anymore, no censoring possible.

"Oh, I'm sorry, Dr. Abercrombie. I…"

"It's all right, Samantha. It's that typhoon. My wife and kids are over there. I haven't heard anything. I'm a little nervous."

A black car pulled up in front of the house that night. He hoped it would be Ron; wanted it to be Ron. It wasn't, of course, as Ron guarded the boys.

Two men in bowler hats and black raincoats accompanied him into the sitting room. "We regret to inform you…" Words he'd expected, sentiments. A folder of photos. "Can you identify?"

He sobbed. No one could have told him those weren't the tortured remains of Clarisse, Jimmy, and Ricky. His wife and sons, all he had in the world. Those *were* their bodies. Ron had told him they would *look like* Clarisse and the boys, not that they would *be* them.

"Oh, my God." Jack wept and his butler handed him a tissue.

"Can you sign this? It is a legal acknowledgment that you recognize the bodies and that they are your wife and children," one of the black coats said.

He signed, unaware. They were leaving when he asked, "Can I have the pictures?"

"No, sir, though I can get you copies, and will, if you request. But better to remember your family as they were, don't you think? They didn't suffer long."

Fuck 'didn't suffer long.' Like he hadn't been suffering long. He'd done nothing but suffer since the day Clarisse vanished.

"Albert, do we have any Scotch?" He asked his driver/butler/ major domo.

"Yes, but your dosage is monitored by Dr. Indra. You may have one shot."

One shot wouldn't soothe a fleabite. Fortunately, he kept a bottle in his room for such emergencies. On his third drink upstairs, he giggled. "It's all a play, a family play. None of it's real."

Alma Bertrand-Elverton, MD was at the door the next morning. She barged into his room. He lay in bed, hungover, blinking.

"What are you doing here?" he managed to say.

"What are you doing hiding alcoholic beverages in your room?"

"It's a free country, isn't it? I thought all Brits were famous for getting soused. I had reason."

"All Brits do not have heart conditions."

"I do not have a heart condition. I had an *episode*."

"Right-o, Jack. Next episode you have may put you in a wooden box."

"I want to be cremated."

"Okay, metal jug. Let's talk about this."

They talked until Dr. Indra arrived with her interns and beeping machines. The two doctors tssked for a while, and then he had to go teach.

"You will not do this again. If you have feelings to express, call Dr. Alma Bertrand-Elverton. She will help you process them… By the way, I am sorry for your loss." The beeping brown princess and her entourage left.

Alma remained for a moment. "Call me any time, Jack." She squeezed his shoulder.

"It's the boys, Alma. I'll never see them again. And they're going to *shoot* Clarisse if she manages to get free."

"I know, Jack. It's hideous. Just awful. But we'll get through it." She bent down—he thought, to whisper something. Her lips brushed his hair. "We'll get through it, Jack."

Well, fuck me. Was his shrink coming on to him? Ron had said to act like a single man.

Not so fast, compadres!

The word was out. Jack Abercrombie was a widower. Every woman from the teaching assistants to his female students to the entire professional staff smiled at him with enormous compassion. *Fuck.* They probably thought he was rich.

"I'm not rich! You have more money than I do! Your cleaning lady makes more! Forget it!" He felt like screaming. "My wife and kids are really alive; they're just in a fuck-up limbo where I can never see them again. That's because there's a clandestine plot with the president of the United States and world leaders to create a fail-safe escape to another reality because they're planning global atomic war!" This was exactly what Ron had told him.

He wanted to go shrieking though the streets. He called Alma.

"Jack, I must tell you something before we start. This is our final session. I behaved inappropriately this morning. I'm no longer the best person for you to see regarding your situation. I've made arrangements with a colleague to…"

"I don't want to see your colleague."

"He's very professional."

"I don't want to see him if he can tap dance on a nuclear warhead. I don't want anyone but you."

"I can't see you anymore, Jack. I've developed inappropriate feelings for you. I need to terminate our professional relationship."

Well, fuck me.

Jack attempted to buy another bottle of Scotch on the way home from teaching. Albert intercepted him. "Listen, mate, that Dr. Indra is gonna move in with us if you don' give up that. Oxford gave you time off to grieve. You've used it. Now you're doing *this*... I know it's rough what you're going through."

"No, you don't. It just got real for me, all of this fucked-up mess." Albert tried to get him out of the car. He was just a little loaded. Jack had found an unexpected resource—the liquor service in the faculty lounge. He'd found it several times since he'd been back at work.

"Jack, if you go around drunk—and you have been seen drunk in the faculty club more than once—Oxford will bounce you. *We* will bounce you. You have to suck it up and deal with it."

Albert took him to the gym below the house and pulverized him until he could go to sleep—if not peacefully, as least gratefully. He'd been working out with a personal trainer since he'd gotten there, courtesy of Dr. Indra's orders. Between that, the diet she'd put him on, and not being able to eat because he *really was grieving*, he looked much different than he had when he'd arrived.

Albert looked at him appraisingly. "You're gonna be a chick magnet, mate; just don't blow it. Get through this, you'll be a happy man."

Fuck that.

He sat at a big conference table in a staid legal office somewhere in Oxford. A very serious barrister sat on one side of an almost deranged-looking-he-was-so-serious older barrister. On oldie's other side was a sober female secretary, or something of the sort, and a suitcase full of documents, with a couple of DVDs on top.

"We don't get cases this large very often," said the cadaverous old attorney. "We've been very careful to include everything. This is your copy of the trust." The suitcase. "Ansel, summarize this for me."

"Well, it's a complicated trust, involving multiple layers; multiple documents. Locations of assets in tax-protected jurisdictions…"

"Such as Switzerland and the Cayman Islands," the woman piped up.

"Right-o! All the Hull assets are held by a blind trust. They can only be owned or accessed by members of the Hull family, as determined by DNA tests. Any claim to ownership must be accompanied with appropriate testing.

"The Hull mansion, by the terms of all the trusts, cannot be sold, even by Hulls. In the event of no direct descendants of the Hull family being available to claim the mansion, it will be turned into an institute for further study of the patents and achievements of the Hull line. We also have a copy of a prenuptial agreement that you signed with Clarisse Hull. As you know, the agreement stipulated that you were to be given a bequest to be determined by her father, Benjamin Hull, MD PhD, at the time of his daughter's death. Before that, your financial needs would be taken care of by Clarisse Hull. The DVDs are messages to you from Clarisse and Dr. Hull, obviously made before their deaths. We will withdraw so that you may see the videos."

"Wait a minute, what is the value of the Hull estate? Am I permitted to know that?"

"Well, what we can account for that's not in the legally protected accounts is quite a lot. Previous generations of Hulls were wealthy, and Dr. Benjamin Hull and Dr. Eleanor Hull, as well as your wife, Clarisse Hull, have patents on various medical and electronic devices. They were defense contractors, too. Dr. Eleanor Hull was an expert on the use of nuclear power. Hull House is worth twenty million or more in today's market, being an acre and a half in downtown Palo Alto…"

The old guy busted in, "We're talking in the high hundreds of millions of dollars, young man, but that is not your concern. Benjamin Hull built a clause into the trust specifying that anyone who disputed the terms of the trust agreement we're explaining now would not receive anything. If you would sign here, giving your assent to that," he shoved an open folder to Jack, "we'll leave you so that you can watch the messages from your wife and father-in-law."

"What did he do for the boys?"

"The boys are deceased. However, the Hull descendants are taken care of by legal mechanisms that were established generations ago. They would be fully supported, if they were alive."

Jack signed. He hadn't really been surprised when old Benjamin's will had been read four years earlier. His father-in-law hadn't left him a cent or even mentioned him. That fit his position in the family. Nowhere. Jack expected that Clarisse would have set him up somehow; he'd have nothing to worry about. Even if old Ben had left him ten cents, that was better than nothing.

He watched the videos.

For her videoed dagger-throwing session, Clarisse sat in their living room with her back to the bay window. The mullioned panes of the window created a white grid behind her. He could see the trees and lawn sparkling beyond that. She wore that pale blue cashmere sweater set that he loved and a pleated kilt. This video had been made some years before; her hair was shorter now, and a little grayer. Details. He always noticed the details.

Her voice was soft and sweet, almost as though she was talking to him in their bedroom—not about lovemaking, but about important household decisions. She looked into the camera.

"Jack, I'll always love you; I've never loved anyone, or had anyone, like you in my life. You're the most stable, nurturing person I've ever known. I thank you with all my heart for everything you've done for me and the boys."

Details: the way her intelligence projected from her eyes. The nervous way her hands clasped each other. She was hiding something, not saying what she wanted. The planes of her face and the way her dark hair curved forward, emphasizing her strong jaw. Astonishingly beautiful. Then she got down to it.

"I had no idea of how difficult making this video would be." Tears sparkled in her eyes, by way of proof. "I can't face doing it again; I won't update this recording when my dad dies because there's nothing to update. My dad is terminally ill; you know that. You also know that our family is as much of a corporation as a family. Legally, I don't hold the reins. Whether he's dead or alive, my dad has control of the Hull fortune. He's set up the financial instruments—corporations, patents, trusts. I don't know what all. He's made all the decisions regarding money. I will not be able to change anything once he's gone. My income from the family wealth will be doled out by some bank. You know that from the pre-nuptial agreement he insisted that I get you to sign.

"That's why I feel comfortable making one go at this video. Please don't feel like you're being passed over or disparaged. How do you think I feel? I've known all my life that I'd never be trusted enough to really control our wealth." She shrugged. "Being a Hull is a curse, Jack, not a blessing."

All the time, she looked lovely in that pale blue sweater, the lawn sparkled green outside, and the window's moldings carved an elegant grid behind her, framed by draperies.

Jack didn't catch the betrayal quite yet, but he got that she was saying her dad handled the money and that she didn't have the balls to fight him.

Clarisse phrased it as, "I've never been able to influence my father about anything financial. I know that he loves and respects you, Jack. I have to trust him to make a fair dispersal of the family wealth. He will do that before he dies and his decision will be uncontestable. No matter what he stipulates, remember that I love you."

She loved him, but not enough to fight for him or make sure that he was treated fairly. Or even find out what the old codger had in mind for his son-in-law.

Ben came on with the hubris that Jack had come to loathe. He spouted about the Hull dynasty and genetic pool, and their contribution to the country and the world. He sat in his wood-paneled study, in his leather wingback chair, pipe in hand, and pontificated. Even so, Jack could see he was ill. This had probably been shot just weeks before he died.

"If you're watching this, Clarisse is dead and so am I. My death will come soon; I am dying as I speak. Given that, you're aware that I did not mention you in my will or living trust when I died. It wasn't necessary. Clarisse will continue to support you with family funds, as we have all the years you've been together.

"I only need to speak or provide for you if she's gone, too. She must be, if you're seeing this, and you must have heard her wishes regarding you. You know how our family works. Membership is earned, not given.

"The boys have come to love and accept you as their father, Jack. But the truth is, you *aren't* their biological father and aren't part of the Hull line. What a shame that you and Clarisse didn't have children.

"I appreciate the good influence you've had on Clarisse and the boys. Given that, I'm bequeathing you the sum of $500,000. You're in command of your faculties and highly employable; you should have no problem managing with that. You have your earnings as a professor, which are regrettably low due to your chosen field, but you've never been concerned about earning a living, have you? Time to face the music and do something with commercial value. We all have to grow up some time.

"I do thank you, Jack, on behalf of my family." The old man's fat face split into a condescending smile.

You stinking, putrid, self-satisfied piece of crap. You couldn't buy an outhouse in Palo Alto for $500,000! He had devoted his life to keeping Ben Hull's delinquent daughter from running amuck, and the fat cheapskate had left him five hundred grand. He'd slapped Jack in the face and told him that he was supremely worthless in one comprehensive gesture. And what he'd *said*. Tears burned in his eyes. *He's hated me all this time.*

Jack went down into the basement of his house and worked out until he was silly. He sat on a bench and drank mineral water, a towel wrapped around his neck.

This was the scene where the kid got that it was real. The blood dripping out of the nose meant death was right around the corner.

FUCK! FUCK! FUCK! FUCK!

He sat back on the bench, bent over, sobbing. "Clarisse, I loved you.

I've never loved anyone the way I loved you. Couldn't you give me *something* back? Didn't you care about me at all?"

She didn't. Not enough to grow up and take on her father for him. The great martial artist was under her daddy's thumb.

And he had been, too. No matter how biting Ben Hull's comments might have been or how he might have expressed his disdain for his son-in-law, Jack had thought the old man would take care of him. That he'd be folded into the Hull largesse and held up in a big, warm blanket of money-love. He could live in a palace like Hull House and have his needs met. He could write beautiful books that made no money. He was secure because he was Clarisse's husband and she was rich.

It's a family play that we're all part of. He'd written those words, and here he was, ejected from a fantasy he had created and lived in for years.

What was he going to do for money? Ben was right; the Hulls had set him up in style when he was in California. He'd been paid decently as a literature professor—the university was one of the highest paying in the United States. But *literature* professors made peanuts; their market value outside academia barely existed. That's why the university provided subsidized housing for his fellow faculty members; they couldn't afford the rent in Palo Alto. But he'd lived in Hull House. His food had been paid for by his in-laws. Clarisse, with her double—or triple, as it turned out—salaried career, had bought everything else. They'd lived well.

He felt like ice, crunching and tumbling out of the refrigerator, dumped into the real world. Oxford was his dream, but it paid much less than he'd gotten in the good ol' U.S.A. He could pay for a decent flat and a night out once in a while, but barely. No more expensive tweed jackets and cashmere sweaters. No more affectations like his collection of ivory carvings. No more…

The real crunch was that, sooner or later, the government or whatever was putting him up would want him to pay them back. He hadn't been required to sign a contract or anything legal, but no one got what he'd been given without strings. What currency would the repayment be in? Would they want him to be a spy, like Clarisse? Did he belong to them already? His shoulders dropped as he realized it. He knew so much that they wouldn't let him quit.

If I tell you what I know, I'll have to kill you. It wasn't a joke. They'd kill him if he wanted to leave. The Oklahoma cowboy was already an international operative.

FUCK! FUCK! FUCK! FUCK!

Anger hit him like a wall. What was he supposed to do? Jack made his way upstairs to his room. His guards were watching a rerun of *24*.

"Stop!"

"There's no time!"

"Trust me!"

Crap like that made millions.

"Daddy." By the time he made the call, Jack was so distraught that he didn't care that he'd called his father "Daddy." He also didn't care what time it was in Oklahoma.

"Son? What's the matter?"

"It's Clarisse and the boys. They're dead."

"Oh, son. I'm on my way. Don't you worry."

"Daddy. I love you."

"I love you too, son."

"Can you bring my saddle?"

"Your stock saddle?"

"Yeah, and as much Bourbon as they'll let you carry."

THIRTY-TWO

RICKY & JIMMY COME OUT

"THEY'LL OFF US," Jimmy said. "And Mom, if she gets free."

"Yeah. We need to get Mom back and get out of here. There's only one way to do that."

"Make another set of those box things and get them to her," Ricky said.

"I've finished the little booster I made for the boxes we installed, but we don't know how to make another one, or how to get it to her. I don't think the aliens will come back to get the dojo again so we can sneak ours to her, even if we could duplicate what she did."

They sat glumly for a while.

Then Ricky smacked himself in the forehead with the heel of his hand. "Talk about *duh?!* We should tell *Mom* to build another one on her side." Ricky said. "You know what's in Ron's office. It's 'Dead Computerville,' plus 'Tech and Munitions Packrat Land.' Ron is a hoarder. Robots, guns, and old computers. What couldn't fit in his house is stored in his office."

"Mom will have everything she needs on her end."

"Maybe. That's old tech junk he's got. And I wonder if she can remember the specs of those boxes and how to make them?"

"We'll feed what's on her computer to her."

"That's a lot for that little game board to handle…"

"It's that or death."

"You have a point, Jimmy. I'll start feeding the code now. You get a hold of El and tell him what's happening."

Jimmy sat in his chair, looking dreamy. A short time later, he opened his eyes. "I told him everything and that we were uploading the specs to the game console; that they needed to transfer them to Ron's computer before it overloads." Jimmy was silent.

"Ricky, have you noticed anything lately?"

Ricky was working like crazy on their computer. He looked up. "What?"

"I always mindspeak to El now. I haven't talked to Mom… that I can remember. We used to do mindspeak all the time."

Ricky sat quietly and closed his eyes. "I can feel her. She's alive." He went back into his interior space. "But Ron said we shouldn't mindspeak with her."

"I'm going to try, anyway, just for a moment."

Jimmy closed his eyes, then sat up in alarm. "I can't feel her."

"What do you think, Jimmy? Is she dying?"

"I don't know." In a panic, Jimmy closed his eyes again and was silent for a few moments. When he opened his eyes again, he was smiling. "It's Elias. He's shielding her mind. If it weren't for him, Pops could hear every thought she has.

"El will tell her everything we tell him, word for word. They're going to the gym to get started building one of those things right now."

"So we wait for Mom to build her incredibly sophisticated, beyond high-tech apparatus out of Ron's 1990's computer junk."

"And then install it in the computer on their side, under the noses of murderous, psychic aliens."

"And then bring the entire computer here, somewhere. Where? Where is it big enough for it to land?"

Jimmy bit his lower lip. "That is a problem. However, that's a longer-term problem. While we're waiting for Mom, we need to give the people at the base a demo of what we can do with the computer. Something that no one else can. Then they'll really want to keep us alive."

"What?" Ricky asked.

"I don't know. We'd better get into her code, and the machine."

They booted up their mom's laptop. A black screen appeared, covered with line after line of mostly white writing interspersed with multicolored writing and mathematical symbols. Their mother's code. They started at the top, reading it.

"Man, our mom can write code better than anyone," Jimmy noted.

"'Code is poetry.'"

"Code is more than poetry; code is fucking life."

"Don't swear. Mom hates it when you swear."

"She swears like a sailor. And she's not here."

"There—that's it." Jimmy pointed to a few lines. "That's what could generate a force field like the homeless guy said she went through. Mom was so close..."

"It's too bad her boss in the physics department couldn't see this."

"She couldn't show him this, dummy. It's top secret."

"Don't call me a dummy."

Jimmy laughed. "That's like 'motherfucker' in the Hull family."

"Worse. How do we rig this so we can bring something over here? Something showy?"

"We're not ready yet. They have to get set on their end. That will be a while. I'll have to think of something else. Give me a few..."

Jimmy thought, while Ricky inserted a line here and there. He laughed. "That should do it."

"What did you do?"

"Fucked up Mom's computer. It's going to scream like crazy and then shut down. I'd say Ron will be down here in ten minutes. That will give me time to tell you the rest of what El told me. News." He frowned, looking at his brother's face. "Not good news. Something bad happened. Óskar Erland is there."

"*Dr. Óskar Erland?*"

"Yep. He died, but he's young and strong there. He's after Mom..."

"She's scared to death of him. He's the only thing she's afraid of."

"Yes. Elias said she has nightmares every night. He helps her. He's like us, Jimmy; he really doesn't need to use words and he can do things with 'no hands.' He's helping her, but he's not as strong as the freak who runs the place. Mom calls him 'Pops.'

"What Mom said on that first message is true. They are planning on coming over here, a bunch of them. But not an army—just a hundred, maybe. Only the good ones will come with Mom and El. They won't have weapons and they won't be hostile.

"But everyone here thinks they'll be alien freaks with super powers. They'll kill them the minute they see them." Jimmy's lips quivered. "The worst thing of all is Óskar Erland. He did something to her, years ago. No one talks about it, but he did."

The metal door began to rattle and they switched their computer screen to a lurid tabloid. The boys jumped when they saw the image covering most of the page. "It's Dad!" Their father was skinnier and looked stronger, but his face was drawn and lined. He hugged a tall, older man who looked like him. That was their Papa Jack, the only person in the world they loved as much as their mom and dad. Both men wore Stetson hats.

"Hey, guys." Ron Weistheimer walked in. "What's happening?" He looked at the screen. "Your dad."

"He's picking up our Papa Jack—our grandpa—at the airport. The article says Papa Jack came to England to be with Dad because we died," Ricky said. "Mom had all these freaks stalking her. Now that she's supposed to be dead, they're stalking him.

"When they told Dad we were dead, they got pictures of him crying and put them in the paper. Now they're taking pictures of Papa Jack and him." Jimmy bristled with indignation.

"Dad knows we're not dead, doesn't he?"

"Yes, he does, but he's taking it hard that he doesn't get to see you until this clears up."

It will never clear up. Plus, they're going to kill Mom if she reappears. Dad would figure that out right away, Ricky thought. His brother nodded, hearing his thoughts.

"They're saying on the internet that we have magic powers and all sorts of shit like that."

"Yeah. That's one reason we've got you down here, to keep you from being grabbed by crazies for experimentation," Ron answered.

"That's a relief." Ricky's voice took an edge. "It's good to see you, Ron.

It's been a few days. We thought you'd been transferred. Nobody around here tells us anything."

"In the works, boys; the world moves slowly. They're making it harder for me to see you, or I'd be here more often."

"How's the computer working, Ron?" Ricky asked, eyes bright and innocent.

"I came to see you about that. The computer started flashing like crazy, scared everyone to death. Then it shut down. They can't get it to boot up again. The techs wanted me to ask you two about it."

"Sure. Let's go take a look."

"Now?"

"Why not?"

The vast machine filled its cube, dark and dead. The big cylinder cut out of the middle was still, as was everything else. No lights, no throbbing, and no thrill of danger, knowing how much power ran through it. Its silence was more ominous than its normal tornado of light.

They stood on the computer's ground floor, looking up at the sleeping behemoth—Ricky and Jimmy, Ron, and a handful of techs.

"It just started flashing and then died..." one explained. They looked gravely concerned. "Nothing we do gets it powered up."

"We'll take a look." Without hesitating, Ricky scampered up the ladder to the middle level and stepped onto the scaffolding ringing the machine, making his way so that he was as close as he could get to the cylinder's empty hole. Jimmy was right behind him.

I'll attach the turbo I made for Mom's other gizmos, he thought to his brother. Ricky had made a little booster for their mother's previously installed, jeweled cigar box, using the little hair bow things she'd left. That improvement should make it capable of dragging the other computer to it from anywhere.

Go, Ricky. I'll create a diversion.

Jimmy dramatically lost his footing and seized the railing for support. He shrieked, then scrambled and grabbed, suspended a hundred feet over the hangar's concrete floor for breathless moments. Ricky dashed into the cylinder with their add-on. He installed it in seconds.

Piece of cake, he thought.

They climbed down, the entire staff of techs clucking and Ron having a hissy fit.

"Do you know how much energy that machine processes? You could have been burned to ashes, Ricky."

"Less than ashes, Ron. It's rated at ninety-five Tera joules. Says so right in the documentation. The atomic bomb that exploded over Hiroshima had sixty-three TJs. But it's powered off."

"Don't ever do that again, boys," Ron scolded.

"I can sure tell how you got to be a secret agent, Ron. It was by squawking like a chicken."

Ron jerked. "What did you say?"

"I get crabby, Ron, when my friends keep me locked up and lie to me. Do you want the fix to the computer or not?"

"You can do that?"

"Of course," Jimmy replied. "Let me get to the console and take a look at the code."

"No, that's not going to happen. This isn't something for kids." The techs massed behind Ron, shaking their heads.

"We're not kids. If you don't want my help, don't ask for it." Ricky said. "Jimmy, give me your iPad." He typed some figures and mathematical symbols on the pad and emailed it. "I sent the code to you," he said, pointing to the head tech. "I also indicated where it goes. Plug it in and the problem will be solved. Our mom's machine won't quit for *anything.*

"Take us back to our cell, Ron. Then you and the geniuses can figure out what to do."

We've got to get out of here before they put us somewhere we can't escape. Ricky looked at their grey, lifeless room with the steel door. *This place is a piece of cake.*

Yeah. It's practically a sieve. We need to decide where we want to be and go there, soon. They'll probably figure out we can get out of here soon. And then they'll really lock us up. The boys had gotten tired of debugging their cell, so they'd stopped using spoken words to communicate.

Where were you happiest in your whole life, Jimmy?

At Papa Jack's Montana ranch. It was like Christmas every time we were there.

Yeah, thought Ricky. *The big log house, the barn, and all the trees. And him. I love him.* Tears sprang to Jimmy's eyes.

Mom and Dad always were there with us. We were a family, for once.

They were happy when we were up there.

Papa Jack showed us how to shoot guns and fish.

And he let us ride horses.

Let's go to Papa Jack's ranch. Nobody knows about it. You practically have to parachute in. Maybe we can get him to come with us.

The boys looked at each other, faces softening and eyes filling. *We've still got Papa Jack. Nothing will take him away.*

Let's get the coordinates of the ranch. Ricky heaved a sigh and logged on to his computer. This was so hard. Because something *could* take Papa Jack, just like it had taken their parents. *We've got to stop them, Jimmy. We have to fight.*

They worked for a while, communicating solely in thought.

Let's go back to the main problem. How did they grab Mom? Ricky thought to his brother.

Through a "force field."

Like that one? They could see into the computer through Clarisse's laptop. Something appeared in the center of the cylinder. It looked like a sheet of water running down a flat surface, except that there was no surface. Just a ripple in space and time. A visible ripple.

Yeah. Like that.

The device I just inserted made it work. Mom was almost right—she just needed that tweak.

The boys worked with the field a little more, using the tablet and laptop. The "sheet of water" widened and grew smaller as they wrote. It disappeared instantly as Ricky plugged in a word of code.

Okay. We're ready. We should be able to put things there and bring them back. We need to test it with something real.

I'll tell Elias to put something in the middle of the cylinder of their computer to send back here. We'll match coordinates.

Jimmy and Ricky knew they were about to launch the greatest innovation ever conceived by the Hull family, or anyone else. Ben Hull, MD, PhD, their not so favorite grandfather, had bred them for intelligence and something else. Paranormal powers, produced by generations of selective breeding. They were Ben Hull's gift to humanity—or, well, to the Hull family. That's all the old man had ever thought about.

Ricky and Jimmy had larger aspirations.

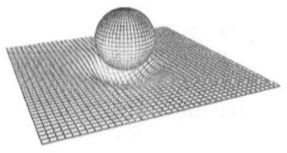

THIRTY-THREE

EL COMES OUT, TOO

CLARISSE OPENED ONE of the cabinets in Ron's office. As neat and tidy as he was in his personal appearance, every nook and cranny of his home—and especially the dojo office—was crammed with an eclectic array of stuff. Not junk, unless you considered thirty-year-old computers junk.

"This must be his sword storage zone." Clary said of a tall cabinet full of *katana*—Japanese swords—and other long-bladed weapons. "Nice in a pinch, but not what we need now." She quickly ran through the drawers and cupboards, finding treasure troves of early electronics.

"There are some useful pieces. I'll have to build the device from scratch." Ron's junk had yielded soldering equipment, an array of motherboards, cathode tubes, and obsolete components that most would have totally forgotten ever existed.

"This is going to take some time. Will Pops get suspicious if we're in here a long time alone?"

"Yes. He's always suspicious." El looked lost at sea. She realized he knew the theory of what she did, but he'd never applied any of it and he couldn't invent anything. "Can I help you?"

"Can you read the code they sent over?"

He looked at the black computer screen with its white lettering and bursts of color indicating commands. "I can follow it."

"Can you improve on it? Or figure out ways of using this stuff," she indicated heaps of electronic guts of extinct generations of computers, "to make the device shown in the specs?"

"No. I can't."

"Maybe you can help another way, El. You told the boys that you had been shielding my mind, preventing Pops from reading my thoughts." He nodded. "Why didn't you tell me that?"

He heaved a huge sigh and got that "whipped dog" look for a moment. "Because I knew you wouldn't like me knowing what was in your mind."

"You're damn right!" she flared.

"I had to; he would know how to get to you, and hurt you."

Clary tightened her lips. "Okay. So you know what I think about. What do I think about?"

"Mostly Jack and Ricky and Jimmy. You miss them. You think about how to get out of here. And about why you're here and how it happened."

"Nothing else?"

"Not really."

She seemed appeased. "All right. Can you divert Pops' attention? Make him think we're doing something that will keep him out of here, and keep him from suspecting anything I'm actually doing? Something that he won't be able to resist…"

"I can think of something. I'll start right now." He went over to the big sofa and lay down. "I'll look like I'm asleep."

"But you're not; you're doing mindspeak." She smiled and turned to her piles of electronic parts. "This could take a few hours."

"Don't worry, I can keep him busy."

El relaxed on the sofa, knowing exactly what to do to grab Pops' attention and guarantee their absolute privacy. He made himself comfortable with pillows and a blanket, and dropped into the type of fantasy that had occupied him since he'd known Clarisse Hull existed.

He lay on the sofa, drifting into the dream state. Clary was doing something. He could smell the pungent odor of soldering flux melting. She moved; he could feel her movements almost as though he occupied her body.

He didn't hear her approach, but just felt her lips on his cheek. She sat on the couch next to him, leaning over him, softly rubbing her lips on his face. Kissing him, so sweetly. Her breast touched his chest as she leaned forward, kissing and kissing again. But not on his lips.

She pulled away and sat up straight, loosening her hair so it fell over her shoulders. "El, I've wanted to do this for so long. I think of you when we lie next to each other at night. I'm married to Jack, but I can't stop thinking of you. Would I be a bad person if I did this?" She kissed his mouth, softly at first, and then harder, more vehemently.

"No, no, Clary. You're not bad at all. You can kiss me. Do whatever you want." He slipped his hand down her chest until he was cupping her breast. His fingers found the nipple. "You like that, don't you, Clary? I remember."

Clary stiffened, and then relaxed. "Yes, El, I love it. I love you. I've loved you for ages, but I..." She didn't say anymore, just kissing him, her lips and tongue exploring. "Oh, El."

El knew all about sex. He'd been submerged in it in the white room. Used for everything, done everything, been everything, and become everything to more lovers than he could count. Not what he wanted, maybe. Or maybe he had. Whichever, he could make his partners' bodies sing.

He made Clary's body sing, writhe, and moan. He made Clary cry out and beg him not to stop. He looked at her curves and crevasses and praised them. He said and did everything he'd wanted to on all the nights they'd lain together.

"I love you, Clarisse Hull. I'll always love you. Every night when you laid in my arms, I could hardly stand it. But now..."

He kissed down her body—her throat, breasts, belly—ending by nuzzling the V between her legs.

"I'm almost done, El," her voice intruded. "It was easier than I thought. Keep Pops occupied for a few more minutes and we'll be able to install it."

El came back from everything he'd ever wanted. He lay alone on the sofa. He had never allowed himself to indulge his fantasies, knowing that they'd never be realized, except in his dreams. If he let them out, he'd be tormented, wanting the real thing.

Once in a while, he'd leave their bed, after she slept, and go into the closet. Those were the barren, cheerless times when he couldn't stand lying next to Clary any longer without knowing her in a way she wouldn't permit. He'd let his spirit and body fly, alone at night, letting himself have her the only way he could. In his dreams. With his own hands.

"Oh," he groaned. He'd opened his mind to Pops while he fantasized and let him see and feel and *know* what he was doing to Clary with his mind. Pops had watched avidly, as El had known he would. Pops was a king of voyeurs, and would have thought what he was watching was real. Pops wanted it with all his putrid heart and vicious soul; Elias' most important job in the white world was to impregnate Dr. Clarisse Hull. His session with her certainly would have done that, if it had been real.

"Okay, I got it. This one doesn't look like the other one, but it will do the job." She hefted a sizable plastic box, the chassis of one of the defunct computers. No flash and glow like the other instrument. "I even got the add-on that the boys designed incorporated into this thing. And it *will* work. The learning curve, El. The learning curve." She smiled at him as though he should know what that was.

"The Boston Consulting Group came up with that from studying industrial output. The more of anything you make, the lower the cost per unit, with no limit. Applies to inventions, too. The more you make of anything, the better and faster you can do it.

"Let's get that big computer shut down so I can put this where it belongs." She went to the laptop, which now contained all the controls of the computer, and typed a few lines. "Pops should be here any minute to tell me the computer crashed and they need me to restart it. I'll tell him I discovered a design flaw and only this will fix it." She indicated the plastic case. "Easy, peasy."

She was so cheerful, trotting toward the office door. As she'd predicted, Pops' face appeared on the wall, looking worried and delighted. "Dr. Hull, I'm sorry to interrupt your afternoon's entertainment." Elias cringed when Pops *winked* at him. Clary didn't notice. "The computer has ceased functioning suddenly. The technicians can find no reason."

"Don't worry, Pops. I've got the solution right here." She held up the plastic case, an Apple PowerMac G3 from 1997. "Never throw away anything, Pops. Everything can be recycled." Clary was ebullient, packing the heavy device in its antique case.

El wasn't happy. He slipped behind her, so furious he could have thrown her newly assembled bit of genius on the ground with her on top of it. His fantasies had stoked a physical desire inside him greater than all the light and power of the huge computer. Nothing he'd experienced in the big hall had been like this hunger. Nothing with *anyone*.

She didn't know it had happened because he shielded her from everything. *Especially* his love.

"El, you stay here by the controls." Clary stood in the instrument room, just outside the computer's boundary walls. The space was filled with screens and instruments of all sorts, all dead. Newly hatched techs looked at them, mystified. "I'll install this patch in the central core and be back in a flash." Clary swung the big box around, cheery and energized.

"Do you want me to carry that for you?" he asked. It looked heavy.

"Nah. I lift ten times what this puppy weighs in the gym every day. You stay and talk to Pops."

El's teeth ground together involuntarily. His hands clenched, along with his jaw, but he followed Clary's orders.

"I say, Elias, I didn't know you had it in you. Great job with Dr. Hull," the old face looked down from the wall. He cocked his head toward El and winked hard. "I'll expect you to keep up the good work, now that I know what you're capable of doing." He laughed heartily, his head moving as though the body to which it was attached thrusted its pelvis.

"Great fun, humans have. I knew you were good from watching you in the hall, but not like that! You've shown your true colors!"

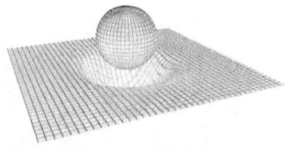

THIRTY-FOUR

A LITTLE TIME TO THINK

CLARY LOOKED UP at the metal armature forming the spine and ribs of the computer's cutout central cylinder. It arched overhead like an ultra-modern cathedral. Glass panes filled the spaces between the stainless steel supports. She walked along the narrow floor installed at the bottom to allow workers to maintain her creation. The thrill she always felt when inside the machine overcame her. She loved her computer. She loved its size, power, and surging energy when it operated. She loved it like this, quiet and seemingly dead. Finally, a place she could be alone, if only for a few minutes.

She made her way to the center of the cylinder bisecting the machine, admiring the LED lights and colorful wiring under the glass panels. When she got to the spot Jimmy had suggested for the installation, she set down the old Apple chassis housing the turbo she'd built. It fit perfectly.

"I thought of a couple of other places, Mom, but this was the best for a fast set-up," Jimmy said in a videoed set of instructions detailing what he'd done with her invention and the booster he and his brother had designed in the other computer.

She'd brought the video game containing his notes. Clary stroked Jimmy's face on the screen. He looked older and more somber. Those words were the first direct communication she'd had with her son in what seemed like ages. Ricky stuck his head into the screen's frame for the last seconds. "We're behind you, Mom. We've got your back!" Serious and sad.

Her men: *Ricky. Jimmy. Jack.* A pause. *El.*

But El wasn't really legit. He cared for her every night when she awakened screaming because of the bedbugs and terrors, unformed and nameless. His arms around her were a balm. He was a balm. Turning to him one night and giving him what he wanted would be so easy. What he wanted and what she wanted. *No!*

Ricky, Jimmy, Jack. Jack. Jack.

She swiped her lips with her tongue, leaning back against the curved side of the computer's inner surface. The power would ripple strongest, right over there, in the center of the center. That's where they should be to go home. The device she'd made and just installed would allow her to go home. She could coordinate with the people in Moffett and they would transport her home. Home. What was home? *Who* was home?

Ricky, Jimmy, Jack. Jack. Jack. ... El.

El was good. So many horrible things had happened to him; he should have been like the blond surfer and the others she'd dispatched. He wasn't. He was good.

And he was changing her. El touched her when they slept together. Never in a sexual way, but still... She felt like she melted around him, feeling his goodness. The warmth spread into her day. She smiled without reason. The shape of his head came to her, and the way he moved. His thoughtful expression.

The melting warmth spread to people and things she hadn't noticed, too.

After all this time, she saw her "troops" as human beings—terribly mistreated kidnap victims with huge deficits in their personal development—but people, all the same. She'd stopped yelling at them as much during the training sessions, only blowing up when Pops was around, to maintain the illusion that she was a badass.

More things came to her in free moments. Like now. Away from the white world and its corridors and brilliance and menace, she could see clearly. Things about Pops didn't add up. The oddities had been there all along, but they were finally registering. He seemed amused by the notion of an attack on Earth. *Always, from the first time I mentioned it.*

She was the one who'd insisted that the crew in the hall were an army assembled to take over Earth. She'd thought they'd kidnapped her to lead them and their human captives, with her martial skills and computer expertise. Pops had *never* said that—simply agreed with what she said, amused.

Clarisse had assumed they wanted to attack because that's what *she* would do. Maybe they wanted something different, with their prizes and parties and disappearing soulmates. Killing women who got pregnant. Kidnapping famous scientists. Nothing in that spoke of conquering worlds... just sadism and bizarre entertainment.

"Did *I* set up the attack we're training for?" She stood up, and got her tools and gear together. "What *does* Pops want?" Clary had no idea, other than what she'd planted in everyone's minds. She knew whatever Pops wanted wasn't good; people dying was the common thread in this place.

Knowing Óskar Erland was around somewhere freaked her out, but he wasn't coming forth with any speed. She'd seen him that once, but he hadn't reappeared and he hadn't pressed her for the meeting he'd threatened her with. That terrified her, but it hadn't happened. Maybe she could stall, or put it off.

Maybe coming back from the dead is as hard as it sounds, she thought, cracking a smile. *Maybe Erland won't be able to bother me.*

Yeah, fat chance, she thought, remembering what she knew of him. *He probably came back from the dead just for me. Whatever he's got planned is just a matter of time.*

"Dr. Hull? How is the installation coming?" Pops' voice destroyed her solitude.

"It's done. I'm packing up."

"All set!" She marched into the control room. Pops smiled benevolently from the wall. The techs seemed more edgy, probably from having to spend that time with him alone. El wasn't there.

"Okay. Here we go." She instituted the protocols for powering up the computer. It took a while—sometimes an hour. But everything booted up correctly.

The grinning Pops practically bounced with joy from his perch on the wall.

"You're in a good mood," she said.

"I had the most marvelous day. Humans are highly entertaining." His tone and unctuous smirk made her feel dirty.

"Since you're so entertained by us, you should know that you're likely to lose the whole bunch of us. Then where will you be?"

He jerked, but kept smiling happily. "What are you talking about?"

"I spent hours with a girl yesterday. She had a high fever and was lying on the concrete floor with *nothing*. Not a blanket or mattress—nothing. I sponged her off with that swill you call water. You don't have any medications—or medical staff. You're lucky the whole bunch of them haven't caught something and died."

The expression on Pops' face alternated between revulsion, disdain, and mirth over the messy fragility of the human species. A strange combination, even for him. When her tirade ended, he smiled with that mysterious, knowing sneer.

"What's so funny? She could have died."

"But she didn't, thanks to your kind ministrations, Dr. Hull. You're becoming quite the guardian angel. Loved as a savior by those you haven't killed." He chuckled.

"Why is that funny?"

"*You* are hysterically funny. I've had such a delightful time since you've been here, lecturing me, killing my people much more effectively than I could, and now becoming the mother of devotion. I remain amazed at the range of your behavior.

"But I will leave now, since my good humor is so distressing to you. The computer seems to be performing its usual dance. Cheerio! Carry on as well this evening as you did this afternoon!"

He faded, leaving Clary more confused than ever. What was he talking about—"this afternoon"? Did he know the equipment she had just installed could lift the entire computer out of there?

Most of the techs were still in the control booth. She trusted this entire batch, unlike many of the others. All her troops, trusted or untrusted, thought they were going on a military mission to Earth in a few weeks, albeit a mission that would probably kill them.

She wanted to tell them her new plan. She'd get the computer to take them back to its mate at the base and lead them out of it to safety. She wanted to go over and whisper, "Pops is pretending that we'll attack Earth in a few weeks. That's not going to happen, but let's act that way. I'm going to try to set the computer up so it can get us out of here. We'll be *going home.*"

She couldn't do it. No one could know. If anyone said a word or even *thought* about what she was planning, Pops would pick up on it and sabotage the escape. She had confidence in this group and a few more out on the floor—confidence, but not trust. They couldn't block Pops from intruding on their minds. Clary thought to them instead, *I'll do what I can to get us out of here. I won't have anything to do with the* bugs. Her name for the thugs still among them.

Clary wanted them to like her, and she wanted to get to know them better. *Her* people. A little smile crept to her lips as she watched the techs leave. It might have been hope. Or love.

She locked up and jogged away from the control room, confusion buzzing around her like a swarm of flies. What did *they* really want? What did Pops want? What was he talking about, saying 'this afternoon'? Her mouth dried as she jogged back to their room.

El would be there. Who was El really? What did *he* want? Besides getting her to love him?

She felt something opening inside, a new and dangerous sensation. *I'm the muff too tough,* she thought. Clary had been that all her life. Too tough, too hard. Too analytical to be conquered or give in. Nothing but a mind inhabiting a woman's body. But she wasn't anymore. El had changed her.

Why had they sent *him* for her? Obvious—he reminded her of Alex. She'd known that from the first. The way he moved, the shape of his head and neck. She hadn't been able to resist Alex. How did they know that?

Once she let go of the idea that what Pops wanted was to attack

Earth, *nothing* made sense. Anxiety built, tension rose. Her head felt like rigid bands circled it. She was changing, and resisting it.

"The muff too tough." Disgusting way of expressing the concept, but it was true. She was unconquerable, but she was softening, changing inside. El was doing it. Oh, God! What if she gave in to El? What if she loved him?

What if something happened to him?

When she opened the door to their room, he stood at the end of the bed. The light from the lamps on each side fell on his back, outlining his slim form. Slim and muscular and beautiful.

"Oh, you're here," she gasped, running toward him.

"Where else would I be?" He had an edge to his voice.

"I don't know, El. I got scared." She grabbed him, the first time she'd done so. He put his arms around her.

"What's the matter? You're trembling."

"I was afraid you'd be gone."

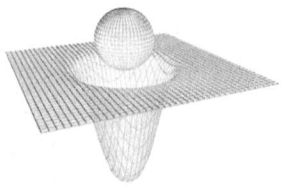

THIRTY-FIVE

PAPA JACK

"THIS IS THE best I could do, Jack," Jack Abercrombie, Sr. held a bottle of 101-proof Wild Turkey bourbon whiskey by the neck. "They'd only let me bring in a single bottle without charging me an arm and a leg at Customs. I thought I'd better bring in something that would bite back. And drink it while saying something important. Tell me, son, what the hell is going on?"

Jack led his father through the entry hall of his house. His stock saddle—a big old roper's special with a wrapped horn and a high cantle rimmed with rawhide—had been installed like an object d'art. He took Jack Sr. to his library.

Then he closed and locked the door, sat down in a wingback chair opposite his dad, and told him everything that had happened—classified or not, unbelievable or crazy or not, the whole thing.

"Well, Jack, all I can say is you're really up shit's creek." His dad took a sip of the bourbon. Couldn't swallow a slug; Wild Turkey had a kick. "Only one up a creek further than you is your wife. And the boys. If they take those boys, that's a real loss. Those are fine boys.

"Oh, son. What can I say? I never liked that Ben Hull. Only met him the once, at your wedding. Stuck-up bastard. I expect he thought I was a hick farmer. Well, maybe so, but I can tell a son of a bitch when I see one."

As they spoke, an electronic picture frame on Jack's desk caught Jack Sr.'s eye. It displayed a picture of Clarisse with her radiant smile and sparkling dark eyes. "Beautiful woman, Jack. So alive. And brilliant, of course. I can't imagine being with a woman like that. She could beat me at anything I did. But I figured she had something you needed. I hope she did, son, because she didn't treat you right, and neither did her father or mother. But those are fine boys."

Jack Sr. got up and fetched the picture frame. The photo display rotated to show an image of Jimmy and Ricky. He gazed at their faces lovingly.

"These boys could do anything. And they are *nice* boys. Did you ever meet their father?"

"No, Ricky's father died before he was born. Jimmy's..." Jack got himself together and told his father about Clarisse's escapade, getting loaded, running away, and coming back pregnant. "Jimmy's father is Dr. Óskar Erland, a guy who's an MD and a PhD like Ben Hull was. The genius crowd. He was in on Clarisse's wild week. Ben had DNA tests run that prove it."

"That's a lie, Jack. Clarisse would *never* do anything like that. No. Those boys have the same father. Look at the structure of their cheekbones and foreheads and jaws. It's not close; it's *identical.* How do you change the pictures on this thing?" He held up the electronic frame.

Jack showed him how to pause and advance the images. They looked at a slideshow of the boys.

"Same skeletal outlines, shapes of their limbs. These boys show the mark of a dominant stud. I've spent my life breeding cattle and horses. I look for uniform, superior quality offspring with the stamp of the sire. These boys have the same father."

"They can't have the same father. Alex Caldwell died before Ricky was born. He's dead; Ron saw his body. He can't be Jimmy's father."

"Oh, son, you *needed* your daddy to come and set you straight. Do you know which of my stallions is most fertile?" Jack shook his head. "Roanoke's Grand Parade. He died in 2003. Froze a lifetime supply of his semen before he passed. That stuff defrosts with more swimmers than cross the Rio Grande from Mexico in a year. He impregnates more mares than any stallion I've owned all my life. Dead since 2003. How many years is that?"

"Thirteen. Do you mean to say that someone impregnated Clarisse with frozen semen from Alex Caldwell?"

"Yeah. Exactly. Son, this is what I do. I breed for type and stamp. That Alex is a top producer and very dominant."

"But why?"

"Why would any cattleman breed to a bull? Because he's the best money can buy and makes the best babies. He'd repeat the breeding if the first one turned out good. Those boys have the same father or I'll eat my Stetson." He glanced at his hat. "That's a good hat, too."

"But Ben said he had DNA tests done."

"Did you see them?"

"No. I just believed him."

"Because he was Ben Hull, MD, PhD. Boy, what you can pull off with that alphabet soup behind your name! That ol' rascal was a liar and a half."

"But why would he lie?"

"I expect he had something to do with what happened to his daughter, and wanted to shift the blame to her. Make her look like the bad, crazy one, and not him for wanting to breed her to a dead man without her knowing it."

Jack's chest collapsed. "You think..."

"I do now. Jack, you can thank the good Lord that you're shed of that family. I think Clarisse pulled up on the wrong beach when she was born a Hull. Nothing to do for her now, son, but lots to do for yourself. And we'll figure something for the boys.

"But, Jack, *son*, I need to tell you something. I'm not much of a reader, but I finally read *Realms of Magic*. I've never read such a beautiful book as yours. I didn't know my boy was so smart, or so good. Clarisse is a beautiful woman, but she's not for you. You deserve one that loves you as much as you love her."

He started the screenplay that night. The idea came out of him in a jolt, five pages, single-spaced. He completed the pilot in two days. He wrote the next episode in another day. In a week, he had five episodes. Writing them had been a piece of cake. And they were good.

People would love the series. It was about a beautiful physicist who discovered a way to go to alternative realities. She's Jack Bauer on meth, a secret agent, unbeknownst to everyone. She gets grabbed up and her family's life is ruined. Meanwhile, she kicks butt all over the universe, trying to get home. He knew that's what Clarisse was doing.

He wrote and kept writing until he had a pilot and twelve episodes finished and formatted as screenplays—a full season of the series. Ideas kept coming for more. He wrote those down as notes. Nothing had ever been so easy.

Jack got the screenplays and supporting materials ready to email to his literary agent. He needed a film agent for the series, of course. Literary and film agents belonged to separate tribes. He asked his agent to do what he could in the unfamiliar territory of film.

Jack sat reflecting for a moment. Should he send them to Ron to go up channels for approval? Probably, but the screenplays would disappear into the maw of the military/government/clandestine establishment and so would his hopes of Hollywood contracts. Besides, what could they do to him? If whomever was supporting him stopped, he could find an apartment or even a room. Downsize like crazy. He could make it on what Oxford paid him and not touch the money from Ben Hull. He had nothing to lose.

Jack pushed the send button.

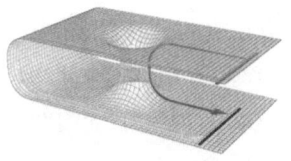

THIRTY-SIX

UNCLE!

E L PICKED UP the game board. Clary worked on the laptop at Ron's office desk, intent on figuring out how to blast off with the gigantic computer. Linking the newly installed devices in both computers and using the combined power to eject their system through a portal between worlds was serious business. Plus, they had to go back to the *right* world, Palo Alto or somewhere close in 2016.

El had offered to help, and she'd refused. He didn't want to, anyway. Since his imaginary lovemaking session with her, anger tore through him every time he saw Clary. He wanted to scream at her, shake her. Mostly, fuck her. He could barely sit still; his skin felt like it might leap from his body and surround her.

He acted all cuddly and sweet when they went to bed, and then ended up in the closet to sooth himself as best he could. Then back to her when the nightmares began. This wasn't what he'd expected when they'd told him she was his soulmate. This was shitty. Anger and frustration fought for his attention. She didn't care about him and never would.

He chatted with Jimmy instead, using the videogame board. El's fingers flew; he played the game faster every time he picked it up.

El typed to Jimmy:

I remember more about my mom. I can see her in my dreams. Her face is a blur, but I can hear her voice. She was talking to her sister on the phone last night. Her sister is Gerillyn Caldwell. They were Jessellyn and Gerillyn. We were going to see Aunt Gerillyn at Christmas.

Gerillyn Caldwell? Jimmy typed back.

Yes, her sister. Cha-cha. This was their code for 'I've got to get off.' Pops' scowling face appeared on the wall of the office.

"Hard at work?" His smirk said he suspected they were putting one over on him.

"Always, Pops! Working for the good of the cause, keeping records like a good girl," Clarisse said.

In their bunker at the base, Jimmy pushed the laptop over to his brother. "Look at this, Ricky. El's mom had a sister named Gerillyn *Caldwell.*"

Ricky sat up. "*Caldwell,* like *Alex* Caldwell? Like—my father's name, Alex Caldwell?"

Jimmy nodded. "Yeah. Do you think that Alex's mom and El's mom were sisters?"

"I don't know. Lots of people are named Caldwell."

"But Gerillyn and Jessellyn? They rhyme. And they're dopey names. Do you know anything about Alex Caldwell's mom? Where she was from?"

"I know a little. Mom told me that she and my dad laughed about his mother's name. She said that no one would name a kid Gerillyn. He said that they name babies stuff like that all the time in the South, where they were from. But Mom never said anything about Alex's mother having a sister *Jessellyn...* We've been sloppy, Jimmy. We should have investigated Alex's family tree."

"It wouldn't have meant much until we knew about Robert Dalton being kidnapped and Elias being Robert. Or that his mom, Jessellyn, had a sister named Gerillyn Caldwell. We didn't have enough pieces to see the puzzle."

"Now we do. But what is it?" Ricky put his hands to his head. "Who are all these people? And how do they come together? Bobby Dalton was born in 1946 and snatched in 1956. We know he's 'Elias' and ended up in the world where our mom is. *His* mom is named Jessellyn Dalton. And

Alex Caldwell is my dad. He was killed in 2000. His mom was Geril-lyn Caldwell.

"If those sisters really were Alex Caldwell's mom and El/Bob-by's mom..."

"Then Alex and Elias are first cousins."

"And El is *my* uncle."

"This is really big." The boys were still, stunned at the implications. "We need to make sure they were sisters."

Ricky and Jimmy tore into research mode, setting up accounts on the multitude of family heritage websites.

In short order, they established that Gerillyn and Jessellyn were indeed sisters—the only two children in the Bertram family of Hog-sneck, Georgia. Their father had been a career Army man at a nearby base, an engineer known as "the Light Bulb" for his intelligence. Their mother had stayed at home raising her children, when not winning national chess championships.

The guy they knew as Elias, and recently as Robert Dalton, *was* Alex Caldwell's first cousin and Ricky's uncle.

"What were they going after, Ricky?" Jimmy was thoroughly confused.

"Alex Caldwell, I think. They couldn't get him because he was dead."

"Was he the last in his family?"

Looking at more genealogy charts... "Yes. Only child. Deceased 2000."

"They stole El because he was as close as they could get to Alex Caldwell. There's been a mastermind behind all of this. Snatching Mom and El wasn't random at all. They were collecting DNA."

"They traced Alex's family tree to find his aunt and then traced her to Bobby/El. His genes are as close as you can get to Alex Caldwell. But they didn't live at the same time." Ricky's eyes widened.

"Whoever did this went back in time from 2000 to 1956 to grab Bobby. They can move through time."

"And through different realities."

"Holy shit. How will we stop them?" Jimmy's head moved from side to side. "There's nothing that can stop them."

"Did they know that Alex had died, so they went back in time and grabbed Robert as a spare? Or did they grab Robert and have him on ice until they found Alex? Did they plan on taking Alex to that other world, but he died, so they couldn't?"

"I don't know. But Jimmy—he's my uncle! *Elias is my uncle!*"

The boys were silent. Other than their mother, they had no blood relations. The hunger for connection, for close relationships and family, blazed.

"What about Gerillyn Caldwell and her family? Is she alive? Is her husband? Do they have more relatives that we don't know about?"

After a bit more work on the computer, Ricky said, "None of them are alive."

"No one is alive on Robert's side, either."

"El is all we've got. You know what else?"

"Huh?"

"Look at the number of people identified as really smart in El's background. As many as in ours: the old records talk about 'They called him The Brain' and 'She could be president—if she wasn't a girl.'"

"That's why they snatched El. For his DNA."

"We have to save him."

"We have to save El *and* Mom."

"You know what else, Jimmy? We've got the genius blood concentrated even more than anyone. They'll be after us."

"They probably already are, Ricky. We'd better get busy."

"Yeah. I bet Óskar Erland is involved in this. His whole thing was the genetics of genius. He approved of Alex Caldwell as my dad, and so did Grandpa Hull. He could have been an axe murderer and they wouldn't have cared as long as he was super smart."

"Let's hope El isn't an ax murderer."

"Let's hope we can outsmart Óskar Erland."

They looked at each other helplessly.

"Jimmy, I don't think their objective is attacking Earth, like Mom thinks." Ricky spoke slowly and softly. "I think that's a trick to throw us off. El said something about their not being able to breathe down here. And not having bodies, so they can only move around and do things in their world. Even if they somehow put their souls in those people in the warehouse, a hundred or so aren't enough to take over anything. Guns will destroy human bodies even with aliens in them, don't you think?"

"I don't know." Jimmy shrugged.

"I think its DNA they're after, and people who can do what we can do."

"Mindspeak."

"Yeah. They want mindspeak. Being able to talk without words. Knowing things that are *always* right that no one told you… Wait a second, I'm getting something." Ricky closed his eyes. Both boys knew that mystical state where knowledge seemed to download from nowhere. "They want an army of people like us, but with part of *them* inside. Then they *will* have enough soldiers to attack Earth and win.

"And they can get that from Mom and El's baby, if El is one of them."

"Making an army will take a long time. It takes nine months to make a baby."

"Not with cloning. What was Óskar Erland famous for?"

"Cloning an orangutan or something. Cloning lots of different animals."

"From one cell of the parent. He was supposed to be cloning a mastodon from a few defrosted cells in a tusk."

"What are you thinking, Ricky?" And then Jimmy got it, too. His eyes popped open and his hand went to his mouth. "They'd only need one baby from Mom and El to make an army."

"You're right! The human body has about fifty trillion cells, plus or minus a few trillion."

"They could create an army of fifty trillion people from one baby."

"Yes, if they used the whole baby. If they just took an arm, or a leg. Or tissue that would regenerate, they could use the baby forever to make mindspeak soldiers who were part of them."

"That's awful. Who would do that?"

"Them. Pops, from what Mom says. And then they could use her work to come to Earth, as perfectly adapted Earth people. The attack isn't in a few weeks; it's when they can clone Mom and El's baby. Nine months, at a minimum."

"No!" They stared at each other a few moments, too aghast to speak, even mentally.

"We have to stop them."

Ricky got that "download" look again and threw up his hands. "Wait! Wait! We're getting crazy. Mom isn't pregnant. She loves Dad and would never do anything with El."

"And El isn't an alien." Jimmy looked relieved. "But now we know what they're trying to do. The grand plan."

"Yep. That's it."

"Hey, you guys," Ron's voice came through the intercom from the corridor. "I've got a visitor for you. Can I come in?"

"The door is locked on *your* side, Ron. Do whatever you want." They quickly stowed whatever might look incriminating, putting a picture of their mom on the laptop screen.

Ron seemed apologetic, entering the cell with another man—a tall, obviously military man in dressed in black. "Hey, guys. I told you I was going to be transferred. It's come through. I wanted to stop by and say 'so long.'"

"You can't tell us where you're going?" Ricky asked.

"Sorry. No can do." Ron's mouth tightened.

"Well, anyway, Jimmy, Ricky, this is Johnny Herbert. He'll be replacing me as your guardian and liaison with the rest of the people who are trying to get your mom back. I know you guys will give Johnny all the cooperation you gave me." He smiled a hollow smile, with dread right behind it. Johnny couldn't see his expression.

"Hi, Mr. Herbert! It's nice to meet you," Jimmy piped up in his best "I'm an adorable little boy" squeak. He'd had the best "cutest little kid in the world" act all his life. At thirteen, he was stretching its credibility.

"How do you do, sir?" Ricky echoed.

What Ron's face and stiff posture didn't tell them, Johnny Herbert's face did. Johnny was a prototypical all-American: blond and blue-eyed, with a bearing that said he'd been born in the service. He was a commando who followed orders without scruple or moral examination. Tall and handsome, the man was a killer assigned to shepherd them through their last days on Earth. Their escapade on Clara Dr. would cost them their lives, if they let it.

"Don't forget everything I told you and everything you know," Ron said, his face rigid. He clasped their shoulders when he left, forgoing the big hugs he would have given them if their new guardian weren't there. And then they were alone. They had no way to contact their father. Ron was gone.

Johnny Herbert didn't smile as he left the cell. They heard the lock to their bunker turn from the outside.

"Jimmy, they're going to off us soon. We need to give everyone on the base and in this black-ops world a demonstration. They need to know how valuable we are, and how we can help them. We've got the force field set up in the computer. If we can bring something from the world where Mom is here, they won't want to get rid of us."

"Yeah. Something showy and big that they can't ignore."

"Like what?"

"No clue. I'll ask El what he thinks when we talk next. Something that will really rattle their cage."

"Should we tell El who he is and that he's our uncle?" Jimmy asked.

Ricky thought for a moment. "I don't think so, yet. It might make him feel worse."

"Might make him feel better, too."

"Let's sleep on it. There are a couple of other problems."

"What?"

"Is Elias an alien? If he was an alien and... you know. With Mom. And she had a baby..."

"I don't think he's an alien, Ricky. I play the game and mindspeak with him all the time. He feels just like us, nothing else inside. I would know. *You* would know. Mindspeak to him more. And besides, Mom would *never* do that. She loves Dad."

They looked at each other over the bald truth. Their parents thought they could keep things from them, but they knew how things were. Their parents hadn't been happy since Grandpa Ben died. Shadows existed around them. Were the shadows too deep and dark to penetrate? Could they fall in love again?

"I don't think she even read Dad's books," Jimmy whispered.

"He didn't go to her TED talk…"

Their mom *could* fall in love with Elias. Maybe. If they made a baby, the aliens would win—if Elias was an extraterrestrial.

"But she'd never do it if Dad was alive." They knew that much about their mother. They fell silent for a moment.

"Why *did* they send Elias to Clara Dr. in Palo Alto in 1956 instead of going straight to the university to grab Mom? Why did they send her there, too? Why the two-step thing? I never got that."

"Me neither. That's another thing to figure out."

"We need to plan, too." Ricky sat up, brow creased. "Where can we go, Jimmy, where the bad guys—*all* of them—won't find us?"

"I don't think anywhere, Ricky. I think that they'll find us eventually, but we should go to the place that we'll be happiest while we're free."

"That's Papa Jack's Montana ranch. Dad can go there, too. He can fly from Oxford." A shadow seemed to come over him. "But what about El and Mom? El's in love with Mom, I know that. I think she loves El, too, if she's being honest with herself and isn't hung up on thinking he's twenty-two."

"I wonder what she'd think if she knew he was seventy?"

They laughed, but it was a short, brittle burst of mirth.

"Getting them here will take a miracle."

"Getting us out of here will take another one."

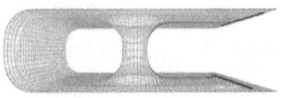

THIRTY-SEVEN

ÓSKAR & CLARY
SITTIN' IN A TREE

"OH, MY DEAR, how delightful to see you again." Óskar Erland sat across from Clary at a round white table in a white room—one of those specially-constructed-out-of-nothing places in the white world. Plates containing a leafy salad with chicken and croutons and what looked like goblets of wine sat before them. He wore a tweed suit and tie with a carnation in his lapel. "A lunch date! What a charming way to reunite!"

"Cut the crap, Erland. What are you doing here?" Clary's eyes narrowed and her muscles clenched for battle.

"My, how testy you are. I see that you haven't changed since our last meeting," he smiled. It didn't come across as an oily Pops smirk, but more like a carnivore's grimace before a fatal attack.

Once again, she was dumbfounded by Erland's appearance. They'd brought him back, transforming him into a virile man in his mid-forties—the same age as Jack, but much fitter. And stronger. He bristled with vitality.

"You're surprised at how I look. So am I, but our friends didn't lie. They promised me a full resurrection if I followed their orders. Which I did. Adjusting my age once I was here took longer than anyone expected, or our earlier visit would not have been cut short. But here I am, fully restored and functional. Ready for anything." He smiled broadly.

"What are you doing here?"

"The same thing you are, continuing my research. Creating the perfect human specimen. You are close to perfect, and your offspring with Alex Caldwell are even better. We'll bring them here next."

"Like hell you will!"

He chuckled. "They are proving difficult to capture. They're well hidden. Obviously Alex Caldwell offspring. Smarter than you and harder to catch."

"Alex's offspring? *Ricky* is Alex's son." She drew herself up and looked at him, nostrils flaring. "Jimmy is *your* son. You know that."

"Ah, but he is not. He is Alex Caldwell's son. Would I intervene and spoil such a perfect genetic pairing?"

"Alex died before Ricky was born. How could Jimmy be his?"

"This is so tiresome, Clarisse. Erik—you call him Pops—has set up this lovely luncheon for us and all you want to do is talk business."

"Jimmy's father isn't *business*."

"Ah, but he is, my dear." He was charismatic, with thick, curly, dark hair, oozing masculinity from his tight, muscular body. She felt a little dizzy around him. "My business is genetics, the genetics of genius. Jimmy is Alex's offspring, too."

"How could that be?"

"Easily. I was Alex's medical officer. I collected and froze semen from all of my soldiers with IQs over a certain level. Alex topped the charts. Alex has made a number of interesting specimens around the world, though none as interesting as his offspring with you."

"My father had DNA tests done. Jimmy is yours."

"No, Clarisse. I hope you are not as gullible as this in all aspects of your life. The genetics of genius was a subject your father and I agreed on. He set up the ruse, that Jimmy was mine, to hide the part he played in your abduction and insemination. He knew all about it. Your father was quite the coward. Couldn't admit that his interest in having another genius grandchild contradicted your personal rights and the law.

"Alas, my dear, I'm sorry, things got out of hand. It was supposed to be a simple, scientific procedure, but we got carried away, my colleagues and I. Quite the Bacchanal for days. I did enjoy you, my dear. A number of us did. But I didn't make you pregnant. None of us did anything that would do that to you. Just Alex, via artificial insemination. We kept you drugged until we could be sure the pregnancy had taken. And we enjoyed you. You would have been more fun if you'd been conscious, but much more dangerous to us if you remembered. You're a good fuck, darling, even insensible."

She leapt to her feet and at Erland, reaching for his throat. She was stopped as though by a glass wall.

"Oh, my goodness, my friends are so helpful. They said you'd try to kill me. But you can't, Clary, any more than you could defend yourself then. Or now." A wolfish smile, dripping with malice and lust.

She continued to stand by the table, breathing hard, clenching her hands. "Why did you do that to me?"

"You've made enemies, my beautiful, brilliant friend. So successful, so arrogant, so much a Hull. I think we saw your father in you; we were doing what we did to him as much as to you. *Everyone* wanted to stick it to the great Ben Hull. And we did, through you.

"Regrettable that the motel where my colleagues dumped you had bedbugs. I understand you've had nightmares about them. Residual memories. Good you can't recall the rest!" He laughed.

"I don't understand. I don't..." She felt dizzy and sick. Something dragged her down, made her... What? She couldn't remember. Why was she there?

He studied her. "You're not well. What a shame. We'll have to finish our meeting later. I wanted us to have a business meeting before our dinner date. You do want to eat dinner with me, don't you? An exquisite evening for two. Nod if you can hear me, Clarisse."

She staggered to her chair and plopped down, her limbs heavy, too heavy to move. Clarisse blinked at Erland.

"Do you hear me, Clarisse?" His voice was sharp; he regarded her the way a cat might watch a wounded bird.

"Yes, I hear you." Drunk, barely able to speak. No thoughts.

He chuckled. "You are inebriated, good. Just what Erik and I wanted.

Erik is my friend. You call him Pops. A little cheeky, I think, given his station and powers. We planned this place together, and what will follow next on Earth. Erik has been my mentor for years, teaching me that I could have what I wanted. I've put together an amazing master plan, which guides our destiny and all that happens in this world. Indeed, it will determine the fate of the planet Earth.

"You stupidly assumed that he was planning an attack on Earth. Nothing so small! So petty!" Erland stood up and walked over to her, glaring down at her.

"You think you're here because they wanted you for your martial skills and your stupid computer and your brain. Fool! They brought you for *me*. This is my project and always has been. I've been feeding them scientists for years."

"Where are they?" She looked at him stupidly, as though he were talking about an infestation of insects.

"They are everywhere, my dear. They finally brought you to me so I could finish my work. You're the one *I* want, the perfect genetic specimen. You and your sons by Alex Caldwell will create a flawless world. I wanted you to be mine exclusively—my wife—but I concede that your children by Alex and his cousin Elias will be superior.

"You will have *many* children, Clarisse, for many more years than a normal human woman because of what Erik and his people can do. You will have an infinite number of babies.

"Eventually, you'll be reduced to a blob of flesh, fed and maintained by life support, a baby in your belly at all times. You'll writhe in labor periodically, only to be refilled and begin the process again. We have planned that future for you. You'll be a genetic donor who happens to be human. Or, somewhat human, at the end."

Clarisse's mouth dropped. She could barely think. That wasn't what... Her mind was blank.

"You're in an altered state, my dear. You will remain so until this evening, when we have our tryst. I wanted you for my wife, filling your belly for eternity, but Erik convinced me it would be better to let Alex Caldwell's cousin, Elias, fill that role. He'll be nothing but a living sperm bank soon.

"But until he is, you hate him. Do you understand that? You *hate* Elias. Make sure he knows it. He will impregnate you, but never have your love." Malice filled Erland's face, flowing into the room like a physical substance.

"To console me, my friend Erik has given me one night with you, a night like our earlier tryst. I will do nothing that could put you with child, but everything else I can think of. Special clothes will be left in your closet. Wear them, Clarisse. I want you to look like the slut you are."

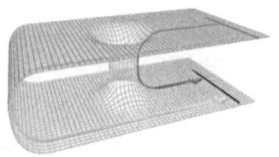

THIRTY-EIGHT

LOOK AT ME!

"OKAY. GIVE ME ten, all of you." Clary had her troops arrayed in rows in the main hall, the one place big enough for her to drill all of them at once. She'd come back from lunch ready to kill. "No! Make it twenty! Now! Hit it!" Whatever kindness she'd shown toward them earlier had evaporated.

Especially kindness toward *him*. El kept his eyes straight ahead from his position in the front row. He dropped and gave her the twenty most precise push-ups ever executed. She got on his case harder than anyone else. But she never seemed to be aware of *him*, as a man or anything else. She didn't seem to look at him long enough to know what he looked like. Now, she seemed to hate him.

Look at me, Clary! See me! He'd held her all night, absorbing her screams and suffering. Getting her through it. He knew she had met with Óskar Erland. She'd come back one of the emptied-out ones he'd seen returning from time with Pops. He knew all about what Pops and *they* could do. Change your mind, make you hate what you loved, make you do or feel anything. Make you fuck anyone. He'd seen it in the hall. They could inflict enormous emotional pain. They could kill.

They were killing Clary. They'd started in earnest at that lunch. Clary was fading. Her original belligerence was based on bravado, and that was running out as they threw greater horrors at her. She'd crack soon.

At night, she would cling to him, running from phantom bugs that grew bigger and bigger, attaching to her like vicious beetles the size of oranges and sucking her blood. Leaving it running down her body and staining the sheets. He had trouble making them retreat into the tortured realms of her mind. Pops allowed memories of the men who had used her to seep through. Dark shapes clustering around her, touching her.

When it had happened, she had been drugged, silent and inert. Now she screamed.

He muffled her cries and killed the surveillance devices they kept putting in their room. The only traces he left them were sounds of his own passion, which he gave himself from his isolation in the closet. He never got to give her his love. All he had was his own desire and her beautiful body, frozen or shaking in terror. She clung to him, wild-eyed, unable to do anything but survive. Every night was like that.

He'd been communicating with Jimmy. They'd gotten mindspeak to where their minds almost melded. Jimmy and Ricky were planning something that would blow the minds of people at the base. Elias could almost see the base through Jimmy's eyes—the computer lab, identical to the one on their side. The dreary bunker where they were the rest of the time. They were in jail, just like he was.

The boys had an experiment planned for that night. They had decided that Clary shouldn't know. "She can't give up what she doesn't know."

Jimmy and Ricky seemed to have a much better idea of what *they* were capable of than Clary. She wandered around in a haze of terror, which had flipped to rage during lunch.

She hadn't come close to experiencing Pop's fury. But she would, if the experiment he and Jimmy and Ricky planned didn't work out that night. If they were found out. If she kept going the way she was, which was half-crazy. El marched to her shouted orders, as afraid of her as everyone else was.

"March! You are an *army, not a bunch of pussies!*"

Round and round the hall, El marched while Clarisse yelled. He could take her drills, and meet her impossible physical demands. He was stronger than he'd ever been.

El glanced in the bathroom mirror once in a while. He had muscles now, more than anyone else. He was lean, hard, and fit. He suspected that *they* had something to do with how he looked, wanting him to appeal to Clary more. But he didn't. She never looked at him once she pulled away from him in the morning.

"Okay. Let's leave this stinking hole and hit the computer," she shouted to the group, heading out of the hall. "You idiots remember what a computer is, don't you?"

Clary was off, up corridor one to the end, turning left at the double set of doors and on to the lab, the crew streaming behind her.

"We're going to do a full drill, all of us. So you'll be triple manning each station and doing the maintenance protocol, taking turns. Go!"

What he did next was crucial to the mission he was carrying out with Jimmy and Ricky that night. The hardware to do it was in place in the old computer case carrying whatever Clary had made a few days earlier. But it needed a bit of programming, a tweak Jimmy and Ricky had written to make it work. Jimmy had sent the code to him on the electronic game and he'd put it on a memory stick.

El sidled up to the control panel on the big computer. He had to log on—using Clary's passwords that he'd deciphered and memorized—and install the new code. Who knew what she'd do if she caught him? He inserted a memory stick bearing Jimmy's programming into a USB port and began to download it. It would take thirty seconds at the most to download and install. Hopefully, she'd be busy terrorizing the rest of her soldiers and not notice.

"El, stop stargazing. Get over here and help me." She'd noticed him.

Once he installed the software, they should be able to move something from one computer to another. The boys wanted him to put something big and showy in the central opening of the computer so they'd impress the people on the other side. Jimmy had told him they were about to shut their computer down and give up. El knew what they'd do to the brothers if that happened.

Twenty seconds. Nineteen. Eighteen. The download from the memory stick crawled along. *Hurry up!*

"El, *get over here* and help me!" Clary barked, eyes blazing at him. He looked down, waiting out the final seconds.

"What are you *doing*, El? I need your help. Get over here."

He had to install the code and get rid of the data on the memory stick once it downloaded. El stood there, doing what had to be done, while Clary screamed at him.

"*Who do you think you are, you idiot!* You work for *me!* When I say *come here*, you *jump!*"

She raved, with all others looking at her as if she was nuts. She was nuts. Pops had taken over in her. El had seen it before as lovers were turned against lovers in the big hall for *their* entertainment.

El turned toward her, memory stick clutched in his hand. She'd find it if he had it on him. He turned toward her, stumbled, and ended up on his knees. He slid the stick under the console. Hopefully, she hadn't seen. In her state, she'd tear up the control room to find it.

"Get over here!" She waited for him, eyes bulging, hands in tight fists. "I ordered you to help me."

"I thought I saw something wrong with the code."

"What? There's nothing wrong with the code. And that's not your call." She swung at him, her fist a knot. He wasn't quite fast enough to dodge the blow. She grazed his cheek, knocking him back and splitting his skin. And then she was on him. He blocked her punches, again and again, finally grabbing her fists. He wouldn't hit her.

"What are you doing, Clary? It's me."

Wild-eyed, crazy. He could see that Pops and Óskar Erland were in control. She slammed her forehead into his face. His head flew back. Stars popped everywhere. Ringing filled his ears. He fell onto his back.

She was on top of him, punching him methodically in the midsection. "Soldier. Do. Not. Do. *Anything*. Without. *My*. Permission. *Do you understand?*"

She didn't help him stand. He rolled over onto his hands and knees and got up, dizzy and dazed, gut aching, blood from his face splattering the white floor.

"Didn't expect that, did you? You need to remember who you work for, pretty boy. Get out of here."

He went back to their room, blood running down his cheek. He sat on the bed and cried. Men weren't supposed to cry. But he'd never been a man, anyway.

He'd tried to help her, and he'd failed. She hated him.

She didn't look at him when she came in after the day's drills, heading straight for the shower. Clary dodged into the closet with a towel around herself afterward.

"Sorry about this afternoon," she barked when she exited the closet. "You needed to learn who's boss."

She came out wearing a white lace dress, one he hadn't noticed before. Tiers of lace and sheer white cloth formed a billowing skirt. The top was cut low. Her boobs pushed up out of it. He'd never seen her dressed like that. When she walked toward the door, he could see her legs and torso through the filmy skirt. Tiny white panties were clearly outlined under the fabric.

"Don't stay up for me, sugar."

"Where are you going, Clary?"

"Out to dinner with Óskar Erland—not that it's any of your business."

When the door closed, Elias sat frozen on the bed. They had won.

He leapt to the door and shook the handle. Locked. He went to her briefcase and tried every device she had in it. Nothing worked. He was locked in and couldn't save her.

Clary would go over to the enemy tonight. Óskar would do whatever he wanted to her. And he would destroy her.

He looked at the clock on the wall. The demonstration he had planned with Jimmy was in three hours. The big surprise he'd planted in the computer would be transported to Clary's world.

Except he hadn't planted any surprise. All that the center of the computer held was air. No one would notice anything when it appeared at the base.

He'd failed.

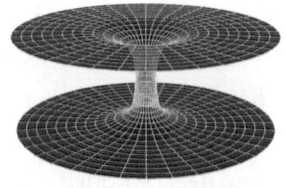

THIRTY-NINE

ÓSKAR & CLARY
K-I-S-S-I-N-G

"YOU'RE LOOKING LOVELY, my dear," Óskar met her at the end of the corridor. He held out his arm. "All in white. Virginal. You look like a bride. Tonight, you will be my bride." He smiled broadly. They turned left into the abutting corridor and headed toward the computer.

She blinked, walking in a daze. The change was so subtle; she didn't notice it. Or remember that she'd been furious with El, or even how she'd gotten where she was. Her belly ached, as did her breasts and the triangle between her hips.

He paused and looked into her eyes. "Ah, I see my friends have done what they said they would—eliminate your unfortunate penchant for violence. They're almost magical in their control of the human psyche. Of course, they've had eons to practice.

"Rather than a bellicose harridan as you were at lunch, you are my completely willing companion." Óskar ran his hand over her breast to test his assertion. He rubbed her nipple and it became a hard pebble. "Lovely, my dear. We will have a marvelous time, with no need for drugs.

"Come with me. I have a very special treat."

Clarisse walked next to Erland, not minding his hand on her arm and his occasional stops to run his hands over her body. She'd been think-ing of him since their lunch. Had it been that afternoon? She couldn't remember. Voices were whispering to her, telling her what to do. How she felt about him. Clary's mouth opened. Everything loosened inside her. She looked at him. *What a handsome man.*

They reached a set of elevator doors in the sidewall. "I find climbing all those ladders difficult, my dear, so our friends constructed this little convenience for us." The elevator doors opened and he led her in, crowd-ing her into a corner and rubbing his belly against her.

"I've always wanted to take a woman in an elevator, but if I did, it would spoil the surprise. Here we are."

They stepped out of the elevator onto a ramp that led directly into the heart of the computer's cylindrical core.

"See, my dear. Our hosts have set up a little trysting place for us." The center of the cylinder was a flat walkway. A table sporting cham-pagne flutes and fine linen was arranged in the middle of the open space. Next to it was a single bed, and a few objects, such as manacles, not nor-mally associated with love nests.

"I even had them lower the lights so that all that flashing wouldn't disturb us. Sit and eat. Look what we have. My favorites—venison and wild boar. Those wretched vegetables that you like so much. Caviar. Snaps. Champagne. Tonight, we feast… in all ways."

Something stirred in Clary. She shouldn't eat with this man, but she couldn't remember why. Something about him had been bothering her. It was gone. Shouldn't eat or drink anything. Something had happened when she did so before. But she couldn't remember what. Nothing both-ered her at all. She ate and drank.

"More wine, my dear? You're so pale. Your cheeks could use a lit-tle brightening."

She drank. He was terribly funny. She had no clear memory of who he was, just knew that he was very attractive. He kept talking, making her laugh. He was a very intelligent man; her father would have liked him. He filled her glass again, bending over her and nuzzling her chest.

"You're just about ready, my darling."

Clary was drunk and intoxicated with something else, though she couldn't say what. Voices whispered inside her brain, wisps outside consciousness, giving her orders as powerful as electric shocks. She would do what they said. All she noticed consciously was how handsome the man was, whatever he had said his name was.

"I'm so glad that we had a chance to talk at lunch today. That cleared up so much. You do understand that Jimmy is Alex Caldwell's son? Yes?" She stared at him, blinking stupidly. He kept talking. "You are inebriated, good. Just what Erik and I wanted. Erik is who you call Pops. Do you remember that?" She blinked again.

"Good. You're the stupid little tart you really are. I'm going to tell you a few more details of our plan. Erik's and mine. Then we'll go over to that bed and I will collect my reward for being such a good soldier and giving you to that Elias cretin. However, you must be compliant. Now, open your dress, just a little. Yes, that's lovely. In good taste, but alluring. A little more." She unbuttoned her dress another notch.

"Oh, Dr. Clarisse Hull, what a lovely bitch you are. Now you are going to hear the truth. I told you earlier that you would be a brood bitch on a gargantuan scale, kept alive for centuries and producing brats through my friend's skills and powers. *Your* offspring will attack Earth, with all your intelligence and scientific knowledge and what will result from crossing you with *them*. They've perfected that. The riffraff assembled in the hall never were of any consequence. Erik and his kind have had fun with them; that's all they are, *toys*.

"I will rule the world, Clarisse. Everything in it will jump to my command. I don't need a queen; I have the women in the troops you trained. I've found many of them to my liking already. Flimsy, but compliant. You will be my queen tonight. I will use you as I wish.

"The exciting thing, my dear, is that you don't have to survive the night. Erik assured me of that. All I need are a few living cells to create a new and better Clarisse Hull, one without arrogance and that dreadful Hull superiority." He spat the words at her, and then slapped her face. She felt her cheek redden, but didn't complain.

"Your offspring will populate creation, while Erik and I will rule the Earth the way the planet deserves. And if all goes well, we'll go on to conquer other planets and galaxies. *I will be the ruler! I came back from the dead to claim my destiny."* His eyes were overly bright. He stared at her, panting with excitement. Clarisse gazed at him impassively.

"Do I get to be the queen?" Her breasts felt swollen, as did the area between her legs. She wanted this wonderful man, this king.

"Yes, my dear." He smiled, nodding vigorously.

She thought she heard someone screaming at her, as though from far away, from the end of a tunnel. A voice was saying, "Mom, wake up. Get out of there. It's *Jimmy*, Mom. You have to run."

"Jimmy?" she said. "Who's Jimmy?"

"He's your son, and Alex's. I told you that," the charming man said. "I am Óskar Erland."

She looked at the man across the table. Óskar Erland was an old man. This was not an old man.

Her ears rang. Voices kept shouting, "Mom, it's Ricky. Remember me? You have to get out of there. Run." And another voice resounded, a very familiar voice, someone that she loved very much. She couldn't make it out.

The name Óskar Erland sounded familiar, but she couldn't place it. A wispy, tiny voice came from her. "Alex died. He died before Ricky was born."

Jimmy was screaming, "Run, Mom! Get out of there!"

She whispered, "Jimmy is Alex's?"

"Yes. I told you that."

"My father told me that Óskar Erland was Jimmy's father. I got drunk and pregnant with him. He was a famous professor. I was bad."

"That's what I told him to say."

"I don't understand. I don't..." She felt dizzy and sick.

"You don't have to understand, my dear. Now, my darling, we are going to complete our tryst."

He half-lifted and moved her, staggering, to the bed. "I don't understand."

"You will. We're perfectly safe here. I wanted to make you mine, my dear and brilliant Clarisse, deep inside the computer's soul. Which is your soul, isn't it?

"Take off your clothes and lie down." She dropped the dress on the bed and stood weaving on her feet. "Lie down, my little whore." He looked at her, breathless. "What a beautiful bitch. My bitch. Now you are mine, for the night anyway. Not that you'll live beyond it.

"Lie down, Clarisse, and prepare to receive a real man. Tonight, I am your husband and you are my slave."

He settled upon her. "Open your legs, slut."

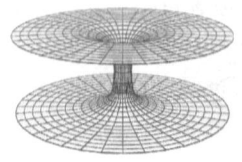

FORTY

DEMO # 1

Ó SKAR ERLAND SAID words that Clary could barely understand. They were bad words, not nice at all. "I'm going to bend you over and take you..." He pawed her and pinched her breasts. It hurt, but the whispers in her head said she liked it.

Her dress was gone; she didn't know where it was. He pulled at her panties, yanking them. "Get them off! Now! I've waited long enough..."

She collapsed on the cot.

"Holy fucking shit, Jimmy. Óskar Erland's got her." The boys received frantic transmissions from Elias, who was locked in his room, unable to help their mom.

"We've got controls on both computers. We've got to be able to do something to stop him. If we can't, this whole thing is bullshit." Ricky sat at the keyboard of the laptop, manipulating screens and typing like crazy.

"Okay. I got sound. We can hear what he's saying to her." They listened for a while, every word upsetting them more.

"She's drunk, Jimmy. Or something. She can hardly talk. Let's see if I can get visuals."

In short order, they could watch Erland pawing their mom, and yelling that Jimmy was really Alex Caldwell's child from frozen semen. That she was going to be a breeder forever. The boys stared at each other.

"You're my full brother?" Ricky gawked. Cause for rejoicing, except that Erland was leading their mom to the bed. She dropped her dress. They could see her back. And more of the rest of her than they wanted to.

"Open your legs, slut." Erland's harsh voice.

"Fight, Mom! Fight him!" She couldn't. Their peerless, undefeatable warrior-mom was disabled by drugs, or something.

"Oh, shit! I can't watch this."

"We don't have to. We've got controls on both ends. We were going to do a demo later. Let's do one now. Send this." Ricky pointed to an object on his bed, a six-inch Bowie knife with serrated edges on both sides of the blade.

The knife had come from Ron's office. They'd brought a few weapons to their cell, in case they had to fight their way out.

"The control code is already written. Just do 'Command, Copy, Paste.' Aim the sensor here and it will copy it to the other side."

Ricky put the knife on the floor and Jimmy pointed the beam at it. In one instant, it was gone.

The screen showed a gleaming knife on the floor of the other computer, within their Mom's reach, if she reached for it. She did not. Her head was rolled back along with her eyes. The whites gleamed in the soft light of the computer's innards.

"She's out cold."

"Quick." Ricky did something and an electrical spark ran across the screen, indicating that the charge had passed through the computer on the other end. The bed leaped into the air as the current hit it. Óskar Erland bounced up and grabbed the frame, struggling to keep his feet. Electricity danced around him.

Clarisse sat up straight, registering Erland, trying to get her bearings. Registering her nakedness. She could barely move. El's voice screamed in her mind, "Get away! Run!" She came out of her stupor. "Get up, Clary. He'll kill you." El again. She rolled off the bed's other side, saw the knife, gripped it, and leapt at her opponent. She was barely able to stand, much less fight.

Erland deflected her rubbery first blow. He grabbed her hand and turned the blade toward her, thrusting it hard into her midsection.

She felt it pierce her flesh, vaguely aware of blood drenching the white dress on the floor. "*Fight*, Clary!" El's voice screamed at her. The whispering voices that had been telling her everything was all right disappeared. Drunken fuzziness fled. El said, "They're controlling you! Fight them!" Her warrior training took over. She reacted hard, jumping away from Erland and paying no attention to her injury.

She feinted with Óskar for a while. He was a very healthy man in his prime; she was a wounded but superbly trained woman, helped by something. Erland grasped his throat as though he was trying to shout, but no sound came out. Clarisse drove the blade into his gullet, just below his hand. A slash severed the windpipe, carotid, and jugular—the strike she'd taught El so long ago. Erland dropped to the floor, bleeding out. Then dead.

She turned on him, rage barely awakened. She was in Iran again, watching the tire iron smash Alex's face. She was drugged and fighting that terrible abduction and rape when Jimmy was conceived, with assailants she didn't know.

She attacked his corpse, first cutting out Erland's eyes, making fast circles with the blade and then a popping motion with her wrist. The eyeballs flopped on the floor. One rolled; the other hung by the optic nerve. She slammed the blade in his torso where the ribs joined the breastbone, cutting quickly. His abdominal cavity opened and glistening sausages still shimmering with peristalsis rolled out.

She kept cutting, severing everything. A medical examiner would have been hard-pressed to do a more exact dissection. The computer's floor looked like the site of a mass murder.

Clary pulled away, looking around. "Run, Clary. They'll get you. Get away." El's voice. Her side was awash with blood, her blood. She looked toward the opening of the cylinder where the ramp joined it to the corridor and the new elevator.

Clarisse took a few staggering steps, looked back at Erland, and collapsed.

"Go, Mom! Run!" The boys monitored the screen in horror.

Then she began to eviscerate Óskar Erland.

"Oh, Mom! Don't do that!" Ricky cried.

"Turn it off, Ricky. I don't want to see what she's doing."

"No." Ricky's expression hardened. "She deserves revenge, Jimmy. He wouldn't have shown her any mercy. You heard what he was going to do to her."

When it was over, they were frantic for another reason. "Mom, you have to go! They're going to get you!" Jimmy cried.

She seemed to hear him, looking toward the opening of the cylinder. She fought her way to her feet, and then she fell, not moving.

"Oh, no!" The boys jumped to their feet, and screamed to the only person who could help their mom.

"El! El! You've got to get out. Mom's hurt. She can't make it. They'll get her."

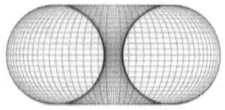

FORTY-ONE

A DINNER PARTY

J ACK DRESSED IN a tweed jacket, wool turtleneck, and slacks. He wanted to present himself exactly as he was, even though his staff was appalled. His butler sputtered about formal dress and a black tie as the only appropriate garments for dinner. Nope. No more pretense. Pure Jack was what she'd get.

His dad wore a suede sport coat, his usual Western shirt with its snap-buttons, and a big bolo tie. The tie had a silver buffalo at front and center, with a fist-sized chunk of turquoise stone. This was a sartorial travesty of such magnitude that it rendered his butler barely able to speak.

The bell rang. The butler glided toward the front door in his black and white penguin suit. At least *he'd* risen to the occasion.

"How do you do, Lady Pemberbrooke? It's very nice to see you. May I take your coat?"

Jack's brows yanked together. Who was this? He'd invited Alma for dinner. She wasn't his psychiatrist anymore; they could see each other socially. He got up and walked into the entrance hall.

Alma was there, graying hair neat and tidy, wearing a pale blue woolen dress and jacket that emphasized her blue eyes and fine English skin. His major domo whisked away her coat and bag. She looked lovely, softer than she had while working with him. She wore a refined necklace of sparkly blue and white stones. After hearing the title 'Lady Pember-brooke,' he suspected they were real.

"*Lady* Pemberbrooke?" he asked.

"Yes, Jack. Members of the nobility work and do things besides running charity auctions. And we go to school and educate ourselves." She smiled and held out her hand.

"You knew me by my professional persona, Alma Bertrand-Elverton, MD. I am also Lady Alma Bertrand-Elverton of Pemberbrooke. Pemberbrooke is our ancestral estate. Not a large one. I work to augment its income, and to serve my country. Now, who is this interesting man?"

She turned to his father, who was lit up as if he'd swallowed a string of Christmas lights.

"I'm Jack Abercrombie, Sr., Jack's dad. Though, in the family, they call me Billy Jack. I like that better than Senior."

Jack was shocked. His father was called Billy Jack *only* by the family. He had invited Alma to dinner because he wanted to ask his father what he thought of her. He didn't trust himself to pick a woman after his unfortunate choice of Clarisse. He'd gotten his answer.

"How do you do, Billy Jack? May I really call you that?"

"I wouldn't have told you my nickname if I hadn't meant you to use it, ma'am." He would have tipped his hat, if he were wearing one.

They wandered toward the living room, but Alma spied Jack's big roping saddle.

"Oh, my goodness, is this yours, Jack?"

"Yes, ma'am. I put all that shine on the seat." The saddle was worn, obviously used for work. The leather was scuffed by lariats and brush, and shiny where Jack's jeans had rubbed it—as authentic as they came.

"Not really a saddle appropriate for fox hunting."

"If you jumped anything," he said, "you'd get that horn in your belly, but I've done lots of hunting in that saddle. Haven't we, Dad?"

"I'd say so, son. Elk, deer. Mountain lion. Raccoon once in a while."

Jack thought she'd grimace at the thought of blood sports, but she didn't.

"I take an elk every year, ma'am. Fills my freezer and feeds me until the next hunting season." His dad shrugged helplessly. "Of course, my freezer is already full of beef, so I had to buy another one."

She laughed at that. "Well, Jack and Billy Jack, perhaps you'll be able to come out to Pemberbrooke for the grouse season next year. I take it you both shoot?"

"Well, ma'am..."

"Please, call me Alma..."

"Well, Alma, I'll shoot anything that isn't already dead, but Jack takes a different view. More on the side of the game. I think he'd rather they could shoot back."

Jack blushed at that. His father had never put a positive spin on his hatred of hunting before.

Alma smiled. "We English are a bloodthirsty lot, I'm afraid. My family has never eschewed blood sports. Our country home looks like a taxidermist's dream, with trophies stretching over generations and species from around the world. I must confess to adding a few specimens myself."

"Well, Alma, seein' that's the kind of folk you come from, I'd like to invite you to my Montana huntin' ranch as soon as you can make it. You'll be able to add to your collection. Won't have to bring your own guns, either. I got plenty. They're gettin' so persnickety about firearms at the airports these days. I wouldn't want to put you through none of that. What do you shoot?"

"Almost anything," Alma smiled with real pleasure. "It's in the blood." She looked at Jack. "I'm sorry if I'm surprising you."

She was, very much, as she endeared herself to his father. "It's a cultural tradition."

"Dinner is served," the butler announced. He stood in the doorway like a black and white stagehand. Jack found him charming now. Alma's presence had changed everything, despite her revelations about her bloodthirsty inclinations.

Dinner went like that, with more chatting and finding out about one another.

The butler entered, bearing Alma's handbag. Distinctive bell chimes came from it.

"Excuse me, Your Ladyship. I would not intrude, but I know that these calls cannot be ignored."

She changed expressions immediately, jumping up to take her bag. Opening it and glancing inside, she said to the butler, "Do you have a secure area?"

Jack and his father looked at each other. He'd told his dad he'd invited a friend to dinner, not that she was someone he couldn't get out of his mind, despite being hustled by every female in Oxford. It was a strange experience. The more he worked out and dieted, the more intense the interest of the fair sex grew around him. But his interest in Alma never wavered, and now she was back.

"Who is she, Jack?" His father beat him to the significant question.

"She used to be my doctor. We, uh… she doesn't see me profession-ally anymore."

"Good thing; now you can… I'd say *spoon*, but that's too old-fash-ioned. Whatever people do now."

"You like her?"

"She's a dandy, son. You know I'm a great judge of cattle and horses; the same is true of people. You ever see a horse with a kind eye like that? That's the one to buy. And her conformation's not bad, either. Plus, she shoots."

Jack blushed. "Yeah. Let's not get ahead of ourselves. Clarisse could come back."

"Yeah, and antelopes may fly and it may rain Brillo pads. They told you to act like a single man for a reason, Jack."

"I know. She may already be dead." *And the marriage was dead long before.*

Alma wasn't smiling when she came back. Her face was white. "We need to talk. Is your study still secure?" He nodded and she headed for it with-out looking back.

Leaning against his desk, she didn't wait for them to be seated. "Something terrible has happened."

"Clarisse and the boys?" He could feel the blood drain from his face before he saw her nod.

"Yes, Jack." She turned to his father. "I understand from Jack's staff that he has informed you of what's going on with his family."

"Yes, Alma, he has. What's up?"

"A dead body was discovered inside Clarisse's computer at the base."

"No!"

"How?"

"Are you familiar with the configuration of the computer?" Neither man was. "I'm not, either. Ron described it as a huge cube about two hundred feet on each edge. The center is a bored-out cylinder, a big one, perhaps fifty feet across. A naked man's eviscerated body was found on the floor in the middle of the cylinder. The corpse had been viciously mutilated."

"What does it mean?"

"That's hard to know, Jack. I was talking to Ron…"

"Why didn't he call *me*?"

"He can't. All of his calls are monitored. He could only reach me through mutual, trustworthy friends. You won't hear about this officially. The boys got out of control a while back while he was watching them. Made quite a brouhaha. Ron was demoted and pulled off their case."

"What they did on Clara Dr.?" Jack barely sat in his chair. He wanted to run for the next plane stateside.

"It really put them and Ron in the soup. They're locked up now." She shook her head vigorously. "It's so stupid. They are the best researchers we've got in trying to figure out where Clarisse is and how to get her back. Ron told me they've created a device that allows them to communicate with someone there. They were able to hear and see part of the attack on their computer screens.

"And then the computer techs found the remains this morning."

For a moment, she couldn't go on, but straightened up and forced herself to explain the rest.

"The murder scene was lifted from the other computer, the whole thing, set up exactly as it stood on the other side, down to blood and fingerprints. Clarisse's fingerprints were found on the murder weapon, a very large knife. This was a place created by a psychopath as a venue for killing. I know something of this professionally. I've been called in as an expert to try to unravel what some of these maniacs are thinking and where they'll strike next. Serial killers kill according to a ritual. They perform acts in a specific order and have particular objects they need to utilize to satisfy their blood lust. This scene bore all the marks: a bed, shackles, various instruments of torture. This place was created to kill someone—Clarisse. She managed to fight off her attacker and kill him. She also did a lot more than that." Alma sighed, shaking her head.

"It's a nightmare," Jack said.

"Yes. Jack, she's dead."

"What?!"

"There was so much of her blood at the scene that she could not have survived. It trails off, as though she tried to escape, but the trail stops abruptly. Her body wasn't in evidence, but without top-notch medical care and many transfusions, she inevitably would have perished. I'm so sorry."

He sobbed while Alma and his dad held him. "Poor, poor Jack. You didn't do any of this. You've been caught in a drama far bigger than you."

Her phone rang again and she went to the secure port on the desk. "Okay. I see. Do you have plans, Ron? What is the next step? ... All right."

Alma turned back to the two men in the room. "DNA testing has revealed the body to be that of Óskar Erland, MD, PhD."

"That's impossible. He died years ago. What was he doing in a set-up like that?"

"Setting it up, most likely."

"He was already dead."

"Yes, I recall reading of his death. A famous man."

"A terrible man."

"Yes. His body appears to be in its late forties."

"That's impossible. He was in his eighties or nineties when he died."

"Not when he died the second time, Jack. Whoever our adversary is, brought him back from the dead, reduced his age by forty or fifty years, and set him up in an outpost of another world. We're talking about supernatural power. Power we cannot conceive of or control.

"But that isn't our problem. They're going to destroy the computer completely. No trace. Clarisse is almost certainly dead. They think the point of entry to the alternative universe is the computer at Moffett Field."

"Why haven't they done something to try to save her? Used the computer to get to her?" Jack cried.

"I don't know," Alma said. "Ron was very hurried. She found portals to other worlds, but her staff doesn't seem to know how to replicate her work. Frankly, they seem incompetent."

"Great. Incompetent fools break up my family, and can't use my wife's carefully documented work to find her. Or even use her computer. What about the cloud? Everything's on the cloud, now, isn't it? Why destroy the machine?"

"*Nothing* about that machine is on the cloud. It's far too easy to hack.

"Jack, you don't know very much about secret projects, but I do know something. The government backs projects verging on insane because they think they have strategic or military value. Clarisse's project was in that class, Jack. You know her funding was always precarious.

"I'm not like Ron or one of the people truly in the clandestine world. Your staff, for instance. I do know shutting programs like Clarisse's down and disavowing their existence happens all the time. They're covered up, disguised, given a clever cover story that the press covers exhaustively. Everyone buys it. Like the story about the tsunami killing your family." Jack choked at her words.

"You know what I'm saying is true—a mysterious explosion that takes out half a block somewhere. There's a deadly fire, or a plane crash. You read about them all the time, and never the real reason they happened. I expect that there'll be an explosion in the hangar at the base and the computer will be destroyed. After a cursory investigation, that will be it."

"But Alma..."

"No, Jack. With that much blood loss, Clarisse is dead. Even if they could figure out how to use the computer to save her, there's nothing to save. Given that, the reasoning of the powers that be is close the door to the other world, and our adversaries will be locked out."

"Which is erroneous—if they could grab Clarisse without the computer, they don't need the computer to reach our universe. They can do it at any time, however they did with her."

"But you and I aren't the government. They undoubtedly have more intelligence than we do that they're not telling *anyone*. Maybe they've been behind the whole thing. Or perhaps some senator has backed this project and needs to cut his losses before the public finds out. Maybe he or whoever really is making decisions here, setting you up and all, has *another* pet project that they want to concentrate on. We don't really know who is in charge or what the top level is."

She touched his forearm. "Jack, this is the shadow world. Nothing will be fully explained. Each of us just knows what he or she needs to know. And no one may know everything. Ron's superiors have ordered them to destroy the computer. They think, by doing that, they'll seal the portal and the bad guys will stay out. Earth will no longer be in danger. And, as a matter of fact, since no one really knows what happened to Clarisse, was there ever a problem?" She looked at them then—a droll, sad expression on her face.

"What about Jimmy and Ricky?"

"They're being held prisoner on the base. Their new handler is a monster. When Ron found out who they'd assigned to the boys, he knew what the official solution was. When the machine is destroyed, they will be 'neutralized.' Killed."

"We've got to save them!"

"Yes. But Jack, you've forgotten one person."

"Who?"

"You." She walked toward the library door. It opened. The kindly butler stood in the doorway, aiming a shotgun at them. Other household members clustered behind him, similarly armed.

"I'm afraid you'll be staying here, Your Ladyship and gentlemen."

FORTY-TWO

ELIAS

E L THREW HIMSELF at the door to their room. He yanked on the knob and shook it. Hit the door with a chair. Kicked it. Tried to pry it open with a knife. He pulled out every piece of equipment in Clary's briefcase and tried to open the door with it. Then he tried using the stash of weapons and electronic stuff they'd smuggled in from the office, all to no avail.

Nothing worked. Óskar Erland was going to kill her. El had been trying to tell Clary something since he'd found out, but she'd been so crazy he couldn't get her to listen. Erland had been running amuck with the girls in the hall, fucking as many as he could and beating them when he was done. He had threatened to kill them if they told, and that kept them quiet. Until he killed one and disguised it as an experiment gone wrong. One of those he'd raped had come to El, telling him what was going on.

Pops wouldn't care, but he would care if Erland killed Clary. El yelled to the corners of the room, trying to get Pops to come.

"You've got to hear me. I know you don't like me, but it's *Clary*. You've got to save her. He'll kill her."

No answer. Normally, Pops' vile voice would intrude any time he wanted.

But not tonight. Erland must have told Pops some lie to keep him away. Like Clary wanted him and that he should leave them alone for the night. That Elias would scream and yell, but not to listen, that he was just jealous.

Clary could get pregnant again. They had healed her so she could be bred. Regardless of what he told Pops, that's what Erland would do. But he would kill her afterward. Pops didn't know him. El's intuition flamed hot on that one, along with what he'd learned from Jimmy's mindspeak. The brothers had pierced the darkest secrets of the famous scientist and found that he was a pervert and a murderer.

"Clary! Clary!" He drooped in front of the door, his forehead touching it. Giving up.

A shudder ran through him. He stood up absolutely straight as though he was doing one of Clary's yoga postures. Breathing deeply, he raised his hands over his head, palms touching. Another breath, and he lowered them, reached for the door's handle, turned it, and walked into the corridor.

Then he ran. The corridor blurred as he flashed through it, arms keeping rhythm to his legs. His shadow on the wall was a blur, a barely visible silhouette. He ran.

The elevator doors were open. They were in the computer; he could feel it. Elias dashed out of the elevator, across the bridge, and into the computer's giant heart. He could smell Erland's disemboweled entrails before he could see his body. One glance took in the bed, the old iron shackles for hands and ankles. The prods and electric devices. Erland might have planned on sex with Clary, but he'd have tortured and killed her eventually.

"Oh, Clary." The area around the disemboweled body and the bed were drenched with blood. She laid in a red pool a few steps from the bed. She'd bled so much that there wasn't much more in her still form. "Clary."

He picked her up and *ran,* shooting through the corridors.

They were back in their room seconds later. Elias looked at her. She needed blood. He had blood. He carried her into the bathroom and searched the cupboards. What did they have that he could use to put his blood into her? There was a bottle of water with a nozzle. He grabbed it, dumped the water out, and laid Clary on the floor. No razor to create an opening in her flesh. He went into the bedroom and got one of her ultra-sharp knives.

"I'm sorry, Clary." He made an incision on a vein in her neck and inserted the small end of the nozzle into it. Elias lay next to her and cut the vein inside his elbow, positioning the other end of the bottle cap over the cut in his arm. He let his blood trickle into her. "I'm a universal donor, Clary. For anything; you don't even have to be human."

He gradually drifted lower onto the floor, eyelids drooping. *Stop,* something in his mind said. *Don't give her too much.*

Maybe it was already too much.

When he woke up, El was lying in the bed. His arm was bandaged and so was Clary's neck. She had a scar along her side, a recent one, bright red and wide. It indicated a deep, large cut. But it was healed. He felt dizzy and weak, but so happy. She was alive!

"Clary?" She didn't answer, but her breathing was full and normal. She was alive. He had no idea how this miracle had happened. He leaned over her, intending to kiss her forehead.

"Elias! Dr. Hull!" Pop's enraged face erupted into their room. "Where is Óskar Erland? What have you done with him?"

El pulled himself on top of Clary. She was wearing nothing but the little panties that went with her dress. "I haven't done anything with him. I'm finally doing what you wanted me to, and you break in here." He moved his hips against Clary's leg. "Get out of here and let me finish."

"No... Oh. What are you doing?"

"What do you think?"

"Oh, good. Carry on. We'll search for Dr. Eland. He said he wanted some private time with her. We obliged him. And then he disappeared. I thought he wanted *her.*"

"He's probably with one of the girls in the hall. Ask them about him. He's sort of a dine and dash kind of guy."

"What does that mean?"

"Drill 'em and kill 'em."

"I don't understand."

"Think about it, Pops. Leave us alone."

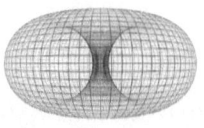

FORTY-THREE

LADY ALMA

"**W**HAT IN HEAVEN'S *name do you think you're doing?*" Alma exclaimed.

"What we've been ordered to do," the butler stood stiffly, the shotgun's stock nestled into his shoulder.

"You're going to kill a famous author and Oxford fellow? A well-known American cattleman? And a member of the nobility? Are you *idiots*? Do you think the world won't notice our absence?"

The servants shifted, and glanced at each other, but did not lower their arms. "Not you, Lady, just the others," came from the back.

"Oh, that's wonderful. I'm so grateful. But you think *I* won't talk about this? I do not report to the same people you do. Do you think that I'm here without anyone knowing where I am? I just spoke to Her Majesty's secretary. He's undoubtedly watching this place."

The silence in the hall became deeper, and a tad less ominous. Alma continued.

"Gunshots will attract every copper in Oxford. The police will break in with fanfare and tape off the area. The public will become aware that something's happening. All the recording devices installed in this house by your employers will broadcast to your various handlers. You do come from the world's most elite intelligence forces, yes?" The servants rocked back the tiniest bit.

"Those agencies wouldn't care if you killed a couple of civilians, I suppose. Whose orders are you following? Official channels? Or black-ops? Our *Sovereign* ordered *me* here."

Alma spoke with utter calm. Her upper-class English accent lent gravitas to the consequences implied in her words. The crowd facing her seemed to deflate; they didn't drop arms, but were on the verge of it.

Seeing her opening, Alma shot across the study at the butler, who raised his shotgun's barrel to keep it centered on her. The whites of his eyes flashed in terror, as though he was the one running at a loaded gun. She grabbed the barrel from underneath, yanked the firearm from his hands, and whipped the gun's stock into his temple. The butler fell, leaving her facing the remaining staff. She raised her weapon.

"If I shoot, I won't kill all of you, but the scatter will wound the majority. Your various keepers' alarms will go off, and this place will be a circus in minutes.

"Put down your weapons." She took a step closer, facing an assortment of pistols, shotguns, and automatic weapons. "There's no need for this." Lifting her chin, Alma addressed the air, "Whoever is listening, it's time to intervene. Your Lordship, I need help."

"There's no help, Lady Alma." Jack's chauffer, Albert Jordan, moved forward. He raised his pistol, firing three shots past Alma into the study. A silencer took care of the report.

She fired one barrel of her shotgun directly at him, then turned and fired the other in a wide swath at the servants. They dropped, some screaming, some beyond making a sound. She moved quickly forward, taking the chauffer's pistol, while the butler groveled at her feet, hands raised.

"Put down your weapons," she said, holding the pistol expertly. None of them could hear her. The shotgun blasts had deafened them, and her. But her words registered. "If any of you move, I'll finish what *you* started." Then she startled, realizing what had happened, "Oh, God. *Jack!*"

Alma turned around. Billy Jack was bent over his son, keening.

"Oh, my boy. They killed my boy." Jack lay on the floor, gaping wounds in his chest.

She shouted, "Billy Jack, hit the panic button on the desk. Help will be here in an instant." She turned back to the wounded servants. Dare she go to Jack? Or would the ones who weren't mortally injured come after her?

As she pondered, the erstwhile cook struggled to her knees and tried to raise her weapon. Alma cut her down.

The front door opened and a group of people clad in black slipped in silently. Their heads were hooded and they carried even more weapons than the servants. She told their captain an edited version of what had happened, as operatives picked up the wounded and dead, removing their weapons and whisking away blood and other signs of mayhem.

As Jack's onetime household staff—the ones who could walk—were marched off by the hooded rescuers, Alma darted forward.

"Wait!" She approached the butler. "Why did you to this? I thought you were Jack's friends."

"No friends in this business, My Lady. They're closing the operation down. That meant he and his father had to go. And you, if need be. I serve my country."

"You're a sociopath."

"Perhaps, but I still serve my queen."

"No, you don't! Her Majesty would never countenance this!" Alma railed.

"Well, Your Ladyship, we did what we did to save the world. He *threatened to expose* our activities. No one does that and lives to talk." He nodded at the office where Jack's body lay and then went off into the night, one of the black-clad sleuths stalking on each side.

The masked captain approached her. "We'll need to debrief you, Your Ladyship."

"Indeed. I will fully reveal everything I saw. However, I report to the Lord Secretary. First, I must care for Mr. Abercrombie, Sr. He is distraught over the death of his son. Dr. Abercrombie suffered a fatal heart attack before any of this happened."

"Are you sure?"

"Yes, I am an MD, officer. Dr. Abercrombie had a heart condition; his records will show that. He collapsed in the study before any of this occurred. His father has been with the body the whole time. He saw nothing. They were uninvolved."

"All right. I'll leave the body with you, Your Ladyship, if you're sure the death was not the result of this…" A gloved hand took in the hallway. The commando moved toward the study door, wanting to see the body for himself. She moved faster, closing it.

"Nothing to see, Commander. Just a dead man with the blue skin coloration that marks a heart attack." She looked him in the eyes. "If you'll excuse me, I need to call His Lordship, Her *Majesty's* secretary. Thank you for your assistance."

She saw him out, and then reopened the study door.

"Oh, no. Oh, no." Jack's chest was torn open, his heart and internal organs visible, blood splattered everywhere. The bullets must have exploded on impact; they could have killed him many times. Jack had never had a chance of survival. She could do nothing for the man she'd hoped would share her life. Except what she was going to do.

Alma knew what would happen to Jack if her story didn't stand. They would take his body and rip it to shreds, looking for evidence of *something*. Some high tech something implanted in him. Something related to Clarisse. They'd take every shred of anything in this house that he had touched and it would never be seen again.

He had told her he was working on a new manuscript. A new book perhaps, stories. Poetry. Those would be seized and destroyed. She couldn't let that happen.

Alma wanted to give in to the horror and grief she felt, but she wouldn't. Not now. She pulled out her encoded cell phone.

"Yes, Your Lordship. That is exactly what happened." She told him the truth, nothing left out. "They'll need to leave immediately."

They spoke a while longer, Alma taking directions and filling in information. "Thank you, Your Lordship. As you say."

Billy Jack was on his knees, bent over his son. When Alma approached, he reared up, raging at her.

"What are you, Alma? A spy?" Billy Jack stood next to his son's corpse, his face red and contorted, streaked with tears that seemed etched into his face. "Are you here on business? What was my son to you? A *case?*"

She stood across from him, not daring to look down at the body. "Billy Jack, no matter how it seems, I am *not* here on business. I expected a wonderful meal with you and Jack. I expected to get to know you better." Her powder blue eyes fixed on his, brows contracted with concern. "I didn't know any of this would happen."

"Are you here because you were watching and reporting on Jack?" Billy Jack's chest rose and fell; he blinked his eyes as though tears stung behind them.

"I am a spy, of sorts. I am a noblewoman, and the nobility is pledged to serve our queen. I have skills that Her Majesty can use. She employs me for sensitive matters. Your son, for instance."

"Why Jack? Why not the kids and Clarisse?"

"Billy Jack, you must realize that Jack was as important in the scheme of all this as either Clarisse or the boys."

"Why?"

"Because they love him. Eventually, they'd come to him. He was the magnet. Our covert ops knew all about their vacations with you and how you loved each other." Her face felt drawn. She couldn't tell him that they had photos of them fishing and hiking at his ranch. Satellites could photograph anything above ground.

"But why are you here? Now?" Billy Jack roared. "You and your stinking country and your fancy accent. Why did you go after my *boy*?" His clenched fists and rigid stance said he wanted to kill her.

Alma began to tremble. Her lips first, and then her face, shoulders, everything.

"I fell in love with him! I wanted to marry him!" she burst out, tears filling her eyes and quickly bridging their lower lids. Rivulets tracked down her face just as they did his own. "Oh, God! They killed him." She bent at the waist, as though she might break, but she didn't. She stood tall and spoke, rapid-fire.

"Billy Jack, Her Majesty and His Lordship the secretary sent me to be your son's physician when he was so ill at the beginning. Uprooted from his family, finding out so many secrets, was too much for him. I *am* a well-known psychiatrist. Her Majesty was particularly interested in your son's well-being."

"Why?"

"I'm not at liberty to discuss what my sovereign says privately, but let us say that many people have read your son's works."

"The Queen of England has read my Jack's books?"

"I'm not at liberty to say, Billy Jack." As she spoke, Alma nodded her head. "She wanted him to be well cared for. I did care for him, too well. I fell in love with him and recused myself from his case. I thought that would be the end of it.

"But it wasn't. Since I wasn't his psychiatrist, I could see him socially. And, he invited me to dinner! A new start. That's the only reason I'm here." Her mouth puckered and her eyes blinked convulsively. She seemed to shrink. "I really hoped that we would..."

Billy Jack placed a hand on her shoulder, and gave it a little pinch. "I knew. The way he acted when he said you were coming to dinner told me that you were someone special."

"Oh, God," she fell on her knees, examining Jack's torn and bloody form. "Oh, look what they did to him! How could they do that! He was the most wonderful, talented, kind man I've ever known. Oh, God. Look what they did to... my Jack."

She took off her jacket and placed it over his chest, covering the gaping wounds. "They shot him like a dog. Oh, my God." Billy Jack bent over to comfort her, but she jumped to her feet.

"We have to work fast. Pick up every scrap of paper that has anything in his handwriting on it. Any scribbles." She moved around so fast, picking up his calendar, note pads. "He liked to work in pen—'first drafts,' he said. Scribbles might be important. Get it all, they'll destroy it. He was writing something new, he told me." Then she grabbed Jack's laptop, iPad, a handheld voice recorder, and whatever other electronic devices she could find, and stuffed them in a backpack.

"They'll be here soon. We have to make it look like a heart attack."

"Why?" Billy Jack was bewildered.

"Because they'll take his body and all of his work, everything, and destroy them if this is seen as part of a covert op. You'll never see them again. You won't get to bury Jack; you'll get nothing. They'll say the body was lost.

"If we're going to get you home to bury Jack's remains in peace, it has to look like what I said was true. You had nothing to do with this, in fact, and don't know what happened. You were with your son, in this room, grieving.

"Go upstairs and pack his things, Billy Jack. But bring me a suit and everything he'd wear for a dinner party first. See if you can find more of his writing or anything pertinent upstairs."

Alma dashed around, removing Jack's bloodstained clothes, padding his body with layers of towels to keep any uncongealed blood from betraying her story. She and Billy Jack wrapped his bundled torso in a plastic shower curtain and dressed him in a suit. Tears dropped from her eyes, but she did not sob. She cleaned up the floor like an accomplished housekeeper and threw the bloodstained clothes in the fire.

Alma went to the door when it rang. Billy Jack watched, ashen-faced as uniformed men arrived.

Someone handed a folder to Alma and said, "Dr. Bertrand-Elverton, please sign this death certificate and we'll let you go on your way."

They placed Jack into a body bag, and then into a limousine waiting outside. The limo didn't block the traffic; the street was barricaded. People piled up at the barricade, wondering what was going on. Billy Jack took out the vial of pills he'd carried since his own heart attack and slipped one in his mouth on the sly. He thought he pulled it off without anyone seeing.

"Will you be okay?" Billy Jack asked Alma. They drove through the night. "We headin' for an airport?" Blackness surrounded them. She nodded. "You gonna be okay after all of this?"

"Yes. His Lordship will help me." Her shoulders rose and fell, shaking. "I killed two people tonight, maybe more. 'In Her Majesty's service,' as they say." She patted her eyes with a handkerchief. "Oh, God, why did this happen…"

They drove for a while, and then Billy Jack spoke. "I doubt we'll see each other again, Alma. Tell me about you and my son."

Then she broke, but not entirely. *Stiff upper lip*, Billy Jack thought. He liked it. She'd make a good rancher's wife. Tough.

"I told you what I wanted. I hoped that one day... things would work out so that..."

"You got married," Billy Jack said the words. She nodded. "Good. Jack never went with Clarisse, smart, rich, and beautiful as she was. Her family thought we weren't good enough for her and they never appreciated him worth a damn."

"That's not true! He was wonderful, and the music of his soul! His words. Oh, how could anyone not appreciate that? I fell in love with him, Billy Jack. Crazy old Englishwoman that I am. He was classy enough for *anyone*."

Billy Jack's face surprised him by splitting into a grin, but his chest was out of his control, leaping with breaths that came convulsively. "Alma, I just met you. But I would have *loved* to have you in the family, even if it meant that Jack and Clarisse, God bless her, split. Any English Lady who could cold-cock that butler like you did with that shotgun is worthy of Oklahoma! The whole U.S.A.!"

They wept silently, leaning their shoulders into each other, grieving.

"Oh, shit!" Billy Jack sat up.

"What?"

"I forgot something. I've got to stop something. Right now. Can I get a call through to my lawyer from this car? One that's not bugged?"

"Yes, use my cell phone."

Jack got through to his lawyer. "You've got to stop the sale of the ranch in Montana," he said. "Stop it right now. Tell Will I made a mistake. I need it for my family. Tell him I'll..." He searched for a word, "... *brief* him fully when I get home. He'll understand. I'm on my way."

He turned to Alma when he got off. "Lord have mercy, I almost made a huge mistake. Those boys will need that ranch." She looked at him blankly.

Should I tell this black-ops woman the truth? Billy Jack thought. He was a fine judge of horseflesh and every other living thing. Everything about Alma said she was true-blue. *Besides, if these fuckers are what they seem to be, they already know about my ranches.*

He told her about his working ranch in Oklahoma and his real ranch in Montana, where his heart lived. "It's in the mountains, and it's big—twenty-five thousand acres, almost. I keep it the way God made it. Used to go out and hunt and fish there, ride through the forest. Jack and his family came out for a few weeks every summer. Best times of my life." He wiped his eyes.

"But they haven't been out much in the last few years. The ranch is a responsibility. Not too much expense; I paid it off years ago, but it's a responsibility. And it's lonely by myself. Those boys loved it more than any place on Earth. And I love them.

"That's why I didn't take my neighbor's offer when he first made it. All those memories. Mostly summer. Damned cold up there in the winter. My neighbor kept pushing to buy the place, but I figured I'd hold onto it. I don't need the money. That's one thing the Abercrombie Blue Tomorrow bulls done for me. Set me up good. Finally, he made such a good offer that I took it."

"I see," Alma said.

"But I think I need to be there now. The deal isn't signed off. I can still back out. That's why I think I'd better go home. My neighbor doesn't need my ranch; he's already got four hundred fifty thousand acres."

"Who owns four hundred fifty thousand acres in Montana?"

"Will Duane."

"*The* Will Duane? The richest man in the world?"

"Former richest man in the world. Still damn rich. Didn't used to be my neighbor, but he bought out everyone between over the years. Must be planning on taking over the state. I've gotten to know him pretty good. Taught him to fish. He's a terrible fisherman, but it slows him down some. We spent some time on the river, talking about life. Both of us having lost a lot; me, Jack's mother. Him, pretty near everything.

"I think he can help me with something. Something he knows how to do, and maybe *only* he knows how to do. But my ranch belongs in the Abercrombie family, waitin' for those boys to come back. An' their mom.

"I'm going to take Jack back there and bury him. I can see the spot now, out on the meadow where the river forks. That's where I need to be. Something's going to happen soon, I can feel it." He felt that stabbing ache in his chest, then fished a tablet out of his pocket. He could take another. He needed them.

"You have a heart condition?" Alma asked.

"Jus' a little one. These pills keep 'er down."

"I need to check you in the airport…"

"No, you don't. I don't care if your tests say I'm going to die in ten minutes, *nothing's* going to keep me from going home. I need to be in Montana now. I don't know how I'm going to get there with Jack…" Tears had been falling all this time, so the gush that came then wasn't much different.

"Let me make a call, Billy Jack," Alma patted his arm and smiled. "We're heading to an RAF base," she said when she got off the line. "You'll be taken from there to Montana. Many people loved your son, Billy Jack. You have friends in high places. They'll take care of you."

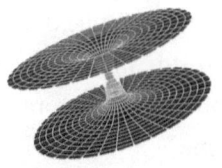

FORTY-FOUR

FREEDOM EQUALS NOTHING LEFT TO LOSE

R ICKY FROZE. HIS eyes froze. Hands, feet. Breath. The scream arose around him, but he bit it back. Choked it down. They'd hear if he or Jimmy made a sound. He lunged for his brother and they grabbed each other, pawing, hanging on. They knew the instant it happened.

They grappled like that, tears bursting forth. Silently. Cries. Screams. Shrieks. All mum.

"They killed Dad."

"We're next, Jimmy. We've got to get out of here." The keypad on their door engaged. Someone was coming in. The boys sat next to each other on the bed, rigid.

Johnny Herbert, their keeper, walked in. He saw that they had been crying and offered no comfort. "Your mother's dead. The sooner you accept that, the better off you'll be. She's dead and this research is terminated. We'll be moving you tomorrow."

He smiled viciously. "New place. Some of Óskar Erland's students heard about you being here when they came to get his body. They know all about the experimentation done on you years ago—Erland was in charge. They want to see how their new instruments measure your *brilliance.*

"That old guy getting killed made the brass lighten up on who knew you were here. The world will get something useful out of you after all."

Johnny Herbert's narrowed eyes and tight face said that he suspected they had lots to do with Erland's death. He walked out without another word.

"They don't know Dad's dead," Jimmy whispered. "He would have said something. We have to get out of here before they find out. They could do *anything* to us if we had no one."

"Yes," Ricky said, "but we also have to figure out how to save El, and what happened to Mom. We saw her fall. She might not be dead. Maybe El was able to keep her from dying." Ricky's mouth tightened. *Maybe we still have a mom.*

I've tried to contact El. Nothing. Jimmy mindspoke.

Did you try the game, if you can't get him directly?

Yes, with no results. But that could just mean he's not in the office.

Send him code to pick up, right away.

I already have, Ricky.

Let's work on something else until El answers. We have to think or we'll go nuts. What else do we need to handle to get Mom back here?

We need to understand why they used two steps instead of just grabbing Mom, Jimmy communicated. *I've been thinking about it. I bet it's for calibration—the first step, you move someone to make sure you've got the right place and time. They sent El to Palo Alto with the house on Clara Dr. as his target, though the time and place wasn't quite right. Then when he was there, they grabbed Mom and sent her to the same place.*

How do we do that?

I have no idea, but we moved a dead person from one computer to the other. I bet we could do it with a living person.

But we're stuck in a cell that's I don't know how many stories underground. The computer is in the hangar on the base at ground level. It's guarded by half the Navy and we can't access it. Ricky was hopeless, almost to the point of being paralyzed. He couldn't fathom his father's death. Their world had collapsed.

If we moved Mom and El and anyone else in their computer, the soldiers on the base would think they were aliens and kill them. We couldn't stop it.

Could we move the computer somewhere where we'd have access and control?

I suppose. We could retrieve the device we planted in our computer and move the other computer with it. But getting that device back would be almost impossible. The computer's huge. Where would we put it that we can access?

Ron's dojo?

The base is right next door. That's not far enough. And the dojo isn't big enough.

To Mom's garden? That's big. If we were fast...

Yeah. Right. I'm sure the neighbors wouldn't notice a two-hundred foot, flashing cube materializing in our backyard. The cops would be there so fast.

Well, what?

I don't know. Why don't you try El again?

El, are you there? Jimmy lay on his bed and sent thought messages to El. They'd been able to communicate this way easily in the past. Jimmy did reach El, but he was barely able to talk. Jimmy wondered what had happened to him, and if he even understood what Jimmy was saying.

I'm sick, El communicated, his mental voice thin and vague.

What's the matter?

I'm dizzy. I feel like falling down.

Where are you?

In the hall. I could barely make it here.

Is Mom alive?

Yes.

She's okay?

She's screaming at everyone. Something happened to... His "voice" faded. *We attack tomorrow. You need to get ready. We will go to the other computer... your computer... there...* His psychic voice was barely discernable.

Is Mom sick?

No. She's crazy.

El, Mom can be tough sometimes, but if you're sick, she's the best. Tell her you're sick. Show her it's real. Throw up or something.

"El, get over here," Clary shouted at him. She'd been furious with him since waking up. "This is not the time to lollygag around."

"I'm sick, Clary. I don't feel..." As if to prove how sick, he dropped slowly to his knees and fell on his side, eyes rolled back.

She ran to him, feeling his pulse and counting his respiration rate. "What happened to you? Why didn't you tell me? You're white as a sheet. You look bled out." She jumped up and pointed at some others.

"You and you, carry him to our room and put him to bed. No, I'll go, too. The rest of you, jog around the hall. Double-time!"

"Just a minute, Dr. Hull." Pops' ugly face scowled from the wall where it had been hovering. Elias could barely concentrate on what was going on, his vision and awareness wavering. "Don't think you can walk out while we're conversing." Pops' face practically shot flames of rage. He ogled the downed Elias from the wall, then continued speaking to her.

"I want to know what happened to Dr. Erland. You were the last to see him. You had dinner with him! Where is he!? There's no trace of him, anywhere! He is a valuable property, not some toy for your disposal. Where is he?"

"I don't know," Clary shouted at Pops' scowling visage. "I don't know what happened last night. I don't remember dinner with Erland. Or *anything*."

"You, Elias. Where is Dr. Erland? You must know."

El heard his name and struggled back to consciousness. "I was locked up. I don't know..." His eyes rolled back and he fainted for a few moments. When he awakened, an invisible giant seemed to grasp Clary by the ribcage, slamming her into the wall.

"Don't hurt her..." El was so weak he could barely speak.

The face, livid now, turned to him. "I'll hurt her whenever I want. And you, too, you stinking worm." Something slammed into El's belly. The air went out of him. He lay, gasping, while Pops turned back to Clary. Her body rose and slammed into the wall, again and again. El could hear her ribs snapping with each impact. Dull thuds told him she had internal damage.

All of her troops watched, aghast, too frightened to do anything.

"What's the matter with you, worms? Won't you fight for your mama? Well, you'll get the chance soon. The mission is *tomorrow*!"

A gasp went up. They weren't ready and they knew it. No one dared object. Clary lay on the floor near Elias. She tried to roll onto her hands and knees, and couldn't. Blood came out of her mouth.

"I *know* you did it, Dr. Hull. Whatever happened to Óskar Erland falls squarely on your shoulders. I blame you entirely. You've wanted to leave here since you arrived. And you will. You're going into the computer tomorrow. I'm sick of you."

He screamed at the humans, shaking the walls and causing the floor to tremble. "I don't care if you die on route or they shoot you the minute you walk out of the computer! I don't care if the computer blows up and kills all of you! You're storming the base. Tomorrow! That's it.

"And Dr. Hull, you arrogant ass, will be first on board. You've not performed to expectations on any level. *YOU HAVE FAILED, YOU IDIOT.*" He shook himself as though trying to regain control, and continued. "Anyone who tries to stay here, I will destroy. You're all dead. You humans are a waste of time. We should have taken your planet ourselves. We had the means. You are *failures. All of you! You will get what failures get!*" He noticed Clary and El on the floor. "Lock them in their room."

Elias opened his eyes. Clary lay next to him on her back. She grimaced in pain, but noticed him moving. "El, are you all right? You look so sick."

"I'm okay, Clary. What about you?"

"Not so hot, El. I'm really hurt."

"Where does it hurt?"

"The whole middle of me." Her head rolled to one side, a rivulet of blood escaping her lips.

"Let me look, Clary. Let me see how bad it is." She didn't fight him. A blue-black bruise covered her belly from the ribs down. Broken bones showed as indentations in her ribcage. The red trickle continued from her mouth. Her internal organs were ruptured and bleeding inside. She would die. "Oh, Clary."

She shook her head, something more important on her mind.

"El, what happened last night?" she whispered haltingly. "I was supposed to have dinner with Óskar Erland. I think I went. He told me something, but the rest... I can't remember anything. Did he do anything to me?"

He shook his head. "I was locked in here. I couldn't get out. I woke up in bed, sick."

"El, you're white as a sheet. Get some sleep. I need to sleep, too." She felt his pulse. He didn't feel himself slip into unconsciousness.

He was sleeping when he felt Jimmy calling to him urgently.

El, we've got to talk. How is Mom?

She's sleeping, Jimmy. Pops hurt her.

Oh, no. He hurt her? My mom?

Yes, Jimmy. He can hurt anyone.

Can you feel her pulse? Will she be okay?

El felt Clary's pulse. It was good and strong. He lifted her shirt, and the bruises and lumps in her ribs were gone. He didn't understand how that could be, but it had happened. *I think she'll be okay, but she needs to sleep.*

I need to sleep… Weariness came over Elias. Clary was well, but he wasn't.

Not yet, El. Something bad happened. The worst thing in the world. Jimmy couldn't hold back his tears. He dug at his weeping eyes furiously with his knuckles. "Damn it!" he said.

What's the matter?

They killed our dad. Don't tell Mom. She can't handle any more.

Oh. El was stunned. Jack was his rival for Clary, but he'd never wished him harm. He was part of El's fantasy about Clary and her lovely, idyllic family. He had studied photos of Jack almost as long as those of Clary and the boys. A father. Elias had no memory of a father. Jack was a good father. *I'm sorry. I don't…*

El, we're next. We've got to get out of here fast. They're going to do experiments on us. When do you think you'll be ready?

Tomorrow. We have to be. Óskar Erland disappeared from here. Pops blames your mom for it. He moved the mission to tomorrow. He doesn't care if we die. And we will die. If we try to stay here, he'll kill us. If the computer blows up, we'll die. If we go into the computer and everything works, they'll kill us when we get to your side.

We have to get you out of there today.

Yes.

Shit. We're not ready, either. We're working on it, but we have all these questions to answer. El? You there? Jimmy could feel his counterpart fading.

Yes... sick. El's voice was barely audible.

I'll make it fast. Why did they send you to that old Palo Alto first, instead of just getting my mom without you being involved?

I don't know. They told me she was my wife. They showed me pictures of your family. Clary was beautiful and so smart. And happy. I fell in love with her. All I could think of was if she would love me. When I was supposed to get your mom, they took me into a room. They told me to remember my life before and what I loved best. I remembered my mother. I felt how much I loved her and missed her. They told me go to my mother, and I did. They said Clary would be near the house with the red door.

Clary wasn't there. I searched for her. I didn't know how to get back or *to find her. Finally, I saw her. I told her I was taking her home. They said a portal would appear and we could go through it. When we found it, it went right into the hall.*

You didn't need the computer?

No, but I think you do to move more people.

Why?

There are one hundred and forty people in the hall. You need the computer to move that many.

But not for one or two. How do you think you moved?

I don't know. I'm dizzy, Jimmy. I'm sick.

You're going to be dead, El, and so are we, if we can't figure out how to get you out of there. How do you think you moved between realities?

I think it was because I missed my mother so much. I got to where she had been because I loved her. And with Clary, I loved her so much; I would have searched the whole world to find her.

El's end of the conversation died and Jimmy couldn't revive it.

"Let him sleep, Jimmy. He needs to. What can we figure out from what he said?" Ricky asked. Less than a minute later, both burst out with the answer.

"Love. That's it! Love powers the movement from one universe to another. That's why the two-step. One step to get him out of the hall—he jumped universes because he loved his mom. He loved our mom and attracted her to him because of that. His love pulled her from the portal on the path at the university to the phony Palo Alto. He attracted *her* to him. That's why the two-step.

"The power isn't physics or machines; it's love."

"And more, Ricky. It's El. El was the one who went, not anyone else. They could have picked anyone to get Mom, but it wouldn't have worked."

"She loved Alex Caldwell. El's energy must be like his. Like what you and I have. And her."

"They picked El because they knew they'd love each other so much that it could pull them from one world to another."

"Plus, they both have some other power. They're geniuses, but they have more than that. Personal power. Spiritual power. Why can she get people to do things and inspire them? And work so hard and be productive? How can she know what we're doing, no matter where we are?"

"She's got something, and so does he."

"And so do we and so did Alex."

"The way we get out of here is through love—and its power."

"The reason they need the computer to move more people is that there's no love involved. They're going somewhere because they're *sent*. Given orders, not looking for a soulmate. Or their mom."

They jerked at an unexpected sound. "Open the door, boys; it's time to go. They're moving you now." Johnny Herbert's hard, detached voice sounded from the speaker on the wall.

They manipulated a few controls and got ready.

"How did you lock the door from the inside?" the commando demanded when the door swung open. He stepped into the cell. He should have been sharper.

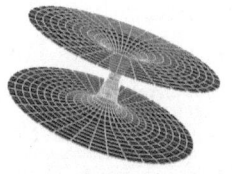

FORTY-FIVE

ON THE LAMB

J IMMY AND RICKY dragged themselves down the broad street
outside of Ron's dojo. They pulled wheeled suitcases and carried
backpacks and briefcases, heavier loads than two boys were likely
to ever pack. Two and three-story concrete buildings—tilt-ups—sat
back from the street, surrounded by lush landscaping. They could see
a freeway overpass ahead. A big sign for the Google Global Headquarters loomed above it. The whole scene looked more like a college campus
than the beating heart of Silicon Valley. Sweat trickled down the boys'
faces as they hustled as fast as they could, given their burdens.

"Don't feel bad about what we did to him, Jimmy. Think about what
he was going to do to us."

"I don't feel bad about it, Ricky. I just don't know how we're going to
do the rest."

"We'll do what Alma said."

Someone named Alma had called Jimmy via his computer. They
were suspicious of her; they'd never heard of her. They were old hands
at smoking out people pretending Ron sent them, though. Someone
who'd said he was from the State Department had been the first to try
to get through to them. He'd said that Ron gave him their contact info
and that they needed to talk to them, that it was a matter of national

security... but he hadn't known the passwords. They'd reported him. He was a black-ops drone.

"Why are you calling us instead of Ron?" Jimmy asked.

"Ron Weistheimer gave me the plan I'm going to share with you," said Alma. "I've known and worked with him for many years. Ron's phones and devices are monitored; he can't contact you in any way. But he *can* speak to me safely through mutual associates. And I can contact you through my own channels. Ron is not safe, boys. And this will be *our* only conversation.

"But first, the preliminaries. Your passwords and questions. The most important password," Alma said in her cultured British voice, "is 'a Hull lot of shaken goin' on.' That's your family's motto. July 27th is your parents' anniversary. Adolf, your grandfather Benjamin Hull's dog, peed on your Grandpa Billy Jack's trouser leg at your parents' wedding."

She had all the passwords and knew the answers to the secret questions. Their mother had insisted that they have such safeguards and use them.

Alma also had the keys. She said that she was a friend of their dad's from Oxford and that Papa Jack was on his way to meet them at their final destination. "It's a safe place, but I won't name it. This is supposed to be a secure connection, but..."

"Will he have our dad?"

They could hear her struggling to maintain her composure.

"Yes, he has your father's body with him. I'm so sorry, Ricky and Jimmy." They teared up, but so did she. They could hear it in her voice. "We need to get to work. Boys, can you escape your assassin and your cell?"

"Yes, ma'am."

"It's doctor, actually. Or 'Lady,' but call me Alma. Do whatever you need to do to escape. The fewer bodies, the better, but that can be dealt with. Get free. Can you get from where you are to Ron's office in his dojo?" With her high-toned voice, she sounded like someone on *Downton Abbey*, but who was talking about murder and black-ops.

"Yes," Ricky said. "There's a tunnel from Moffett Field to Ron's office in the dojo. We used it all the time."

"You can find your way to it?"

"Yes. We know all the combinations. Unless they've changed them."

"Then we can blow them." Ricky had to get into it. "I've made some plastic explosive."

"Not advised, Ricky. The place is loaded with detection devices. All right. When you get to the office, Ron has packed a number of cases with your mother's inventions, and things you've created while 'doing your homework' in his office. You have the patents on them. Taking them is not stealing. He also retrieved the linked devices that you installed in the computer that allowed Óskar Erland's body to be moved. He called them 'the jewelry boxes' and 'hair bows.' What you added recently."

The boys looked at each other. No one was supposed to know about those; they'd installed them on the sly.

"Ron is a master of the clandestine, boys. You would have a hard time getting past him. He noticed the devices when they were removing Erland's body, and snuck them out. They're in your pack. Do not lose the backpack. It's crucial to saving your mother.

"Take the bags—all of them—and your laptops, and walk casually out of the dojo's front door. If anyone is there, they will know you and won't question your presence. If they ask about the packs, say you're going camping.

"Here are step by step instructions for the rest of your journey. You'll go to the Fish Inc. terminal in San Jose. I want you to load an app on your cell phone. I've also got credit cards set up for you." She gave them the necessary numbers and downloads. "A car to carry you the next leg of the trip will be parked on the street, three blocks from the dojo. Good luck, boys!"

"Wait! Where is Ron?" Jimmy had to know.

She was silent for a moment. "Ron is gone. You will never see him again."

"Did they *kill* him?"

"No, Jimmy. He left. No one knows where he is, nor will they ever know."

When she got off the line, the boys looked at each other. "He's gone dark."

"Darker than anyone, ever."

Johnny Herbert wouldn't bother anyone for a long time. "I hope we didn't kill him," Jimmy said. "We've never done that before." They'd hidden Jimmy Herbert, as Alma had said, and then followed her directions exactly. It was a little more trouble than expected, but they ended up where they were supposed to be.

"There's the car up there with a driver."

"That's good. We're too young to drive."

"Legally."

A plain black sedan waited in front of the address Alma had given them.

"We're going to Fish Inc. at the private terminal at San Jose Airport." Ricky took the role of speaker in dealing with the driver.

"I didn't know you'd have all that stuff. That's a lot to put in the trunk." The driver's eyebrows scrunched together as if he was mad.

"We'll help you."

"No. I have to lift luggage. It's in the rules. You got heavy stuff, though." He hefted the backpacks and cases Jimmy and Ricky had hauled for three blocks after they'd walked out the front door of Ron's dojo. That didn't count the hundreds of yards through the tunnel to get to the dojo after they'd left their cell. But they hadn't gotten to the heaviest stuff until they got to Ron's office.

"This is *really* heavy." The driver raised a long case that might carry a guitar or automatic weapons.

"It's not so heavy. *We* carried it. How about if we give you a twenty-five percent tip?"

That put him in a better mood. But not for long. Traffic was at a dead stop.

"We've got to get there fast. A plane is waiting for us."

"This is as fast as I can go. If you want to get there faster, have a helicopter pick you up in that parking lot." His sour face said, "Fat chance, bozos."

"That's a great idea." This was Silicon Valley. Anything was possible. Ricky got on the cell phone that had been left for him in Ron's office. He looked up aviation services and ordered a helicopter. "They're coming. Pull over and wait."

"I'm charging you for this." Their driver looked to be in his mid-twenties; he had a buzz cut, and a roll of fat bulging over his collar. He wore an air of permanent irascibility.

"That's fine. Charge away," Ricky said.

The driver sat impatiently, yanking the wheel as if he wanted to pull it off. Finally, he spoke, "Who are you? Junior billionaires?"

"We're venture capitalists," Ricky answered. "This stuff is our product. We're heading for a presentation."

"Venture capitalists! You're kids! I have a PhD in engineering and six patents. I can't get a return email from anyone on Sand Hill Road! I'm twenty-five, too *old* to make it in Silicon Valley!"

He continued to swear, until his Über screen told him of his next ride. "You better make this fast or I'm gonna have to leave you here."

"It's okay; there it is!" Jimmy pointed at a small helicopter landing in the parking lot. Someone ran from it and grabbed a load of their stuff from the trunk. "This way, sirs." They pulled out the rest and started to hoof it for the chopper.

"Wait a minute; you gotta sign for this."

Ricky did while Jimmy headed for the waiting aircraft.

The Fish Inc. Terminal was at one end of the new private airport owned by Silicon Valley bigwigs. It was small, relative to the rest. A couple of planes were parked beside it. They were a bright blue, with a giant, crazy fish painted on the side—along the *whole* side. The fish was black, rimmed with bright-colored zigzag outlines. It had feet, huge fins, big bulging eyes, and a zany grin. 'Fish Inc.' was painted on its body.

"Look at it, Ricky. It's crazy."

"A privately held corporation." Ricky consulted his iPad about Fish Inc. "Mostly held by Will Duane. Do you remember him? He used to be the CEO of Numenon. Here's a picture from back when they kicked him out. That was 1999."

"The richest man in the world."

"Not anymore. How are we going to get to Papa Jack's from here?"

"I guess they'll pick us up. Alma's instructions didn't say anything more than to go to the Fish Inc. terminal."

A short, squat Native American man with long braids climbed down the stairs of the smaller jet. He had a jaunty gait and a big smile. His shirt was a bright turquoise, printed with fluorescent pink coyotes.

Ricky and Jimmy eyed him. *"Jimmy, that's Willy Fish,"* he whispered to his brother.

"The Willy Fish. He's super-famous. He invented the flat-screen TV and..."

"Every kind of wireless anything. He was ten years ahead of anyone when Will Duane found him at a Native American retreat. I've seen him talk on TED and in all the commercials."

"He's waving at us, Jimmy. Why?"

"Hi! Are you Ricky and Jimmy?" He had kind of a high-pitched voice for as big as his chest and body were. They nodded warily. "Come in; we're ready to go. Oh, I'm supposed to tell you all the passwords." Which he did. "Your mom is really smart. A lot of kids wouldn't get stolen if they had passwords."

The inside of the plane was more like a regularly luxurious, private jet plane. Jimmy and Ricky had never been in one, but they'd seen commercials on TV. In this one, all the seats were bright blue and had that crazy fish woven into the material.

They sat down where Willy indicated. "Buckle up." He was very cheery, but more than a little eccentric, starting with his clothes. "We're going to Will Duane's ranch in Montana. I'm going to work there for a while. Mr. Duane will be here in just a second. He really wants to meet you."

Someone they'd seen on dozens of magazine covers walked down the aisle. He'd been most famous a long time ago, but they were still writing books and making movies about him. It was Will Duane.

He took a seat opposite the boys. The jet was set up so that some seats faced each other while others were in rows. He had white hair and he looked about sixty.

"Hi, I'm Will Duane!" he held out his hand. They didn't take it. "Oh, I'm supposed to say 'a Hull lot of shaken goin' on' and July 27. Your parents' anniversary." He kept smiling, with his hand out. When they didn't respond, he reeled out more passwords.

Jimmy froze, smiling endearingly, and spoke into Ricky's mind. *The TV special said he was sixty-four when he left Numenon. That was 1999. He should be eighty-two.*

Their eyes widened. No way this man was eighty-two. They sunk down in their seats, trying to think of a way to get out of there.

"Um. Do you think we could just take Über to our grandfather's ranch? Montana isn't that far." Jimmy smiled his adorable child smile.

Will laughed. "You are as smart as Billy Jack said you were. I don't go out in public much for fear people will notice how I look. Don't worry about my age. We have more serious things on our plates." He also eyed their packs with the rabid interest of a fellow techie.

"We're about to take off, Mr. Duane. Seatbelts," a stewardess said.

"Always rules," Will noted. "Billy Jack—my neighbor and fishing buddy—just left New York. The Brits got him a ride to one of the bases there. One of my jets is bringing him to my place in Montana. He's got your dad's body with him, boys. I can't tell you how sorry I am."

No matter how cool they tried to be, they couldn't stop the tears.

"Take a moment, boys. I'm going to keep talking. We'll rendezvous at my ranch. Plans to retrieve your mother are underway. Chief being, finding something large enough to house the computer. We're working on it. We'll extract her tonight, if we can organize it. I've got a full lab at my ranch—top secret, *my* secret, not any government crap—and scientists. Plus, we've got you and Willy. If this thing can be done, we'll do it.

"You and your grandfather and your mom will stay at his ranch, though you're welcome at my place as long as you need it. Billy Jack is planning a..."

They were surprised when Mr. Duane stopped speaking and leaned forward, pulling out a handkerchief and wiping his eyes.

"I didn't know your dad well; I met him at the ranch a couple of times when you were little. But I read all of his books. To lose such a fine mind. And soul. You could hear his heart speak in his words. Billy Jack is planning a memorial service, when we... uh... have recovered your mother."

Or had failed to save her, the boys knew he was saying.

They flew silently for a while. Jimmy tried to do mindspeak with Elias, but with Elias. But he couldn't reach him. Had Pops beat him up? What was going on there? They needed to talk to someone they could trust; big things were happening.

"Do you boys fish?" Will said out of nowhere.

"No. Our mom doesn't allow it. Well, catch and release, maybe, but she doesn't even like that."

"Huh. Your granddad, Billy Jack, taught me to fish. I don't know your dad well, but Billy Jack's my fishing buddy. He says I'm the worst fisherman he's ever seen."

The boys laughed.

"I wanted to buy Billy Jack's ranch, but he wouldn't sell it. I understand why now, meeting you two. I wish I had grandkids. That's the only thing I can complain of in life." Will smiled, and they could see how hungry he was for family. "I'm rich and famous, but I'm just an old man, too." They looked at him. He *was* just an old guy, but a safe old guy.

"Do you know Alma?"

"No. I spoke to her once." They lapsed into silence, but a kinder silence.

Willy Fish started the conversation up again. Jimmy had heard people call him an *idiot savant,* but that seemed cruel. He was a tech's tech discovered by Will Duane at a spiritual retreat. His story was Silicon Valley history. He stared hungrily at their backpacks and the cases.

"Oh, please, Jimmy and Ricky. I know it's not polite, but can't I see one thing that you made?" Willy Fish said. Jimmy recognized the longing that he and his brother often felt. The urge, the *need* to see a beautiful piece of electronics.

"Can I show him what we used on Johnny Herbert? That's simple."

Ricky thought a moment. "Okay. We didn't want to hurt the guy who was guarding us, but we didn't want him to kill us or let them experiment on us. So when he came into our cell to take us away, I hit him with this." He took a small metal device from a backpack, what appeared to be a bulbous pistol.

"It looks like a taser," Willy said.

"It is. It puts the person out for as long as you set the dial. But when they wake up, they feel really happy."

"A taser that makes people happy?"

They nodded. "Yeah. It would be very good for police forces. They couldn't be accused of brutality. And they wouldn't hurt people."

"The police might want to use it on each other for job stress." Willy Fish held the device, turning it over in his hands. "This is really a good idea."

"It's fun. That's how we tested it. We set it as short as possible and tried it on each other."

"But we set it for eight hours for Johnny Herbert. As *long* as possible."

"And we made it as happy as it would go."

Will Duane burst out laughing. "I love it! Ingenious and nonviolent. But let's get you to your grandfather. We can talk about all this later."

Will's ranch was much different from Papa Jack's. Ricky and Jimmy had only seen it a few times when they were little, and it had changed a lot since then. They landed at his... well, it wasn't a landing strip so much as it was an airport, with big hangars, a real terminal, and control tower. They taxied toward a hangar. Another jet had just arrived, jockeying in front of a big metal building. That was Will's jet; their grandpa was in it. Will's jet wasn't painted in wild colors like the Fish Inc. plane. This was plain, off white, and had just a few numbers for identification.

Beyond the hangars and planes, they could see a huge log house, like a palace made of first growth pine. More buildings were beyond that— a village out in the woods. Who knew what else might be out there that they couldn't see; the place was so big. And grand. They'd heard about the 'Will Duane style.' This was it.

"It's Papa Jack," Jimmy said. Their grandfather walked down the ramp of the other jet to the tarmac, bent over and gray. He put on his Stetson, and then took it off again when the baggage compartment opened and men took out a casket.

"Oh, no! It's Dad!" The boys rocketed toward their grandfather. He directed the workers.

"Be careful. That's my son." The old man raised his hands up to the casket being lowered to a flatbed truck. The casket was magnificent—rich mahogany finished to a satiny sheen with fine bands of brass wrapping it. He saw the boys and held out his arms to them.

"Oh, boys. I never thought we'd see this day…" He embraced them. The three clutched each other. Everyone else looked away.

"Can we see him, Papa Jack?" they said it almost at once, when they could talk.

"Oh, I suppose. But not right now. I can't take any more. I want to bury him at my ranch, on the hill above the fork. He always loved it there." He circled them with his long arms. "Ain't that a nice coffin? His friend Alma gave him that. Goodbye present. Bull crap. But, it beat a body bag. I might have liked her, if she wasn't one of those black-ops piles of shit."

"Oh, Papa Jack." Ricky burst out. "They *killed* Dad."

"Yes, they did, son. Right in front of me. No way for him to get away." Billy Jack stood, teeth clenched. "No way for him to live, his heart shot out. Stinking sons of bitches!" The old man cursed his best, giving them a display of Oklahoma's finest blue vocabulary. "No good, useless assholes. Acting like life is a game. Like they can kill and get away with it. Break the law. Lock people up without due process. Torture and maim! Animals are better!

"I swear to you boys, I'm going to live to see you grown and doing fine. I'm going to…" He touched his chest and turned around, fishing out his pills and taking one. "Don't mind this. My ticker's good enough to see me through what I have to do.

"Damned sons of bitches. Black-ops! Secret police! Assholes. People make movies about them as if they're heroes, but they're not. They're lying, cheating killers. Even the best of them are shit. They have no respect or common decency." Billy Jack looked around. The boys, Will, and Willy Fish stared at him.

"You're right, Billy Jack," Will said. "Now let's bring Clarisse home and shut our lives to their stench. Clarisse is not dead."

Billy Jack jerked. "Alma said she was *dead*. No one told me anything different."

"No, Papa Jack," Jimmy said. "I talked to El. Something saved her from Óskar Erland. When I talked to him last, El said she was yelling at everyone and that they're attacking tomorrow."

"El is the person you talk to on the other side?" Will said.

Jimmy nodded solemnly. "Yeah. I think he saved her somehow. He's like us, Papa Jack." The boy looked at Will warily. How much did this stranger know about them?

"I know something about people like you, Jimmy. My wife is one; so is Willy Fish and a bunch of our people. Is El on our side?"

"Yeah." Jimmy's lips tightened. "I think."

"Let's get this party started," Will said. "We've got your mother to save and maybe some others, too. You'll be staying with me until we bring her home. This way." He led them into the airport's main terminal and then into an elevator.

"I don't hold much with secrets, boys, but I've got a few of my own. This is a working ranch, but we don't raise cattle. You'll see."

They got to the bottom level. The doors opened to a huge, brightly lit computer lab/office facility of cubicles and maze-like walkways. People looked up when they passed by. "Hello, Mr. Duane!" rang out a dozen, twenty, or more times.

Will brought them to a control room bigger and more modern than anything at Moffett. "Here's where the big kids play," he said. "Let's see what we can do. Do you have the controls for the computer with you?"

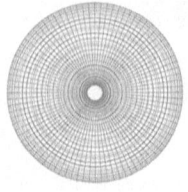

FORTY-SIX

LAST CHANCE FOR LOVE

P OPS RAVED ON at her terrified troops; she had heard him, even in their room, even asleep. Clarisse pulled herself out of bed and ran back to the hall. She and El had been lying next to each other. She left him there, sleeping, and ran back to stop Pops. Somehow.

But she'd been hurt. Clary remembered Pops screaming at her when she was in the warehouse before. He'd thrown her against the wall a dozen times.

Before reentering the hall, she pulled up her shirt. Her belly was perfectly fine. No bruising. No nothing. No memory. Just like with Óskar Erland. Pops ranted on. No time to think about it.

"*You attack tomorrow!*" Pops' face covered the hall's widest wall. He spit when he screamed, the spit having no substance and not leaving the flat image of his face. In his fury, he seemed not to have noticed her absence.

"*You did it, Dr. High-and-Mighty Hull! Óskar Erland's disappearance is entirely your doing!*" Clary stood and took it, wearing her toughest commando face, muscles on the ready. For what? He could kill her in an instant; he almost had. She was in deep doo-doo and, for once, didn't know anything about it.

El had to have had something to do with Erland's disappearance, but Clary didn't know what. She hadn't been able to talk to him since they'd both gone to bed. He was so pale; he looked as though he'd lost half his blood.

He was the key; he held everything together. She didn't remember the night before. And how could those bruises be gone and her broken bones healed? It was El, but how?

"*You will attack tomorrow!*" Pops shrieked.

"*We're not ready,*" she shouted.

Pops noticed her presence again. "Oh, I see you've recovered from my disciplinary action."

"Yeah, Hulls are hard to kill." He smiled.

"Not as hard as you may think. You'll see tomorrow. You're as ready as you are going to be. If you didn't use your time well, that's no one's fault but yours." He smiled with malicious delight. "Your stay here has been a trial to all of us, and soon, it will be over. Tomorrow, you storm Earth and take over, or die."

As Pops glared from the wall, Clary addressed her pseudo-army with words chosen for his benefit. "We're going to climb into the computer tomorrow and be transported to Earth. There, we will attack and subdue whoever we meet, and acquire our target, the Moffett Federal Airfield. When we acquire that, we will continue our expansion until we have taken over Earth. Our benefactor here, Pops, as I call him, and the rest of them will insure that we succeed.

"Questions?"

The questions didn't need to be asked. They knew the answers; Pops had yelled them while screaming at her. They would get no assistance. They would be slaughtered the minute they arrived at Moffett Field, if they weren't killed when their computer powered up.

The ones she'd selected knew Clary's answers, too. She'd try to protect them. She'd try to convince whoever met them that they weren't hostile. She'd try to help them create a real home, somewhere they could be safe and live good lives. She'd give her life, keeping her promises to them.

"We will meet here at 09:00 in full battle gear." She'd been planning to have them gather at 04:00, but why should they get up early to be killed?

Clary didn't think about El again, until she was almost at their room. What had happened to him? She couldn't remember anything. Just snippets. A white dress. Óskar Erland telling her something important. All gone.

"El? Are you okay?" She slipped into their room. He didn't seem to be anywhere. "El, are you okay?" Fearing he'd collapsed in the bathroom, she dashed in to discover him naked, toweling off from a shower.

"Oh, my God, El. I was so worried about you." She grabbed his shoulders and pulled him to face her. "You look so much better. Your color, everything." Pressing her finger against his arm, she noted the healthy blush returning as she pulled it away. The indented flesh refilled with fluid. "Everything's better. I'm so glad. I was so scared."

She grabbed his head and pulled him close, kissing his cheek.

El dropped his towel and embraced her, meeting her mouth with his, pulling her closer.

"Stop it! Not that! We don't do that! I'm married!"

"Oh, *you* can kiss me and touch me and see me naked, but nothing more, and *you're married*." She couldn't read his expression. His mouth was tight and his face hard, but his eyes misted with tears.

"Yes, I'm married. You know that. Why are you angry?"

"Get out of here and let me get dressed."

Clary didn't understand why he was so hostile. He knew their arrangement. They were friends. They loved each other, platonically. She was married to Jack and would not betray him.

Dinner arrived and she arranged it on the table. He was slow emerging from the bathroom. When he came out, he was wearing black jeans and a black shirt. His wet hair fell forward dramatically.

He looked like Elvis, or James Dean—*really* pissed off… and shaken to his depths.

"Tomorrow is the day. We're going to get in the computer and…"

"I know. Pops announced it on the intercom. So what?" He blazed at her. "We've known what was going to happen. It's happening." He picked up his plate and ate at the coffee table.

"Are you scared?"

"No."

"You ought to be out-of-your-fucking-mind terrified, going into battle the first time. That's normal. It's also normal all the following times." Clary tried to be flippant.

"I'm not normal. I haven't been normal since I came here. Even if we don't die tomorrow, I won't be normal, and I won't *ever* get what I want." He turned toward her.

"What do you want, El? Why are you so upset?"

"*You'll* never marry me."

"Oh," her eyes widened, "I told you I wouldn't marry you because you're too young. There's fifteen years' difference…"

"I don't care how much older you are than me. I love you. I've told you that a thousand times. There's a greater than ninety-nine percent probability that we'll die tomorrow. Thinking about how things will be when I'm fifty is *stupid*."

"*But I'm married, El. I'm married to Jack, and we're faithful to each other.*"

El pulled away from her, a snarl on his face. "I know that you're married. But are you married to Jack for *Jack*, or for *you*? Are you faithful because you love Jack so much you would never betray him? Or are you faithful because you're too chicken to admit you don't really love him? That you just wanted a nice guy to cover up your secrets? Would you want me if Jack were *dead*? I don't think so. You'd come up with another excuse to keep away from me."

She stood, paralyzed. *Was* she faithful because she loved Jack, or because she didn't want to be the slut her father had said she was? Could she love anyone after losing Alex?

El grabbed his pillow and stomped into his closet. She could hear him settling in.

"You're sleeping in there? *Tonight? Our last night?*"

"Yes. Why shouldn't I?"

"We sleep together."

"Yes. That's all we do. Sleep. And hug. And cuddle. You need a teddy bear, not me." He closed the door from the inside.

She followed, entering without asking. "What is this about?"

"I want to marry you. Mostly, right now, I want to love you so hard that you won't be able to move afterward. I've wanted you since I first saw your picture. I think you're too chicken to take my love and love me back. But there's no more time. We'll be dead tomorrow and Jack won't matter at all. I wish you'd stop thinking of me as an abused kid. I wish you saw me as I am." El stepped into the middle of the closet so she could see him, head to toe.

Fully clothed, he was beautiful, his once emaciated body transformed by working out and good food. His dark hair was long over his brow and trimmed tight in back. His elegant bone structure made him look like a Renaissance statue.

"Take a good look, *Clary*. Check out what you've been missing." He unbuttoned his shirt and stepped out of his pants. "See me, for once. I'm not a little boy."

Her eyes brushed his lanky frame, registering his white skin, lightly covered with a sprinkling of dark hair. Tight strands clung to his chest and belly, ran over his arms, and down his legs. Almost-black hair against his pale white flesh. Muscles rippled everywhere. He wasn't all whiteness. He had an erection, which jutted from a thick mat, curled like a pelt.

"I'm big, aren't I? *Aren't I?* They fought for me out in the hall." He turned from her, so she could see the dimples above his buttocks and the curve of his spine. El turned back, showing her his profile.

"I love you more than anyone ever will, Clary. I want to love you tonight."

"But I…"

"Last chance, Clary. If we die or end up floating around between universes, I want to have been with you for one night."

He turned so she could see him. It rose out of that tangle of hair, dark, muted red, so different from the rest of his pale skin. Impossible for her to resist.

She didn't count the steps it took to reach him. He put his hands under her shirt and felt her breasts while she pulled at her buttons and zippers.

"No. Go slow. I want to see you. Show me your skin, Clary. Every inch of it." His eyes gleamed as her nakedness was revealed. "Oh, God, you're so beautiful."

The first time was on the cushions.

"Oh, El." She took him in her hands, working him with knowledge she'd gained in her marriage, and in her wild years. "Oh, oh. El, fuck me. Do it now."

He didn't let her stop until she was sobbing and mewling, begging. "Please. Again. Oh, God, El."

That's when they moved to their bed. El was a lover like no other. He'd been a whore in his life before her, but Clary didn't think about that. She thought about his fine skin and the pale light illuminating it. She thought about its soft texture and his hard prominence. She thought of his mouth and hands, parting her and giving her what she hadn't had since...

"Oh, Alex, I love you so much."

He didn't stop even when she called him Alex.

"I want you to love me more than Alex, Clary. I want you to love me more than you know you can love anything. I want you to speak to me with your heart, Clary, not your mind." He kept going. She was beyond exhausted, beyond needing to sleep.

She had no thought of the battle in the morning.

She was Clary and he was El. She loved him more than she'd loved Alex. She had never loved Jack like she did Elias, and finally admitted it. Every pore, every opening belonged to him. She looked at him, a little afraid. He had so much stamina. Much more than any man...

He sat between her legs, his own folded under him, examining her. "Spread farther, Clary. Let me look at you." His face flushed as he separated her, unfolding petals and exposing her heart, the center of the flower. His eyes opened wider. He blinked, awed.

"I've never seen anything so beautiful." Opening her, he inserted a finger tentatively. "Look. You're wet. And your perfume is so exciting."

She didn't notice anything different at first. It was El. She loved him. He could do whatever he wanted. But he didn't seem so sure of himself, like the boy who did it all or had had it done to him. He wasn't a natural denizen in the house of love. Yet, he was natural enough. Sweat burst out all over her as she reacted to his touch. How could he make her turn over like that, so many times?

"Oh, my God. El, do me. Do me now. Hurry." Her chest heaved and she begged him.

He stayed, kneeling between her legs, looking bewildered. She had to guide him in.

His back arched as he entered her.

"Oh, Clary. Oh, my. I didn't know. Nothing. Nothing is..." He came rapidly, not that it mattered. She was a thousand times satisfied and her body was on the same wavelength as his. Her torso lurched and shuddered with him.

"Oh, Clary." He fell on top of her, bursting into tears of gratitude and ecstasy. "Thank you. Oh, thank you, my love. I didn't know. My dear..."

A primeval instinct awoke inside her. Something was wrong. El's voice wasn't as deep as this man's. And El didn't talk like this. He didn't call her *my dear* or *my love*. El was a better, more mature lover. Her brows knit. Something had changed. What?

"El's" head rolled back and his eyes closed. He was unconscious. *Le petit mort*, the little death, the French called it. She'd seen that in other lovers. But El hadn't done that at all, nor had he reacted so strongly to his orgasm. He'd known how to enter her and hadn't been awed when he got a close look at her. This wasn't El! The fucking aliens had done something to him!

She rolled out from under him, grabbed her weapon from under the bed, and stood with it aimed at his head.

"Who are you? Where's El?"

He continued to shudder, unable to speak. "Please, give me a moment." His voice wasn't El's. This was a man, full grown and powerful, who had just had sex for the first time.

"What kind of bullshit is this?" she pressed the muzzle against his head. "Who are you? You're not El. What did you do to him? Where is he!"

"My name is Robert Dalton." He raised his hand, a gesture of conciliation. "There's a lot you don't know. Jimmy thought it would be better if you didn't know who I really was. And he didn't know all of it. He and

Ricky worked out who Elias was, piece by piece. I'm Alex Caldwell's first cousin. Our mothers were sisters. They stole me when Alex died."

"What bullshit are you talking about? Robert Dalton? How do you know my sons? Who are you?" She poked his temple with the gun's barrel.

"I'm Jimmy and Ricky's uncle. They stole me from my mother because they were collecting DNA. Our mothers were sisters. I'm Alex Caldwell's cousin. That's why they did all this. They wanted to create a genius army by combining us, you and me. And what I am; there's more to me than a human named Robert Dalton. They wanted to take our baby and clone a million more of us. That was the army that was going to take over Earth. That's why they brought Óskar Erland here. To do the cloning."

"*What are you talking about? Who* are *you?* You better explain fast, bozo, or your brains will be wallpaper."

"If you kill me, you'll kill Elias. And every chance of happiness you have."

"What the...!" She rocked back. "El. Are you in him? Give me a sign."

His head rocked back and his eyelids fluttered. She didn't hear El's voice, but she knew he'd answered. He was inside the dick who had just fucked her.

"You're one of them. El told me that he was the only one who survived their 'beat out the human.' He said something like a tornado came out of the sky and touched his chest, but he didn't feel anything and he didn't think he was changed. You stinking piece of shit, you've been hiding inside El all this time, lying to me. Conning me. What was all this?" She indicated the rumpled bed. "A learning experience before you send me off to war? You asshole." Surprisingly, her bravado slipped. Tears leapt to her eyes, but rage burst out again.

He shook his head. "No, that isn't what we were doing... I am one of them, though the concept of one of a group doesn't fit us." His voice was deeper and more serious than El's could ever be.

She pistol-whipped him with the butt of her revolver. His head rocked back, blood spurting from his forehead.

"Oh. That hurt. Don't..." A brilliant scarlet stream flowed down his cheek.

"Explain yourself, or you'll…"

Her weapon was in his hands. She didn't know how he'd gotten it.

"If you want my help, I'd like you to exhibit better manners." He spoke formally, despite sitting in their bed totally exposed, blood running down his face. Odors of semen and female secretions permeated the air. Their bodies dripped with the detritus of sex.

"Better manners?! You want *better manners*? You're the enemy! You *stole* Elias! You lied to me, or got him to lie to me. You're going to kill us all, aren't you? *This* is Pops' big plan. *Infiltrate.* FUCK!" She jumped up, raving. "What an idiot I am to trust *anyone. Goddamn it to hell.*"

Clarisse exploded, swearing venomously, despite having had uncountable orgasms and being stark naked. She paced the room, screaming and cursing at him. His eyes widened and widened again, as the vocabulary that could be earned only by military service, life in a ghetto, or occupations involving drugs or rock 'n roll spewed from her lips. "You stinking fuck. You…"

"I suggest that you be quiet. I can only dampen their devices a certain amount. You're approaching my threshold."

"WHAT?!"

"I'm the one who kept them away from you and Elias. Yes, you and he are good at manipulating the technology you have, but you don't have ours and you can't possibly understand it. You've had your privacy because of *me*."

"*You! You stinking rat fuck.*"

"You swear excessively and unnecessarily. You would be more effective in your communication if you simply expressed your thoughts and feelings in words. And you'd appear less crass and vulgar."

"Crass and vulgar? After what you just did to me? Fuck!" Clary spun and pounded her forehead against the wall.

"Stop that!" She stopped immediately, whirled, and walked toward him as though he commanded her silently. "We need to talk and you need to get some sleep."

"Sleep! It would take a bucket of Ambien to put me out now. But that would kill me. Which will happen tomorrow anyway."

"You're not going to die. You're going to listen to me." He looked down, apparently realizing he was as naked as she. "Get those robes for us."

She went into the bathroom and pulled them off the door without question. "I smell."

"So do I. Put the robe on and get into bed with me."

"What?! Why should I..." She did what he said, sputtering.

"You're about to go into shock. I need to hold you to heal you."

"Heal me? How can *you* heal me?" He cupped her body from the rear. The sweet balm she'd felt in El's arms was a thousand times more intense coming from him.

"I've been healing you since you've been here. Pops beat you so severely earlier today that you would have died had I not healed you. I saved you after Óskar Erland savaged you. You're alive because of me. You're going to lose consciousness, but you'll be able to hear me. You need to sleep, and so do I, so I can't tell you everything now. I will when I can."

Her eyes closed and she drifted off, whimpering and jerking at first.

"That's good, Clary. You're so good. You need to know that I'm the one that chose you to come here, just as I chose Elias. Though the term 'I' is not appropriate for my people, who are really one entity, one consciousness. Not plural. Not separate.

"I am a traitor, Clary, like the worst of your traitors on Earth. I separated myself from them while seeming to be part of the *one*. We are just one spirit. We don't have bodies. That's how the botched experiment with the humans started. We wanted a body; I wanted a body. We/I wanted a home, Earth, the beautiful planet that your kind is ruining. We/I didn't think you deserved it.

"We thought we'd take care of Earth, but the truth is, we're predators. We'd take over Earth and steal everything good about it, then move on. We've done that for histories beyond history, roaming the universe and destroying whatever we took.

"We are *spirit*, with no attachment to anything. Spirit is not all good. Your kind seems to think the immaterial is better than the corporeal. It's not. We've destroyed planets from our end of the universe to yours. In the name of liberating your planet, we created the hideous travesty that was the hall. We permitted and encouraged your natural sociopathic tendencies."

She jerked.

"We can discuss that later. Your genes attracted us. The Hull brilliance and legacy. We wanted you and your boys and whatever children we could produce with you. Óskar Erland told us about you, and the brilliant individuals his research had unearthed. We wanted Alex Caldwell, but his body was so badly damaged when we found him, we couldn't use him.

"I picked the child Robert Dalton because I could see his genes were similar to Alex's. He was a happy, healthy child living in a little house with his mother. But none of you humans in those days knew what his genetic code carried. I could put it all together with your past and present. And Alex's.

"I am one being, no separation inside of me. I am Pops, Clary. I am of the same stuff as Pops, but I separated myself because I wanted a human life. I wanted your life, Clary, the one we showed the boy Elias, our captive and creation. I wanted all the videos, images, and peeks into your life and heart that we showed him to make him love you.

"It wasn't hard to make him love you, Clary. *I* fell in love with you. I know your life as though I lived it. Spirit can go anywhere. I'm a spirit, and I am the creature Elias. I am Pops. And I am Robert Quinn Dalton, the little boy stolen so many years ago. My mother was Jessellyn Belle Bertram Dalton."

She was barely sentient, but her lashes fluttered.

"That's right. You recognized something about the name when Elias said it. Alex Caldwell's mother was Gerillyn Caldwell, my mother's sister. Cute, Jessellyn and Gerillyn? I am Alex Caldwell's first cousin. I told you that earlier, but that longer explanation may make it more real.

"Elias worked this out with Jimmy using mindspeak, piece by piece, over all the time you've been here. I prevented him from telling you. Stupidly, perhaps. I wanted you to love Elias. I wanted you to love him as much as he loved you. Then, I thought maybe I could reveal myself to you, and you could love me.

"Life isn't of the mind, Clary; it's a matter of the heart. Heartspeak, not mindspeak, will win in the end. Or so I thought. I kept you in the dark, thinking you'd love me if I gave you enough time."

Clary drifted so deeply into unconsciousness that she could barely hear his voice. She would have been in shock, had he not been holding her.

"Robert was ten when we took him. He was born in 1946, right after your World War II. In your time, 2016, he'd be seventy years old, not twenty-two." Her jaw relaxed and her mouth opened. She relaxed totally, comprehension fading. "Do you understand? Robert Dalton is Elias and *me*. We're the same human, except I'm not human.

"We'll discuss it more tomorrow. You and I will have to work as a team, closer than any humans ever have. Or we'll lose. Clary, you and Alex were made for each other, as was El. By me, for the most part. The rest of me, the blob of consciousness that I turned away from, wants you and your boys, Ricky and Jimmy, to use as slaves for the rest of your lives.

"I want you for my family. I can compel you to love me, but I don't want to. I want you and the boys to love me for myself. If you can. I love you. I fell in love with you, seeing your bravery in doing your research against all odds. You were correct, but none of your people could acknowledge it. I fell in love with you, seeing how you coped with the hell we'd created. I loved you for how you healed El. You taught me what love is, and courage. I want you for my wife."

Her eyes opened a bit, pupils rolled back, lids fluttering.

"Well, now's not the time to talk. Tomorrow's 'show time,' as you say. We need to sleep."

He wrapped himself around her, feeling the bliss that he always felt when near her. He whispered in her ear. "I've wanted this for so long. Now I've gotten it, but I haven't. I'm holding you and have known the ecstasy we could create. But you're beyond communication. I don't know if what I said reached you. If you hate me, if you understand what I am. I gave up immortality for you, Clary. Power you can't imagine. I love you.

"But that's how it's been, eh? Me hiding in Elias, you hiding from his love. Elias working as hard as he could despite everything. Pops trying to sniff me out. No one knowing what's really going on. Mindspeak, Clary, blocking heartspeak. Hear my heart with yours. It's time for the heart to take command."

FORTY-SEVEN

SHOW TIME

"OKAY. THIS IS it. What we've trained for," Clary spoke loudly. "We will enter the computer and be transported to the twin facility at Moffett Field." Clary held forth in the corridor leading to the machine. From the other side of the glass doors, it flashed and beeped as always.

"Form ranks!" No one moved. She looked around. Elias had been right behind her. They'd awakened and made love with aching tenderness. She'd heard what he'd said the night before. As bizarre as it was, as wonderful as it was, as incomprehensible and strange as it was, he *had* reached her heart.

"I love you," she'd repeated over and over. They'd gotten up and dressed for the last day of their lives. When she'd walked out of their room, he'd been on her heels. She wanted to call out to him for support now, but he wasn't there.

Pops' face appeared on the wall near her, radiating joy. "What's the matter, Dr. Hull? Aren't your troops obeying you?"

"They will." She turned to the group, which was about one hundred and forty strong, including those she trusted and those she didn't. Clary shouted, "If you want to spend the rest of your lives listening to this asshole, stay here. I don't care. He'll have you back to eating dog shit the minute I leave. The bullies will take over and fuck up everyone else.

Pops will finally dump you off somewhere on Earth and tell you to fight and win.

"But you won't. Because you don't know how. If you don't go with me, you're too chicken to take a chance on a better life. You know what chickens do? What?! Tell me!"

None of them could remember seeing a chicken.

"They do this." Clary did a tolerable imitation of a chicken, circling around, flapping its wings, and squawking. "They do *that,* until they get their heads chopped off and they're *eaten.* Oh, they also lay eggs." She squatted and let out a piercing squawk.

The group laughed, despite themselves.

"We got chickens, bullies, and warriors. The warriors go with me. Form up. Now! This is a timed event! Elias set the timer for ignition last night." She hoped. "Show time is coming fast. We have to get in and get settled."

A bunch of them, maybe forty, started toward the elevator that would take them to the computer's empty central core. They would pack in there for the journey.

"*Do not take anything metal with you!*" she shouted.

"We won't have any weapons!" The cry went up. Most had home-made knives they'd fashioned. Sharpened serving spoons were prized.

"That's true. We've never had weapons. We played guns with brooms and serving utensils. Pops never intended to arm you, *did you,* Pops?" She turned to his face on the wall, which registered no emotion—just that haughty stare.

"We were never going to have weapons! This is all a charade! Not only that, if you had weapons, they might explode and kill you when the computer accelerates. It's not going to be like that," she waved at the benign, if flashy, behemoth.

"It's going to be working. It's magnetic. It will pull firing pins and depress levers. It could blow up our ammunition. The whole thing may explode the instant the ignition is tripped. No one's tried this before. If we're bearing metal, we're a million times more at risk."

The group pulled away as though she'd offered them tickets to a leper colony. They retreated up the corridor.

"If we aren't seen as the enemy, we may be offered refuge on the other side. As long as I'm not seen as hostile, my people want me back. They may accept all of us and not attack.

"So, go with me in peace and have a decent life, maybe, or live here with what you know and get fucked by the next big kahuna that takes over—or Pops."

No one moved, so she upped the reality level a bit. "I understand Óskar Erland was a little rough on some of you. Oh, but those people aren't here. They're dead. The rest of you know what he did. Who do you think they'll bring in next? Are you stupid enough to believe that Pops and his friends will change? They'll *never* change."

Clary scanned the crowd for El. He wasn't anywhere. He was a traitor to his own... *self* by wanting to go with her. Could he change back? Or, what if they found out and captured him? They could be torturing him right now.

Pops picked up on her distress. "You're looking for Elias? Robert Dalton? He said he had a wonderful time with you last night, but he won't be making the trip. Thanks for the memories. You'll have to go without him."

She staggered.

"Yes, that's how human relationships are. Fickle. He's off with someone else, doing what he did with you. Quite the ladies' man, Elias."

Clary stood tall, her fists clenched. That was a lie. But Pops would try to make her believe it. Could the lie be used to her advantage?

"That stinking son of a bitch. I knew he was lying." She whirled and faced the others. "Let's get out of there. There's nothing here for us."

She efficiently ushered those who wanted to go into the elevator and the center of the open space in the computer. Counting, she found forty-one were with her. A huge digital clock was counting down when they sat on the flat floor of the machine. 00:11:00. Eleven minutes left.

"Okay. Sit close to the middle of the cylinder, tightly packed. I don't know what's going to happen, but it will be over soon. Whatever happens—will be better than staying here."

A hundred feet away, the opening to the cylinder remained clear.

She kept expecting him to appear. What Pops had said *couldn't* be true. El wouldn't lie. He wouldn't abandon her.

At 00:05:37, a gaggle of ten or twelve more people appeared in the opening. "Can we come?"

"Yes, take seats as close to the middle as you can get." Clary got up and ran to the opening to help them. Standing on a little landing, she could see the remainder of the people she'd been training behind the glass doors to the corridors, jeering at them.

"Stupid assholes! She's going to blow you up! Idiots." Most of what they said was in the slang of the warehouse, dirtier and nastier than English swearing, but almost impossible to appreciate if you weren't one of them. "Y'tom tail! Y'fool's bitch! Y'll eat…"

They didn't open the glass doors or mob the computer because they didn't know what was going to happen.

She stepped out a bit farther, hoping that Elias would appear. He wasn't abandoning her. Was he? She heard his voice, soft and intimate, for her ears only. She didn't see him.

I will always love you. I treasure last night more than anything in my life. I will search to the end of the universe to find you. Trust me. I can't go with you now. They'll follow and destroy your planet.

"El! Is that you? El! Let me see you."

Shh! You won't see me again until I come to you. Clary, I love you. But I am the only one that can stop them.

"I'll stay with you! I can fight!"

No, my darling. You can't fight them. You will keep me from doing what I must for fear of you being hurt.

"What are you going to do, El?"

I am going to obliterate them, Clary. Every vestige of their culture and being. Except what's in me. I am their… flower. Their soul. I will destroy the rest.

"But, El—I love you! I really love you, more than I loved Alex. More than anyone. I want to love you for the rest of my life."

I know, Clary. I feel the same. Take care of Jimmy and Ricky.

"No! I won't leave you. Don't make me go, El. Please." Tears coursed down her cheeks. "Please, please." She felt something like a hand gently caressing her belly.

My darling, you must go. You must guard the life within you.

"What? I'm pregnant? You made me pregnant? I can't..."

Yes, you can. I healed you. You bear my child. Our child must live. Get into the computer, Clary. You need to guide it. I will find you.

The clock counted down. Everyone inside the cylinder watched the time on the machine's interior controls. Everyone waiting in the corridors, and Pops, watched the numbers displayed on the wall. Pops had created a huge stopwatch on the wall so they could watch the countdown.

At first, jeers and catcalls came from those staying behind. Then everyone grew quiet. The numbers changed: 00:04:31; 00:02:53; 00:01:21. 00:00:12.

00:00:00

The lights of the computer went off. The facility went black. A droning noise began deep in the machine's core. It got louder and louder, so that people inside held their hands to their ears. Then they screamed, falling on the floor in anguish.

All the lights on the computer turned on as suddenly as they had quit. Brilliant light! Explosive light! Light to blind and terrify. Then pounding. The lights resumed their earlier patterns, flashing in intricate configurations in the layered guts of the machine.

The central core of the computer began to bang back and forth, shaking itself, and sounding like a giant tennis shoe pounding in a hellish dryer.

Pops could hear the screams inside the machine. A smile lit his face. Alas, his resident genius, Dr. Hull, was a fraud. A few of the traitors appeared at the opening of the cylinder, trying to escape, but he had pulled away the scaffolding and bridge. They faced a hundred-foot drop onto solid concrete. They fell on their knees, holding out their hands, begging those behind the corridor doors for help.

But there was no help. He would offer none. Hull and her misbegotten warriors deserved what they got.

The rattling and banging continued, escalating. Shaking everything, the computer center, and the whole warehouse. Then came sounds of tearing metal and snapped wires, breaking glass. The cacophony of total destruction…

Silence. The computer was still. No lights, no movement, no sound.

"What is it?" The humans in the corridor cried. "What happened?"

Pops could see that something had happened, but what? He moved closer, as close as he had ever gotten to the computer. He didn't like it, and usually contained himself to appearing on the walls surrounding the mammoth structure. Now he flowed into the space between the unholy beast and its enclosure.

The cylinder was gone. The giant rod-like hole was gone, along with everyone in it. So were twenty feet of the computer that had surrounded the edges of the cylinder. Broken metal edges and dangling wires, big bundles of them, broken glass panes, and everything that made the thing work hung there, useless. The beast was dead. Dr. Clarisse Hull was gone, and with her, she had taken any hope of using this monstrous waste of their resources.

He'd have to take the other one, the one at the place called Moffett Field. But why? Bringing Dr. Hull to the warehouse had been a disaster. Why transport more of those arrogant, willful creatures to the world he had constructed for them?

They would destroy the planet from where they were. They always had been able to do that. *Are you with me?* he thought.

Yes! The answer was instantaneous. *Kill them now! Destroy Earth! Kill the humans!*

He felt something… a dissent. "Is that you, Elias? Pining over your lost love?"

Blackness fell like a sheet of molten lead.

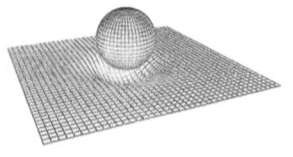

FORTY-EIGHT

COLLISION

C LARY KNELT ON the computer's floor, body folded over her knees, head wrapped by her arms. Glass and metal crashed around her as the ceiling of the tube broke up. Wails and screams accompanied the sounds of destruction. Others didn't escape the cascade of sharp objects and beams as well as she did. When everything began breaking and falling, she wedged herself into the corner between the floor and sidewall. Shards of glass embedded themselves in her forearms. She left them and folded her hands and arms over her head.

Clary had thought the people in its central cylinder would be lifted to the twin computer in Moffett Field silently and painlessly. They'd arrive intact and ready to move efficiently the minute they got there.

El had told her that Óskar Erland had disappeared from the computer the night before. He'd also told her that she had had dinner with him there, but she had only the vaguest notion of it. The table and everything else present at their dinner must have been lifted with Erland's body. She had inspected the computer and seen no damage to it from whatever had happened—or any evidence of anything at all happening. She'd thought that Jimmy and Ricky had managed to lift Erland's body and everything around it to the Moffett Field computer.

This hell of disintegration was unplanned. The computer wasn't supposed to go on their journey with them. No part of the machine was supposed be affected, yet it was breaking up. She hadn't trained them for this. How could anyone train for this? The computer tearing itself to shreds?

Nothing in the physics of it had said this would happen.

Then she got it. They had to be going somewhere else. Not to Moffett Field.

They landed hard, shaking down more glass and wreckage. Then things were still. She looked up. Bundles of electrical wire hung from the ceiling. Glass was everywhere, along with sheets of torn steel paneling and cabinet doors. People moaned and screamed, looking at legs and bodies riddled with steel and glass. Blood coated everyone and everything.

"Everyone. We're here. I don't know what happened, but I'll get help." Clary stood, legs shaking but functional. She picked her way toward the lit opening of the cylinder. The other end was dark, buried in something. Blood ran down her arms.

She held her hands over her head in surrender as she approached the opening. "I am Dr. Clarisse Hull. We are unarmed. We are friendly. We have wounded. We request support. Repeat: Wounded. Request support." She looked over the edge. More shattered metal and glass. It was a twenty-foot drop to the concrete floor. She looked around. They were in a building, but not the white warehouse and certainly not Moffett Field.

"Mom! Mom!"

"We're here, Mom! We'll get you."

Two voices she'd recognize anywhere. "Stay down! It's not safe. Unstable glass and metal. Do not approach." She responded like a robot. But inside: *Jimmy! Ricky!*

"Clarisse, I'm Will Duane." She saw a man with white hair. "You're at a hangar at my ranch. We have equipment to get you down. And medical staff."

She couldn't process all of that. "What?"

"We'll get you down, Clarisse. You're safe."

"I have to make sure everyone is secure. I can't..." Clarisse was on a gurney being wheeled into a big, beautifully furnished bedroom in an extravagant log home.

The doctor was firm. "I need to remove the glass and treat those wounds. I can't do it if you're moving around. I need to give you a sedative so I can work." He set an IV port in her arm.

"But the others, are they…"

"Most of them will be fine. A few perished. Some are in critical condition. You were lucky."

"Lucky." She turned her face away, tears running across her skin, dropping on the sheets.

"Mom!" Jimmy came bounding in, his face white with worry, but wearing a cautious smile.

"Mom, you're okay. Oh, shit, man," Ricky doubled over her bed in tears.

"Ricky, Jimmy, what happened? What did you do? How did I get here? I thought I'd be in Moffett Field. I thought there would be soldiers…"

"We did what you said, Mom. We made the device according to your plans, and some modifications of our own." Ricky struggled to his feet and explained.

"You couldn't alter the destination with your instrument, Mom. So we modified it. You had it basically right, though." Jimmy added.

"We put the device from the Moffett Field computer in Will's hangar here in Montana, on his ranch. That's where we are. Ron got the control panel for us when he helped us escape from Moffett. We programed it to tell your computer to come *here*. It did."

"Oh, Mom, we were so scared."

"We didn't know if it would work."

"Me, too, guys. It was scary," Clary said, words slurring a bit from the sedative.

"Will didn't have a building big enough to put the whole computer in, but he had this hanger for his jet. Ricky and I figured that you really didn't need *the entire* computer to do your work.

"Most of the controls and stuff that made it work were in the twenty feet around the cylinder. So we set the device to take that, and all the people inside."

"It got kinda wrecked, though."

"But we can fix it!" Jimmy beamed, but then looked at his mother's bandaged arms. "Is she okay?" he asked the doctor.

"She's going to hurt, and she's going to have some scars, but she'll be fine."

"We're in Will Duane's house. He cleared a whole wing to be a hospital for everyone. He's nice, Mom. He's Papa Jack's neighbor. We couldn't have gotten away or done anything without his help."

"Clarisse, I'm here, girl," Billy Jack's tall form with its Stetson hat poked over the boys' heads. "Just a little slow these days." His eyes were red-rimmed; he slipped his handkerchief into his pocket.

"I'm here, too, Clarisse. Will Duane." She saw a tall man with white hair behind her father-in-law. He raised a hand in greeting.

"How are you, darlin'?" Billy Jack said.

"I'm fine." Clary winced at an injection of local anesthetic in her other forearm. "Where's Jack? Is he still in England?"

The room froze. No one could speak.

"Mom," Jimmy whispered. "Something happened while you were captured…"

He didn't have to say more.

"They killed Jack." Her face was bloodless. "They killed him because he knew I was alive. Oh, God."

The doctor moved fast, breaking an ampule of smelling salts under her nose. "Get her on a heart monitor. STAT. She's in shock." An emergency team closed in around the unconscious Clarisse.

A nurse asked the others to leave. "We need to get her stabilized. We'll call you."

"Will she be okay?"

"She should be. She's young and looks in good health. It's the shock of hearing of her husband's death, after everything else."

Jimmy and Ricky retreated into Will's house.

Clarisse awakened in a beautiful, high-ceilinged room. A log room. Billy Jack's house in Montana was logs, too, but not like these. These must have come from old forest patriarchs.

Her arms were bandaged. She had a tube in one of them. Then she remembered. "Hello? Hello? Is anyone here? Where's El?"

She froze. Her ribs froze. Her soul froze. A voice came from her that she didn't recognize. A high, tinny voice, empty. "He stayed behind. He's fighting *them*. Where is he? Did he make it?" She knew. Her knees pulled up and her torso shot forward. Sobs erupted. Killing, dying, painful beyond any telling—sobs of grief and desolation. "He's gone. I'll never see him again."

A doctor rushed in, with the boys and Billy Jack close behind. "She needs a sedative. You can see her in the morning."

Oblivion. Relief. Who cared where it came from, as long as it lasted.

Three days later, she lay in a bed at Papa Jack's ranch. Clarisse couldn't feel, couldn't respond, and could barely breathe.

Billy Jack and Will Duane stood on the front porch of Jack's ranch house. It was a big and rambling log place, two stories tall, but not grand like Will's. Older and a little scruffy, but homey and warm.

Will shuffled from foot to foot. Clarisse had asked him to impart a bit of information to his neighbor. She was too fragile to do it—that was obvious, seeing her in bed.

"She needs a psychiatrist," Will said.

Billy Jack nodded. "I know a good one, but I don't think she'd work in this situation." Tears filled his eyes as he thought of Alma and what she and his son would never have. "Sorry. My boy," he shrugged and shook his head, "had a good life shaping up for him in England."

"Jack, I'm really sorry about your son; nothing can bring him back and nothing can lessen your pain. We need to concentrate on those we can save, and right away.

"My wife has an excellent psychiatrist in her hospital back in Woodside," Will continued. "But Clary needs to be here, not there. Until we get the situation more secure, she should stay secluded. The fact that she and the boys are officially dead, and that half the nuts in the world, including the entire clandestine community, would be after her if they thought she was alive, speaks to her staying in Montana. With the boys."

Will put the sentences together coherently, but he was as shell-shocked as the other man. He was stalling on delivering the news.

Debriefing the people rescued from the computer, they had found that Clarisse had defied an entire population of aliens, whipped a force of mostly worthless, abused humans into a cohesive group, improved their nutrition and physical condition, and was considered close to a goddess by those who'd lived through the escape.

What conditions were like in the alternative reality had shocked Will and everyone else speechless.

In addition to all that, Clarisse had engineered the transformation of the captive population from displaced persons into highly employable physicists and techs. They could work for Will in his facility. He could have talked to Billy Jack about that all day. But that wasn't what Will had to say.

"Jack, I'm just going to tell you. Clary's pregnant."

"What!"

Alarmed by the way the old man turned white, Will grabbed his arm. "Come over here and sit down. Do you want me to call a doctor?"

"No. Get me that bottle of bourbon over there on the sideboard. And a glass. Two glasses, if you want." He flopped into a big leather chair. "Lord have mercy. I've heard of Clarisse doing this sort of thing. Her father said she ran off once and came back pregnant with Jimmy, but I never believed it... What the *hell* is going on?"

Bourbon was a great thing. If it weren't for that wonder drug created in the American South for the good of humanity, Billy Jack would have had a much harder time assimilating the truth as Will spooled it out. Clarisse and the boys had told him as much as he could handle. Sipping his own cup, Will passed on the essence of what had happened.

Aliens had snatched up a boy named Robert Dalton back in 1956. He'd turned out to be Ricky and Jimmy's uncle, and their only blood relative, aside from their mother. The boys could talk to him through some magic device they'd made. They knew he was their uncle and loved him.

In that other world, Clary had fallen in love with this Robert Dalton, who was known as Elias by the aliens, and El by the boys and Clary. Dalton had sacrificed himself to fight the extraterrestrials and save Earth. That's why he wasn't here.

Along the way, Clary had gotten pregnant.

The docs had told Will about Clary's pregnancy that morning. He was the first they'd told, since the rescue was taking place on his ranch and he was footing the bill.

Billy Jack sat sipping his best whiskey, trying to put a lid on his feelings. Or figure out what they were. When he'd been at Oxford, Billy Jack had learned about Clarisse's supposed desertion that had resulted in Jimmy. Billy Jack had never believed, though, that his daughter-in-law had run off with a pack of physicists.

What *had* happened in reality was worse than any terror his son could imagine. She was pregnant by a man who was half-alien, and not the undocumented-migrant type.

As he learned more of the situation, Billy Jack realized that things would be worse if her lover hadn't run off to save the planet. If enraged beings from outer space were about to destroy Earth, he found himself rooting for El/Elias/Robert Dalton's success. Only part of the old man wanted to kill him. As painfully as possible. The rest was suffused in sadness. He thought his Jack was lucky he hadn't lived to see this mess.

But Clarisse was in such terrible shape. She was wounded, yes, but her paralysis was grief. Would she grieve for his son in this way?

No. She'd be sorry. She'd cry. She'd be back in the physics lab three days later.

"I need a psychiatrist," Billy Jack said.

SECTION TWO
CLARY'S DESPAIR

OCTOBER 2016 TO MAY 2017

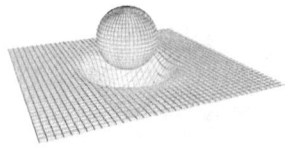

FORTY-NINE

THE END OF THE WORLD

"THIS IS JASON Kingsley, KCBM News, reporting on the torna-does sweeping the state of Washington. You can see the funnel behind us getting ready to touch down. Now *two* have dropped from the clouds... *Three...*" Jason stood at the side of a road, clutching his mic as black clouds dropped deadly scythes behind him. The wind blew his collar up as he struggled to remain erect. Thunder rolled.

"Get in the van, Jason. Now!" The news van bounced away as howling winds made speech unintelligible. Funnels dropped from the black sky like lines and sinkers from a pier. Three, four, five.

The cameraman yelped as all five cones came to a halt before striking the small town of Beeswing, Washington. They skirmished briefly, with three funnels apparently trying to outflank the fifth as the fourth dashed toward the town.

Lightning cracked. Electricity surrounded the van, glazing everything with flashing current.

"Oh, shit, the tornadoes are *fighting*. Drive! Get out of here!"

"I got it! I got it all!" the cameraman had been leaning out of the van as they dashed for safety. "Look. Let me play it back." They watched as one of the tornadoes clashed with the three that seemed to be attacking it. "Look. It *absorbs* them."

The remaining, larger funnel went after the last cyclone, smashing into it and growing larger yet again. It stopped where it was, turning around and leaving Beeswing untouched.

"What the fuck was that?"

"The story of the year. Let's turn it in."

Jason got on camera again, screaming ecstatically. "I can't believe it! I can't believe it! How many tornadoes does the state of Washington experience a year?" A band ran across the bottom of viewers' screens: "Washington State has one of the lowest incidences of tornadoes in the United States, experiencing an average of one tornado per year, with a zero death rate."

"We saw five tornadoes fight to the death over the little town of Beeswing, 'the Sweetest Place in America.' The town is safe, folks! Saved by a miracle in a place where tornadoes almost never happen."

Clary clicked the TV control and changed channels, her face drawn and strained. The storms had started shortly after she'd moved into Papa Jack's with the boys. She'd moved in in October and had been there for months now, not even thinking of going anywhere. The weather made travel anywhere sporadic and dangerous. Planes were grounded, or thrown from the sky if they took off. Every channel told the same story, all around the world.

"Millicent Vander of QKUZ News, reporting on the floods in…"

"Braydon Wolt of WXYU News. The *big one* has struck! A 9.2 on the Richter scale earthquake centered on San Jose, California has caused unprecedented…"

It was El. Elias. Robert Dalton. Bobbie. Fighting to the death with Pops/them. Fighting so hard he was almost destroying the Earth he was trying to save.

"Clary, I've got dinner for us." Billy Jack could not have been nicer. She couldn't meet his eyes. She had been so bad for Jack. She'd been a lousy mother, a lousy wife. She never should have married him. She hadn't loved him enough, or the right way.

Yet, you did love him. And you do. You wish him happiness. A little voice would intervene when she got too hard on herself.

She went into the kitchen for dinner. The diet of beans and meat got to her, but growing vegetables in Northern Montana in the middle of *this* winter was impossible. Christmas had come and gone; it was a new year: 2017. She sat at the table.

"Billy Jack, I'm sorry…"

"Clarisse, if you tell me how sorry you are for marrying my son one more time, I'm going to throw you out in the snow and let you freeze. I knew you weren't a good match when you got married. I also know that he was so in love with you—or what you represented—that you'd have had to grow a tail and horns for him to see it.

"I know a heap of married couples that got along way worse than you and Jack ever did. You didn't do so badly, Clary. You're no worse than anyone else, or any better. Now eat your elk."

That made her smile. So did the boys. They often stayed at Will Duane's ranch, mostly because of the snowstorms that seldom let up. The first day she was well enough to look outside, a wall of black clouds rose from the mountains and obscured the sun. Snow fell for days. The storm was oppressive and terrifying.

If one of the snowstorms struck, the helicopter couldn't bring the boys back from Will's. She couldn't conceive of a ranch so large that you needed a helicopter to visit the neighbor's. The boys loved it, though. They came back more excited than she had ever seen them.

"You've gotta come to Will's ranch, Mom. It's not just a ranch. It's a lab. It's a better lab than you had at home." Jimmy's face lit up.

"They're doing research sort of like yours, Mom. We could all work there, when you're feeling better." Ricky added.

"No one thinks it's weird that kids know what we know. This is a cool place, Mom," Jimmy said.

She smiled wanly, not wanting to dampen their joy.

Sometimes the depression lifted a little. Like the day Will picked her up in his chopper and took her to lunch in town. The town looked like a full employment opportunity for people owning snowplows, but it managed to stay open. The weather was all anyone talked about.

Will took her to a cute little restaurant and then to a western-themed dress shop. "Let me treat you, Clarisse. It will do both of us good."

She bought a bunch of things, feeling very embarrassed not to pay with her own money. Maternity jeans and a western top, a pants suit with pointed yokes and pearl snap buttons. A feminine dress with a tiered skirt. A bathrobe and nightgowns. Slippers. She'd been wearing donations from the staff at Will's house. With her expanding waistline, she needed more.

"Thank you, Will. I'll pay you back…"

"No, you won't."

Then they went to the ranch and discussed her status, but first she'd had to clear up an obvious discrepancy.

"Will, I'm not going to pussy-foot around. There are things about you and this ranch that I don't get. If my boys are going to keep coming here, I need some answers. You were in your mid-sixties when you left Numenon. That was eighteen years ago. You should be in your eighties, but you don't look older than you did back then. In fact, you look younger. How do you account for that?"

"Well, ma'am, I'm afraid that's top secret." Will aped Billy Jack's best Oklahoma drawl.

"That's not good enough, Will."

"I can't say, Clarisse. Not unless you sign on with us. We have a project going here. It *is* top secret, but not for the government. It's a private top-secret project, and we guard it with tighter security than any you've seen. That's all I'll say, except that I would be delighted if you'd join us. You have exactly the skillset we need.

"That's all you'll say?"

"Yes… Well, I'll say that in my golden years, I decided that I should give back what I've gotten. The project we're working on benefits everyone. More than that—if it works, it will save the world."

"That's what the aliens said."

"Do I look like an alien?"

She studied him, frowning. He sat in his office in his magnificent log house with those fantastic looks and that famous white hair. She'd seen him on so many magazine covers in the old days. He looked better in real life. A hunk, at sixty. How?

"Now it's your turn to face the music," he said. "You need to make some decisions, and I am eminently qualified to help you make them. First off, I think you and the boys should come back from the dead," Will said.

"Can't we just live and work here and let things be? I need to find out more about your project, but I could be happy living out here."

"Clarisse, do you know how much you're worth?"

"No. I always let my dad deal with that."

"According to what my attorneys could find, and the copy of your trust that Billy Jack loaned me, it's in the high hundreds of millions."

"What?!"

"Your family works sort of like I did in the old days. I was a defense contractor. It's profitable; that's where I made most of my money. That and the tech stuff. Your parents had multiple patents, contracts, and research pacts. They were rich. Did you know that?"

"Not really. I knew the house was valuable, but we'd lived in it for so long, it was just home. None of us are showy."

"Do you know what's happening to it now?" She shook her head. "Since you and the boys are technically dead and you have no blood relations, the trust specifies that Hull House will be turned into a museum celebrating the Hull genius. It will be that in perpetuity; it can't be sold or used for anything else."

"No!"

"Yes. And your assets are being tucked away for the use of some lucky stranger who shows up and who has your DNA. People are lining up to be tested."

"They'll never find a match."

"That's right. Only our mysterious friend who's causing the weather to go nuts is related to the Hull line. If he comes forward, in a human form, he will be qualified to take over your estate. He's the only possible DNA match."

"So what's the money being used for?"

"Nothing. It's parked in accounts in places like the Cayman Islands. It might as well not exist. All that wealth is being totally wasted, making trust officers rich. Clarisse, let me give you a bit of fatherly advice: NEVER LET GO OF YOUR MONEY. You may need it one day."

"But what about all the spies and bad guys following us?"

"My place is as safe as anywhere on the planet. I'll give you a tour of our security systems and staff. You're welcome to live with us. You'd have your own house. We have lots of room. Or you could live at Billy Jack's.

"Billy Jack and I have become good friends. I finally realized he wants his spread for Ricky and Jimmy, and for whatever may come. I've already extended my security perimeter to include Billy Jack's place. I did that hoping you'd join us, but also to keep whatever's after you from busting in my back door."

"Well, I'll think about it. I hadn't thought of much beyond being in a safe place with the boys. But it does make sense." She had been thinking of more than that, and come up with an eventuality that chilled her soul. What if the powers that be, her old bosses, the real powers behind the government, figured out a way to break the trusts and take the Hull assets? What horror would they fund?

"There's something else I need to discuss with you." Will glanced at her with those blue eyes. He had something big to say.

Her breath stopped. What else?

"It's good, don't worry. I've branched out a lot since leaving Numenon. Smaller projects, like Fish Inc. Nothing so global and all consuming. Among other things, I invested in a film studio."

"Really?" Clarisse could see Will as a studio chief. He had all the flare...

"I'm more of a silent partner. My friend Niles Swanne—have you heard of him?" She shook her head. "Me neither. He's a huge actor in horror films. Never heard of him until we did that Native American retreat together back in the 90s.

"He was sick of playing zombies and vampires; he wanted to direct and produce. And write. He's a very good screenwriter. He'd already incorporated Ragnarök Properties when we met. I put a little money into it; we're off and running.

"Did you know that Jack wrote a TV series when he was in England?" Her eyes widened. Will scoffed. "Of course you didn't; you were abducted by aliens. His agent got it to one of our people, who got it to

Niles. Who went nuts over it. We optioned it. We also optioned all of Jack's books for movies.

"This wasn't a favor, Clarisse. Niles did the deal before I found out about it; he's got an amazing ability to pick hits. I completely agreed with him when I read the screenplays. This didn't involve any patronage on my part; I didn't know you or Jack then. Jack's work is that good.

"With him dead, his living trust administered his assets and intellectual properties. As you agreed when the two of you set up the trust, it specifies you as his beneficiary and executor. Since you were presumed dead, we've been working with his attorney. Now that you're back, you're his heir.

"The initial offer is in the high tens of millions, but we can negotiate more, if you want. We can bump it up, give you a portion of the profits from the films and the series. We can make a documentary about Jack, too. Niles thinks the series is going to be a spectacular hit. It's about you, by the way. A beautiful scientist and undercover agent. He loved you, Clarisse."

"Oh, no!" Tears rushed to her eyes. "Oh, my God."

"Say yes, Clarisse, and we can have the deal done in a week."

"Oh, my God. Jack would have been delighted. Oh. That's wonderful, Will. He was never appreciated when he was alive."

"No, he wasn't, but he will be now. This series is going to knock people over. Have you read it?" She shook her head. "I'll send you the screenplays."

Will's words did it. When she got back to Billy Jack's, she walked around the porch in front of the house, thinking. It didn't take much thought. She marched back into the house, and picked up the phone. "Will, please begin working on my return from the dead. I'm feeling livelier already."

Clarisse decided to put her marriage to Jack and her interlude with Elias behind her. She began the laborious process of coming back to life and bringing the boys with her. They would be a family, just the three of them. Or four, soon. Will's attorneys initiated the steps needed to declare their previous deaths invalid and restore her assets.

Clary placed her hands on her hard, round belly. They'd abducted her last May. She'd been a hostage until October. Six months of captivity. It was May of 2017, now. A year later. The baby would arrive in June—a few more weeks. It bumped and thumped inside her, growing well and apparently very happy.

She was the only one who was sad.

The snow kept falling.

SECTION THREE
MONTANA:
WILL DUANE'S PLACE
&
BILLY JACK'S RANCH

LATE MAY 2017

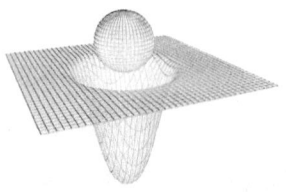

FIFTY

THE DEAD GUY

"DEFINITELY A BREACH," said the technician who'd first seen the object flying past a screen in the ranch's security center. Lights flashed and a siren wailed, indicating that something had tripped the sensors covering the property.

The team's twelve computer stations ringed the room. Every team member had multiple screens, viewing two or more at a time. Larger screens ringed the bunker just below the ceiling. They were subdivided into quarters. Quarter screens displayed strategically significant points around the ranch and beyond. The locations shown rotated around the clock—that many areas needing observation existed.

"There it is," the technician pointed to his screen. "I replayed it. Slow down the image. Freeze it."

He replayed the images of a large, rocket-shaped object hurtling from the sky. It had to have hit the ground on Jack Abercrombie's property. "See. There's the landing spot. That big puff in the snow."

"Yeah, I see it. What is it?"

"I don't know what it is. Could be anything from a body to a missile."

"We have to check it out."

"Affirmative."

"I don't know how we're supposed to keep this place secure," someone complained. "Between the Indian Reservations and the federal lands, the map of the ranch looks like a jigsaw puzzle. It's like trying to do border patrol on a sieve. Where that thing landed isn't even mapped."

"Ours is not to question why, ours is but to do or die."

"Enough talk. We have to figure out what that was and how to defuse it. If it needs defusing."

"And figure out where it is."

Everyone was silent as they played back and magnified the images.

The security station at the Montana ranch was larger than most in Will Duane's installations. When he'd been the richest man in the world, he'd been known as being obsessive to over-the-top paranoid about his personal security and that of his enterprises. He hadn't changed. When he'd started the Montana project, Will's ranch had already contained hundreds of thousands of acres. His original reasons for buying such immense acreage, though, had changed, and changed again.

He had a new family, a new mission, and a use for the gigantic ranch.

As the mission unfolded, he bought more land and went underground. On a spring day, a visitor would see rolling lawns and greenery, and never realize that a research facility as big and modern as any in Silicon Valley lay under his feet.

The security staff had no idea what the place produced—only that they were paid better than their wildest dreams, and that if they talked about it, they'd be out of a job and blacklisted. After a while, that didn't bother anyone. Trying to secure a 450,000-acre spread dotted with federal land and Indian reservations, lakes, and impassable terrain was *enough* to worry about.

"How can we get out to where it landed? It's in the middle of nowhere." The team continued its investigation. Analysis at ultra-slow speeds revealed that it was a body, hurtling downward headfirst. They were able to slow the video and magnify the images enough to get some good ID shots. No one knew who it was.

"He had to fall out of a plane. He's heading straight down. No parachute."

No *nothing*. The guy was naked.

"This is a job for the cowboys." The techs called the beefier commando-types employed at the ranch "cowboys." Experts at wilderness survival, weaponry, and modern warfare, these people were not your traditional cowboys. Most of them had only visual acquaintance with cattle or horses. The *real* cowboys, who handled the cattle, buffalo, and horse production on the spread lived miles away.

"Set the commandos up with electronic guidance and send them out with the helicopter. They can get the guy in a couple of hours." That was the plan.

But the storm came up out of nowhere. It was late May, and everyone should have been basking in the glory of the early May fishing in Montana and getting ready for the next foray to the rivers, but they weren't. All but the techs were sandbagging the entrances to the research labs and digging trenches.

"Shit. The last thing we need is more snow. When this pack melts, this whole place could flood."

"We need to find the dead guy. And we need to tell Mr. Duane."

"He took off for California this morning to spend time with his wife."

"Think he'll mind if we don't recover the dead guy? He won't thaw for a while," said the latest hire.

Everyone looked at him.

"Okay. I'm new. I've never seen Will Duane pissed off. I don't want to, from what I've heard. Fine. Having an unidentified body lying around will make him mad. So how do we get the body? Snowmobiles? That's all that could get out there."

They could hear the wind howling even underground. Snow whipped across the skylights above them.

"No one's going anywhere until the storm clears."

That was it. They decided on the helicopter, when the storm abated enough for them to get near the body's impact site. Otherwise, they'd truck in as close as possible to the site, then use the snowmobiles. Sled him out and begin the identification process.

"Ah, shit. I wanted to use the mules!"

"Very funny. Mules with snowshoes?"

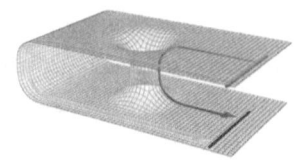

FIFTY-ONE

WRECKAGE

THREE FEROCIOUS DAYS passed before the storm blew itself out. When that happened, the helicopter pilot over at Will's called to say the wind had busted the chopper. Billy Jack knew that the main hangar was occupied by whatever had brought Clary and the others back. *Guess they didn't get the chopper in one of the smaller hangars before the gale flattened Montana.*

When Jimmy and Ricky went over to Will's to do their mysterious work, they usually flew them home the same day. Not this time. Billy Jack would have to go get them, and get them fast. The old man looked up at the sky. Just wisps of clouds. He didn't trust the clear weather for a minute. He had to make this trip because he thought Clary's time was coming. They needed a doctor, which they had at Will's, and she needed to have her sons close by.

The damn freak storm had busted the helicopter and closed the main highway. That wasn't such a bad thing. It was three hours on the main road to get to Will's, but the back road they had cut the summer before was only an hour and a half, assuming you didn't mind a hair-raising adventure.

Billy Jack opened the car barn's wide doors and surveyed The Monster. A truck to match the mountains. Clary called it a "boy toy." True. No man could look at the truck without a sense of joy. Even someone as tall as him had to crane his neck to see the roof. The Monster's floor was four feet off the ground. It had tires that made the rest of it look small, with grooves so deep, they might have been tank treads. Might have been a tank, too, for all the extras he'd had added to it when they'd built it for him. Had a bulldozer blade on the front, winches front and back. A backhoe was installed in the truck bed.

Enough dawdling. Billy Jack reached up and opened the door, tossing the sack of food Clary had made for him up onto the seat. Before Jimmy and Ricky had come, he'd used to use a stepladder to get into The Monster, but the boys had built him a hydraulic ladder that retracted tightly under the chassis and practically buckled his belt after settling him in.

"Time to see if I've still got it," the old rancher said. With luck, he'd be back by noon.

He headed out the back of his spread. Road was okay there, for a dirt road. This easy stretch gave him time to think. Clary was very nervous, fretting about her boys' safety. *And* she needed a doctor. She'd had a hard time over the months she'd been with him. Billy Jack hadn't seen a rougher pregnancy, even with all the cows and mares he'd owned. They usually sailed through making their babies. Those nine months had been a snap for his wife, too, God bless her.

Not Clary. She was as big as *two* houses and carrying low. Her back hurt. The boys were so sweet to her, helping her with everything. The baby was their cousin and their brother. Weird situation, but legal, except that Clary and the father weren't married.

He'd never seen grief like Clary's, though. Like everything alive had been crushed out of her. When she'd first gotten there, he'd wanted her there because of the boys. She was his son's wife. He owed keeping her to Jack, even though he'd never really liked her. Billy Jack always had thought Clary was too smart, too fast, and too sharp, like she might bite. And she had entirely too many muscles. Didn't treat Jack right either. Never was in love with him. Jack hadn't been able to tell, but he certainly had.

When she'd come to the ranch, his son dead and her being pregnant with another man's child, he'd let her stay purely out of human kindness and sympathy, and because of her boys. *And* because of her bravery and what she'd gone through. Stories from the people she'd saved got around. She was a lioness in a situation that would break generals.

Early on, she'd corralled him and said, "Elias and I weren't lovers all that time. I stayed true to Jack. We lived together, because they'd have killed us if we didn't. We were like brother and sister. I *wouldn't* betray Jack.

"Just that last night," she'd looked down, tears forming in her big eyes, "when we thought we were going to die the next day. He begged me, and... we..." Did it, obviously.

He'd come to love her like a poor, broken daughter. Her crazy parents and tragedy had warped her. He liked the broken Clary much better than Commando Clarisse, fighting the world.

This Clary didn't have any more fight. She didn't try to hide how she felt or how much she loved this Elias fellow. All the terror of living in that hell came up now that she was safe. Clary had screaming nightmares almost every night. She cried out for El.

Billy Jack held her; he didn't want the boys to see their mom that way. But they knew. She told him snippets of the life she'd lived all those months, and about Pops. She said that Elias had stayed behind to fight Pops and them. To destroy them.

He was making *this* crazy trip for Clary. She saw the doctor at Will's, but she wanted to be at his place. Billy Jack thought it was because she believed her Elias would come for her there.

"We told him about your ranch, Papa Jack." The boys gave him more information than Clary did, about how they'd communicated with this guy through a game, and how Jimmy had communicated with him psychically. "But that stopped, Papa Jack, when we got here."

"Okay. Now things get real," he said, jolting out of his reverie. He'd reached a sea of rocks and snow. The road was a rocky track at the best of times. Now it was a nightmare. Rocks that had fallen in the storm and small slides blocked it. Snow stacked the hillsides above the road, threatening major avalanches at any time.

He dropped the bucket and bulldozed his way through it. Some of the time, he let The Monster walk its way across the rocky wasteland.

One big front tire ratcheted its way over a boulder and down its other side, only to pick up again at the next giant rock.

His heart started to pound and sweat covered his lip. He'd brought his heart pills, but he didn't take one. What was a seventy-six-year-old man doing this for? Had to be crazy.

He thought things like that, but mostly, he drove the truck.

Then he entered the back gate of Will's place.

"Ricky, Jimmy, we'd better get a move on," Billy Jack stood by his truck in the middle of the "farmyard." This part of the spread was a ranch in name only. The gigantic super-log house did have a barn, bunkhouses, and corrals, but the action was underground in the lab. Covered by snow.

Jimmy and Ricky bounded out of a bunker, carrying packs with their latest inventions.

"What we just made is going to be great, Papa Jack. It will boost your cell reception and internet so it's as good as here."

Which was as good as the highest power station in a major city, he knew, though he hadn't toured Will Duane's underground mega-lab, not being a member of staff and not taking "the pledge." Billy Jack didn't want to get into any of Will's doings. He just wanted to be neighbors and friends.

"Wow! You brought The Monster," Jimmy said of the huge truck, craning his neck to see the top.

"With the weather the way it is, I didn't want to take the mountain route without it."

"Let's see you get in, Papa Jack. I want to see how our ladder works."

Billy Jack smiled through his worry and fatigue. He let their invention lift him up and put him in his seat. "It works just like you designed it. Now let's pick up that doctor and get back to your mother."

He didn't want to say how worried he was for her, but his face must have said it for him. The boys immediately got skittish.

"Have you heard from her?"

"Not since I left. She was okay then, though."

The doctor supervised workers loading boxes of medical supplies and equipment into the backseat of the truck's crew cab.

Billy Jack looked at the man. Dr. Mang. One of those foreign doctors one saw so much of these days. If Will had hired him, he was probably okay. Definitely okay at this point, since he was all they had.

The old man could feel how tired he was. He'd driven The Monster over a pass that had just barely been passable when it was constructed. Did he have it in him to get back? Hell, yes, he did. If that little gal could hang out in a cabin in her condition waiting for him, he'd be there.

"Damnation!" Behind the barn and blocking the exit that went to the mountain road were three trucks, two of them crew-cabs with 4WD almost as beefy as his. They all had winches and the first had a blade on the front. The first two pulled trailers with snowmobiles. Crews loaded all matter of equipment into the beds.

Jack pulled up, "Say, can I get through?" He glanced toward the sky. The clouds had changed from wispy to heavy wispy.

"You just come over the pass?" said one of the workers, probably the supervisor.

"A while ago."

"It was clear?"

"Clear for a rock yard. Should have been riding a mule. But this truck did it, and what you've got should do it, too. Could you move, please?"

"Oh, yeah. Sorry." he turned to the others and had them move the trucks.

"That's a lot of equipment for an afternoon tour," Billy Jack drawled, suddenly suspicious. That was a *lot* of stuff for a normal patrol.

"I can't talk about it, but there was a potential breach of security. Over on your place, actually."

"My place? That's *my* business. What breach? Any danger to my daughter-in-law or the kids?"

"No. Something may have fallen out of a plane. You know how things are these days. Planes breaking apart in the sky. We're going to take a look."

"You better start fast, to beat the blow." Jack hauled ass out of there.

"Are we going to be all right, Papa Jack?" Jimmy called out. They'd been on the road for about an hour. Everyone was belted in tight, even at ten miles per hour. The Monster rolled up to a boulder with its giant tread, crawled its way over, and then dropped down on the other side. Only to repeat the process with the next great rock.

They were holding steady and making progress, but slow progress. They'd be okay if a snow squall didn't hit them. He looked up through the windshield. That *could* happen.

His heart pounded and sweat ran down his face. He was breathing hard.

"Excuse me, Mr. Abercrombie," said Dr. Mang. "Are you well?"

"As well as a seventy-six-year-old man driving this vehicle at nine thousand feet with a snowstorm coming and worried about my daughter-in-law can be. How 'bout yourself?"

"Mr. Abercrombie, I think we should stop. I think I should check your vital signs."

"That's probably right, Dr. Mang. One thing, can you drive this truck?"

"No, sir. I cannot."

"Boys?"

"I get my learner's permit next year. I could try," said Ricky.

"I think I should keep on driving. If I pass out or die, I'll try to hit the parking brake. You can take over. How about that?"

Billy Jack kept driving. His heart hurt, but he let it. Let his hands shake. Let his mouth go dry because he had to breathe through it or not at all.

"Papa Jack, I think we…"

None of them saw or heard it coming. It hit the truck right behind the cab. The truck jolted, bounced, and slowly rolled on its side. The wheels continued to turn for a while, and then all was silent.

FIFTY-TWO

RESCUE

T HE CARAVAN TO find the dead guy set out later than expected. The team supervisor had misgivings about going out so late, but some idiot communications jock had given Mr. Duane his daily update on the ranch and told him about the dead guy.

That was stupid; even worse was telling him that Mr. Abercrombie had been there to pick up the boys and the doctor because he was afraid the baby might be on the way. Dr. Hull was alone. *And* he'd told him that the helicopter wasn't working and the main road was closed due to the storm.

Duane was in a jet, on his way back to the ranch now.

The supervisor was not a newbie. He was one of those who knew what it was like being on the receiving end of Will Duane's rage. They'd better get that body or die trying. Dying might be preferable to what would happen to them if they failed.

"Let's move it," he barked into the shortwave joining the caravan. They were set. Mr. Abercrombie had said it was clear. Plenty of daylight. Clouds weren't bad. They'd be back before dark, or they could stay over at the Abercrombie place. No problem.

I'm fucking out of my mind, the supervisor thought just over an hour later. They were hanging off the edge of the so-called "road" between

Will Duane's ranch and the Abercrombie place. The old man had said the road was passable from the other direction, but that they'd better hurry to "beat the blow." Blow? Goddamned hurricane. Rocks across the road, avalanches, if small ones. He drove first truck with five other guys in the crew cab. It had a blade in front, which was why they were moving at all. They had brought three trucks total, with a couple of work crews.

The crews were jammed in the first two trucks. The vehicles had winches and everything they'd need for a difficult extraction. They also pulled four snowmobiles on trailers. This was a big production to rescue a guy who couldn't say thank you.

The temperature dropped by the minute, too. Isolated flakes of snow drifted by.

"That's it. We're going back," the supervisor said.

A roar covered the sound of his voice. He looked back and saw an ocean of snow and rock roaring down the mountain, heading for them. Rolling like surf, but more terrible. Trees snapped. It ate everything in front of it.

Someone in the backseat shrieked. "It took the last truck!" The rumbling of snow and rock covering the road spoke louder than he could.

He hit the gas. The truck behind him followed, banging over the rock-strewn road. Snow dumped on them like a machine was overhead, spewing it out. Maybe he was yelling. Maybe the others were, too.

The screaming white monster roared past them, down the hill. He kept driving, grabbing to the wheel, holding on as hell passed. Finally, the place was eerily quiet, just echoes of the crashing rock and snow reverberating off the mountains. He slowed and then stopped.

They went back and searched for the last truck and the men in it, but they were gone. The slide had uprooted trees and boulders all the way down to the valley.

"Should we search?" someone asked, looking at the tangle.

"Not if we want to get out of this alive. They couldn't have survived that. You can't even see the truck. It's buried under half the mountain. Someone, call back to headquarters and tell them. We have to go forward now. There's no other way out."

They fought their way around a switchback to see that the road ahead was clear of major landslides, at least around the deep cut into the mountain in front of them and out the other side. They couldn't see past the far ridge.

"When we get past that ridge up there, we should start heading out of the mountains. The dead guy was in a meadow just off the road." He nodded at the GPS's screen. It showed topographical lines and a dot where the guy had gone in. The dot had been added by whoever had loaded the map; nothing of the dead guy was visible on their equipment.

"Drifts might be twenty feet in the meadow." He couldn't help cursing. "I've lived here all my life. We don't have weather like this in Montana. We get snow, but not like this, and not almost in June... Well, no sense cryin' about what you can't fix. Let's get that body."

They made it into the deep cleft of the mountainside and out of the fold, on beyond it. Just around the corner, the super jammed on the brakes.

"Oh, shit."

Abercrombie's monster truck lay on its side. The old man, two boys, and the doctor stood beside it waving at them.

"Thank God!" Abercrombie shouted when they got close. "We have to get back to the ranch. Got a shortwave SOS from Clarisse. She's in labor, all alone."

"How far away is your place?"

"An hour in this slop, if you don't run into what I did." The cause of the tipped truck was obvious. A six-foot-tall boulder that looked like it had been chiseled into a giant bowling ball was lodged behind the cab. A champion bowler might have thrown it, just to hit that spot.

They ringed it and whistled. "Truck's a strong mother, I'll say. It didn't flip and roll all the way down."

The passengers didn't look quite as good as they had at a distance, the team leader noticed. Abrasions, cuts, glass fragments all over.

"We climbed out the windshield. Main injury is Dr. Mang. Busted arm. I put a splint on him," the old man said.

The doctor nodded, pale with pain. He wouldn't be much good to anyone.

"We've got to get to Mom!" Jimmy cut through the chatter.

"Yeah, and fast," Billy Jack said. "Clary sounded bad. Those snowmobiles will be the best way to get there, if you avoid the heavy drifts. I'd say some are forty feet deep, and we don't know where those are. They could swallow us whole."

"*Mom's going to die! We need to go!*"

"*Jimmy and I can tell where the deep drifts are! Let us go!*"

The supervisor cut in, "No, kids. This isn't for you."

"These boys aren't kids." Billy Jack took control. He might croak on this mountain, but he'd be damned if he'd let Clary down. "These boys know more than you ever will about… everything. Get the snowmobiles down. Each of them can take two people." Billy Jack turned to the doctor. "You able to handle an hour in a snowmobile?"

Dr. Mang turned away and vomited into the snow.

"Compound fracture," Billy Jack said. "Nasty." He pointed, "The mountains end about two bends from here. Follow the road. It's flat. Nuthin' more to fall on you, though plenty can drop out from under you till you hit the flat."

They began unloading the snowmobiles from the flatbed trailers.

"Doc, we're gonna borrow all your stuff that we can pack. Who wants to go in the snowmobiles with us? I'm driving one."

Five operatives volunteered, including the boss.

"What about the dead guy?" someone asked.

"What dead guy?" Billy Jack said.

"Well, there was a little more to our mission than I told you," the team leader sputtered. "We're out here to get a dead guy that surveillance showed falling from the sky. He fell headfirst. Looked like he'd been pitched out of a plane."

"If he survived the fall, he'd freeze to death in minutes," Billy Jack said. All of them were cocooned in down and higher-tech arctic gear.

"He was already dead. We've got pictures. He froze in the air. You can see the frost." He pulled his tablet out with the best freeze-frame image showing. It was blurry, but clear enough to identify. "Do you know him?"

Billy Jack shook his head. "No. Boys, do you know him?"

Ricky and Jimmy looked at the screen. They stifled cries and pulled together, grabbing each other.

"It's Elias," Ricky said. "We've never really seen him, but that's him."

Billy Jack took a closer look at the picture. "He looks like Alex Caldwell." He'd seen a picture of the man at Clary's house in Palo Alto, the one time he'd been there. But he also saw Alex Caldwell's image every time he looked at Jimmy and Ricky.

"Is this your uncle Elias?" he asked the boys.

"Yes," they nodded, the rims of their eyes reddening in the cold as they blinked back tears.

"Oh, boy. Poor Clary. Jesus. Well, if we see him, we'll pick him up. Now let's go help Clary." Sweat ran down his cheeks and his heart banged in his chest. No matter. Let his heart bang away as it wanted.

He couldn't stop and didn't want to. If he died out here trying to help Clary, that was fine. An old man for a young mother with three kids was a fair trade. If he lost that girl and her baby, his heart would break anyway.

The four snowmobiles took off down the incline from the road. Jimmy and Ricky acted like bloodhounds, scenting the depth of the drifts and any drop-offs in the ground beneath them that could cause them to tumble.

"Stay on the throttle, boys; don't let them stall out," Billy Jack shouted. "Keep up your RPMs and go forward. We got long tracks on these babies and wide skids. We should get through just fine."

Their snowmobiles blasted across open white meadows, jumping off hillocks and digging the threads in as they turned. The engines roared. They flew toward the ranch, finally making speed.

"What the hell is that?" Billy Jack stopped, panting when they pulled over a shallow ridge. The others pulled up, staring. Down below, something like an inverted ant's nest made a circle that was two hundred feet across. An upside down, very shallow cone, dropped down a few feet in the center. Not a tree or branch broke the cone's finely sifted snow. In the middle, two legs coming up protruded to the knee. The feet pointed slightly upward. They were blue, frozen solid.

"It must be the dead guy," the supervisor said.

"Definitely dead. But why like that?" Billy Jack said.

"Dunno." The super motioned for one of the operatives to investigate. He did, hand on his weapon. "What are you going to do? Shoot a frozen dead guy's *feet*? Christ, I'll do it."

He put one foot into the cone's circle, and the snow fell away, leaving him on a slide aimed at the corpse. "Ahhh!" he cried, trying to scramble back up and failing. The snowpack disintegrated, seemingly mostly air.

The team super ended up jammed next to the body, which was revealed as the snow around it disappeared. He clawed away, climbing to his feet, staring in horror at the corpse.

It was frozen stiff, with hands and arms held out in front of it, Superman style. They were sunken into the ground. The top of the head rested on the frozen dirt. The corpse was frost blue. The dead guy was very dead. He was also very good-looking, a study in muscles and fine anatomy.

"Uncle Elias!" Jimmy cried and ran down the sloppy incline to the body. Ricky followed him, not making a sound. They stood by their uncle.

"What happened to him?"

Billy Jack had a bad feeling. "Something tells me he was on his way home when whatever did this caught up with him. I have a feeling that that same something is headed for my house and Clary, planning to dish it out to her and that baby.

"Leave him here. Nothing can hurt him now. Let's save our girl!"

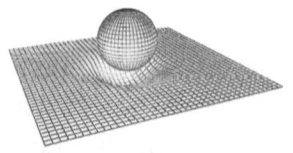

FIFTY-THREE

HARD LABOR

C LARY'S BACK HAD ached for hours. She walked slowly around the kitchen. The baby wasn't due for at least another week. That was according to the charts, but Jimmy and Ricky had been two weeks late. She'd assumed that was how this one would be also. She had settled at Billy Jack's ranch. She felt good around her former father-in-law and loved the ranch as much as she could love anything during these hollow days.

Will's place was hours away by the highway. The mountain route was shorter, but it was worse than she'd imagined riding a horse would be. Billy Jack had tried to drive her to Will's that way over the summer. Her back had started hurting so much, they'd barely made a mile or two on the road before turning around.

Clary was glad Billy Jack had taken his immense, 4WD truck, but she hoped that didn't mean he planned to drive over the mountain. He hadn't told her; she'd been sleeping when he left. She thought no one was crazy enough to go that way after that storm.

It was late afternoon. He should have been back by now. Her nerves had her jumping at any sound. A light sweat covered her face. She couldn't stop pacing.

The first hard pain ripped her back, catching her by surprise. She bent over the kitchen table, resting one hand on the table and pressing the small of her back with the other. "Oh!" The contraction was strong enough to make her cry out.

She looked out of the window at the white ranch yard. Still covered with snow at this time of year. It should have been a muddy mess with spring flowers dotting the muck.

"Oh!" Another ripping pain. *Not now.* She was alone. Huge white flakes drifted by the window, whipped horizontal by the wind. They had an infirmary at Will's. She'd been seeing an OB-GYN over there. Everything was normal with her and the baby. The delivery was all set up for Will's clinic. She had wanted it to be at home, but the clinic was safer. Who knew what special needs this baby might have? Billy Jack must have gone to get a doctor, but been unable to get back.

Could she get to Will's by herself? Wind lashed the house, shaking its log bulk. The wind was too severe; they couldn't use the helicopter. She picked up the phone. The line was dead. Cell phone. Nothing. Service was too spotty out here to count on even in the best of times. Shortwave. Clary had been able to use one blindfolded—in the old days.

Her hands felt like marshmallows; she was retaining water like crazy due to the pregnancy. She powered up the device, fumbling with swollen fingers as she did it. You were supposed to say, "Calling CQ. CQ." And give your call signal. What was it? What was Billy Jack's damn call signal? It was a prize cow's registration number, Billy Jack's lucky number. CQ meant any frequency that was listening.

"Hello. Calling CQ. This is Clary. I'm in labor. No one's here. I'm at Billy Jack's ranch. I need help." Damn it! She couldn't remember the fucking number. Her back ached. Maybe she'd sent a message. Maybe someone had heard. She slumped and walked away from the receiver. She'd been a commando. She'd been able to use any type of equipment or technology, learning on the fly.

What had happened to her? Why couldn't she remember anything? She'd have a thought, and an instant later, it would be gone. Remembering anything was a trial, as was thinking. The doctor at the clinic had said she would be able to remember better when her depression and grief lifted.

Clary laughed, semi-hysterical. Neither hadn't lifted at all! And she wouldn't take the antidepressants offered her.

El's baby was half-alien. Who knew what pills would do to him? He *was* a him; she'd had an ultrasound. She'd named him Robert Jack Elias Dalton Hull, the longest baby name outside of royalty. She took the vitamins and iron they suggested. She should have taken more iron; she was anemic. She got dizzy easily and any little scrape bled like crazy.

This pregnancy wasn't like the others. This was hard and carried with it huge mood swings and cramps in her back and legs. Nightmares. The baby was so big and pressed on her back. She went to the bathroom every two minutes.

Oh, why had she told Billy Jack it was okay to leave when he'd asked her the night before? It wasn't. But she wanted the boys back. Maybe he hadn't been thinking right when he took off; he'd just heard that his ranch in Oklahoma was underwater from the floods. He wanted to go there, but what could he do, anyway? Everything was washed away or ruined.

Elias had failed at his quest to destroy them. The world was devastated. Floods, landslides, fires. Earthquakes. Silicon Valley was nothing but debris from 'the big one.' The TV showed pictures of venture capitalists trying to rescue computers from condemned tilt-ups. Less developed parts of the world were rubble. *They* had won.

"Oh. Oh." She clutched her back. Her back hurt worse than anything when she was in labor. No one had told her about that ahead of time. With her first baby, she'd thought something was dreadfully wrong.

"No, honey, that's just how *you* do labor," the nurse had said. Clary had resented her calling her "honey" back then. She'd love that endearment now.

She was in labor. How could she be so stupid as to be alone *now*? No one knew how long the gestation of a baby who was part of them would be. Why had she thought this baby would be like Jimmy and Ricky?

The pains racked her. Clenching her teeth, Clary grabbed her coat and the keys to the SUV. She went outside and was almost blown off her feet. Gusts of wind swept the yard between the house and barns. The house and garage. The house and anything. She shoved her way into it, holding onto the rail along the porch.

Could she make it to the garage? Could she drive the SUV for three hours to Will's? Was the highway open? Would the car start? Clary got to the end of the porch. "Oh, no!" Liquid splattered on the wooden slats. Water streaked with bright red blood ran down her legs.

That's when she knew. Elias had failed. She and the baby would die, alone. She would bleed to death, and her child would freeze.

She looked up and saw Pops' face floating over the meadow. He smiled at her, a superior and all-knowing grimace.

"Oh, Dr. Hull, I bet you wish you'd sided with us." That nasty chuckle. "Or if you don't yet, you soon will. Your 'Elias' is dead. I killed him not long ago. You know why I'm here, don't you?"

Her eyes shot open. She gasped.

"You are very quick, my dear. I want your baby. Nothing of Elias' can survive. And neither can you."

She turned and ran, barring the heavy wooden door behind her. It wouldn't keep him out. What *would* keep him out?

"El. Elias. Bobby. Robert. El. Elias. Bobby. Robert. El. Elias. Bobby. Robert." She'd been repeating the words like a mantra the last few weeks as her anxiety peaked. *El. Elias. Bobby. Robert. El. Elias. Bobby. Robert.* She repeated silently, dashing around the house's lower floor, closing draperies and shades, locking windows. If only she could go outside and close the shutters. But she couldn't.

Clary knew very clearly that only El. Elias. Bobby. Robert was keeping Pops out. Blood ran down her leg. *This isn't how it was supposed to be. El. Elias. Bobby. Robert.* She had to deliver her own baby. She was supposed to have a doctor. The others were supposed to be here. Clary straightened up as well as she could. She was a soldier. She would do it.

Bent at the waist, Clary made her way into her bedroom, the cheery log haven in which she'd lain awake so many nights, in which she'd screamed in terror from the nightmares.

Pulled off her clothes and put on a gown and bathrobe, the one Will had bought her. Grabbed all the towels. Did she cut the cord? Or not? Scissors. Where? Kitchen.

Oh, no. That one drove her to her knees. She crawled from the kitchen with the scissors, leaving a trail of blood behind her. *El. Elias. Bobby. Robert.*

"Please, Elias. Help. I need you. He's going to take our baby. I'm going to die."

El. Elias. Bobby. Robert. She kept it up as well as she could. El had warned her that she had no idea what Pops could do, or what he would do. Now she did.

No one felt pain like this. Beaten in Iran, raped in Iran, wasn't like this. She shook and groaned, clutching her belly. But she didn't scream.

El. Elias. Bobby. Robert. She made it onto the bed and positioned all the towels beneath her, leaning her back against the headboard. Blood flowed out of her. *El. Elias. Bobby. Robert. El. Elias. Bobby. Robert.*

She would die. He would take the baby. *El. Elias. Bobby. Robert.* She had the crawling sensation she'd had whenever Pops was around. He was in the house.

The urge to push overwhelmed her. Clary screamed, a scream of rage and pain and deliverance. Once, twice, and the baby lay between her legs. She grabbed him and clawed for the shotgun under the bed.

Pops' face appeared on the wall. She shot both barrels into it; the recoil threw her back. She couldn't hear anything; the blasts had been like missiles going off in the small space. Her ears rang. Pops was speaking. She couldn't make out his words, but she knew what he wanted.

"Oh, Dr. Hull, you know your weapons can't hurt me. Give me the child."

She grabbed the baby, not wiping him off, not really looking at him.

"No!" She held him to her shoulder. "He's mine."

"Oh, come, Clarisse. You didn't think I'd let your romantic fantasy play out, did you?" His mouth pinched and he made a tiny pout. "You really didn't think this story would have a happy ending?"

The baby flew from Clary's hands, dangling in the air in the middle of the room. She felt something yank inside her, and then tear loose. Something solid and wet came out, followed by a gush. She didn't look to see what had happened. She knew; the torn umbilical cord dangled inches from the baby's tummy. Pops had broken the cord and pulled the placenta out too soon. She was hemorrhaging. The baby opened his eyes, dark blue-brown, and looked around the room. His eyes fixed on hers.

"Robert! Bobby!" she cried. The child didn't make a sound, just met her gaze.

The infant began floating around the room, moving from one side to the other and up and down.

"Hmm," Pops mused. "Let's have some fun. How about—drop the baby!" The newborn fell like a stone.

Clary jumped up in the bed, screaming and scrambling toward her child. But Pops didn't let him hit the floor.

"That was fun. What else can we do? How about a walk in the woods?" His face floated to the door on the room's far wall. "Where does this go?" The wooden portal opened, letting an arctic-type blast into the room.

"Let's go outside, Clary. That's what *he* called you, didn't he? Clary. How sweet. Will sweet Clary cry and sob for mercy the way strong Dr. Hull wouldn't? You don't look much like Dr. Hull now." Laughter wafted in through the open door.

Clary slipped her legs over the side of the bed and slowly stood. Everything went black. On the floor, she realized she had fainted. She crawled toward the door. She had to get her baby.

"Give me my baby…"

"What's that, my dear? I can't hear you."

She struggled to her feet, grasping the door's frame, and took a shaky step over the threshold. Blood ran down her legs and puddled around her feet. "My baby…" No strength for words. *Get outside and get the baby.* Slipping across the porch, each step a feat worthy of all her military training. Vision blackening, sparkling.

A wide log porch ran across the back of Billy Jack's house. Its overhang framed a garden and view of the mountains. Evergreen trees made it look like Christmas in the snow. The baby's naked body bobbed in the open space.

Her ears rang. Light swam. The baby was in the garden. He didn't make a sound.

"Give me… baby." Just a whisper. Bare feet in the snow blown on the veranda.

"Come on, Clary. I'll give you your baby if you're good enough. You're not good enough. You're not trying. Come down the stairs."

She staggered on the stairs. Made one, slipped and fell forward, landing on her belly in the snow. Clawed the way down. A trail of red followed her.

"Baby…"

"What will you do if I give you your baby back? Tell me?" The baby flew into the air, hurled and then caught, hurled and caught.

"Baby!" Pulling herself forward with her fingers. No snow. No cold. "Baby." The buzzing in her ears diminished to nothing.

"Come on, Clary! Work! Is that all you'll do to get your baby back?"

Lying face down in the snow, she was silent; her nightgown drenched bright scarlet. The area beneath her lower abdomen grew crimson, making a widening circle. Her fingers twitched a few moments.

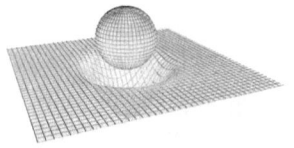

FIFTY-FOUR

THE POSSE

WHEN THE BLAST came, they could see the lights of the house. The caravan of snowmobiles skidded to a stop.

"Was that a rifle?" one of the operatives yelled.

"No, shotgun." Billy Jack said.

The lead operative and Montana native nodded vigorously. Both he and Billy Jack knew guns. "It's a shotgun. You can tell by the deep sound. The snow and the altitude strip off the top registers of the blast. That was inside, too. It would be louder if it were outside. Probably blew the eardrums out of whoever was in there."

"There's a shotgun under Clary's bed," Billy Jack said. "Something's attacking her." He waved to the others, tearing straight across the meadow to the house. No sense in trying to hide the approach of the four snowmobiles, and no time.

Everything was silent when they got to the cabin.

"Jimmy, Ricky, I want you to stay back." They crowded close to him. Billy Jack waved them back. "Boys, your mother wouldn't want you hurt or killed. Stay back. I won't hide anything from you." Billy Jack and the operatives pulled their weapons and charged into the house through the front door.

"Hold up a second," Billy Jack said. He ran to the gun cabinet in the living room; he had one in every room of his house. He pulled out pistols for the boys and a shotgun for himself. "Here. You know how to use these, boys."

"Papa Jack," Jimmy's voice shook.

"What?"

"Blood's coming out of your nose. Your hands are shaking."

"Don't worry about it. I'm old. Stay here."

"Oh, shit. Watch it. I almost slipped," someone said in the kitchen. The bloodstain started there, red, as if someone had squirted a bottle of catsup all over the floor, trailing into Clary's bedroom.

They stood off to each side of the locked bedroom door. The leader kicked the door in and they swung inside, pistols held in two-handed grips.

A thick pad of towels covered the middle of the bed. Blood drenched it, leeching off onto the bedspread. The membranes and placenta were there.

They cautiously made their way to the door. Billy Jack noted the wall opposite the bed that had received the shotgun blast. *Broke through the calking, but the logs held up.*

"Oh, no," he said, walking around the bed. What had happened was written in blood.

The men were silent when they got onto the porch. Billy Jack could see her in the moonlight. Face down in a pool of blood. Blood all the way from the door down the steps. She'd clawed her way over the last bit. Died with her hands outstretched, reaching for her child.

His eyes followed her hand.

"Good God in heaven!" He saw the hole in the ice. The baby was in there! Yanking off his jacket, Billy Jack ran to the pond. Never mind the sweat on his face. The shaking. "The baby's in the pond! Get him out!"

He collapsed before he got to the pool, grabbing his chest, kicking his feet at the pain. Once, twice.

"Where's that doctor? Go back and get that doctor!" the lead operative turned Billy Jack on his back and began CPR. "Get. The. Doctor!" he screamed between breaths into Billy Jack's mouth.

Jimmy and Ricky wandered out of the house, wild-eyed and clutching each other. Looking around, barely breathing. All that was her blood inside. Where was she? Then they saw her.

"Mom! Mom!"

"Mommy!"

They threw themselves down by her. The man working on Papa Jack yelled to get the doctor again.

"Papa Jack!" Jimmy screamed. Ricky dug his nails into his palms and bit his lip.

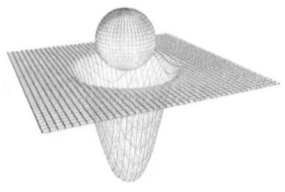

FIFTY-FIVE

THE DEAD GUY, ROUND 2

W HEN BILLY JACK, the expedition leader, and the boys took off on their race to save Clary, they left behind the two crew-cab trucks with all their equipment and seven trained operatives, plus the wounded Dr. Mang. They had the job of retrieving the dead guy, getting him in the truck and hotfooting it to Billy Jack's ranch.

Easier said than done. Whatever formed the "inverse ant hill" around the corpse acted like extremely cold, dissolving sand. Or maybe lightweight Styrofoam chunks made of ice. It collapsed, crunched, and cracked. Wasn't dangerous, really... just weird, and hard to work with. And strange. Everyone had had his share of strange this day.

They shoveled the stuff out of the hole until four of them could get down there to try to pull the frozen body from what seemed like the permafrost beneath him.

The dead guy stood there, looking like an upside down Statue of Liberty with his arms jammed into the frozen turf. He remained just as frozen, and just as dead. Also, big. He was twice as high as a normal man, towering over their heads.

"We could use a winch to pull him down and then out of the cone, but there's nothing to hook the winch cable to." The body was naked.

They thought for a moment.

"Anybody know how to rope? Like with a lasso? There is a lasso in the truck."

For the first time, they truly appreciated their leader, who was a red-hot team roper in addition to being a Montana native. Unfortunately, he wasn't there. Also unfortunately, the lasso was stiff; it wasn't like a piece of rope you could drape over the figure or tie around it. You had to get the loop around the target; that's how it was made.

"I've seen him practice. He swings it like this."

As the sun began to sink into the horizon, they took turns trying to get the lasso's loop around the dead guy. They finally got the loop around his feet, and secured the lariat to the winch on one of the trucks.

When they pulled at him, a wrenching 'snap!' resounded. They all thought that his arms had broken off, but the frozen ground around him had made the noise when it had cracked. The body lay on its side, stiff as ever, but the Styrofoam/sand/snow granules pulled toward him like a magnet was pulling them. Soon, he was buried by a heap of pseudo snow.

They backed out of the hole and stood watching. A blue glow emanated from the mound. The glow grew more intense, until they could see the body shining through the ice stuff. He was turning pink. The snow cover was disappearing.

When he started moving, they ran back to the trucks.

Dr. Mang woke sleepily, having dosed himself with Vicodin. And maybe some other stuff. "What is happening?"

"The dead guy started moving."

"That is impossible," said Mang. "He is dead."

"Not anymore—look."

The erstwhile corpse climbed over the edge of the bowl and approached them. He was a real Superman type. Big and covered with muscles. Unnerving.

He spoke, "You must go to the Abercrombie residence as quickly as possible. Where is the doctor?" Mang held up his hand, his complexion a pale gray. The dead guy frowned. "What happened to you?"

"In the crash. I broke my arm. I took medication."

"Let me see your arm." The supposedly dead guy crowded into the truck, close enough so that those next to him could feel his burning heat.

Way hotter than a regular person. Before the doctor could scream, he had the splint off. "Oh, yes. A bad break. I'll fix it." He pulled the arm hard, causing the broken ends to retract, and ran his hand over the limb, wiping the torn tissues away. "It's healed. Don't take any more medication. You're going to have to work.

"Mr. Abercrombie needs you; you have to hurry. But first, I need a couple of things." When he'd gotten what he wanted from the doc's supplies, the dead guy waved at them. "Go now! Hurry!"

He stepped a short distance away and disappeared.

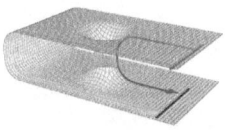

FIFTY-SIX

ELIAS

H E ROSE DIRECTLY into the clouds, through them, and into the infinite calm on the other side. Feeling the cesspool that was what remained of his kind, Elias turned to its dark heart.

"I thought you were dead," Pops smirked. "Did you come back to join us?"

He was a tattered fragment of the force he had once been. Nothing backed up his postured might—no vast spiritual power. No hinted minions. No schemes to invade and destroy.

"I killed her and your baby and the old man. In a moment, I'll go back and get the brats." A hollow laugh, filled with nothing. He was almost powerless, but still capable of a sting. "You think you have defeated me, Elias, but I have defeated you. I have planted my seed in millions of humans. They're just like me: killers, cheaters, thieves. We didn't need the Hull bitch or any of it..."

"Silence, liar." Elias flew into the middle of *him*—and exploded. Pops and his kind were obliterated, their evil gone from the cosmos.

The blast rocked the planet from its orbit for a long instant. The colors, the glory, and the way light shot through the clouds and illumined them—no one had seen anything like it. Like fire, like heaven. Like love. It destroyed, and brought absolution.

Some called it the end of the world; others said it was the beginning. Newscasters played replays of the mega-explosion, interviewed anyone who could talk, and marveled that the storms and disasters playing around the planet had ceased.

As soon as they realized that it wasn't worldwide nuclear war, that it wasn't the harbinger of doom, celebration overcame terror. The people rejoiced. But not everywhere.

When the sky lit up and it seemed that the end had come, one of the people in the two trucks speeding to the ranch said, "It's God."

No one said much of anything about the exploding heavens at Billy Jack's ranch. Grief hung too heavily. The weight of darkness cast a pall on the brightest light.

Elias appeared next to Clary in the snowy yard. Jimmy and Ricky crouched by their mother's still form. No one had touched her. The boys looked up when he appeared.

"El?"

"Uncle Bobby?"

He fired a blast of instantaneous thought at them, telling them what to do. *Do it as fast as you can.* They ran into the house.

He turned Clary on her back and touched her throat, searching for a pulse. Nothing. Looking toward the house, he saw the story spelled out in blood. Following the trail of her outstretched arms, Elias spun and dove into the pond. The ice cracked and water slopped over the banks. He surfaced moments later, carrying his dead son. He put the baby on Clary's belly and picked her up.

"Jimmy!?" he yelled toward the house.

"Here, Uncle Bobby! Upstairs in Papa Jack's room." Jimmy's face appeared in a window. His voice shook when he said Papa Jack.

Elias followed Jimmy's glance and saw the medical tech still giving Billy Jack's dead body CPR. "Bring him. Follow me."

They picked up Billy Jack and stumbled up the wide log staircase with him.

370

"Here, Uncle Bobby." Jimmy stood in the doorway. "I've got the heater turned up, and all the blankets and towels are on the bed."

"Good." Elias lay in the middle of the big king-size bed and put Clary on his right. He pulled two IV sets from his belly. "I need your help in taping these on." In moments, he had the IV in the vein inside his elbow and set up Clary the same way. Dark red liquid flowed from him to her. "Help me tape it. Good. Give me the baby."

Elias turned his child over and pushed his tummy. A flood of almost freezing water escaped the tiny mouth, caught by a towel. "Good. Good, little one."

Billy Jack was carried up the stairs. "Take off his clothes and put him next to me," Elias indicated his left side. "Jimmy, Ricky, cover us with all the blankets and then go. Keep everyone out. Keep the heat up. Don't let that doctor in.

"Make the people happy downstairs; give them food. But keep them away. Only you two can come in. Just to make sure I don't give her too much. I did that once."

"When Óskar Erland got her?"

He nodded. "Go now. We'll be fine."

Jimmy thought it was the longest night in history. He and Ricky did exactly what their uncle said. Keeping the doctor out was a problem until Ricky thought of spiking his ice cream with Vicodin.

Everyone else flopped on the floors and sofas and filled the extra bedrooms. The boys got sleeping bags and camped in front of Papa Jack's bedroom door. Everyone they loved in the world, except their dad, was in that room. They couldn't lose them.

Even in the most terrible calamities, people finally sleep. What awakened them was the sound of water. The natural inclination in these times was to look outside and wonder how long the storm would last.

"That's a shower," someone said. "Upstairs."

They sat around in the living room, staring up to the second floor.

Jimmy and Ricky sat up in the hallway—hopeful, puzzled, terrified sentries.

"Come and see your new brother, boys," said Elias. He wore some of Papa Jack's clothes, which didn't fit, but seemed wonderful to them. They felt like they'd always known the man in front of them. He looked like the pictures of Alex Caldwell they'd seen. But he was mature and more powerful—mighty, even—yet he didn't look any older than twenty-two.

Jimmy and Ricky approached their mom. She lay in bed wearing Papa Jack's T-shirt and one of his sweaters. She looked radiant. Her eyes were brilliant and her hair was softly curled around her face. "Hi, boys. I had a baby!"

"*What happened to you, Mom?*" they said at once. Their mother looked like a girl.

"I took her back before all the bad things damaged her," explained Elias. "She had just met your father and was in love. She knows what happened later, she remembers it, but it hasn't scarred her. She has a new life. *We* have a new life." He beamed.

"Hi, guys! Here's your new brother," she held out the new baby, who was beautiful and looked exactly like both of them.

"He's really our brother!"

"Oh, yes. Very much so," Elias said. "I hope we have many more children. I hope you won't mind if we do."

"Oh, no. Oh, he's so tiny, Mom. Look at his fingers!"

"Your mom's going to feed him now. Do you have anything to eat downstairs? I'm starving. Your grandpa is going to wake up in a little while. He'll be hungry, too."

"Papa Jack?" They noticed his blanket-covered form lying on the far side of the bed. "He's alive?"

"Yes. He's fine. Very sleepy. He'll be up later."

Elias kissed Clary's forehead. "I'll be back in a minute. I think I'd like to eat a whole elk." He laughed. "I knew where you were, Clary. I just had a few things I had to do before I could come." Standing next to the bed, he leaned over and kissed her lips.

"I'm never leaving again, Clary. You're stuck with me."

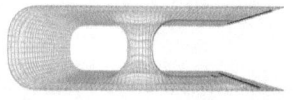

FIFTY-SEVEN

JACK, I'M SO HAPPY

CLARY SAT ON the hill overlooking the river fork. They'd put a bench there, near Jack's grave. Clary came often to enjoy the beauty of the scene, and to talk to Jack. Little Bobby toddled around her, grabbing the bench, pulling at her jeans, hanging from her knees. He pulled up grass and stuffed it in his mouth.

"No, Bobby. That's not good for you. Might have bugs." He kept her busy, for sure.

Riotous flowers bloomed all over the hill. They'd planted some, but she knew that Elias was responsible for the splendor around her. He multiplied everything: flowers, the hay crop, the cattle. Everything. He took to everything, and loved everything. Galloped all over on Billy Jack's horses, scaring her to death.

She looked across the river at the dense stands of pines, spruce, and cedar, remembering the last eighteen months. When he'd first gotten there, El had exclaimed, "Clary! Those are trees! I've never seen trees like those before! They're beautiful!" He'd said stuff like that all the time when he'd first arrived, but he'd settled down recently, only remarking on new species. Of trees, bugs, plants, types of clouds. Everything. No one could be more curious than her husband. Or his son.

"Jack, I'm really happy," she whispered to the mounded knoll before her. "I want you to know that. I always feel guilty when I even think that, because we didn't have what I have with Elias. But who has that? It's the stuff of miracles, Jack. Miracles and fairy tales. I love him without any shadows. The only sadness I've got is you. I loved you, Jack, more than I knew.

"I've talked to Alma. I like her. I wish you could have had a good life together.

"But here's some good news. Your TV series is an incredible success. Millions of people watch it every week. We found the notes you left for more episodes on your computer. The show will continue for years. The fans are clamoring for more.

"The first movie based on one of your books will be out soon, Jack. Because of the TV show, the book has become a bestseller, all over the world. Critics are calling you a literary genius, Jack. An American treasure. Will said all you needed was some good marketing. They've given it to you. Oh, sweetheart, I'm so delighted for you. You're famous."

Tears ran down her face. "Your dad's doing great—Elias fixed his heart when he brought him back. I think he fixed more than that. Billy Jack looks like he'll live forever. And Jack—the boys have never been happier. I know how much you loved them and would want them to be happy. They are, happier than either of us thought possible.

"They spend a lot of time at Will's, working. He's got a big experiment going over there, very hush-hush. Scientists and techs everywhere. He's invited me to work on it and I keep thinking I should check it out. But I've got the baby. I want to enjoy him as a baby..." She wiped away the rivulets rolling over her lower eyelids. She wanted to bawl; her feelings crowded up so hard that they seemed to fill the whole valley. But she couldn't stop to cry; she had to tell Jack the rest.

"Ricky and Jimmy are not freaks here. They've finally found a place where they fit in. The scientists at Will's accept the boys for what they are, geniuses, and their input is treasured. They're *normal* in this world. They're part of a team.

"They're also cowboys. Elias has them riding the range with him, doing ranch things. I'll never go near a horse, but the boys love it. El swears he'll keep them safe. He promised that if I'd let them ride." She let out a trembling sigh. "They love Elias, Jack, but as an uncle. That's what he is, and he's been very careful to stay in that role. Not that they would have it any other way. You're *Dad,* Jack. If one of them has a nightmare, they call out for you, 'Daddy! Daddy!' They'll never forget you, ever, and neither will I.

"So that's how we are. I never thought I'd enjoy staying home and being a mom, but I do. I missed all of that with Ricky and Jimmy. Babies change so fast, Jack, from day to day. I don't want to miss a moment of it. Not a single new word or a tooth … I'm so happy, Jack."

"If you're so happy, why are you crying?" El's voice spoke from behind her. He did that, appearing from nowhere. He really was half-alien. And all human. He knelt in front of her.

"Why does the most beautiful woman in the world have a runny nose and wet cheeks?"

"Oh, El. I'm not the most beautiful woman in the world."

"Yes, you are. In my world. You get more beautiful every day." He stroked her cheek.

"I'm fat as a pig and out of shape."

"You look the way I wanted to see you look: relaxed and happy—to the extent you'll let yourself. You like to worry. But you're not so skinny as you were, and you're not a fitness freak. You've realized that a few six-mile hikes a week is plenty." He grabbed Bobby. "No, buster. No eating wild mushrooms." El looked at the offending fungus. "Got to get rid of these. Too much plenty is not always a good thing."

The field rippled as El removed everything potentially harmful to his child. "That's better." He picked up his son and sat next to Clary. He held the baby over her belly. Bobby stretched out his hands and felt his mother's abdomen.

"Baby Jess…" the child lisped.

"Yes, baby Jessellyn is in there. But don't tell your mother that we picked that name," he whispered. "She thinks it's weird."

Clary laughed. "El, I love you. I will always love you. I *adore* you, actually."

"Stop crying."

"I can't. No one could be this happy."

"Oh, now you've set another benchmark. I'll have to work on making you happier!" He whispered in her ears. "My latest calculations are that I'll live… almost forever. I'm going to spend all that time loving you. Can you stand it?"

"Well, I'll have to go into training, but I think I can."

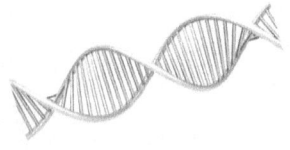

EPILOGUE

ELIAS' PRAYER

Clary nestled into Elias' shoulder, content and ecstatic. Around them as far as anyone could see or think, the planet unfolded in peace and plenty.

"El, what are you, really? Tell me."

"Well, I guess you could call me a god. Just a little one." He kissed her forehead and they began again.

Elias, that most ephemeral and junior of immortals, would not leave his ailing body until ages after Clarisse and their children, and their children's children, and theirs, had passed.

He loved this earth with all his heart, leaving a part of his soul in the mountains of Montana, a living spirit protecting and upholding the glory of nature.

They say if you go there and feel and see that spirit, you will know the glory and peace Elias came to create. If you feel it, you will know what he came to show us—the world of peace.

Pray that we do.

If you see the splendor of the mountain and feel Elias, you will know that we humans came to this planet to create a world of kindness and love, just as he did.

Pray that we do.

As long as the mountain lasts, Elias will bless those who love creation as he does.

Pray that we do.

WHAT'S COMING NEXT IN THE
BLOODSONG SERIES?

THIS IS A very good question. What is next? The Bloodsong Series is both a laid out, written-in-draft-form series and a work in progress. It was supposed to start with a neat trilogy describing the experience of the richest man in the world and his staff at a Native American spiritual retreat.

It should have been three tidy volumes: *Numenon: A Tale of Mysticism & Money* (Bloodsong 1), about the journey to the retreat; *Mogollon: A Tale of Mysticism & Mayhem* (Bloodsong 2), about what happened in the first days of the retreat—roughly described as "they went to hell and back"; and a final volume, setting out the retreat's final days.

But then—out of left field, *In Love by Christmas* (Bloodsong 3) emerged from my brain. This book, if you don't already know, is about Grandfather's grandson, Leroy Watches Jr., and his quest to save his soulmate. Said mate happens to be the daughter of Will Duane, the planet's richest man. Leroy appears at his grandfather's retreat just long enough to be given the task of finding and saving Cass Duane. The quest takes him all over the world. I didn't see *In Love by Christmas* coming; my books are like that: they push their way into my consciousness and don't leave me alone until I've seen them in print.

Meanwhile, back at the retreat that started the whole thing, a thousand people are stuck in a cave at the end of *Mogollon: A Tale of Mysticism & Mayhem*, Bloodsong 2. They've been attacked by the Lord of Darkness and all his minions. Looks like most of them made it. But the week isn't over. What's next?

The Bloodsong Series should have gotten back to those poor folks and at least gotten them to a place to rest and heal—a lot of them are terribly wounded.

So what happens? If you read the Author's Note and the About the Book section of this book, you'll know. I was in Santa Fe, New Mexico, a spiritually explosive place for me, and I had a soul-shaking nightmare… and that's what you've been reading. The way writing works for me is inspiration comes, I write it down. Or it goes away, lost forever. So you're holding a book called *MINDSPEAK/HEARTSPEAK*.

But what happened to the holy man, Grandfather, and Will Duane, and everyone stuck in the cave? What about the demons? Did they just go home? Grandfather's spiritual retreat runs from Sunday to Saturday, seven days. *Mogollon: A Tale of Mysticism & Mayhem* ends on that Wednesday night. Grandfather still has three more days to realize his dream of creating a world where love is king.

Will Earth become a place where people cooperate and work together with mutual respect? Or will violence and corruption rule the day? And how will they get out of that cave?

That's where the story goes next.

An editor might have wanted to wade in with a machete and cut out the "unimportant" people, but I won't do it. I've decided to include all the important characters and stories, but as a series of novellas. Grandfather and Will's story—the real business of the series—will be its own novella. As will be those of Wesley Silverhorse, Doug Saunders, Bud Creeman, Gil Canao, Delroy West, Niles Swanne, Jon Walker, and several more.

Using a novella format, I'll be able to give you the richness of the saga as I know it. Full force, full feelings, full length. So, what's next? A bunch of novellas, which I'll produce and publish as they emerge.

Sign up for my Readers' Club on my website.
www.sandynathan.com
You'll get advance notice of all my work,and often free downloads
orstories unavailable elsewhere.

So don't worry, there's more to come! The suspense, terror, romance,
and miracles you've come to expect reach a crescendo as the
meeting comes to a close. I promise fantasy with a bite, bringing the
gifts of insight and awe.

A SAGA OF QUANTUM PHYSICS, ALTERNATIVE UNIVERSES & LOVE

On the worst day of her life, Dr. Clarisse Hull is denied tenure and fired by one of the world's most prestigious universities. They say her research is fraudulent. Unfortunately, she can't show them her real research... the government owns it.

The government owns her, too, and that's why she's been fired. She broke a student's jaw and gave him a concussion. It was an accident, of course. Clarisse simply did what she was trained to do. She just can't tell the university what she really does.

Heading home to her husband and sons, she walks toward her car—and ends up in a bizarre reality. It looks like her world, Palo Alto, CA, but in the 1980s, not 2016. An emaciated young man approaches.

"I'm here to take you home."

They walk through a slash of light and into a vast white warehouse. Roving spotlights create a blinding glare, concealing the hundreds of people lurking there.

"Hey, Dr. Hull? Wanna get *Hulled?*" They close in, hurling threats.

She discovers that she was right. Alternative universes exist, and they aren't necessarily fun and games. She has landed in the mother of them all, and she will do *anything* to get home.

In the reality left behind, Dr. Jack Abercrombie, Clarisse's husband and a professor of literature, and her boys, Ricky and Jimmy Hull, are thrown into a deadly world of quantum physics and black-ops. They find out what Clarisse was really doing when she left home to attend conferences.

A brilliant physicist, she developed the technology to break into alternative realities. Perhaps more importantly, Clarisse has been a top-ranked secret agent most of her adult life. She's a genius and a member of the brilliant Hull family, involved in the military-industrial complex up to her beautiful eyebrows.

Jack and the boys' lives are in danger from the minute Clarisse disappears. They will do anything to get her back, but will their own government back them up? Every clandestine operation on the planet converges on the family in an attempt to discover Clarisse's secrets.

Clarisse, trapped in a nightmare, uses all of her wits to battle captive humans and a twisted alien civilization. The young man who brought her to the alien world entices her soul, but she won't give in. Is he a friend or foe? Meanwhile, the aliens bring her mega-computer across time and space. With it, she may be able to free herself. Or she may be turned into one of them.

MINDSPEAK/HEARTSPEAK is a thrill ride with no rules and no guaranteed survivors.

ABOUT SANDY NATHAN

I used to be a princess. My parents were born in the hungry days of the Great Depression. They overcame the poverty of their youth by becoming extremely successful. As a kid, I spent my time showing horses and water-skiing behind my dad's obscenely overpowered boat.

That life vanished when a drunk driver hit my father head-on in 1964, killing him.

Not instantly, though. My dad's death was the stuff of horror movies and plunged my family into years of darkness.

My old life disappeared. I lived at close to poverty level for a while. What happened in the following decades opened my eyes. I've seen and lived the over-privileged existence I describe in the Bloodsong Series.

I've seen how it can warp those who are lost in it. I've seen how the power of money can mask mental illness and allow evil to ruin lives.

I know the mental and emotional landscape of the San Francisco Bay Area—Silicon Valley, as it has come to be known. I know the physical geography just as well; I lived on the San Francisco Peninsula for fifty years. I made my home in the iconic cities and towns of Atherton, Woodside, Cupertino, and Palo Alto during that time.

How did such a hothouse flower end up writing the rough and visceral fiction I do? It's because of what happened in those dark years.

My writing has a bite. My life has had a bite. Recovering from what happened to me has taken many years. And I have recovered. What was legitimately mine came back to me, along with the fruit of my own labor. If your life echoes mine, you might like to see how I healed; it's in my books.

My writing isn't for everyone. I write about people getting better and the world working out, but it's not always gentle and nice. A reviewer described one of my books as "equal parts horror, spiritual, romance, and action." If that's for you, you're my reader.

I consider what I write as falling primarily into the visionary fiction genre, which is about psychological maturation and making the world a better place. I have had huge spiritual experiences all my life, as well as gentler, ongoing inner guidance. Whatever is behind these experiences and this earthly life wants me to tell you my visions through my tales: my darkness and light.

Now for my "regular bio": I've been in school a very long time and have two advanced degrees. I've had prestigious careers. My writing has won thirty national awards. I'm very happily married; my husband and I have been together forty-two years. I have three grown children and two grandchildren. My husband and I live on our California horse ranch and love it. We still ride the trails together, metaphorically and on our horses.

Sandy Nathan's Website
www.sandynathan.com

www.ingramcontent.com/pod-product-compliance
Lightning Source LLC
Chambersburg PA
CBHW020507260626
47156CB00006B/1910